The power began in fire just above and behind the bridge of my nose, and expanded, gaining in weight and heat until the pressure forced me to my knees. Blinded by my own sweat, I put one hand up to feel my head. The Crown was cool as always, but my head seemed to glow red-hot like a stoked furnace. Inky shadows streamed back from couches and pillars as my flesh glowed like molten silver. I gave myself up for lost and clung to the floor as it rocked under me.

With a soundless shock I broke through the pain and was free. From a great distance, yet very clearly, I noticed the Magus shading his old eyes, Arixhel clapping her gnarled hands in glee, and the white fluffy hair around Sandcomber's awed face. I tasted for the first time the delight of doing what I was born to do. . . .

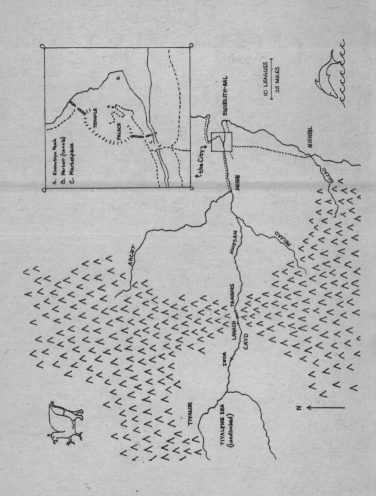

A. Execution Rock
B. Harbor (amaka)
C. Marketplace

TEMPLE

PALACE

← the City →

ENNELITH-RAL

MISHBIL

ELVOD

FELVOD

10 LEAGUES
25 MILES

ARGET

AHISE

AHESAN

LANACH

TAMBORS

CAYD

ISON

TIVALOR

N

TIYALENE SEA
(landlocked)

THE
CRYSTAL
CROWN

B. W. Clough

DAW Books, Inc.
Donald A. Wollheim, Publisher
1633 Broadway, New York, N.Y. 10019

PUBLISHED BY
THE NEW AMERICAN LIBRARY
OF CANADA LIMITED

To My Grandmother

First Printing, April 1984

2 3 4 5 6 7 8 9

 DAW TRADEMARK REGISTERED
U.S. PAT. OFF. MARCA REGISTRADA.
HECHO EN WINNIPEG, CANADA

PRINTED IN CANADA
COVER PRINTED IN U.S.A.

Kings are not born:
they are made by universal hallucination.
George Bernard Shaw,
The Revolutionist's Handbook

". . . the inhabitants of this otherwise charming land are afflicted with a unique custom for selecting their monarch. The Shan King (or Queen) must be pedigreed, as we would say, of the old royal blood. Very proper, you think? But this class is, due to the unregulated proliferation of semi-fictional genealogies, exactly congruent to almost the entire population of Averidan. The country is therefore of necessity subject to the most ludicrous monarchs, sometimes even one who has neither the wish nor the vocation for the august office. Chaos in domestic policy, in foreign relations, and in economic direction would be perpetual were it not for the structure that a tortuous bureaucratic system imposes, itself a source of much discontent. Thus we may draw this moral: that in whatever idyllic situation God may place a nation, their natural folly will at whatever cost contrive endless unhappiness. . . ."

from *Journals of a Scholar's Travels Over Sea*

PART I: UPHILL

Chapter 1: Salad Days

The copper gong tolled when I was in the garden.

"Whoever it is, I'm not at home," I ordered, for I had just finished the most difficult feature of klimflower vine pruning: untying dozens of thorny, sticky green stalks from their trellis and laying them out on the grass. "I'm just at the best part, if I can find my shears."

Ferd bowed and went back into the house. Sap had run over my heavy gardening gloves, and I rubbed them on my breeches. With irritation I saw I had left the shears on the grass, where they were now cloaked by vines. Picking my way over the thorns, I teased the shears free. The sap was turning white and glucy in the late spring sunshine, and a thorn had caught me on the ankle.

"Sir?"

"Yes, Ferd, what is it?" My mind was taken up less with the importance of proper pruning to future klimflower production than with the maddening tendency of my gloves to stick tightly to the shears.

"Sir, it's the Collegium. They're here."

"What nonsense is this, Ferd?"

"*The* Collegium, sir, the Collegium of Counselors to his late Majesty." Now I stared at Ferd, who jerked his head at the house. I turned and saw that the central court was seething with nobles in vivid ceremonial dress.

"The whole Collegium? They won't fit into the house. They'll step on the cat. What about refreshments?" An icy blast of impending doom chilled the sweat on my forehead, as if my cozy refuge had already been riven by the storm.

"I don't think you'll have to worry about that anymore, sir." Ferd grinned until his face was nearly circular, and then twitched it swiftly into a solemn mask as the Counselors approached. They had rearranged their procession to get it up the narrow garden path. I could have looked more calmly at my own funeral cortège.

First in rank was Xantallon, Master Magus of Averidan, in

9

formal scarlet silk robes, followed by a page bearing his glass hydromantic wand. Chief priestesses followed, each preceded by the banner of her Order, and commanders of various armed forces in parade armor. Those unable to approach in procession crowded the terrace. From every window and door, and even the roof, my servants, my relatives, the Counselors' friends and relatives, my neighbors, waited staring. My quiet walled garden shimmered with the crazy brilliance of a madman's mosaic floor.

I had been working in a corner beyond the prostrate vines, but no magus can be deterred by mere thorns. Xantallon simply walked a handspan above. Even his long trailing sleeves disdained the thorns and floated just above.

"We seek Shan Liras-ven Tsormelezok, son of Shan Torverlis Lord Tsormelezok, son of Shan princess Siral-sei Mirtserelok, who was fourth daughter of Shan Norlen-yu Mirtserelok the 517th king. Are you he?" The Master Magus' voice was unexpectedly deep, and carried to every ear. It was impossible to do more than glance at his deep black eyes. I stared instead at my vines, and his long braided white mustaches, which fell to his waist. A scalding-hot blush burned in my face, my neck, and even my hands. I would have given anything to be able to reply, "Sorry, he lives next door," but my tongue seemed stuck sideways in my mouth.

"Are you he?" the Magus repeated, stepping closer. Then he added, in an undertone, "Speak up! and say, 'I am.' " Startled, I glanced up. He gave an almost imperceptible nod. Behind him the page winked at me.

"Ah—I am," I said. After the Magus my voice sounded reedy.

"And you are so listed in the Genealogies of Averidan?"

"I am."

"Then our quest is at an end." He turned to the assembled company. "Brethren, I present to you Shan Liras-ven Tsormelezok, the king of the Children of the Sun." Instantly everyone bowed. Some signal must have passed through the courtyard and passageway, for from the street beyond the gate came the sound of musicians playing an anthem as loudly as possible. The procession broke up as everyone surged forward cheering. I grabbed the Magus' silk sleeve, pressing close enough to whisper, "But what if I don't *want* to be king?

"There's no provision in custom for that," he replied in a very low voice, and then more loudly, "Your Majesty recognizes me, I presume, but you may not have met my grand-nephew Xalan, apprentice to the art Magical.'' The page came forward and bowed. Close up he was older than I had thought, but still younger than I. As he straightened he muttered, ''Relax and enjoy it.'' Then he added aloud, ''My felicitations, Majesty, on your accession.''

The rest of the day I do not clearly recall even now. The entire Collegium was presented to swear their allegiance to me. It took all afternoon, and every name and face had escaped me the next day. I do remember shivering in the sunshine, knowing that what every Viridese half fears had befallen me. I was being drawn into that other Averidan that so closely overlaps our own: the Averidan of history and plaiv-embodied legend. Those of that world are larger than life, brave heroes and bold villains and glorious queens. In their presence my orderly little world was fading and shrinking, like a cheap embroidered shirt after a wash. Soon it would quite burst at the seams, leaving me bare.

I come a little to myself when the procession re-formed to go back to the Upper City. My place was near the end, in the royal sedan chair that is so heavily gilded ten men must carry it. ''Wait,'' I said. ''Don't I get to change? Wash my hands? Pack a lunch?''

A very grand somebody in a blue and gilt outfit (later I found he was Lord Director of Protocol) told me, ''The custom is for the new king to be brought to his Palace as he is, since it will be the last time he wears common garb.'' I shuddered. ''Your Majesty will find everything needful in readiness.''

At the head of the parade someone began a traditional thanksgiving chant which was picked up by the musicians outside. With surprising speed the procession began to move through the courtyard and out the gate. I tried to hang back but the Magus, who was behind me, said, ''You can't stop now.'' As we moved off I looked back. Through the golden lattices of the chair my garden seemed to be tiny but clear, like the engraving of a beautifully arranged landscape on the bezel of a ring. With a pang I glimpsed the shears forgotten on the trampled grass, with my gloves still stuck to their handles.

Averidan has been a nation for ten thousand years. So custom has near the force of law, and of these customs none is more rigid than those decreeing the Shan King's activities from his selection to his coronation. Some previous kings-elect had died before ascending the throne. I was certain they had perished from boredom.

Most of a new king's schedule is common knowledge—a dreary mill of rehearsing coronation rites, customary words and behaviors for court occasions, and being measured for endless robes, tunics, sets of armor. Though much of the business of rule was closed to me until after coronation, I was not spared a sea of titles and names: diplomats, organizations, subjects, magi, all to be addressed correctly. The infinitely complex negotiations of a treaty with Cayd, our neighbor to the west, and the wars there, alone filled a dozen archival scrolls. Although I had lived all my life in the City I had never dealt in politics. Mother had handled family contacts with the court. I was only nineteen, a shy gardener and horseman. So all this new life came very hard, and to me was mostly obscured by pain for the loss of the old existence.

Slowly, over that miserable week, I groped to a decision. I should never be worth anything as a king, it was all a dreadful mistake. Once articulated, this idea begat a bright vision: I would step down and go home, lock the gate and stay there forever with my cat and horses and flowers, while the Collegium chose out some other unfortunate to be Shan King. The picture was so compelling I invited my only possible ally, my brother Zofal-ven, to dinner that evening. Zofal is the eldest of us, and in taking over my late sire's horse farm had nursed the enterprise from a rich man's hobby into a business that nearly paid for itself, if one was not too exacting about bookkeeping. In my own diffident way I had assisted him. All decisions that Mother did not actually settle for me I was accustomed to consult Zofal upon. So in this pass I turned to him.

Whether in my inexperience I worded the order to my scrivener poorly, or whether my relatives had been itching for the opportunity, when the dinner hour came I found to my dismay my entire immediate family gathered in the small green-and-white salon. It was the first time we had assembled since my selection, and the two family factions, each headed by their strong-minded widow, grouped on opposite sides of the long green glass table. But since there is no contest between the two Viridese national preoccupations—food and argument—Mother did not open formal hostilities until the sumptuous meal was over.

"How greatly the loss of your brother must affect you," Mother began, "Yibor-soo, dear stepdaughter-in-law!"

This barb—for the late Shan King Eisen never liked his sister—made Yibor smile toothily. She wore a particularly unfortunate ensemble of bright lime green that heightened her resemblance to a plump angry snake. "Ah! could my beloved brother only be assured of an illustrious successor," she said, "how sound he would sleep in the Deadlands!"

Mother glanced at me to be sure I had caught the innuendo. "Our side of the family has never lacked greatness," she retorted. "At least if, in the cause of family unity, one overlooks certain alliances." Mother turned to the head of the table, where I had been installed on a tall thronelike ebony chair thickly inlaid with curly patterns of silver wire. "Your reverend father, Liras dear, was a man of *chun-hei*, of impractical honorableness. He made his mistakes, but how sad that he cannot see you now!" Taking the traditional silk handkerchief from her wide yellow silk sleeve she blotted imaginary tears, carefully, so as not to smudge her eye paint.

Now that the meal was over I was allowed to rise. Leaving Mother and Yibor to it I drew Zofal to the tall triple windows. But before I could pour out my troubles he took up the long trailing end of my white silk sleeve to examine the emerald-sewn hem. "Nice, little brother, very nice. Any you outgrow, be sure to hand down to me."

"To Ixfel with the robe, Zofal!" I said, jerking the hem away. "Tell me what's happening at home," I demanded. "Have you seen Sahai? Has the new mare foaled yet?"

"She did indeed—it was a little filly, too, gray as a storm cloud and with her dam's one white stocking. But how can you worry about things like that now? I've got something important to discuss."

"So do I," I said, but Zofal cut in.

"I was thinking about the guardsmen," he said.

"What guardsmen?" I said, confused.

"The City guardsmen, you know, your Home Defense. You remember how they've always been infantry? Well, it's about time we had some cavalry too, don't you think? Just the act to start off your illustrious reign."

"And you would patriotically sell mounts to the City for that purpose," I finished. "Zofal, you make me tired. Here I've been abducted and forced into this ghastly role. Turning over a nimble coin should be the last thing on your mind."

"You've always been the stupid one," he snapped. "What are you fishing for, sympathy? Here you are, a reclusive nobody, now Lord of the Shan, child of fire, King of Averidan."

"Oh, Liras-ven, I'm so excited for you!" my sister broke in.

"How dreadfully white you looked the other day—you're much more impressive now."

"Don't tell me," I sighed, "You have something important on your mind."

"Oh, yes! how clever of you, Liras."

"Such an unusual condition for you, Siril, that it doesn't take much perception to see it," Zofal said with fraternal malice.

She ignored him and went on, "Can we live in the Palace with you, Liras-ven? There must be plenty of room, I've always wanted to."

"I don't know the custom," I said. "Yibor-soo never stayed here in King Eisen's time."

"Oh, but you know how he felt about her," she said. "I'm sure my husband would be delighted, he's always held you in such high regard."

"Silly girl, nothing's settled until Coronation anyway." Rosil-eir sauntered up and helped himself to a pear from the bowl on the windowsill. "I've heard stories about kings-elect that would make you think twice. You'd never get *me* on the throne." The fruit was ripe and yellow, and he bit through the rind with a wet juicy sound.

I wanted to ask about the stories but Zofal cut in again. "Relax, now you never will."

"And I'm sure young Liras here was a compromise candidate," Rosil said to Zofal. "There are so many more obvious choices. You, for example."

"Or yourself, you mean," Siril said. "You envious pig! Liras will be a wonderful Shan King, you'll see, and I hope he has you lapidated, for rudeness and spiteful remarks."

"If those were capital offenses we'd all be flat and dry in the sun," I said, wishing all my quarrelsome kin at the bottom of Averidan harbor. I would just have to confide in Rosil and Siril as well; they would have to know sooner or later and Rosil's support especially would be invaluable.

But before I could say a word Mother swept up to me and cried, "Liras, I won't have you listening to the poison of this son of a jealous viper!"

"Viper, am I?" Yibor's silver filigree hair ornaments shook with her outrage. "Heaven alone knows by what error the son of a manipulative old hag was selected Shan King!"

I hissed in Zofal's ear, "We should have kept the conversation general. What can they have been saying to each other?"

"Do something, you're the host," he whispered back.

I reached over and grabbed one of my half-sister-in-law's chubby hands. "Actually, Mother, I'm not sure that dear Yibor-soo isn't correct."

"Correct?" Mother's glare should have killed me on the spot. My sister rolled her eyes at me and began to giggle.

Like a fool I announced, "I'm sure my selection was a mistake, and I'm going to refuse to be Shan King. They can choose someone else."

Icy silence greeted this statement. Zofal stared at me with his mouth open, and Mother collapsed into a chair in shock. After a moment of astonishment Yibor pulled her hand away.

"You must be mad," she said to me. "Rosil, does the Collegium know about this?"

Rosil was silently laughing too hard to reply at first. "Oh, Liras, Zofal is right, you are a ninny. No, mother, I don't think he's told the Collegium yet. I can't wait to see their faces when he does, no one has ever declined the Shan kingship before. They'll have to spend all summer searching the chronicles for precedents."

"Don't you dare!" Yibor pointed at me, focusing the strength of will that makes her such a worthy opponent for Mother. "Don't you dare decline the throne! How can you even consider letting us all down!"

"But I don't want it," I argued. "Why should it be me?"

Mother leaped from her seat, throwing off the shocked expression like a worn-out garment. "Liras, you are the silliest of all my children. Where do you get these foolish notions. You've always been too shy and worrisome. The Collegium selected you, and you are going to rule unless you can offer a really substantial reason against it, substantial, do you hear me?"

"There aren't any reasons," Zofal said in disgust. "Just the usual woollymindedness."

"There are, too," I protested. "I'll have to live here instead of in my own home. I'll have to do things that bore me, see people I dislike, and learn things no one wants to know. And worst of all," I continued, losing my temper, "I'll be so important all my friends and relatives will be around my neck for the rest of my life!"

"Liras!"

"What an awful thing to say!"

Whenever foreign sages comment on our love of division they tell us nations need unity. The Viridese always reply that we do join to face real trouble—that is when the hearers do not split into two parties to debate the assertion. That night I learned it was true. Faced with my lack of nerve the fractured Tsormelezoks united to scold me back into line. Zofal and Siril were genuinely hurt by my assertions and said so at great length, while Yibor and Rosil agreed loudly that though our side of the family was weak no one had actually gone insane before.

I might have weathered their wrath but could not stand against Mother. She had held us all in the rigid yet remote grasp Viridese women wield—for we were a matriarchy once, and will be again. Now she solemnly told me, "We are all counting on you, Liras-ven. You must be responsible not only for us, your family, but for the Shan. I'm sure the Collegium chose you for the family qualities you aren't even aware you possess. You must simply learn to be Shan King."

It was as though she lay crushing stone weights on me, a lapidation under the loads of kingship and responsibility. As usual I bolted, turning and racing for the green-paneled door. My relatives were taken by surprise and I had just grasped the brass door-ring when the door swung in of its own accord, tumbling me flat. With cries of apology and horror the Chamberlain helped me to my feet again, and when I had been dusted off he said, "The Master Magus is here, Your Majesty."

"Is he outside?" I gasped, weak with relief. "Show him in. Mother, you must excuse me, I have business."

Balked victory gleamed in Mother's eye, and I quailed at the sight. "We haven't finished discussing this by any means, Liras. Come, children, come, dear stepdaughter-in-law."

The Magus had brought Xalan with him, and an incredibly old, white-clad Sun Priestess—Arixhel, Guardian of the Crown. The three, ushered in and announced by the Chamberlain, bowed low before me. I nodded, as I had been taught, but did not sit again. Instead I paced, hampered by my long silk robe. "You should have told the Collegium this before," I said. "I do not want to be Shan King. I want to raise my horses, tend my garden, and go home. I don't want to be King."

"And what of Averidan?" the Magus asked.

"Well, let them find another monarch; there are enough of us to search among. Plenty of the Shan want the job." I caught the glance exchanged between the Master Magus and the old priestess.

The old lady poked a skinny yellow finger at me. "The blood runs thin in your veins, boy, does it?"

"It does not!" I had the feeling of being manipulated by these two old adepts.

"No time like the present to prove it," the Magus said. "Come with us."

"Let's not get drawn into proofs and such," I said with as much dignity as I could muster. "I've had a trying day. Besides, the chamberlains will be along soon to help put me to bed."

"I think not," said the Magus. "All this—" he gestured around the room—"All this is the trappings of power. It is time you saw the source."

"That's not quite right, Magister," the old priestess said. "You will find, child, that all these rites and courtesies are necessary. They give both support and restraint, help and hindrance." Her bright black eyes were unwinking on mine, birdlike, as if to search out some flaw in me. Then in a much less kind tone she added, "And then of course you might not."

"We ought not to speak of this here," the Magus said. "Let us go." He turned and led the way without waiting to see if I followed.

"Where are we going?" I asked Xalan.

"The room is called Navel, since it's reputed to be the center of the realm," he replied. "It's above the dome in the Temple of the Sun."

"I've never heard of it."

"Oh, lots of people know of it. But no one but the king goes in, after the coronation. We'll just show you the way of it."

The Magus turned in a swirl of wide red sleeves. "Do not speak of this here," he repeated.

In silence we passed east through the Palace. Although the hour was late, the wide marble halls were all brightly lit—white porcelain lamps glowed from the ceilings, and white candles were supported high on the walls in continuous glass holders cast in the shape of an endless line of torchbearers. In happier times I had seen the Palace at the top of its hill at night, outshining even the zenith moon, staining the sky above it with a smear of diluted night. At the time I had thought it very pretty.

Since Temple and Palace share the scarp of the Upper City we used the Shan King's private connecting door. The sanctuary was empty when we arrived. Worshipers favor the daylight hours, when the visible disc of the Sun can regard their sacrifices and hear their wishes. I looked across the enormous circular mosaic floor to the fire that always burns on the central altar. Then I stared up at the golden dome above. All I could see was the opening that lets smoke out.

"There's room up there?" I asked. "How does it fit round the chimney?"

"The flues bend so as not to let rain in," Xalan whispered. "So there's enough space for a room." We did not cross but went around near the wall to a brass-bound door. The Magus unlocked it with a key from the bunch at his waist. We passed through into a narrow stone corridor, and then through another locked door on our right which led to a dim stone staircase.

"Don't climb too fast," the Magus warned.

We scaled three short straight flights and then started up a long narrow flight without landings that curved ever so slightly to the right. My legs got heavier as we ascended. I used to ride every day, and had felt complacent about my physique. Now I was forced to slow my pace and gasp for air as the stair curved on into eternity. It was discouraging to hear old Arixhel pattering close behind me. "Keep up, kinglet, don't lag," she urged. The Magus had disappeared around the curve above me. Xalan was not so far ahead, and looked back. In the dimness I could not see whether he was laughing or sympathetic.

We caught up to the Magus at a place where the darkness seemed thinner and the air cooler. There were still no landings, but a wider place had been laid on either side of the steps where we could sit. I collapsed, and listened to my own panting breath and the thump of blood in my ears for a while. Then I realized I was the only one so distressed. The magi weren't winded at all. "That's unfair," I said, sitting up. "Using magic to lift while I use muscles."

"You won't have to come up here often, I hope," the Magus said. "But we aren't waiting for you to catch your breath. Look!"

I saw that a low opening on the left wall was a deep-set window. Looking out I could see south to the sleeping city below. Pin-pricks of light shone from scattered windows, and a redder glow marked a party's bonfire to the east. Beyond, the dark sea curved around the headland and into the many canals of the harbor, quiet now as it never is during the day. Directly below me, the glazed tiles of the Palace wall wore a nimbus of light, shining from windows I was too high to see. And above, the sky-dome enfolded us round in starry hands.

We were far higher than the tallest Palace spires. For a moment I could not think where we were. "Ah, I see," I exclaimed. "We're climbing in the Temple dome itself."

"Yes. The stair is built between the outer and inner dome. We have ascended more than halfway, and circled three-quarters of the way around. From here the ascent is easier."

When we started again I noticed the stairway curving in slightly more. The steps became shallower, and the ceiling, which had been too high to see, dropped gradually until I could brush it with an outstretched hand. There were sections now of landings, or perhaps the stair had changed into a corridor with occasional steps sloping inward and up.

Suddenly we came to the end. The corridor took a sharp turn, went up a few more steps, and stopped at a plain stone door. There was no handle. The Magus laid a hand on the stone and muttered some formula under his breath. Then he lifted his hand away slowly, and the door followed, swinging outward.

The Navel of Averidan is a small room hollowed out in the dome's keystone, with no floor to speak of. The walls form a cup shape, and since the room is open to the sky the whole effect is that of sitting at the bottom of a giant's wine cup. A stone ledge runs around the room just wide enough to sit on with care. I edged around to give the Magus space to shut the door. The room was so small I would have been able to lean across and touch him, if there had been anything to hold onto for balance. Rain water hid the "bottom" of the room.

"Aptly named," I said. "It's very like an enormous navel. And certainly no one can overhear us here on the City's highest dome. So tell me about kings and their power."

"No," the Magus said. "It would be more instructive to know of your views. What does a king do?"

Together the official history in chronicles and traditional folklore of plaiv painted quite a clear picture of the Shan King. "He wards his people," I said slowly. "Sees clearly, rules justly, chooses rightly. A hero." Before this mighty golden image, potent yet calm, taller than life, my own self seemed feeble and ridiculous. "Me, I can stay on a horse's back," I burst out. "Dose them when they eat too much, raise fancy peonies, prune klimflowers. I hide in my garden with my animals. I'm sure you made a mistake, you meant to pick a hero. Why don't you choose someone with some special gift—" I was thinking of Norlen-yu my great-grandfather, the best swordsman of his time— "someone who does something useful, and let me go?"

"Nonsense," Arixhel said.

"Only a Child of the Sun can be selected, but not every royal kinsman can wear the Crystal Crown," the Magus said. "The Collegium selected you, but this is the final test, the touchstone."

"Some of the mistakes the Collegium has made, too!" Arixhel said cheerfully. "Embarrasses everybody. But we'll soon see if you're one of them."

I was given no time to ponder the implications of this. The Magus said, "Now, Xalan, the lantern." Xalan passed over a small copper lamp of the sort sold to sailors or travelers, that holds a flame safely. The Magus slid the flap aside, releasing flickering light and a smell of heated metal. The night's darkness became suddenly much more noticeable. He directed the beam down past our feet. "Look!"

Thus I first saw the Crystal Crown. It glowed hotly under the water at our feet, throwing back the lantern light tenfold. The motion of the water, and the lamp moving in the Magus' hand, made the Crown seem to throb with its own life.

"It's yours," the Magus said. "Pick it up."

The water was not deep. I almost expected the Crown to be white-hot as well as glowing-bright. But it was cool as its surrounding water. When I raised it dripping to my knees it flared almost too bright to look at.

"I don't remember the Shan King wearing this," I said, awed.

"He did—that light refraction will pass," the Magus said. "You see why we brought you here at night. Imagine what the Crown would be like at noon." I winced at the idea. "The Crown is the source of the Shan King's power. Your predecessors applied it to different things, as the needs of the kingdom dictated and their own talents took them. There are limits, of course—the Crown confers no omnipotence. You will have to concentrate on a few things. Other realms have charters or commandments, to keep continuity with their past. The Shan have the Crystal Crown."

I didn't really listen, as I turned the Crown on my lap. It was of an attractive substance, neither metal nor glass, white yet transparent, faceted like a gemstone. It was shaped to cover the head from brow to nape like a helmet. Its glow was entirely reflection, and also seemed linked to its warmth—when I cupped one of the angles in my hands that portion dimmed as it took heat from me.

"Power," the Magus was lecturing, "is a heavy responsibility. We magi wield similar talents, but we are many, and can support each other. The Shan King is alone. We direct our powers to goals fixed by custom time out of mind, but each monarch must find his own path. In a culture bound by adamantine tradition, you shall be the most and the least free. We will instruct you, Shan Liras, as best we may, but in the end the King and the Crown must reach an understanding."

I interrupted. "How does it work?"

The Magus sighed. "You simply put it on," he replied.

Without a thought for all the hints I had been given I set the Crown on my head. At first I felt nothing. The Crown had been heavy in my hands, but rested light on my head. Gradually a mood of detachment overtook me. I relaxed, aware of every drop of blood flowing through my veins. The Crown seemed to pulse, in time with my heart. Every muscle loosened, but my mind was alert. I could imagine how I must look to my companions: my jaw slackening foolishly, my body slipping off the ledge into the water. From a great distance I heard the Magus snap, "Grab him, Xalan, you're closest!"

The apprentice took hold of the slack of my robe, but it was so loose he shifted the grip to my elbow where the wide sleeve had fallen back. His hand touched my skin, and with a sudden shock, a sensation of bursting, I was actually looking at my own face. It looked as if I had been drinking—flushed and slack. My eyes were glazing and didn't focus. With interest I noticed that the royal barber had cut my dark hair shorter than I used to wear it.

With a cry of surprise Xalan released my arm, slipped, and fell into the water. When I heard his exclamation twice I knew I heard once through my ears and once through Xalan's. I seemed to be thinking two sets of thoughts at once. One set clamored that I was losing balance, slipping off my seat, and might either crack my skull on the stone ledge or break a leg bone falling into the water on top of Xalan.

The other set was trying to get me to stand up on the floor of the pool. The walls sloped down so sharply there was room to stand only on one foot, the stone ledge got in the way of my knees, and Arixhel was screeching in my ear, "You're not supposed to do that, you wicked boy! Magister, make him stop!" The long sleeves of my red apprentice robe were soaked, dragging at my arms, and I was terrified the king would fall on me before I got my balance.

Above all this the detached bit of myself seemed to float. It had been not exactly conversing, but rather listening to and occasionally commenting on the discourse of someone sitting behind and above the bridge of my nose.

". . . and the people wept aloud and cried, 'How shall we then know the next king, if you indeed perish and leave us? And

Shan Vir-yan replied, 'You shall always choose among those of my get, one of the Children of the Sun. Yet though I have many sons and daughters, as my father does also, only one may rule. Today I declare to you my heir: after me shall my granddaughter, the warrior Shan Mir-hel, rule. For I foresee the need of a mighty defender in Averidan. And against the day of her accession, I and my sons among the Magi have prepared a Crown.' For in the days of Shan Vir-yan he wore no diadem or crown, but carried with him instead the fiery corona of the One his sire—"

"I recognize that," I said. "It's a plaiv, a version of the Passing of Shan Vir-yan. But I never heard the part about the Crown."

The cool beautiful voice ignored me and continued, "And so even from a distance the king was always known. But the Shan, his children and grandchildren and great-grandchildren, had no such glory."

"Just as well," I said. "Otherwise by now we would none of us be able to sleep at night."

"So it came to pass that the monarch is chosen by the Crown, and not otherwise, since the magics laid on the Crown by its maker Shan Xao-lan at the command of their father the king were such that the unworthy, or the evil, or those not born Shan are slain by the Crown when they first wear it. And thus the custom arose—"

"Wait a minute," I interrupted. "Did you say *slain*?"

The voice paused for a moment and then went on, "The custom arose that after a monarch was agreed upon by the Shan he would be brought to a private place to be assayed by the Crown, so that if he failed—"

"If he failed they could discreetly dispose of the body, is that the idea? How many failures have there been? Why didn't anybody tell me how dangerous this is? And why didn't anybody tell *you*—" Suddenly I realized why the beautiful voice hadn't known of my refusal. I had been listening all this while to the voice of the Crown itself.

My nerve shattered. "I told them, I told them," I gabbled. "I never wanted to be king, they just chose me and dragged me away to try you on. It wasn't my idea at all. I don't want any part of it, and now I know all this I absolutely decline. I will not be Shan King!"

For the first time the voice addressed me directly. "Is this your final decision?"

"Yes," I said, and then realized I might have just cut my own throat. "No! wait a minute!" I had to get the Crown off my head, but my arms refused to obey me. With an immense mental effort I dragged my perception back to the Navel Room.

The whole exchange had apparently taken no time at all. My body had shut its eyes and seemed about to faint. Xalan had floundered out of the knee-deep water while the Magus sensibly kept clear of the confusion by levitating up to the dome proper. I turned to him for help, and vertigo swept over me. I became acutely conscious of perching on the top of the highest roof in Averidan. I realized that the earth spun madly on its axis, that the world raced round and round the Sun, and the Sun executed who knew what appalling motion. I wondered how exactly the Crown rid itself of an unworthy wearer. The idea made everything whirl past my eyes, and as my levitation faltered I fell.

Something hard hit me behind, and suddenly I was on my hands and knees. The Crown had been knocked from my head and spun with a musical clink off the ledge into the water. My head was in one piece, whole again. Uncontrollable panic took charge of my limbs and like a scalded cat I threw myself against the stone door. It gave way and I ran down the corridor as fast as I could. My robe was not made for races, and I trod on my own hem. The stair was too slick for me to save myself. I rolled head over heels down into the darkness.

Chapter 2: The Wasteland

In the morning I woke from a troubled sleep with a raging headache and bruised limbs. Instantly the Bedroom Lord Chamberlain was at the bedside, making me jump.

"Good Morning, Your Majesty. Will Your Majesty take breakfast now?"

"No, I'm ill," I said. "I don't wish to see anyone or do anything today—absolute quiet, tell everyone."

He bowed and withdrew. I hid my head under the linen quilts until I heard the door close. Peering carefully between the green silk bed hangings, I saw I was alone. My bare feet made no noise on the mosaic floor as I crept across to the wardrobe alcove.

I couldn't remember it, but last night someone must have removed my after-supper outfit and put me into night clothes. Now I doffed the embroidered linen and searched for inconspicuous clothing, not an easy task. The Viridese—I myself, once—love clothing, and the Shan King has to dress to a standard no one else can afford. The cupboards were packed with hundreds of outfits, all impossibly ornate, made for a king: a rainbow of vividly embroidered silk robes with the wide trailing sleeves that demonstrate leisured status, quilted silk jackets with pearl fasteners, shoes made of thin leather dyed scarlet. Finally I put on what was probably a mourner's traveling costume, black suede leggings and spurred boots over gray breeches. I picked the onyx-tagged silk laces out of the black tunic, replacing them with plain leather ones, and selected a deep green traveling cloak lined with fur and a wide hat. Uncovering the tall mirror, I saw my convincing appearance—the black hat brim hid my eyes, the pallor of my face suggested bereavement, and the bulky cloak blurred the tell-tale width of my shoulders. I lacked only a sword, since arms are stored in the Royal Armory. But I could stop there to get one.

The spurs scraped and jingled as I edged up to the tall triple window. The royal chambers are one floor up, but the ivy and purple klimflowers twine up to the sill. The morning was clear and bright, still early, and no one was visible in the grounds or on the marble terrace. I prayed Viris that the chambers below me were empty also, and opened the casement.

Lowering my aching legs over the sill, I too late recalled the proverb that only a lover is fool enough to climb a klimflower. The thorns caught me even through leather. Gritting my teeth I wrapped the edge of the cloak round my hands and climbed down holding ivy whenever possible, and cursing silently whenever my spurs tangled in the vines.

I had almost reached the terrace when one spur became completely stuck. As I reached down to free it my other hand slipped, and I fell backwards off the trellis.

"Got you!" Strong arms were thrust between my back and the pavement.

"Xalan!"

"Didn't manage it last night, but now I've done a real rescue," he said with pride. "You might have broken your skull on this hard marble. Oh, your foot—allow me." Deftly he freed the trapped spur and I staggered to my feet. "Black is unlucky wear for the Son of the Sun. Who's dead?"

"Me. I died last night." I collapsed cross-legged on the sun-warmed stone, my hands and voice shaking with reaction. Xalan fanned me with the hat, concern in his face.

"You look ghastly, shall I have your people call an herbal?"

"No!" Wildly I snatched the hat and clapped it to my head. "How do you come to be here?"

"As a matter of fact, I descried you." He settled himself in a comfortable position on the white marble balustrade and raised a black eyebrow at me. "Daily scrying practice is set for apprentice magi in the mornings. Today, bored with my exercises, I shopped around and happened to glimpse the uncovering of a mirror by a familiar figure, dressed very oddly indeed." He looked me over with a mischievous smile. "Impelled to resolve the mystery, I ran across the gardens and came round the corner just in time to see your valiant battle with the trellis end in defeat."

"Ixfel!" I forgot about scrying. In despair I hid my face in my hands. Although mirror-to-mirror scrying is easiest, with enough incentive a trained magus can see (though not hear) almost anywhere in Averidan. With the entire Order of Magi on my trail unobserved escape would be impossible.

"Where are you going, alone in that weird outfit?" Xalan asked. I wondered then whether some affinity had been set up between our minds last night, but now I believe only Xalan's natural speed of thought supplied the answer: "You're running away!"

Leaping to my feet I grabbed him by an arm and hauled him bodily over the balustrade onto the lawn. The thousand triple eyes of the Palace seemed to bore holes in my back as I dragged Xalan across the grass and into the shrubbery beyond. Safe behind a screen of ornamental yew I halted, panting, and gasped, "I am. And now you know, you'll have to come with me."

I expected argument, perhaps even violence. To my surprise Xalan nodded his assent. "When do we leave?"

"Now." A little dazed, I led the way through the shrubbery. Kingship had been so full of unpleasant aspects that this new, convenient power—to command and be obeyed—had not occurred to me. The grounds were unfamiliar and I quickly lost my bearings. Xalan pointed the way to the little gate out of the private gardens.

"So you don't want to be Shan King?"

"I do not!"

"And the Crystal Crown didn't convince you otherwise? It's supposed to."

"I failed the assay," I confessed. "I told it what I told everybody, that I never wanted the role."

"Not conclusive." Xalan dismissed my words with a wave of his hand.

"What would be conclusive?" I watched his countenance carefully as he tried to frame a reply. "It's conclusive if I don't drop dead, is that right? Well, the only reason I'm here now is because the Crown fell off my head before it could fry my brains."

For a moment Xalan did not reply. At my touch the well-tended wooden gate swung quietly back. Now I was truly a fugitive. "If you're sure about that," he said at last, "then it's completely against custom. The Crown is supposed to definitely confirm kingship. Or deny it, and supply a final solution."

"You're saying I'm not supposed to be alive." I shivered, but when I glanced back the myriad eyes of the Palace were empty.

The stableyard was busy, and it was simple for Xalan to lead out two plump donkeys. I would have preferred horses, but such beasts are both rare and conspicuous in Averidan. We rode them round eastward to the courtyard of the Sun Temple and were instantly hidden as leaves are on a tree in the bustle of departing worshippers who had attended dawn sacrifices and then lingered for counsel or wishes. For the deity does grant wishes, and now I whispered to Xalan, "Would it be easier to just wish myself out of the role?"

"Don't waste your time," he hissed in reply. "The Collegium consults the Sun in selection. You're defying not only your country but your ancestor god."

This truth was too awful to consider. Viridese can hold conflicting beliefs in separate watertight mental rooms, and now I pushed Xalan's words into one of these chambers and locked the door. Perhaps when I got home I could think of some way to placate the One.

We ambled down the wide road that zig-zags back and forth along the scarp from Upper to Lower City. The way at the bottom of the hill was clogged by spectators watching an execution, and we had to sit hemmed in by the crowd until the show was over. No one paid attention to us. Our mounts slipped effortlessly into the sort of waking doze donkeys are subject to, and Xalan leaned over to ask, "Have you given any thought at all to the mechanics of this? Where are we going?"

"Home," I said. My haven of reality was not far—in an hour I should be safe forever.

Xalan laughed aloud at this. "You'll have to leave the country, nothing less."

"What? Are you certain?"

"Of course," he said. "You think the Collegium will just look under the bed and around the garden? There'll be a nation-wide hunt like never before. In fact, if you're serious you ought to take a long sea voyage or something. Get far away, obscure your trail—magi can't scry over oceans. You could cross the Mhesan and go south to take ship at Mishbil."

I was appalled, and said so. "You'll have to hide for the rest of your life," Xalan continued cheerfully, kicking his donkey forward. "Never a dull moment. The excitement of the chase, the thrills of foreign travel. Always wondering if the Collegium is a day, a league, a city behind you. And what will you live on?"

I had no idea. My family property could hardly be drawn on, and I knew no trade worth speaking of. Was it possible to support life pruning vines? "Maybe I'd better consider that point," I admitted.

"It does bristle with difficulties," Xalan agreed. "It's obvious you've never worked a day in your life."

"In our family that's considered a virtue," I said.

"Where you're going it won't be."

Then I glared at him. His milky, innocent gaze met mine, limpid and leaf-brown as a forest pool, but I was not deceived. "You're trying to scare me."

His teeth shone white in the Sun as he grinned, not at all ashamed. "It was worth a try," he admitted. "You scare easy. But all these obstacles are real."

"I'll think of something," I growled, and applied myself to guiding my donkey through the press onto the teeming main road out of town. The day was sunny and warm, ideal for a tidy lapidation, and our mounts sneezed softly at the smell of the blood being rinsed off the road. Outside the West Gate the daily market was bustling with business, and Xalan nudged me again.

"So are we going to Mishbil?"

"I suppose," I said reluctantly.

"Then we'll need water for the trip. And are you armed?"

I was not—in the excitement my visit to the armory had been forgotten. Xalan grumbled at this oversight but hoped we wouldn't need weapons. From a potter's booth he purchased four stone-

ware water jugs, curved to fit comfortably on either side of a
beast, and after filling them at the fountain we strapped them on
two and two behind our saddles.

With the traffic we ambled west and then south on the road to
the bridge, reaching it by noon. The Mhesan is deep and very
wide here, and the bridge humped up a good way above the
strong green water in many black marble arches. Bored guardsmen
in their black-barred outfits patrolled the span, keeping traffic
flowing on its own side in each direction and watching for
purse-slitters. Though the possibility of recognition was very
remote I tipped my hat over my face.

On the farther shore the road passes south through vegetable
fields to make a triple fork. Left and east is the way to the holy
city of Ennelith-Ral on the sea; westward lie wide barley fields
and rich estates, league upon league right up to the knees of the
mountains. This was the road to my home. I avoided my eyes
from it and looked rather at the third road—straight ahead south,
through farms and then sandy wastes to the distant port of
Mishbil. Nearly everyone turned either east or west. We rode
ahead alone.

The Sun was molten gold in a sky of glass above us, and the
donkeys plodded along nearly asleep, with a crunching sound of
oystershell-and-lime paving. "We should turn back," Xalan
announced. "I know what the problem was last night." In the
dappled shade of the trees lining the road his eyes gleamed merry
as a fox's. "It was Granduncle."

"What about him? He was above us, on the dome."

"You remember worrying about breaking an ankle?" I looked
sharply at him but he didn't meet my eye. "You must have
begun to read him, because when you got dizzy you muddled his
mind enough to spoil his herognomical lift. So he fell off."

"He fell off the *roof*?"

"Oh, toward the Navel," Xalan said. "Not off the dome into
the street. Only two or three times his height, but he was off
balance and knocked you over as he came down."

"And broke an ankle?"

"Well, a small bone in his foot, anyway," Xalan said. "The
bonesetters were looking at it. It was no joke, let me tell you, to
carry both of you down those stairs. For protocol's sake we took
you first."

"He'll never forgive me," I said with remorse.

"He'll never forgive you if you give up without finishing the trial," Xalan said. "Don't you see, that was the problem, the Crown hadn't completed the assay."

"And it never will!" The very suggestion of donning the Crown again made my hands on the reins shake. "If I disappear before the Coronation rites the Collegium can give out that I died. Or lost my mind, which would be true enough. They could choose someone else. We're going to Mishbil."

Xalan shrugged. "Pity we didn't plan it better. We haven't even any provisions. You didn't take breakfast, I suppose?"

"No," I said. "But surely there are inns?" Even as I spoke I doubted it. Houses and smallholdings had imperceptibly given way to scrubby thorn brush in sandy valleys that scraped itself thin at each hilltop in a vain attempt to hide the rock beneath. The trees lining the road had become smaller and scrawnier, and at last nonexistent. Sand and stone were the identical pale yellow-brown, glittering with almost invisible chips of mica, so that one could not tell whether the rock was born of compressed sand, or whether wind and thorn scoured rock into grit. The shuffling hooves soon raised enough powdery dust to cover both of us in a hot, unpleasant ocher coat. Armored in gold, the Sun slowly stooped low enough in the west to throw glowing spears under my hatbrim, and of course Xalan's peaked red magus cap was no protection at all.

Xalan squinted at the road before us, a pale yellow streak in a landscape of yellow-brown, and wiped his sweaty brown with a dust-streaked handkerchief. "At the Halfway Stone, perhaps," he said. "To get there we'll have to press on well after dark— most travelers to Mishbil leave the City at dawn to avoid being benighted."

"I should have planned, you're right," I apologized. The drawback to command, I saw, was the responsibility for consequences. With hungry regret I thought of last night's delicious meal—scallops sliced with ginger, fowl roasted with little shining fish impaled on their beaks, and an enormous redfish. The line of meditation was unwise. With an audible growl my stomach reminded me I had not eaten in a day and a night. Since in Averidan those who are able eat four or five small meals a day I had never gone so long without food in my life. My gastronomic dreams so occupied me that in spite of our gentle pace when my beast halted I nearly tumbled off. "What's wrong?" I demanded.

"Look." Shading his eyes Xalan pointed ahead. We had just passed the crest of a hill, and a good deal of the road unwound before us as it curved down into a thorny valley and then up the opposite slope. There, descending toward us, was a party of perhaps ten men on foot. Dust and distance hid all fine detail, but the setting Sun shone down slantwise and reflected little ruby sparks from their forms.

"This is a lonely stretch of road," I said nervously.

"Nothing for it but to press on," Xalan said. "But keep your hand on your knife." From its sling on his back he drew out his wand. It was a slim core of black stone, long as his torso and reinforced with silver bands for strength.

"That's right, you're a geomant!" I exclaimed with relief. The Magi are loosely divided into four specialties to master the four elements—earth and air, fire and water.

"Apprentice only, remember," Xalan said. "It's difficult to turn geomancy toward the mastery of others. I must say I wish I had devoted more time to my studies." He pulled in his donkey a little, falling back so that we rode side by side.

We went on a little way downhill, and I saw that the approaching party had turned off the main road and halted in the brush below. "Why don't we turn aside too?" I suggested.

"And then what, wait till morning? If we see them, they see us." At a maddeningly slow donkey-walk we descended. The Sun dipped through its bath of scarlet and with dismaying speed slipped below the horizon. In the stuffy valley night reigned, though light still gilded the hilltops. It was impossible to see what sort of folk crouched waiting in the brush.

Suddenly we were nearly among them. I kicked my donkey, hoping to make it run, but it only hopped forward a pace or two before settling into an amble again beside its fellow. No one hailed us, and Xalan and I did not speak. In tense silence broken only by the multiple crunches of hooves on oyster-shell paving we passed, knee to knee in the twilight.

I took a deep breath and leaned back in the saddle to relax. Nothing had happened. "Mother always says I'm a worrier," I said to Xalan, when suddenly his donkey stumbled heavily, lurching against my leg.

"Cabbage-head!" someone shouted to my right. "I *told* you to spare the beasts, there's half our profit gone!"

"He moved!" another rejoined indignantly, even as Xalan's hapless donkey sagged. The javeline that had missed both him and me stood out from the beast's side, and my left leg was red and wet with its blood. As it fell Xalan struggled out from under the corpse.

"Get down," he hissed at me, "you're a mark for spears." I

felt almost sick with fear as I did so, but Xalan's grimy face held only a frown of concentration. As the robbers closed in he took off his cap and dusted it against his leg so that its red color was plain once more. "Change your minds now," Xalan shouted cheerily, "before it's too late." He set the cap on his head again and our assailants muttered at the sight. Magi are very bad enemies. Thankfully I peered between Xalan and my mount, hoping that our foes were as terrified as I was.

"He's only one, and an apprentice at that," someone said.

Clicking his tongue in impatience Xalan raised the black wand. As its butt left the ground the pale sand rose silently with it, evenly, steadily, mounting like wine filling a cup until it was high over our heads. Only a small circular area around us remained clear. All around us choking curses and sneezes marked our invisible foes. Xalan grinned at me, gesturing for silence, and pointed at his dead mount. I unstrapped the water jugs and laid them on my donkey. Taking my hand, Xalan led the way through the fog as quietly as possible. The crunch of the road would betray us, so we threaded our way through the thorn bushes, Xalan keeping us in the right direction by geomantically feeling for the earth currents below our feet. The clear dustless area crept along with us. "As long as we don't trip," Xalan whispered, "or shout, or blunder on to one of these ruffians, we're safe."

"How far shall we go?"

"Up out of the valley," he replied. "Let them look for us all night."

The sand that had been so irritating now cloaked and carpeted us through danger. Then without warning a grubby thickset man tottered into our circle onto my toe, spitting and rubbing his eyes. He recovered from his surprise before we did. "Here!" he shouted. "They're here, everybody!" Shouts and yells answered him. Encouraged, the fellow raised his club at me. Frozen, I did nothing, but the black wand gestured and a finger of sand flicked into the man's face. With a howl of enraged pain he turned and struck at Xalan instead. Unaimed the weapon glanced off Xalan's head, and he crumpled. As the wand fell the friendly sand fell with it. All at once I was standing alone on the sandy slope, revealed to my foes.

Old instincts took over. I leaped to my donkey's back and lashed it to an unwilling trot. Unfortunately because of the four water bottles my seat was extremely precarious. The donkey shied away from a snatching hand and I slipped right over its back to the sand, knocking myself breathless. I heard my frightened mount cantering away, stirred at last out of a walking pace. The balked robbers swore as they gave chase, but one must have stayed behind to deal with me. I heard nothing of the blow that felled me.

Much later thirst brought me slowly to myself. Cold moonlight shone down on my face. I was alone, tangled right up to my eyebrows in a snarl of thornbush. From pure spite, probably because I had carried little money, our assailants had thrown me down the slope. Donkey and water, even my clothes and knife, were stolen. I pried myself free, and the motion made brazen gongs thrum in my skull. Feeling my head I found the hair matted with sticky blood from a cut near the nape of my neck. I plucked out a few thorns and sucked the bloody cuts, but the salty, dusty taste of my skin made me thirstier than ever.

I crept over to Xalan and turned him gently over. There was no blood on his face in the moonlight but he did not wake. His hands were cold, clutching their black wand so tightly I dared not remove it. I supposed the robbers had not dared either. Nor had they stolen his clothes—they could not be sold since that shade of deep red is worn only by magi. But his shoes, belt, purse, and knife were gone.

There was nothing to be done, no rescue to seek. A white and empty despair filled me. I sat beside Xalan in the indifferent moonlight and watched the blood from my scrapes seep into the sand. "The King ought to do something about these gangs," I said aloud foolishly. "There's really no getting to Mishbil anymore." Then I realized *I* was the King. Hunger and weakness were allowing the locked mental chambers to pop open in my head, and from each a new accuser emerged, snakes sliding from the inner darkness into the lurid light of the Moon.

All by myself I had wrought Xalan's end and my own. At my command he had exiled himself from guild, city and kin to die here. I had defied the same, with the god and the government thrown in for makeweight. And for what? All my roads seemed to lead to the Deadlands. Was it better to die in an attempt to claim the Crystal Crown, or in the wilderness of thirst and exposure? At least if I had been a little braver in the Navel Room Xalan would not have walked the deathward road with me. And at the last when he had been struck down in my defense I had left him and run, shamefully. All my conflicting errors rose up and stared at me, mutually unsolvable yet as one demanding resolution, and in the face of them I could not stand. I sagged back onto the friendly sand and stared at the night sky. The stars trembled cold and bright, as if through a veil of tears, but their sympathy was no comfort. "If I ever get out of this," I muttered to them, to the Sun, the White Queen, whatever deity that could hear, "I'll make amends, change my life."

It seemed a poor offer. Yet the Moon above me spoke in reply: "A very common promise, I should judge, from someone in your melancholy situation. No doubt this is why God allows tribulation, so that new—if evanescent—devotees may be constantly won."

I knew it was the moon because it spoke Viridese with a weird clipped accent, one I had never heard before. Naturally a sky-rider gets little opportunity for conversation with the earthborn. Then I blinked, focusing my eyes. Not the Moon, but a round face haloed in white with white moonlight full on it. I started up and almost fainted. "Steady, steady! Flops, if you would—" Strong hands supported me and helped me up.

"Who are you?" I croaked through dry lips.

My vision cleared a little, and I saw that despite the odd name the one called Flops was Viridese. "We all serve the weird foreigner," he said cheerfully. "How lucky your donkey escaped to run over the hill! When we saw it the master knew someone had been waylaid."

His master whacked Flops none too gently on the head with his cane. "No conversation now, Flops," he ordered. "Help him to the wagon and send the others for this one."

On the road waited a conveyance, not what we would call a wagon at all. To my dazed perception it seemed to be a neat little flat-roofed house complete with doors, windows, a balcony, and a ceramic stovepipe, all set high on great wheels of solid wood and drawn by eight donkeys. My own beast was tied behind. Flops and his fellows hoisted me aboard and poured water for me. I gulped down the first delicious cupful so thirstily that Flops advised, "Slowly!" So I set down the mug for a moment.

"You can't really be named Flops," I said.

"As a matter of fact I'm a Melekirtsan," Flops said, "but the master's country holds by nicknames and he dubs everyone anew when they enter his service. Though I never thought I should say it, I've got quite used to being called Flops."

"What is his name and nation?"

"No one can pronounce his name, and he came to Mishbil from over the Endless Mountains, believe it or not."

At that point Flops' master appeared with Xalan, so gossip

ceased. "You must sleep," our rescuer advised me in deep booming tones that filled the little room. "We shall travel north all night but you shall be snug enough in the bunks." Narrow shelf-beds were let down and Xalan tucked into one. "Sanitation must give way to prudence," our host said, brushing off the sandy sheet before tucking it in. "Victims of head wounds ought not to be bathed. In any case we have little water to spare and even less space for a bathtub."

"Wouldn't think of it," I muttered, anxious to please, and fell asleep.

Chapter 3: Assay Question

Pulling this tremendous weight the eight donkeys traveled very slowly. When I woke next morning we had retraced only half of yesterday's road. I hurt all over, and was indescribably dirty, but my head and the worst of my thorn-stabs had been cleaned and anointed. I sat up and examined my surroundings. The little wooden room was exquisitely tidy, everything stowed neatly in its place. However, it seemed snug as a foxglove's blossom since it was painted in vivid tones of yellow, green, black, and blue, with touches of white and red on doorknobs or window-latches. The effect was cheerful but dizzying, especially when a wagon wheel lurched over a rock or into a pothole. I rose, balancing myself against the wagon's motion, and put on a gray linen robe laid out ready for me. On the other side of the room Xalan was still asleep or unconscious, his face pale against the bright paint. The other two shelves were occupied by Viridese servants. I tiptoed past them and tried one of the yellow-and-green doors. It gave onto a view of the east—ocher hills rolling up and down to the horizon. A stepladder which could be lowered for disembarking was folded up and latched to the door frame. I closed the door and tried another. This opened onto a short steep stair, really almost a ladder, up to the roof. I went up, closing the door carefully behind me. The exterior of the wagon gleamed as bright in the morning Sun as the interior, in a scheme of blue and yellow diagonal bars adorned around the upper edge with curlicued railings painted red and purple. At the back, on the awninged balcony-platform, lounged my host, eating breakfast.

As well as I could for my headache and the lurching of the wagon I bowed. "We owe you our lives," I thanked him shyly.

"Join me," he said, tossing over a cushion. I did so, and as he poured me some tea I looked him over.

He was of no race I had ever seen or heard of in chronicle or plaiv. White hair stuck out in a deep fluffy halo all around his head, continuing on down around his chin in a beard. His skin was deep brown, not tanned but brown in itself. He was tall and broad with a powerful sort of fat, perhaps sixty, with a lined yet zestful round face. As I had last night I asked, "What is your name and country?"

"Hah! Flops, do you hear? Shall we wager again?"

Flops, who was perched on the front seat driving, glanced back at us. "No, master, I've no more gold to lose."

Grumbling, my host said, "Pity, I was beginning to enjoy your Viridese custom of wagering. The bet is always as to whether anyone can repeat my name. I never met a Viridese who could. Flops is an avid gambler, but he's backed so many losers now he's quite shy." He looked at me. "Would *you* care to bet on it?"

"All I have now is yours," I pointed out. "How would you profit?"

"Knowledge! You shall stake knowledge! What do you know? Not much, I daresay, you're too young."

"My story is perhaps unique," I suggested. "In fact, I shouldn't mind wagering you've never heard the like."

"Very unlikely! I've heard many stories indeed. But so it shall be. Your story is your stake. And when you cannot pronounce my name, and recount your tale, if it is unique you shall have any boon of me that I can grant." I assented, and he continued, "Good, then! My name in my own tongue is—"

He said it and my jaw dropped. No Viridese tongue could ever get round those twisty consonants and liquid vowels. It was not a Caydish name, nor Viridese, nor even a term in the incomprehensible sacred language of Ennelith's rites. I could not begin to try repeating it. He bellowed with laughter at my expression and said, "So! I win, eh?"

"Then what shall I call you?" I asked. "Who are you?"

"Mmm—I am a scholar, you might say, and I travel to far lands and then publish my journals so that those too lazy to leave home may taste all the pleasures of voyaging without the accompanying labor. My country is south and west, on the other side of the mountains your folk erroneously name Endless, but I shall not burden you with its name. This is the farthest I have ever journeyed, and should make a most lucrative tale, to which your story (if unique) would be a welcome addition. You shall call me, let me see, Sandcomber—for I did search the thorny sands for you and your friend last night. Ugh, what a dreadful spot that was! And now—your stake!''

"Wait," I said. "What about Xalan?"

"Your friend?" He sighed. "You should solicit advice from your own people—bonesetters? herbals? But I should say his skull is cracked.''

"Will he die?"

"Possibly. Console yourself that we are hurrying as fast as we may to the nearest possible help.''

But a dreadful guilt seemed to crush me down, an invisible lapidation, and as the garish little wheeled house crept up and down the ocher hills I poured out to Sandcomber my "story" all the tangle of trouble I had somehow wound myself in. It took a long time, punctuated by many cups of tea, and I concluded by begging, "Advise me, you aren't Viridese but a foreigner. The webs that hold us do not bind you.''

He thought this over, staring meditatively out at the passing hills. "You Viridese are the most unreasonable race I've ever encountered. By which I mean you don't use your reason in daily life. If your foolish friend had used his head he would have instantly perceived the inconsistency in obeying the commands of a self-deposed monarch.''

"Xalan is the quickest person I know," I protested.

"Hum! I owe you a boon, by the way. I must admit I have never met, let alone succored, renegade royalty before. As to your plight—it is dangerous, you say, to become Shan King?''

"Yes.''

"Yet it is dangerous to travel to escape anything, as you now know from bitter experience. Danger is inescapable—life of itself is perilous.''

"It wasn't before," I mourned.

"I should judge, from your account, that what you call the passage between myth and reality is like certain gates, that lock behind you. One may go forward, but not back.''

"Then what should I *do*?''

"Formulate goals, and then set about achieving them, of course," he said, obviously quoting some proverb of his people.

"There are many ways to discern one's goals, but perhaps the simplest for one of your race would be this: What would you wish for, if at this moment you were at the famous Sun Temple of Averidan to beg a wish of the god?"

I considered, searching my heart. To not be Shan King? But as Xalan had pointed out, the deity had chosen me—if only by passing the Collegium's choice. A sort of politeness restrains us from wasting the divinity's time on fruitless wishes. And on second thought there was something I wanted more now. "For Xalan's recovery," I said.

Sandcomber sighed—apparently my wish did not please him. "Even if achieved, that would do nothing whatever toward resolving your other difficulties," he grumbled. "But I will concede that it is at least a goal within your grasp. I do my part: carrying you both to the City. What shall your contribution be?" When I could not reply he said, "There may genuinely be nothing for you to offer, but you should bear the question in mind. I will now go down and inspect your friend—oh, please don't follow, there is not room in the cabin for both of us."

With the assistance of the curly wooden rail he hauled himself to his feet. He wore a long white linen robe, not Viridese in style but simple enough to pass here unremarked. Descending the little stair, which was just wide enough to receive him, he looked like a plump white rat being engulfed by a brilliant viper.

The blue and yellow trap door shut behind him, and then popped open again. "Did I complete my own assessment of your plight? No? Remiss of me. You may recall your resolve last night to change yourself. That was relatively enlightened of you—in our country we always consider problems as functions not of circumstance but of internal flaw. In other words, to address your situation, what lack in yourself has gotten you into trouble?"

The door banged shut again, and I leaned back on the cushions. The answer to that was obvious: courage. Lack of it had driven me from one peril to another, like a mouse skittering from cat to cat until it collapses in terror. Had I only the courage either to grasp my destiny and die, or exile myself properly! Put like that it was plainly easier to go back and be slain by the Crystal Crown. And now I had decided Xalan was the first priority I had to return, to ensure his proper care or at the worst to explain his death to his kin and the Master Magus.

The patient donkeys had dragged us back to pleasanter lands, the mosaic of tidy vegetable farms surrounding the triple fork of the road. We were nearing our destination. Then, as they some-times do after long thought, the answer to part of my problem came to me. Raising the little trap door I descended, crouching on the bottom step. "I know what to do for Xalan," I announced. "When we come to the City I'll send for the Crystal Crown, and heal him by its power if it doesn't kill me first."

Sandcomber looked up and raised his eyebrows. "You mean to say it has real powers? Hah! You astonish me! I would have said rather that the voices and so forth were supplied by your own overheated imagination."

"Absolutely not!" Here I was, alas, all too sure of my ground. "The Crown is very powerful and ancient magery, as well as the symbol and sign of the Shan."

"At least you propose a positive step." He frowned down at Xalan's white face. "You can assuredly do no harm. But you will need to act promptly. The lad is sinking." But these words made me not fearful with dread but stubborn. I should fight as long as possible, now I knew what to do.

It would take all afternoon for the faithful donkeys to drag the heavy wagon up the steep main road to the Palace. So when we came to the triple fork I suggested turning west, to my home. Sandcomber greeted the proposal with a sniff and a warning: "One can never go back, any more than smoke and heat can creep back into the burning log." But having no better idea to offer he directed Flops to turn the wagon up the west road, and in less than an hour we drew up into my own street. I leaped off the wagon and ran ahead to my own gate. No sight was more cheering than the afternoon sunshine turning my gate-gong into a molten copper disc, and taking up the stick I made it sway in its stand with my blow.

"Hey, open!" I shouted. "I'm home!"

The wicket swung open sharply and Ferd glared for a moment before recognizing me. "Sir, is it really you?" he cried. "What happened? Everyone's been going mad looking for you."

"Ferd, go immediately to the Palace and bespeak the Master Magus," I commanded.

"Impossible, sir," Ferd said. "Didn't you hear—the Colle-gium's going into session right after the evening sacrifice."

"To choose another Shan King?" For a moment I was sorely tempted to do nothing. Let them select some other victim. But I felt Sandcomber's sardonic gaze on my back, and remembered Xalan, who would never survive to be healed by another wielder of the Crystal Crown. "That makes it even more vital," I decided. "Run, and get the news of my return to the Collegium any way you can. And it's very important that the Magus bring the Crystal Crown here instantly."

"Here? Yes, sir—" Without further words Ferd dashed off.

"What obedient servants you have in your country," Sandcomber remarked, signaling to Flops.

"We reserve arguments for our families," I replied. I held the wicket open while he and Flops carried Xalan through.

Viridese gates are traditionally double, the outer of solid wood or metal and the inner carved and pierced in openwork designs linked by a thick arched passageway. This is so that tenants may examine visitors before letting them through into the garden and so around into the house. However, doors had been let into mine, giving into either side of the passage. This spoiled the entry for defense purposes but rendered daily life much more convenient. Xalan was borne through into one of these side rooms and laid tenderly on a couch.

"Wine," I ordered. "Let someone fill a bath—no, two baths, you would like to wash too, Sandcomber. Send for a herbal to examine Xalan. Prepare some guest chambers, this gentleman will be staying—"

"Liras!" At the door stood Yibor-soo. "Where is Rosil?"

"How should I know, isn't he with you? And what are you doing here in my house?"

I thought this a perfectly reasonable question, but Yibor screamed high and thin, dashing over to strike at me inexpertly with her hands. "What do you mean? How dare you! You dreadful, irresponsible brat, Rosil is in prison and it's all your fault—"

She could not really damage me—Yibor is well over forty, and was always flabby—but the blows on my scratched and sunburnt skin hurt. I ducked away and ran to the inner door, Sandcomber neatly sidestepping out of my way. Before I could touch the latch the door opened. It was Mother. She took in my presence with one gimlet glance and said, "No doubt, Yibor dear, the authorities had other charges after all. Here is my beloved Liras-ven safe and sound, but poor Rosil is still incarcerated. At the least, I was always confident your son would never stoop to actual murder."

"And you'll aver, I suppose, that your vixen of a daughter had no part in this?" Beside herself, Yibor tugged at my sleeve. "Liras must go to the guardsmen immediately and give himself up!"

"Why ever for?" I demanded. "Why is Rosil in prison?"

"He's not in prison," Mother corrected. "Just held for questioning. He's suspected of being involved in your disappearance."

Definitely I was not myself. I was both sticky and gritty all over, and my many scrapes and scratches were still painful and raw. Sandcomber's disturbing conversation had been unlike any other I had known—the arts of analysis and philosophy are minimal in Averidan—and the final assay of the Crystal Crown was approaching me far too rapidly. So my first reaction to this preposterous development was laughter. I collapsed to the tile floor and almost wept with mirth while Mother and Yibor traded insults and recriminations over my head.

"Ladies, ladies!" Sandcomber stepped up to me. "My young friend, should you not present me to your kin?"

Pulling myself together I rose and made introductions, adding, "Sandcomber is a foreigner who gave us a ride home."

"How very kind of you," Mother said graciously. "Your name is not Viridese, I believe."

A little suspiciously Yibor-soo asked, "Where exactly did you meet Liras?"

Leaving Sandcomber to cope with their questions I went over to the window. All these days I had hoped someone had finished pruning my klimflowers and tied the plant up properly to its trellis again. But when I swung the shutter aside I could not suppress a cry. "Viris above us!"

A deep excavation lined with rock had been dug in the middle of my lawn. The marble garden paving had been pried up and stacked on the peony beds, crushing the plants. The trellises had been demolished, and some sort of building was being erected in what remained of the orchard. "My garden! What have you been doing in my garden?"

"Now Liras," Mother soothed. "You can't live in the house anymore. We were redoing it for Rosil when all this trouble started."

"He's planning three fish ponds," Yibor added with maternal pride. "And a little fountain, over there."

"But it's mine! That's five years of intensive gardening spoiled out there!" I leaned my forehead on the window frame.

"You mustn't be so selfish," Mother said. "The gardens at the Palace are four times the size of this one, and are filled with dozens of lovely things—roses on pear trees, as they say."

Too overcome to reply I turned away. Indeed there was no

returning for me. Then sharp needles stabbed my calf through
my borrowed robe. "Sahai!" I exclaimed, bending to detach her
from my leg and pick her up. My cat was glad to see me, purring
and writhing in my arms, and I asked, "Has she missed me?"

"She's a pest," Yibor complained. "She spoiled a lovely
robe of mine the other day by clawing the embroidery."

Somehow Sahai's furry gray body against my chest was an
infinite comfort, and when Ferd panted in to announce the arrival
of the magi I was able to remain quite calm. The Master Magus
limped in, with a flurry of red sleeves, almost on Ferd's heels.
He leaned heavily on his wand, since his foot was swathed in
bandages. Magi are supposed to cultivate moderation and inner
peace but I could tell Xantallon's control was being severely
tested. In tones of grievously injured dignity he demanded,
"Where has Your Majesty been?"

Softening the truth as much as I could I said, "I went for a
ride with Xalan."

"And why did you not bring your proper attendants, or at
least leave word?"

Before I could work up a plausible reply Arixhel darted for
ward from behind the Magus. "What has happened to you,
Majesty?" she cried, patting my scratched face. "Look at you!"

A little put out by this usurpation of her role, Mother said,
"Did you fall, dear?"

"We were waylaid by bandits," I explained quickly, "and
Xalan was hurt."

The Magus was so upset at this intelligence he forgot his
official role's questions. "How did this happen?" he exclaimed.
"What shall I tell his mother?"

"There isn't time for details," I said. "We must hurry with
the assay so that I can call on the Crystal Crown's power to heal
him." Too late I recalled that the existence of a test is supposed
to be secret. But if the Magus did not scold me for blurting the
vital word likely no one would notice.

"That's not the proper order of things," Arixhel objected.
"You have to pass, and then study all the chronicles on the
subject before attempting healing."

But with feverish haste the Magus was hurrying everyone else
out of the room. "That would take days," he said. "The rite is a
state secret, ladies, so I must ask everyone to leave."

My family and servants fluttered with curiosity—all Viridese
love exciting events—but allowed themselves to be shown out.
But emerging from his corner Sandcomber refused. Fixing the

Magus with an ironic brown eye he said, "Now, what would my readers say to me if I left at this thrilling juncture, eh? I have never seen the terrible Crystal Crown, but from my young friend's incoherent descriptions I should surmise it to be a heat-fueled brain-power transformer. Think, of departing without confirmation of my guess! Impossible!"

"Is that what it really is?" I said with interest.

The glass wand slipped clattering from the Magus' hand—fortunately it was reinforced with bronze, too thick to shatter easily. He stared at us with real horror. "You foolish boy!" he exclaimed. "How did you come to babble this?"

"You must not blame Liras," Sandcomber said. "He was, after all, overwrought from his unpleasant adventure, and also we always tend to trust our rescuers. Would the assurance that I should never so abuse the Shan King's trust by publishing his secrets be of any comfort to you?"

The Magus collapsed onto a couch and pulled at his white beard in anguish. "Who is he?" he asked me.

"Sandcomber," I introduced, "a foreigner." Hoping to console him somewhat I added, "He saved Xalan too."

When (as etiquette demands) the Magus offered thanks, Sandcomber swept them aside in a mellifluous flow of words: "Do not think of gratitude, dear magician! In our country it is counted a particular virtue to rescue the humble so that all may know thoughts of reward did not inspire the kindness. The appearance of your monarch was particularly misleading last evening. . . ."

Putting down Sahai I drew Arixhel aside. "Did you bring the Crown?"

She held out a wooden casket adorned with chased-gold plaques. "This isn't the way it's supposed to be done," she told me. Ignoring this I set down the box and lifted the lid. I had avoided this encounter for so long I dared not hesitate now for fear of losing my nerve.

Remembering the hot white glow in the water—was it only night before last?—I was ready to shield my eyes. But to my surprise only soft white light shone gently out of the box. Perhaps my own fears had veiled my sight. How else had I not noticed that the Crown was beautiful? The Queen of the Dead is so lovely, they say, that death is only the fair price to pay to look on her face. Now I understood that tale. I held in my hands perhaps the oldest work of the Shan in existence, and it had always been beautiful. My death by it if I failed would be unimportant, would not sully that loveliness. And this was as it should be. In a spirit almost of reverence I lifted the Crown and put it on.

As before there was no effect at first. Arixhel drew back a few paces, her bright black eyes glittering, and Sandcomber was explaining to the distracted Magus his people's theories of treatment for head wounds. Then without warning my own form stood before me.

My spine crinkled with slow horror as I looked the eerie arrival over. He wore a robe exactly like mine, and my own face, but no Crown. It was like looking in a mirror, except that his movements did not ape mine. He stood unsmiling, hands on hips, and stared at me as I glanced sidelong round the room. Arixhel did not appear to see him at all, and the Magus was just being maneuvered into accepting a wager on Sandcomber's name. My heart thumped in my chest as this most obvious peril entered my head—that the double would simply snatch the reins of my personality, become me. The Shan have been a nation for ten thousand years. Was this because they had had only one ruler in all that time? An immortal, bodiless being, usurping mind after mind. Involuntarily I looked down at myself to be sure I was still me. The familiar sight of my own dirty hands steadied me, and wiping them on my borrowed robe I approached my twin.

"Who are you?"

"It was thought you might be less unsettled with a visible and familiar figure," my double said, with precisely my own voice and inflection.

"Silly but effective," I said. In spite of my new apprehensions my stomach unknotted and my nerves slackened as I looked the image in the eye. It's not quite possible to feel threatened by your self, any more than you can tickle your own ribs. The Crystal Crown sat warm on my head, but I could ignore it while I had a speaker in front of me.

"You are a silly young man," the image said.

My fears were seeping away, to be replaced by assertiveness. I said, "I liked your other voice better, mine is rather thin."

"At our other conversation you were asked your final decision. Your presence now indicates your choice, does it not?"

"It might." I considered lying but it seemed pointless. "If you must be told, I nearly got away. I came back because I needed something more than escape.

"Good." My image smiled. "To take the first step of your own will is unnecessary, but propitious."

"Propitious for what?" I demanded, but the image had vanished. Yet its voice still lingered in my head to reply, "For your career as a hero."

"Wait a minute," I protested. "I'm no hero. And what about this assay?" But almost before the words left my mouth the power descended. It began in fire just above and behind the bridge of my nose, and expanded, gaining in weight and heat until the pressure forced me to my knees. So the ore must feel in the crucible, as it is melted down and poured into the mold. Blinded by my own sweat I put up one hand to feel. The Crown was cool as always, but my head seemed to glow red-hot like a stoked furnace. Inky shadows streamed back from couches and pillars as my flesh glowed like molten silver. I gave myself up for lost and clung to the floor as it rocked under me.

With a soundless shock I broke through the pain and was free. Riding the surge as I would a powerful but well-trained horse, I tasted for the first time the delight of doing what I was born to do. I felt, to turn the saying, like a pear tree when it gives up trying to produce roses and sets pears instead: a relief of strain, a rightness of destiny, a return to nature. From a great distance, yet very clearly, I noticed the Magus shading his old eyes, Arixhel clapping her gnarled hands in glee, and the white fluffy hair around Sandcomber's awed face.

In this new clarity it was easy to see what was wrong with Xalan's head. Tracing the crack line with a finger seemed to be enough to persuade the bits to reunite. It was pleasing to smooth a disorderly spot away, but when I had done I felt a new imperative to move, to go. Sandcomber had been right. My return had been as foolish as a moth trying to climb back into its silky cocoon. Of their own accord my feet took me out the door into the arched passageway connecting the gates. I paused in confusion, shining in the dimness like a misplaced fallen star, and across the way at the farther door my family cowered back. Then beside me the Magus spoke in low and soothing tones. "Let's take a turn round your garden," he said. "Sandcomber, if you might take his other side—" He led me to the left, and pushed the openwork gate aside.

So arm in arm we paced my ruined domain, avoiding the deeper excavations, while I tottered on my first fumbling steps toward the dual management of distant body and newly augmented mind. Nobody spoke, and as the Sun set in a pool of crimson and gold the unearthly white fire on my head waned. By then the presence, above and behind the bridge of my nose, was warm and ponderous but no longer disabling. I was still myself, so far as I could tell. I could think my own thoughts around that presence, even speak, as one would speak round a mouthful of chewy candy. "How is Xalan?" I carefully enunciated.

"Let's go see," the Magus suggested, and we strolled back.

Inside seemed stuffy after the cool evening air, and intolerably busy. Mother held a basin of water and was washing the grime off any portion of Xalan's body she could reach. The herbal had arrived and had let a smelly headache potion boil over on the glowing copper brazier while she argued with Xalan over her fee. And for reasons known only to herself Yibor had ordered an elaborate company supper, ensuring an unceasing flow of servants to carry tables, cloths, plates, and tableware in and out of the room. Since the passageway door was ajar we went in, but as I entered the bustle faltered. Truly, wearing the Crown did not alter my usual self—tongue-tied and shy I fidgeted in the door way while everyone stared.

Xalan came to my rescue, rising from the couch and bowing before me. "I'm honored to be Your Majesty's first healing," he said. "My powers in your service!"

"How do you feel?" the Magus asked him.

"I've a terrible headache," Xalan complained, "and this herbal wants to upset my stomach as well. I want to go home."

"But what about supper?" Yibor cried, just as if we were guests.

For the first time the Magus glanced at me for the decision, and I said, "Yes, home." While sedan chairs were summoned I offered Sandcomber the family's hospitality here. He agreed, to spare his donkeys who had worked so hard the further uphill trip to the Palace. Yibor-soo did her best to seem delighted at the unexpected guest. Then I sent for a covered basket. "Here, Sahai," I coaxed, "come along." She allowed herself to be lured down from her perch on the lintel, not appearing to notice the Crown at all. Indeed if she had recoiled I would have been hurt.

When the chairs arrived we took our leave, but Mother said to me, "With that thing on your head on a trip to the Upper City they'll overcharge you." It seemed a petty economy but she insisted, so taking the Crown off I returned it to its box. Not until then did Mother hug and kiss me good-bye.

"It's not all that far," I protested when I saw how upset she was. "I'll see you very soon." Yibor made me promise to order Rosil's release as soon as possible. But now that my head was my own again I was realizing what I had let myself in for. Making the bearers wait I beckoned to Sandcomber and asked in a low voice,'' What about the rest of my problem? How *do* I learn to be a hero? Where does one acquire courage?''

''Certainly it is not a commodity one finds in the market,'' he replied. ''Nor have I ever in my travels met a purveyor of bravery. No doubt this is why it is so rare! But I will consider the question for you, and if I find an answer I will set myself up in the profession. Hah! That would be lucrative indeed, particularly in the more unsettled parts of the world!''

With this unsatisfactory arrangement I was borne away. As the bearers trotted to the West Gate I gloomily reflected how after all my labor to scale the slope I had succeeded—only to see the real mountain before me. It was a depressing prospect, becoming a hero. But Sahai's basket on my lap was some comfort, as was the thought of a bath, hot food, and sleep in my own bed.

The pavements must have been hot after a day baking in the Sun, but the bare feet of the bearers spurned the white lime and sharp oyster shells. Back and forth we tacked, until the steep natural fortification of the Upper City was ascended. Once through the upper gate my bearers followed the Magus' chair around to the right, through the silent Palace gardens. For the first time I noticed—I was able to notice—how big the starry night sky looked here on top of the hill, and how deeply arched. A yellow Moon smiled high above the white marble Palace, the two great lights thinning the night north and east to a milky purple-blue. The gardens, though well planned, did not seem to contain the marvels Mother had said.

We descended our chairs at the very terrace I had fallen onto two mornings ago. ''Those klimflowers need pruning,'' I said, craning my neck to inspect them. ''I think I'll plant some peonies, too. If Rosil hasn't squashed all the old ones they can be transplanted.''

Xalan nudged his granduncle, laughing at me. ''Who would have believed it? Welcome home, Your Majesty.''

PART II: THE ROAD TO IEOR

Chapter 4: The Caydish Treaty

On the first official day of my reign I rose full of good intentions. The three-day coronation rite and thirty subsequent days of holiday had been fun, but now I looked forward to learning the business of rule. So I was suspicious when the Master of Wardrobe and his assistants appeared before breakfast with a fancy suit of parade armor.

As they lined up against the wall, each holding a segment of worked golden scales on gilded leather for my inspection, I eyed the stuff. "Didn't I wear this for that military review of honor the other week?"

"Oh, no, Majesty, that was the enameled set." The Master stood in front of his subordinates like a rooster before his hens. "We would never suggest a repeat appearance so soon."

"Isn't it a bit ostentatious?"

"Accept my assurances, Majesty, armor is completely appropriate. After all, Prince Melbras is the Warlord of the Caydish Army."

"So he is. What does that have to do with it?"

"Why, you're to sign the treaty with him today. And it's proper for you to be in military dress."

Since I knew nothing of the treaty there was no further argument to make. I allowed myself to be dressed. "Send someone to see if the apprentice magus Xalan is here yet," I ordered. We had formed the pleasant habit of breakfasting together after the abortive escape attempt.

Xalan shaded his eyes in a pretense of awe when I came clattering out to the terrace. "Dazzling!" he exclaimed, imitating the rhetors' florid narrative style. "The Son of the Sun arises!"

"Stop laughing, it wasn't my idea. What is this about a treaty with Cayd?"

"The embassy was in town for months," Xalan said. "Negotiating with your predecessor. No one told you the signing was today?"

"No," I grumbled. "I suppose no one tells the King anything

49

so that he can enjoy his coronation.'' Then I looked at him. Xalan wore that milky look I had learned to associate with mischief. "All right, out with it. What are you planning?''

"Invocation first,'' he said. "You'll need food to ballast you.''

I rattled through the formula, invoking the Sun our ancestor to bless and guard the day. Then as the servers brought out bowls of sectioned fruit Xalan began, "You know about the old pact between us and Cayd.''

"Certainly: to war on the Tiyalor and destroy the dam at Ieor.''

"Yes.'' Xalan's face darkened for an instant. The waters of the Mhesan River are important to our irrigation system, but not vital, since Averidan has three rivers. But our neighbor Cayd has only the one. When the Tiyalor dammed the river at Ieor they inconvenienced us, but held Cayd by the throat. Such a subtle work would never have been conceived by the oafish lake-men. To the magi's shame the dam had been planned and built with the geomancy of a renegade magus, one Xerlanthor.

"And we gave Cayd money and arms and food the last few years, while they did the fighting,'' I remembered.

"Right. Well, it seems the magery laid by Xerlanthor makes his dam almost impossible to destroy. And he's using his powers against the Caydish too. They're losing. So we'll take a bigger hand—send the Sisterhood of Mir-hel and the army. That's what the pact will affirm.''

"How exciting, I've always wanted to see war.'' Sitting on white linen cushions with the morning Sun tinting the marble balustrade to the exact gold-pink of my peaches, it was hard to believe war was not anything but what is told of in plaiv: entertaining, exciting, but not really perilous. "Sandcomber will be sorry to miss the trip. The northern coasts won't be nearly as picturesque.''

"Oh, you won't be going either,'' Xalan laughed.

"Why ever not?''

"There's a provision in the treaty especially for you.''

"Now we come to it,'' I said. "Is this the reason I have to be dressed to the teeth to affix my seal?''

"Surely. Prince Melbras, after all, has a right to expect a show of honor from his future nephew.''

Xalan put down his cup and hooted at the sight of my dumbfounded face. "But my sister Siril already has a husband,'' I said stupidly.

"The Prince's brother the King of Cayd has many children. I understand his youngest daughter Melayne was at first to wed one of your predecessor's sons. Of course it fell through when he died. They say the Caydish embassy was relieved and delighted to learn the new Shan King is a bachelor."

"I'm getting married?"

"To seal the treaty."

"My appetite was gone. The juicy peach turned to dust on my tongue. "Why didn't anyone ask me? Shouldn't I have been told? What is she like? When will it be?"

Xalan laughed at my discomfiture until he choked. "Actually," he said at last, "it is unfair you didn't know." He wiped his eyes with the trailing end of one red sleeve. "This custom of not confusing a new king with affairs has its bad features."

"I can't get married now, my mother wants to handle that," I said.

"Don't be silly, you're Shan King now." Xalan grinned, remembering the proof of it. "You have no private life."

I assented with a sigh. "Besides, she would have been sure to pick out some awful nagger," I said. "She picked out Yibor-soo herself." This reflection renewed the flavor of my breakfast a little, and I refilled our teacups. "What's the girl like, what's her name?"

"Princess Melayne of Cayd—they don't use family names or generational syllables. No one here has met her—they keep high-born ladies close. But you'll meet her uncle today."

"And she isn't Shan."

"Well, no, but that's not anything to worry about." This was true enough. Our nation has vast assimilative powers, and strangers who marry in, conquer, or simply live nearby eventually become Shan. Of course this quality would not help me if my wife turned out to be uncongenial. Since there was nothing to be done about that I resolved now, while heart and mind were still clear, to like my wife if it was at all possible.

"Very accommodating of you," Xalan said when I told him this. With a glint of irony in his eye he quoted, "No one of discernment resents the inevitable."

In my chambers the Lord Director of Protocol waited for me. We navigated the wide halls to the Treaty Chamber while I listened with half an ear to his advice on what to say and do. Some of my family were in the antechamber when we arrived.

"Hallo, Liras-ven, I hear you're to be married!" Zofal whacked me on the back in a gesture of brotherly congratulation.

"Why the bridegroom is last to learn of it I'll never know," I said. "What does Mother say about it?"

"She doesn't like the idea of a foreigner, but she'll adjust."

Rosil-eir came forward also, saying, "Hope you'll be very happy, Liras. When do we meet her?"

"I'd like to know that myself," I said. "Xalan, what did the treaty provide?"

"The betrothal now, Majesty, the wedding to take place over the winter, and the new Tiyalor offensive to initiate in the spring."

I sighed. Events were moving too quickly for me. "Let's go in then, and sign the thing." But I was not deemed ready yet. The weapon bearers buckled a gemmed sword on my hip and slung a shield enameled in scarlet at my shoulder. Then I beckoned for the Crystal Crown. In a moment of nepotism I had appointed one of my younger cousins, Fisan-shi Tsormelezok, Bearer of the Crown. The honor had made her nervous—she was more of my temperament than Zofal's—and as she approached the casket almost slipped from her hands.

"You should have named someone older," Rosil criticized, and the poor girl blushed.

"Cousin Fisan is inconspicuous and quiet," I said, and put the Crown on.

Of the unimaginable powers of the Crystal Crown none is more useful or better known than its enabling the wearer to read hearts. The Shan King's duties—doing justice, selecting bureaucrats—would be impossible without it, and the turbulent affairs of other, lesser nations are certainly due to the lack of a trustworthy method of divining the truth.

As one my family retreated behind the others in the antechamber. Siril-ven my sister had been the only relation tactless enough to tell me the Crown made the family nervous. My enhanced perception seemed to inflame guilty consciences, and, as Siril assured me, I didn't seem myself.

"You mean I'm not so easily bullied," I had said at the time.

Now I watched as if from some remote window as the procession formed to enter the Chamber. The Sardonyx Council, in charge of conducting the negotiations, looked very fine indeed. The Master Magus wore formal scarlet and the Vizier of the Army, General Horfal-yu Dariletsan, had bronze links under his traditional green and white cape. But most impressive of all was the Commander of the warrior Sisterhood of Mir-hel, Silverhand. She wore hammered copper plate armor of a style that the Shan

Queen Mir-hel herself might have borne. Though it was green with age, plainly for show and not protection, the Commander's seasoned and competent manner made the General and me, in our silly parade armor, look like amateurs.

"But you *are* an amateur," the Crown told me. "In war, at least."

"An opportunity to change that is imminent," I said mentally. Much of my relatives' unease stemmed, I am sure, from my speaking to the Crown aloud. To forestall arguments about my sanity I had taken to conversing with it silently.

" 'When Shan Mir-hel had triumphed at the battle of Mishbil Ford, and the frontier of her empire had been fixed—when the armies of Averidan had trodden their foe into the sands, and slew until day became night again—then she threw down her scarlet spears and cried aloud to the One her great-grandsire, "What madness is on us, your children all, that we slay our kin and spare not?" And from that day she forswore death and the dealing in death.' "

"And founded the arts of unarmed battle," I finished. "You oughtn't quote so much from plaiv, you must know how it really happened if Shan Mir-hel wore you."

"Plaiv shapes itself to the needs of the hearer," the Crown replied.

"I hope you're not trying to tell me this treaty is imprudent."

"Majesty! Sir, it's time!" With an effort I turned my attention outward again. The Director of Protocol did not quite dare to prod me forward, but hovered behind clucking in my ear. Everyone else had gone. I hurried jingling into the Treaty Chamber.

The Chamber was not crowded. It never is, since it is proportioned for giants with plenty of space for even the largest delegations—red marble columns carved to look like palm trees supporting a many-arched ceiling. I seated myself on a painted porcelain chair of state and nodded to the assembly when they bowed to me. Then I rose again to greet the Caydish Warlord Prince.

As he approached I saw that though I stood three steps up on the dais Prince Melbras could look me in the eye. He must have stood two heads taller than anyone else in Averidan, and broad in proportion: rippling muscles straining at the straps of his worn corselet, hairy calves thick as my waist. Red hair thatched his neck a bristly red beard hid his chin, and thick red eyebrows jutted above green-yellow eyes. A copper necklet, the insignia of a Prince in Cayd, circled his throat. His foreign and to my eye barbaric clothing, made of hairy wool, metal, and leather, left large portions of his body bare. It seemed an immodest, not to say uncomfortable fashion, and I wondered with apprehension whether my betrothed would take after her father's side of the family.

The Caydish Ambassador made the presentation, and I replied, "Be welcome, Prince Melbras of Cayd, to Averidan." The interpreters translated his response: formal, correct, and of no information. A chair was brought for the Prince, and the royal scriveners, kneeling, offered us copies of the new treaty. As the herald read the lengthy text aloud to the assembly in both languages, I breathed deeply and called on the power of the Crown as I had been taught.

Reading hearts is not unlike standing on the Palace terrace at the cliff to look over the Mhesan valley. One gets a broad view of the countryside, and with practice buildings and crops can be identified, but recognizing a face is possible only by leaping over the edge. Slowly I had learned to gather impressions of my subjects' general character, but I avoided fishing for actual thoughts. I had worked often at this primary royal duty, since it is a conveniently quiet skill to practice on review stands, at dedication ceremonies, and so on. I had discovered that language was no barrier. Now, with some confidence, I focused my attention on Prince Melbras.

A hard and competent general, I decided. I got the impression of many battles, in mountains or near the river, bloody and indecisive. Frustration; stubbornness; vindictive fury toward a cunning and vicious foe; fiery ambition. I resolved never to offend my future uncle-in-law. But my main interest was Princess Melayne, and I pressed closer to catch a glimpse of his personal life. A wife. Sons. Mistresses, on campaign. A glimpse of a royal seal on the shaky hands of an ancient, balding man in a white fur cloak—the King his brother, my prospective father-in-law.

Suddenly my perception was seized by a sucking, slipping sensation. I knew I had gone in too far and struggled to escape before I fell off the edge. But before I could break free I was looking up at my own body, and thinking strange thoughts.

The portion that was myself tried to calm my panic, and slip discreetly back into my own head. But the other thought was watching a pale and dandified weakling, propped like a toy on a fragile porcelain chair. How useless that pretty suit looked! Plainly never even worn outdoors, never mind in a fight. A shield that could turn only drafts, a sword (admittedly with real rubies on the hilt) that probably wasn't even honed. My left hand crept down to fondle the worn handle of my own axe. Now there was a good bronze edge. My arm remembered all at once the dozens of ways to maim, sever, disembowel, kill. The costly and foolish armor of my host could never stand against me.

How long-winded these wordsmen were! But it would never do, to look bored. Perhaps it would pass the time to enumerate the weak points of that outfit. The way the fishscale stopped to accommodate the bend of the elbow would allow one to hack the joint through. The neck was vulnerable, with no throat-piece around it. The pit of the thigh, where the big artery runs, was covered with only one layer of armor, which might turn a sword-thrust but surely not an axe-blow from a powerful opponent. The chest, near the armpit—

With horror and active nausea I wrenched myself free. Safe in my own head I panted and shivered, sweat cold on my upper lip, and hoped that no one had noticed anything odd. My violent exit had affected the Prince also—he swayed in his chair and put his hands to his head. I wondered if he would suspect what had happened but the idea of again reading him to find out made my stomach turn over.

"Stop a minute," I commanded in a shaky voice.

The herald paused in the reading, and after a moment General Horfal-yu said, "Your Majesty has a question on this clause?"

"No," I said. "His Highness seems to be ill." And indeed the Prince had gone pale under his tan. I hoped I had not seriously hurt him. His entourage gathered around him, exclaiming and questioning in their own tongue, and I signaled the fanbearers to come forward. "Some fresh air, perhaps, or a drink? Let the Chamberlain order wine."

The ceremony halted in confusion, as I had hoped. No one paid attention to me and I was able to secure a cup of wine from the servers. Xalan, however, edged up and offered me his handkerchief. "You need this? What have you been doing?"

"Research," I said, mopping my face. "Tell my Scheduling Director to have Commander Silverhand call on me after this is over." The sweet wine settled my queasy stomach, and seemed to hearten my guest also. "Xalan, am I undersized?"

"The Prince is reckoned tall and broad even in Cayd," Xalan said, answering my unspoken question. "Height and strength are considered kindly traits there."

"Viris, what will the Princess be like?"

After a while the Prince recovered sufficiently to continue, and the reading was completed. Ink blocks and brushes were brought and the copies were signed and imprinted with the seals of Averidan and Cayd. I was now formally betrothed to Melayne of Cayd. Protocol demanded a betrothal celebration but through the interpreter the Prince pleaded the necessity of harassing the Tiyalor forces before winter closed the passes. Gifts of honor were exchanged—I presented the Prince with a high-bred horse, a beast of almost fabulous rarity in Cayd, and sent for the Princess a coronet of Viridese pearls. Now I had seen Caydish fashions I regretted that my staff had not selected silken robes for her. In return I received from the Prince some of the loot won of Tiyalor: silver bars marked with the Tiyal seal, amber in fist-sized chunks, and a thick round silver-backed mirror in a bronze case.

"That doesn't look like Tiyal work," I said. "Magister, come and see. Where did his Highness get this?"

The Master Magus turned it over in his hands, while the interpreter passed my question to the Prince. "This is a magic mirror," the Magus said. "Smelted right here in Averidan."

The Prince's brow had knotted, and he growled an angry reply which was translated. "His Highness captured it, in an assault on Ieor, from the encampment of the evil magus himself."

There was a murmur of astonishment from my court, and I said, "Commend for me his Highness' valor. A magus defends only his wand more stubbornly than his mirror."

The Prince bowed. In a low voice the Magus told me, "Keep it carefully, Majesty. It may be useful. And keep it covered!"

"I'm not a complete dolt," I muttered back.

From my betrothed I received an unusual gift, a long hooded cloak woven of fine blue goats-hair yarn, softer than a kitten's fur. It was embroidered at the hems with silver thread. "The Princess gathered the fleece from her own goats, spun and wove the cloth, and embroidered it with her own hands," the interpreter translated with pride. I tried to look delighted, but couldn't imagine a princess tending goats and spinning yarn.

At last it was over. Prince Melbras took his leave in the formal and ritual phrases, and I withdrew. It was a relief to stretch my legs and take off the Crown.

Rosil-eir waited until the Crown was safe in cousin Fisan's casket and then said, "Just what we need to strengthen the Tsor-melezok line, a strapping barbarian goatherd girl. Ho, ho,

Liras! If she's anything at all like her uncle she'll be able to fold you in half with one hand!''

"You'll certainly have healthy children," Zofal consoled me, and then began to chortle also. "But what will they do to you when they're big enough! You'll need a bodyguard to visit the nursery!''

"What will you gamble, Zofal-ven, that she'll be bigger and taller than poor Liras here?''

"No bet, nephew! But I wouldn't mind a wager on whether the goats will come with her!'' They roared with laughter together. Furious, I left them to their humor and stormed down the wide corridors to the private area of the Palace.

In my own rooms I began removing the armor. The Wardrobe Master appeared and said, "What do you wish to wear now, Majesty?''

"Anything," I said. "I don't want to wear this set again, ever. Sell it, melt it down, do whatever you do with discards— but never let me see it again, understand?'' Ignoring protests and questions I donned my favorite old gardening outfit and went out into the grounds.

Under the stimulus of my interest the gardens surrounding the Palace had been greatly expanded in size and complexity. On the south side of the hill screened by formal plantings were the kitchen gardens, devoted to fruits, cooking herbs, and vegetables. In one of these areas some gardeners were spading a raised bed, turning under the remains of spring vegetables and smoothing the earth before setting out a crop of cabbages. They recognized me as I came up, and paused in astonishment.

I took the spade from the nearest hand and said, "You may all take holiday for the rest of the afternoon. I'll finish turning this one.''

They goggled at me and whispered together, but did not dare argue, and left, taking their tools with them. I set my foot to the shoulder of the spade and gave myself to the rhythm of the work. The late summer Sun beat on my neck and shoulders through the thin old tunic, and the soil smelled good.

The shock of the morning's incident was wearing off. I realized I had never really thought what bravery meant, when I had resolved to learn it. I had no more chance of ever learning to be like Prince Melbras than I had of leaping to the Moon. Yet here at hand was the ideal opportunity: a just war, with my own armies, in a foreign country. It also came to me that a new wife would supply plenty of practice in courage, especially if she resembled Melbras. Whatever deity is in charge of such things had been very prompt in replying to my wish.

My tunic grew damp with sweat and began to chafe my ribs. Sticking the spade upright in the soil I pulled the garment over my head and turned to hang it on a vine-stake across the walk. To my surprise I saw a woman seated cross-legged on the low retaining wall. It was Commander Silverhand.

"You should have spoken up, Commander, have you waited long?"

In one easy movement she rose. "I didn't want to interrupt, Majesty. I could see you were thinking hard." She had changed into the everyday garb of her Order, the loose shirt and trousers of coarse brown linen, and her black hair was tied back in the traditional knotted club. "Worried about your wedding?"

I looked at her with suspicion. "Why do you ask?"

"Because that's outside my range of knowledge." She smiled, and indeed the Sisterhood of Mirh-hel is vowed to valor, loyalty, and virginity.

In relief I admitted, "I was recovering from meeting my new in-law. An intimidating fellow."

"Size, Majesty, isn't everything."

"*You* can say that." For although she was fifteen years older than me, and not quite as tall, an aura of invincible power and victory radiated from her. Like every Commander of the Sisterhood she had won leadership by fighting for it, so she was the best warrior in the Order and therefore very likely the best in Averidan. "Sit, please, and if you don't mind I'll continue digging," I said. "Tell me, Commander, when you admit a novice into the Order how can you tell she has courage?"

"She may not. But after three years' training in the novitiate she will learn it."

"I thought a person is born brave."

"No." The Commander smiled. "Your Majesty confuses the terms. The brave know no fear. The courageous may be afraid but do not let that fear affect their deeds. Courage is learned and maintained, but bravery is a grace."

"Then I have a chance," I said, greatly cheered.

"Your Majesty doubts your mettle?"

"Well, it's this war with Tiyalor."

"We'll take care of that," she said, with complete confidence.

"I don't doubt it," I said. "But I'm coming too."

She stared. I avoided her eye, watching instead the earthworms push themselves back into the newly turned soil at my feet. "No monarch has ridden to war since Shan Norlen-yu the Merciful," she said.

"He was my great-grandfather," I said.

"Your presence isn't mandated by the treaty," she pointed out, "so why not let the Sisterhood and the Army deal with it?"

"Because I know already I'm not brave," I said. "Where else shall I learn courage?"

"You can learn courage here in Averidan," she said. "It's a long journey to Ieor, and Xerlanthor is no ordinary enemy." Then her dark eyes narrowed, calculating. "Of course you might be just what we need against him. Have you ever heard or read of your great-grandfather's deeds with the Crystal Crown?"

"Only the official chronicle," I said. We both knew that while the official archives are sometimes adjusted for expediency's sake, plaiv is also curiously flexible in the service of color. Viridese history shapes itself to the people's needs to such an extent that what truly happened is sometimes lost. "Why didn't he like to be called 'the Merciful'? It's a nice epithet."

"That's not told," she said. "But in the Order our plaiv tell that the Shan King carried an invincible sword of white flame in battle."

"Did he really?" I exclaimed. I had not realized the Crown's powers could be turned to kill as well as to save. But I recognized the 'white flame.' "I could do that, now I'm Shan King."

"If you could it would be well worth the risk of bringing you along," she said. "Xerlanthor couldn't possibly have a defense. If we sprung it on him right—" She rubbed her hands in anticipation.

"Yes, we'll have to keep it secret," I said. Only a fool would disappoint Warlord Prince Melbras, and I was too shy to painfully explain through an interpreter the powers and limitations of the Crystal Crown. Furthermore, tradition demanded that the Shan King's powers be discreetly kept. A romantic vision, of unveiling my prowess in the field to the astonishment and applause of three armies seized me. I said, "We must do it. I'll brush up on my swordplay and get Zofal-ven to give me a warhorse."

"I still don't fancy the idea," she said, uncertain again. "You've no experience whatever."

"It's consonant with *chun-hei*," I said. "Brimful of impractical honor." Firmly I changed the subject. "What I had really intended to discuss with you, Commander, was armor. Did you mark the set I wore today?"

"Surely. It was very grand."

"But completely useless." Suppressing a twinge of conscience, I continued, "There were weak spots: the elbow joints, the armpit, the hollow of the thigh—"

"Majesty!" She closed her mouth, which had opened in surprise, and leaned forward to look at me more closely. "It's true enough, but where did you learn it? Have you been hiding all this time your skill in war?"

"Ah, I have my sources of information," I evaded. "I don't know anything about armor really, just about that one set."

She cast a shrewd glance at me. "Your informant is too passive. Any disciple of ours could have told you the best armor can't substitute for training in offense."

"I think I'll need good armor too, though I don't intend to neglect training," I said. "I was hoping you and General Horfal-yu would assist me."

"Your Majesty has only to command," she said.

"Good." I turned over the last spadeful of earth and stepped down to survey my work. The rich black soil was free now of lumps and stones, uniform in texture as a bowl of steamed barley. "What do you think of it?"

I could see her shuffling through possible replies for a tactful one. "It's an unusual skill, for a king," she said at last.

The thought had never occurred to me. Jauntily I swung the spade over my shoulder. "And my bride keeps goats! What an interesting couple we'll make!"

Chapter 5: Nerves

Viridese bureaucracy is vast and convolute. The smallest village has its tax collector or chronicler, even before one begins to count the herbals, the magi, and the dozen or so religious orders, all government-directed at a slightly further remove. The most enervating duty of a new Shan King is to confirm in their posts the four thousand-odd bureaucrats he employs. My main function in years to come would be to appoint, direct, and if necessary execute them. I was able to regard the hateful prospect with resignation and only occasionally now complained to Xalan that there must be a less agonizingly dull way to give my life to my country.

For reasons unrecorded in chronicles—though probably some plaiv supplies a colorful reason—the confirmation reviews must begin with the Office of City Roadworks. The maintenance of the City's oyster-shell paved streets is not skilled labor, and the Office traditionally hires strong peasants for the work. Thus the Director and his nine underlings dealt more in payrolls than paving-shells.

The morning after my betrothal was bright and warm, without even a hint of the gentle autumns we get in these parts, so I ordered that the reviews be held this day in the pergola. I would spend many days in the Hall of Audience, the traditional locale for such work, and for my own equilibrium it was important to set an outdoor precedent. The pergola was secluded in its own grove of larch and holly, built two hundred years ago by a Shan King who fancied outdoor copulation. Klim-grown trellises roofed the room thickly over so that the purple blooms and green leaves cast a watery, green-purple light on the marble floor. Pale marble fretwork let the scented breezes flow through. I had had the gilded royal bed removed and a chair of state set up for me. My staff would stand behind; the reviewees would kneel. It is a less formal occasion only for the Shan King—the bureaucrats were never at ease talking for their lives and jobs.

The Director of Roadworks had the dubious honor of discovering how strict the new monarch intended to be. When he and his staff filed in I leaned forward on my seat, the Crystal Crown resting light and warm on my head. The Lord Manager, who supervises all City functions, presented them to me. As custom dictates, I said, "Tell me, messirs, of your duties."

The least important clerk, prodded by his master, began. "Your Majesty, my work is to assist the Director in the collection of suitable oyster shell from the trawler fleet. Every week I receive from the Harbormaster the lists. . . ."

By the time he had got that far I had reached into his heart with the Crown's power. A zealous worker, who genuinely felt that the oyster fishers and pearling industry existed only to supply shells for paving. I waited patiently until he had finished a rambling and confused account and then said, "I confirm you, Naranshi, in your office. Serve me as well as you did my predecessor."

The man blushed with relief and pleasure but etiquette allowed him only the customary reply: "It is my honor to apply myself in your service, Your Majesty."

I worked thusly through all nine assistants, learning far more than I would have believed existed about the wide, slightly crunchy roads I had trod all my life. Some were less efficient than others—the man who toured villages hiring strong young workers, for instance, had an intense interest also in visiting discontented wives, of whom he had a lengthy list. But it was no part of my duty to regulate my subjects' personal lives, and the Crown advised me, "His work is done well, that is your only concern."

But when the Director spoke I felt a difference. "Our beautiful durable roads may be completely laid to my credit," he began. "For the past eight years my constant labor has been . . ."

". . . to skim the gold and labor we entrust to you for your own benefit," I interrupted. With the Crown his perfidy was obvious. He had diverted roadworking funds into family investments—his son's silk-dyeing business—and only this past winter had roadworkers laboring not on pavements but on repairs to the wall of his house outside the City.

He stammered, "Rumors vilely spread by my daughter-in-law's family—"

"No one dares lie to the Shan King," I said. "Confess instantly, or shall I explicate your dishonesty?"

The man burst into tears, sobbing something about his aunt's weak nerves, the pressures of ungrateful offspring, and the malign geomancy of his house. Everyone stared at the marble floor in embarrassment. Silently I consulted the Crystal Crown: "What ought I do now?"

"Lapidation," the Crown said in its beautiful cool voice.

"What? Execution is so permanent! Surely he repents his ways—" I looked again into the man's heart. He loved his grandchildren, his house: a home tucked outside the City's West Gate notable for its unlucky placement of door and window. Perhaps he was right about malign influences. He had been honest and industrious when King Eisen had appointed him, but little by little dishonesty had crept over him. I could not help remembering the last lapidation I had seen. The condemned had been laid in one of the bathtub-shaped depressions cut in Execution Rock, at the curve of the steep road between Upper and Lower City, and a panel of wood exactly the size of the hole was laid over him. The people, demonstrating their concurrence in the sentence, came forward to pile the stones over. The condemned man was pressed to death. Drainage holes are cut in the depressions, and when after a week or so of sunny Viridese weather the stones are removed the corpse is tidy, flat, and dry: a human raisin exactly in accordance with fastidious Viridese ideas. The very flavor of the atmosphere came back to me—horror, fascination, and also righteousness. For only the Shan King or his viceroys command lapidation, and they were always right.

Now I was not so sure. The man was too close. I knew too much now of his heart, his little, obscure life, so much like the one I had once hoped for. Such a minor rank would have suited me exactly—neither too great nor too difficult, just prestigious enough to placate ambitious kin. I said to the Crown, "I can't do it."

"Every Shan King must," the Crown warned. "Justice demands that you at least depose him from his office."

But when I repeated this to the offender he fell flat on the marble floor and begged for another chance. "The shame will mark me forever, if I am ousted," he wept, and again I was too much in sympathy. In Averidan fall from power is absolute; one never regains a lost rank. Indeed this accounts for the popularity of lapidation—problems buried under rock never rise again.

So I yielded, creating a merciful precedent for first offenders: "I will have mercy on you this once. See that you mend your ways."

I could read only relief and gratitude in the man as he cried, "Oh, I will serve you well all my days, Your Majesty! Thank you!"

But the Crystal Crown said, "You are unwise."

Mentally I argued, "If he errs again I'll catch him sooner or later," and signaled the Lord Manager to show the next batch of bureaucrats in.

All menchildren are taught swordplay. In the upper classes this only means the management of sword and scabbard so you don't trip over them. The real art was surprisingly hard work. General Horfal-yu was well-born enough so that the idea of attacking someone with a sword or spear was faintly distasteful to him. This is not a good quality in a general but not sufficient cause for lapidation. There was no way for me to oust him and appoint a better until he died or stepped down. I hoped in the spring the Tiyalor would reveal to him the joys of retirement.

Far more useful to me was the instruction of the Sisterhood. The Commander supplied me with a special dispensation so that

I could in defiance of my sex and rank attend novitiate combat classes. These were of course in unarmed combat—the Sisters never let their sky-fallen weaponry out of the Order's hands. Since I was at the bottom of my class I was not threat to the novices' virginity; they could individually and collectively break my arms if I took liberties. Rosil teased me about getting in all my romping with women before marriage, until losing patience I inflamed his imagination with hints about wrestling bouts with slim young maidens, and singlestick classes run by a teacher who had developed her chest muscles to superb proportions. Then I invited him to a morning's round of exercise. He got away with bruises, a black eye, a sprained wrist, and a bloody nose, since his previous calumnies (which I had repeated to the novices) had offended their pride in the Order's threefold vows. After this he was more subdued.

So summer passed into autumn, and autumn faded into early winter. In the mornings I slowly worked through the City's civil servants, and then began on the provincials and the armed forces. I never had to lapidate anybody, though I deposed a few recalcitrants, and it was universally agreed I would be a clement and peaceable Shan King. The afternoons were spent in warlike exercise. By that time I had almost forgotten why I was learning all this. The development of skill had become sufficient, and I did not consider what I would do with them after.

The season of my wedding came before I was ready. I had handed over all official preparations to the Director of Protocol, but as the cold advanced to my annoyance distant family connections, relatives I hadn't seen in years, came to town anxious to help dear Liras-ven get married. After wasting several evenings in painful small talk I learned the trick of pleading work and referring everyone to Zofal or Mother.

On the afternoon of her arrival the entire city gathered to meet the Princess at the bridge over Mhesan. It is just the sort of occasion the Shan adore. The day was blustery but not quite raining, and chunks of ice bobbed past on the green river, washed downstream from the wintry hills. The Caydish party was traveling by barge east from Mhee, but post-riders had given us warning so that everyone had plenty of time to shiver in the cutting wind and regret warmer clothing foolishly left at home. Baked chestnut vendors did a brisk trade, and an enterprising glover who had brought his entire winter stock sold every mitten and glove.

Mother had contrived to have a brazier brought along, and we huddled around it at our end of the market square. "If it's this cold near the sea what must it be like upcountry?" I said.

"The old hydromants' plaiv say ice on the Tiyalene Sea gets so thick in winter you can walk across the water to the home of the West Wind," Xalan said.

"And you're really going there?" Siril-ven giggled. "Will your wife let you go so far, Liras-ven?"

"She will obey her husband, as a good wife ought," Mother said.

This is not an unusual sentiment in the well-born, where the Sea-Reaver strain runs strong, but it was unexpected since Mother herself had been a matriarch of the old school—not what one would call submissive. With veiled malice Yibor-soo said, "Of course a foreigner might feel differently about it, but a nice Viridese girl, such as I hope to find for Rosil, is always biddable. You must be sure, Liras-ven, to convey this expectation to your bride to ensure a peaceful union."

It was far more politic not to reply. I concentrated on untangling my wind-blown sleeves so that they would hang properly. Mother cast an icy glance at her stepdaughter-in-law and said, "Of course since Liras will live a long life he will have plenty of time to instill proper attitudes in his wife."

Disaster was imminent—in a moment they would be accusing each other of driving my late stepbrother into his early grave—but Xalan, who had been well-briefed in the family factions, stepped in and said, "The Princess will receive such inspiration from the good examples before her that I'm sure His Majesty will have no difficulty. Besides, Caydish ladies are brought up to meekness."

Rosil-eir did not quite snicker, but winked at me instead. Zofal-ven said, "You could always keep her at the weaving." For I was wearing her gift cloak.

I grinned, refusing to be offended, and said, "I'm probably the only one here who's warm."

The lookouts on the wall behind us released long turquoise silk streamers and flags, signaling the barge was in sight. Cheering, the people crowded to the river-bank to catch their first glimpse. The musicians struck up a gallant tune on gongs and bone flutes. In the thin cold air the noise was deafening. I had to wait as propriety demanded, with my court at the far end of the square.

Passage was cleared by the guardsmen, and I could see the Caydish. Their duller garments were easy to pick out in the brightly colored multitude. As they approached I scanned the faces and forms, but in my anxiety my eye could not take in the foreign dress.

The Shan favor flowing, trailing styles in brilliant or rich tones. Of these visitors, the men wore stiff coats and vests of hairy fur or leather, bulky natural woolen jerkins and breeches, fur cloaks, and many metal ornaments on throat or arm or finger. Prince Melbras was easy to pick out, the tallest of all. The dozen women were even more outlandish—full, stiff-petticoated skirts of thick dark woolen, felt vests crossed in front belted with big metal plaques, over full pleated blouses.

Determined to spot my bridle, I remembered now to look for one wearing the gift coronet of pearls. Before I could begin they were upon us, towering over my Director of Protocol, who said, "Your Majesty, may I present her Highness the Cayd princess Melayne."

Before me was a buxom young woman: pale, flower-petal skin, intricate coils of braided red-brown hair pinned behind with long rods of silver and further adorned, rather incongruously, with a delicate pearl coronet. With a clash of earrings and necklaces she curtseyed in the Caydish style. As she straightened I met the cool stare of gray-green eyes. She came just up to my brow, in the thick-heeled boots worn by Caydish men and women alike, and in proper shoes would no doubt stand even shorter.

I resisted the temptation to glance at my brother or half-nephew, and took her hand. It was warm in my own, which felt cold and sweaty by contrast. Wiping the other hand on my breeches I switched, and said in as enthusiastic a tone as I could, "Be welcome, Princess, to Averidan."

Under eyebrows as fine as a moth's feelers the even glance did not alter or shift, and in the moment of plunging silence I felt a fool. Then the interpreter translated, and her eye lit up.

"Viris!" I exclaimed. "She doesn't speak Viridese!"

"Don't translate that," Xalan hissed to the interpreter, and trod on my toe.

Pulling myself together I listened to the interpreter's propitious phrases, and recited the replies I had had to memorize for the occasion. We were put into an ornate carved double sedan chair to be carried up to the Upper City in state. There was no room for the interpreter to ride along but no conversation would have been possible anyway because of the noise. Close up she smelled not unpleasant but very foreign, of wool and mountain herbs. I could tell my subjects thought we looked well together, and were delighted by the idea of the marriage.

At the Palace she was whisked away to the Lady's chambers which were to be hers. Abandoning my retinue and family I grabbed Xalan by a sleeve and dragged him into the wet garden.

"Xalan, I can't say a word to her, how can this work?"

"Her uncle couldn't speak Viridese either," Xalan reminded me. "So it's not surprising."

I sat on the grass and leaned my head on a marble wall. "I wasn't going to marry her uncle. Maybe I should invite the interpreter along on our wedding night. Why on earth didn't they teach her the language?"

"Well, for that matter why didn't you learn Caydish? It's easier than Viridese by all accounts. For the long term you should have her take lessons. And for the needs of the moment do you really need words?"

"I suppose not," I said in misery. I could not imagine not being able to speak to my partner. For us the words of love weigh almost as much as the act.

"Or why not use the Crown?"

"No! I'd almost rather have the interpreter," I said. "There's such a thing as getting too close."

An icy wind tugged at our clothing. Xalan said, "Let's go in. You got to sit all the way uphill. I had to walk, and I can't sit on the grass in this outfit, I'd ruin it."

Snug in the goat's-hair cloak I was warm enough but I would have to go in sometime. I rose and said, "Now I know how poor old Dosal-yu felt."

"Your deceased stepbrother?"

"Yes. Mother always said he died of being married."

"Well, but that was to Yibor-soo. Don't be so negative!" Xalan exclaimed in his most encouraging tone. "Most marriages turn out fine, how else did we all come to be here?"

Weddings in Averidan are celebrated if at all possible in the coastal city of Ennelith-Ral, sacred to Ennelith the fertile. Mine was the only exception. For the Son of the Sun, Child of Fire, the entire Sodality of Ennelith would journey west to celebrate the rite here. It is only a day's ride, but because the Mistress of the Sodality refused to allow her hundred charges to use the high road it took them almost two days to walk from their seaside temple up the gravelly beaches to the City. I didn't envy them their chilly wet trip, and ordered a gift of fifty copper braziers to be prepared for their arrival.

During those two days I became more and more nervous. I clung to the familiar—my horses, Sahai my cat—and drew up a colossal scroll-chart of the Palace and Temple grounds with all the current plantings marked in four colors of ink. I was no longer allowed to practice combat, for fear of hurting myself and disappointing the Princess on the wedding night. If it hadn't been so cold and wet I would have gone out and dug up something.

Because of some Caydish custom I was unable to see the Princess again, and had to content myself with inviting her uncle to dinner. Unexpectedly I had an informative and pleasant evening discussing the war through the interpreter. The Prince had with great bloodshed recaptured Ieor and the dam. His second-in-command (one of the Princess' brothers) had laid in great stores of food for the winter, so that the dam should be secure even against siege. In the spring even if we could not destroy the dam the sluices would be opened to let the water through. I listened attentively to the language, and tried to pick out words and phrases.

The wedding day dawned red and cold. I woke early. Icicles weighed down the vines outside my window and the ground crackled with frost under the feet of gardeners hanging blue pottery lamps on the trees to light the processional path. I lingered at the window to watch the preparations with Sahai in my arms until I was hurried away to be dressed.

For this very important occasion my clothes were so ornate there was almost no moving in them. A blue-green brocade robe trammeled my legs, pearls encrusted sleeves trailing long enough to step on, and a pearly collar stiffened with silver wire stuck out far enough behind so that sitting would be impossible without help. Over all this was a gemmy blue vest that touched the floor. The mirror was uncovered for me, and I remarked, "I look like a monstrous butterfly stuck in its cocoon."

"Oh, no, Majesty," the Master of Wardrobe objected. "Blue-green is particularly favored by Ennelith, and pearls are her special gem."

"But what's the point of clothes you can't walk or sit in?"

"The style is traditional," he replied, uncomprehending, and of course there was no more to be said. Like an invalid I was assisted down the stairs to the ceremony hall, and handed over to the Sodality.

For me the long rite passed in a blur of nervous exhaustion. The incenses used in the ceremony are stupefying, and the chants are so old they drone in the ear like bees. When we were led outdoors after noon to be shown to the people the cold air cleared my vision. But in my befuddlement I could not for a moment recognize the figure whose wrist was bound to mine with purple thread. You've given me the wrong one, I almost exclaimed, but then I recognized the clear smooth brown over gray-green eyes. She was as painfully garbed as I, and further muffled from head to toe in a long blue veil.

We were waiting for the Mistress to finish aspersing the crowd with seawater. How frightening it must be, not even understanding the prayers, I thought, and although she could not comprehend in a low tone I said, "Don't worry, it'll be over soon." And when I could not tell if she even heard me over the noise I raised our bound wrists and kissed her softly where the pearl sleeve cuff bared the thin skin. The veins were blue on the back of her hand, and her fingerbones felt as small as Sahai's. For an instant she returned the pressure of my hand, and I smiled shyly at her. Then the Mistress signaled us to come forward.

We were taken on paths scattered with little clam shells to the Sun Temple where after a complicated offering we were pronounced indissolubly wed. The brief winter day was fading, but we were not through yet. A long wedding feast followed, to which everyone of note in Averidan had been invited. I picked at the endless courses, dishes of nearly legendary rarity and excellence that I knew I would later regret not remembering. The wines were poured freely but I dared only taste each glass.

Of course we were expected to retire early. Now that the time had come I felt a hysterical impulse to delay, but inexorably my wife was gathered up by my immediate female relatives and taken away. Zofal-ven and Rosil-eir appeared to take charge of me.

"Come along, uncle, it's time." Rosil was in the best of spirits. "Mustn't keep the Lady waiting."

"Any humor out of you and I'll take you to Ieor with me," I said. They helped me to my feet. A fiery blush had taken up what appeared to be permanent residence in my face.

"Ignore him, Rosil," my brother advised. "All bridegrooms are snappy." With what I felt was undignified speed we bustled down the halls. "How sensible of you, Liras, to keep clear of the wines. I had planned to warn you of them but never got the chance."

Zofal's concern touched me but all I could say was, "Everyone knows intoxication is a handicap in the end."

The Lady's rooms are far out in the rambling Palace, looking northwest over the fortified cliff face. The wedding celebrations which would continue till morning could not be heard through the long corridors and quiet rooms. In a secluded bathing chamber the Master of Wardrobe waited, and I was divested of my finery.

"How often does he wear this?" Zofal wanted to know.

"It depends on how often he gets married," the Master said.

"Is that an unlucky thing to say?" I asked, my teeth chattering, but, muffled in the robe, no one heard me.

"You mean it's just a wedding outfit?"

"It's the royal wedding costume, sir. This robe is almost two hundred years old."

"No wonder it's so uncomfortable," I said, scratching the chafed places.

"Don't do that, it'll show. Into the water with you."

The bath water was hot and sweetened with herbs. Somewhere in this wing Melayne was sitting in a similar bath with similar assistants offering conflicting advice. At least she couldn't understand it. I slumped down until the water filled my ears and I could no longer hear Rosil and Zofal debating whether in their experience women do or do not like men to be domineering.

I sat in the water until it was tepid. Dried, shaved, and dressed in night attire I must have looked so racked that Rosil had pity and said good night quite kindly. Zofal said, "You're alone from here—sleep well!"

They left but did not shut the door, since I would soon have to make my way to the bridal chamber. Now, handicap or not, I could have done with a drink. I examined the dressing table under the tall arched window but found only bath herbs in the red porcelain jars. Looking up from them my heart turned over when I saw a ghostly face floating outside the glass.

Recovering, I unlatched the casement. It was Xalan. "What are you doing out there, you must be freezing."

"Somewhat," he admitted. He floated in head first. Only a magus could wait at a window three hundred feet up. "This just arrived by courier from Mhee, and I knew you would want to see it right away." He handed me a small bundle wrapped in oiled silk.

"What a shock you gave me! Is this a wedding present?"

"From one of our western brethren. I haven't even looked at it, but it was the best we could do. Open it now. If you don't mind I'll exit this time through the hallways. I was terrified someone would recognize me looking in windows and have me thrown out of magery!" With a grin and a wave he was gone. I shut the window again and opened my package.

Within were two scrolls, of the half-size convenient for travelers. I slipped one out of its red-figured case and unrolled a bit to see the title panel. "Phrases in Viridese from the Caydish, with a Supplemental Word List and Tables," I read. "By a Merchant of Quality."

"Thank the One for faithful friends!" I exclaimed aloud. The other roll was titled similarly, "In Caydish from the Viridese." Closing them back up I slipped on my shoes and hurried down the hall to the bridal chamber.

Inside, large windows let a chilly winter moon peep in. White porcelain night lamps stood beside the wide bed, and braziers warmed the air. Outside the covers in the exact middle of the bed my bride sat in a blue silk night robe, her hair flowing down her back and forming a dark mass on the quilts and pillows.

"I have just the present for you," I announced without ceremony. I handed her the second scroll. "Get under the covers, you'll get a chill." She did not understand and I gave her a quilt. Wrapping a coverlet around my shoulders I sat on one side of the bed and unrolled the book, tilting it to catch the candlelight.

At first I thought I had by chance selected an unhelpful phrase. On one side were the Caydish sounds and on the other the Viridese meanings: "Does that include the import duty?" "How much is that sheep?" I turned to another panel and got, "I have bribed you once already." Is that water for drinking or for washing?" Searching backwards and forwards, I slowly realized that the "Merchant of Quality" had noted phrases useful only to himself. The Supplemental Word List was made up of money and commercial terms, and the Tables converted units of measure.

In frustration I hurled the scroll across the room. A faint gasp reminded me I might have startled my bride. She held her scroll in both hands and stared at me with wide wary eyes as if doubting my sanity.

"I suppose yours is the same," I said. "Let me look." Gently I took it from her and read one phrase: "This goat is insufficiently hairy." Holding it out to her so she could see I said, "It isn't even a graceful translation." She looked with mild wonder at the parchment, reaching one finger to touch the characters, and it came to me she couldn't read. "Can you read this?" I pointed to the Caydish side, and she was patient and interested but obviously not able to extract any meaning from the words.

The blankness of my dismay was unreasonable, I knew, and I

said, "I suppose there's not much call for books in Cayd. What a lot of lessons you'll need, I hope you won't mind."

Her patience came to a sudden end. Flicking the scroll out of my hand she sent it flying after its companion. "We don't usually do that," I protested. "I'm setting you a bad example." Then it occurred to me she was not imitating me, or at least not with polite intent. She swirled the quilt off her shoulders and, dropping it over my head, pulled me over backwards. Before I could wrestle the padded linen off my face she had wriggled under both her coverlet and mine and put warm arms round my neck. The vitality and sweetness of her mouth on mine astonished me. Though I am frequently slow to grasp the obvious, this hint was unmistakable, and I decided words after all are not necessary.

Chapter 6: Dinner Incident

She delighted me. I had not suspected that my mild interest in sex had held the late-blooming seeds of such passion. Blessing the whim of fortune that had brought her to me in the next fortnight I spent part of each day, and every night, with her. This was held to be entirely proper for a newly-wed man, and the Lord Scheduling Director cut my ceremonies and duties down to a minimum.

Her dignified silence and illiteracy did not disguise her intelligence and will. When I woke that first morning and found beside me only a warm, sweet-scented nest in the covers, I sat up. She stood at the window, combing out the tangles in the red-brown tresses that were her only garment. When she saw me awake she approached, saying in very fair Viridese, "Good morning!"

Startled, I exclaimed, "Where did you learn that?"

She pointed at the chamber door, and said, "Breakfast?"

"Ah, I see, you listened to the maids." It was uncanny, after at most two hearings. "You're quicker than I—you must teach my Caydish, too." We took to telling each other the words for various items around the room.

Since I could not express my pleasure in words I turned to gifts. No flowers were in season, and Caydish lovers do not give beautiful seashells as we do. So I poured polished sapphires into her hands, and went with her to Zofal-ven's horse farm to choose out a young riding horse for her. Of course she could not ride. "Not even many Viridese do," I told her, as she stroked the white nose and sleek arched neck. "Horses were brought here only about a hundred, two hundred years ago. They're still a luxury."

"Luxury?"

"Uh—" I turned through Xalan's scrolls, which I had reclaimed from ignominy, but could not find the word. "Curse it, we'll have to ask the interpreter. I looked up from the book and almost dropped it in shock. Melayne had tugged her gift a little closer to the stableyard wall and from there was hoisting herself to the horse's bare back. Though it was almost certainly safe enough—I had gentled and trained the beast myself in the days before I was Shan King—incautiously I cried, "Melayne, don't do that!" At the sudden shout the horse danced nervously away, and with an effort I lowered my voice to say, "Horses can be dangerous if you can't ride." Of course she could not understand me, and when the animal bore her through the gate and across the pasture she squealed with delight, not fear.

But the terror I would have felt in her place muddled my judgment, and without so much as a rope I ran after them. The pasture had been mowed before winter, so that dry yellow cut grass lay in swathes on the green sward. Entering into the spirit of the supposed game the horse paced before me around the field so that the trailing blue hem of Melayne's skirt fluttered just out of my reach. Fortunately Zofal was in the other field and seeing my plight came to the rescue waving a piece of hard barley bread. I had tamed the horse well—wheeling round it trotted eagerly over to claim the treat. Zofal captured the bridle and yelled at me, "Have you taken leave of your senses, putting her on bareback? She could fall off and kill herself!"

Melayne had clung tight to the white mane, but when I panted up she slid to the grass and kissed me, saying, "Thank you, Liras dear," in accented Viridese.

"I had nothing to do with it," I gasped to Zofal.

Melayne took the bread to feed her horse herself, leaving Zofal free to exclaim, "She doesn't know how to ride, probably never seen a horse in her life, how did she come to get on his back unless you put her there?"

"I tell you I don't know," I said. "But isn't it clever and brave of her?"

Zofal's rage melted away and he looked at me with only mild exasperation. We sat on the stone wall and watched Melayne ply her horse with more stale bread. The air was mild and cool, a pleasant winter day in Averidan. "One would think you had known nothing of women before," Zofal said to me.

"It's different when you're married," I explained in superior tones—Zofal was still a bachelor.

"It's embarrassing to watch you."

I kept a careful eye on Melayne as she stroked the horse's shoulders and boldly picked up each white hoof as she had seen us do, though she did not know what to look for. "Melayne is the one creature that belongs completely to me," I said.

"What about Sahai?"

"If you had one you'd know you can't own a cat." I had not devoted much reflection to this before, so I spoke slowly. "I share the horses with you, the Palace with the government, the Crown—well, you could say the Crown owns me, just as well."

"If you knew anything at all of women you'd know you can't own them either," Zofal said. "I prophesy it won't last."

"You're jealous," I grinned. Zofal had never had anything to envy me for before. "We must search around for a nice wife for you too. Maybe I'll put it to the Sardonyx Council—they do nice work, don't you think?"

"Don't you dare!" But we didn't finish the discussion, for Melayne tried to ride her horse again as we both intervened. Zofal took charge of the horse and I held Melayne while we explained too quickly for anyone to understand that she had to learn to ride first. I saw for a fleeting moment the glint of stubbornness in her eye, but she submitted with good grace.

The magi and their elemental powers made her somewhat nervous—Xalan assured me that the defeat of Xerlanthor would change her attitude—but she liked cousin Fisan and learned from her the Viridese for items of feminine attire I never knew existed, and which I then had to order for her. I also took her to the Monastery of the Sisterhood east of the City, to meet Commander Silverhand and my novitiate combat friends.

"So, you are happy in marriage?" the Commander asked me, as we toured the exercise halls.

"Very much so," I said. "It doesn't matter at all that I can't talk to her." Then I blushed at my own words, remembering that Sisters did not marry.

Silverhand was too kind to laugh at me but a smile quirked her lips as she said, "We Sisters don't go about with our heads in wicker crab-pots, Your Majesty. Everyone knew you would have to wed someone, the fascinating question was how you would like your Lady.''

I had long since given up my nostalgia for privacy. ''You mean because she's a foreigner,'' I said. ''She's nicer than any Viridese wife they would have chosen, so everything worked out very well.'' I thought of Yibor-soo and could not resist a smug glance at Melayne. With gesture and pantomime she was helping to bind padding onto the butts of singlesticks, for the practice bouts. Her ruddy hair and pink silks were bright among the brown-clad novices, and when they told her Viridese words she repeated them carefully, stringing them into new and sometimes unusual sentences.

''It's a pity we can't converse with her,'' Silverhand said. ''The Lady would make an excellent Sister, I'd like to know of her life.''

Impressed, I asked, ''You can tell just by looking at her?''

''It's my job.'' It was rare for Silverhand to think aloud, and I kept quiet as she continued, ''One learns to sense the attributes we need in the Sisterhood: fortitude; will; pride. And above all the capacity for violence. That is what our foundress was, you know. The Shan King can evaluate people with the Crystal Crown, but other commanders learn to sort of smell quality.'' She fingered her wind-burnt nose and smiled at me. ''For that matter you have the nose too, Crown or no. Your wife, this child here—'' She turned to indicate Fisan-shi, who followed me as always with the Crystal Crown. ''The potential is there, as it is, say, in rats but not mice.''

''Melayne isn't at all like that,'' I objected, laughing. ''She's a sweet and winsome little thing, and keeps me amused, but she would never hurt so much as a fly.''

''I'll bet you,'' Silverhand offered.

I was tempted—the Shan love to wager—but I asked, ''How should we settle the winner?''

''Look into her heart sometime when you wear the Crown.''

''No,'' I said. ''I couldn't do that. Besides, I like not knowing what she thinks, it lends mystery. Like with cats—I would never read my cat either.'' So the Commander sighed, and turned the conversation to other topics.

This idyll was doomed to end. Scarcely two weeks had passed since our marriage when I had a dinner in one of the smaller dining rooms. On a whim I had decreed that to accommodate

Melayne only Caydish should be spoken. This quashed my relatives completely, and it would have been a silent and glum meal had I not invited the Caydish embassy as well. My progress in Caydish had not the flair of Melayne's into Viridese, but by dogged concentration I had a rudimentary vocabulary, and now if the flow of words was not too quick I could grasp the drift of most of my guests' speech.

The Ambassador was recounting to me, slowly and with frequent pauses to substitute simpler words, a tale of his first trip to Ennelith-Ral, when my Lord Chamberlain came in and hovered at my elbow. "Your pardon, Ambassador," I fumbled in Caydish, and then in Viridese, "Yes, my lord, what is it?"

"Emergency messengers, Majesty, from Cayd."

"Send them in immediately," I said.

"Does that mean we can talk properly again?" Siril said to Rosil in a whisper meant to be overheard.

"Yes, it's all right," I conceded. "And call the interpreters, my lord, I don't suppose the messengers are bilingual."

I was wrong. There were two: one Viridese, a soldier from our garrison at Mhee, but the other, incredibly, was a Caydish archer: filthy, red-eyed, and reeling with exhaustion, carrying a box. We gave them chairs and wine, and the dinner party split each to hear its own.

Our soldier handed me a sealed scroll-case, saying, "I'am sorry, Your Majesty, we told him he could trust us with his tokens but he said he was sworn to deliver them to the Warlord's own hand."

"Never mind, you did well," I said, slitting open the wax and shaking the scroll out. "I hope he didn't slow you down."

"It's unbelievable, Majesty. He'd never seen a horse before, but when my captain told him horses would be faster than a boat he said he would ride. Asked us to tie him into the saddle."

"Viris above us!" Zofal exclaimed. "What happened to the horse?"

"That's not important now," I said. I held up the scroll. "This says the Caydish have lost Ieor again. Xerlanthor has sealed the sluices of the dam, and if they're not opened soon none of the spring snow-melt will get to Cayd—or us."

My hearers were silent, stunned. Abruptly across the room the Caydish cried out or screamed. The deep bull-voice of the Prince roared out a course, damning Xerlanthor to some complicated fate for all time, and my wife darted over and threw herself into my arms.

"Melayne, what is it?" She trembled in my arms like a frightened bird, but when I tried to go over to see she set her jaw and followed me.

The Caydish had fallen away from the box, which stood on the carpet. The archer knelt beside it, hiding his face in his hands, and the Prince towered above him, black as a thundercloud with rage. I tiptoed up to peer past them into the box, and gulped.

A parchment-white mask stared up at me, gaping and smeared with dried blood. I recognized it for a severed head, and forced myself to be calm, to observe. The hair was straw-colored, the eyes gray—not one of my dark-haired, dark-eyed subjects. The teeth were broken and the tongue protruded dry between them. "Who is it?" I whispered.

Behind me Melayne wept into a handkerchief Mother handed her. The Prince roared out Caydish I could not understand, and the Ambassador said, "It's Masgalor, one of the Princess' brothers. His Highness had left him to hold the dam for Cayd."

"And who sent it?"

The Prince spoke slowly, in fury not grief. "That magus, that Xerlanthor." He turned to the archer. "No other word?"

"No, Warlord." The archer seemed on the verge of collapse, shaking as if with ague.

"Then you know your fate." Without a word the archer dropped his clenched hands to his sides, kneeling back on his heels. From his belt the Prince unhooked the battle axe which never left him, and before anyone could interfere, swung it in a glittering circle and beheaded the kneeling man.

The body slumped, spouting blood in a ghastly crimson pool that spread over the woven yellow carpet. The severed head bounced sideways from the blow and rolled across the room. Rosil scrambled out of the way, green in the face, and Fisan-shi leaned over the arm of her chair and was sick.

"Why did you do that?" I asked, almost fainting myself.

The Prince did not reply, but took up the edge of the tablecloth and wiped off his gory blade. On either side of him Mother and Yibor-soo shrank back. The Ambassador told me, "Only Xerlanthor could compel someone to travel night and day to bring a token. The evil magus set a geas, a compulsion, on the unfortunate, to bring the head to his Highness."

"Xerlanthor can do that?" Sickened, I glanced at Xalan.

He nodded, his face broken with shock. "It's pyrolurgy," he explained. "Constraining the soul-fires to certain courses of action. To kill the man immediately was necessary. The geas might have included all sorts of injunctions—to betray at some crucial moment, or to assassinate the Prince,. or even you.''

"Oh.'' I knew my face was also green-white but remembering Silverhand's words I refused to give in to the fear. Signaling for the Chamberlain I said, "My lord, call someone to have this corpse removed. And have the carpet cleaned.'' The Chamberlain obeyed, staggering to the door. I turned to the Prince and said in stilted Caydish, "Such an evil must be stopped. When shall we leave?''

For the first time the flinty face relaxed a bit. "Immediately,'' he growled, and held out his big hand. It was spattered with the archer's blood, but I took it, steeling myself not to flinch. When the iron grip loosed my hand also was bloody. I restrained the instinct to wipe it off on my robe, for I knew it was an omen.

Chapter 7: Grave-gift

Of course we could not truly leave immediately. The Prince did depart the next morning to start the offensive, taking his gruesome token with him, but I would muster Averidan's forces and follow as soon as possible. Frantic preparations were made: vast amounts of food were packed, hundreds of weapons selected and honed, armor repaired, messages sent west for the countryside to prepare for our arrival, and taxes raised. It promised to be a hard journey. In Averidan it was almost spring, but upcountry we would be climbing the Lanach Mountains back into winter again. The Army and Sisterhood would march, but I hoped to go horseback at least as far as the Tambors, and perhaps even over the pass into Cayd. Horses are not often brought upstream past Mhee, but I planned to extend the courier lines and leave Zofal in charge at the Tambors. His assistance would be invaluable to nurse a string of horses so far.

Planning, doing double-quick confirmation reviews—for the country must be in order when I left it—I got up early, worked without pause all day and into the evening, and late at night collapsed into my bed alone. My holiday with Melayne seemed to belong to another person, long ago.

The first hint of trouble appeared when Fisan-shi came to me one afternoon and begged for a few words.

I looked up from materiel lists and rubbed my eyes. "What is it, cousin?"

"I'm coming with you, Liras-ven, aren't I? After all I'm the Bearer of the Crystal Crown."

The idea startled me. "I don't see how it's possible," I said. "This isn't a pleasure-trip. I'll depose you and appoint a soldier."

"You can't do that, it's not the custom," she said. "You gave me the position and it would dishonor me to be ousted."

This was true enough but I had no time for minor considerations. "To bring you might be dangerous," I decided, and turned again to my list.

But she put both hands over my scroll, smudging the ink, and said, "Commander Silverhand said I had potential."

Exasperated, I said, "Get her to take charge of you and you can come." This satisfied her, and she left. I made a note to tell the Commander to do no such thing, and put the incident out of my mind.

Two days later I was signing letters of requisition, and ordered a quick meal since the supper hour had past. Looking up perhaps a hundred signatures later I glimpsed beyond the lamp's light a server with a tray. "Set it down here," I ordered, pushing some rolls aside. She came forward, and I saw it was Melayne. I lay down my brush and pushed my chair back. In the warm light her red hair with its silver rod ornaments shone scarlet as frosted autumn leaves. I had almost forgotten how good she smelled.

She snuggled onto my lap and fed me bits of barley cake dipped in sauce. "Don't kiss my dress," she admonished in her charming accent. "Sticky." So I transferred the attentions to her mouth.

"We're leaving day after tomorrow," I said at last. "How shall I ever do without you?" For I realized that all this time I should have been laying in a store of Melayne, so that when I went away I should not hunger too soon.

I expected no reply, having become used to talking without her comprehension. But she understood, and said, "Take me with you."

"What? Never, I couldn't risk you."

"I will help."

"Nonsense." Her body through the thin sky-blue gown was a little plump, but so lightly boned she felt as perfect a lapful as Sahai, who had already stolen an oyster from my plate. "I know

what you'd like," I whispered into her ear, and plucked the two
Caydish fastenings from her hair. It tumbled down around my
face, over the papers, and down to the floor in a silken fall, and I
wrapped a handful round my throat and wondered whether any
other husband in Averidan was so happy.

"Return those," she commanded, but I wouldn't. The rods
were heavy, I noticed, but not heavy enough to be solid metal,
about the thickness of my forefinger. Melayne wriggled away
and insisted, "You will need me, bring me with you."

"Yes, I need you," I murmured, "but no, you can't come
with us."

She tried to rise but I held her waist and hair, and her
slippered toes could not reach the marble floor. She could not
even glare at me, for I was filling my lungs with the exciting
odor of skin and scalp behind her right ear. She poked me hard
in the ribs and accused, "You bring Fisan-shi."

"I do not!" I said, but with a pang remembered the forgotten
note to Silverhand. "Don't tell me that girl persuaded the
Commander!"

"I want to go, too," Melayne repeated.

"I'll deal with Fisan," I promised, "but no matter what she
does you may not come with us. Now be reasonable. In Cayd
proper ladies stay at home." I swept the tresses off and stood up,
setting her on her feet. In frustration Melayne shifted to Caydish,
arguing and explaining. I did not understand a syllable, and
taking her in my arms again put a finger over her mouth, saying,
"Now, no more talk. I've done with work, it's time for bed." A
stabbing pain in the finger made me jump. She had bitten me.
"Ouch!" I cried, as she twisted free of my arm. "That really
hurt!"

It was actually bleeding a bit. In a fury she snatched the ink
block and shied it at me with deadly accuracy. Then she took up
the paperweights, her hair flying back behind her like a comet's
tail. One hit me on the knee and the other in the stomach.
Bruised, bewildered, inky, and hurt in my feelings, I retreated to
the antechamber and slammed the door, leaving her victor of the
field.

The Chamberlain looked up in mild surprise and said, "Are
you retiring, Majesty?" I was too upset to reply and hurried
away before Melayne could emerge from the inner room.

I slept poorly and next morning sent for Xalan. He had been
made a full magus at last, and was helping the Master Magus

select the specialized magi to combat Xerlanthor's geomantic works. I recounted the entire episode, expecting sympathy.

"Of course she was angry," he said with typical Viridese relish. "What a pity no one translated for her, Caydish profanity is said to be notable. She must have been accusing you of sneaking off to the wars and other women."

"I should have invited the whole court," I snapped. "It would be less nerve-wracking to fight the Tiyalor. And what is this about Fisan?"

"I heard about that. She told the Commander that a trustworthy person had to keep the Crown in hostile country, and the Commander made a place for her in the Sisters' staff tent."

"Then it's too late. I did promise." I held my aching head in my hands and asked, "What should I do?"

"How about a present?" Xalan suggested. "For the Lady, I mean. Tell her you love her, reassure her of your regard. It's unlucky to go to war on bad terms with a wife."

Taking this advice I had a bale of silks sent over to the Lady's rooms. Preparations for our departure next day kept me too busy to call, but I refused to work late and after supper with the officers and magi retired. After a bath I donned a vivid green night robe and hurried down the maze of bright-lit corridors to her rooms.

In the outer chamber my sudden appearance woke flutterings and whispers from Melayne's Caydish maids. It was unusual for so many of them to be present in the evening, but I brushed past and opened the door to the inner chamber.

To my surprise Melayne was wearing her Caydish clothes, which I had only seen her in that first day. She seemed at first not very pleased to see me, but then came forward into my embrace.

Contrition, I felt, would be appropriate even if I didn't know my fault. "I'm sorry I offended you, Melayne, last night," I told her. She did not answer, but reached up with both hands to tilt my face down towards her own. Taking this hint I kissed her, and a tide of desire rose in me at her touch. The wooly, foreign smell of her clothes was distracting, and I said, "How do all these things come off?" The gray-green eyes narrowed for an instant, and then she laughed and showed me how the belt of metal plaques latched around her waist. One item led to another, and in the delights of the present I forgot to inquire into the reasons for last night.

When I awoke the next morning I thought for an instant I had overslept, for yellow light shone on my face. Blinking, I realized it was a light from the door, not the window. It was not yet dawn. The place beside me was empty and cold, and in the outer room I heard hushed Caydish voices. Wrapping a linen quilt round myself I got up to see what was going on.

The ladies were bustling about in their night robes, tying up satchels and wrapping parcels. Beyond them Melayne, fully dressed in her Caydish clothes again, was adjusting a furry hood on her bright hair. A maid brought her a long sheathed knife, and she belted it at her back and swung on a fur cloak. To my horror I saw that there was luggage enough for only one person, and Melayne was going to each maid with final words of injunction or command. Forgetting my appearance I threw the door open and shouted, "Melayne, what does this mean?"

The women squealed with surprise. Melayne met my eye and set her jaw but her words were lost in the others' babble. In my best Caydish I thundered, "Out, everyone, go away!" They glanced at Melayne, who nodded, and scurried out. I slammed the door behind them. "Where do you think you're going?"

"Liras, take me with you to Tiyalor." From her tone she did not expect me to give way, but she glowered at me in defiance.

"So that's it! and how long have you been planning this?" I remembered her discomfort at my arrival last night. "Were you planning to go last night?"

She nodded, and stubbornly repeated, "You will need me, I want to go."

I was hurt, and angry, realizing that when I had surprised her in her packing she had kissed me to keep me from seeing her luggage, and lulled me to sleep with sex. "You deceitful creature," I cried. "I absolutely forbid you to leave this Palace!"

She became angry in her turn, and said, "I am not deceitful, you are stupid!"

Remembering my family's advice I snapped, "You are my wife and you will obey me." She tried to scurry past me to the door, but I caught her arm. Writhing in my grasp she kicked at my bare shins with booted feet. I yelled with pain and let go. She retreated but before she could find a missile someone tapped on the door at my back.

"What is it, I'm busy!"

"You wanted to be called at dawn, Majesty," a meek voice reminded me. "The army marches in a few hours."

"Curse it." Opening the door quickly, I slipped out and pulled it to again. My lord the Scheduling Director gasped and looked away. I had lost my quilt in all the fuss. I said, "Lend me your cape for a while, my lord, I seem to have mislaid my robe." Averting his eyes he unclasped the garment and handed it to me. It wasn't long enough but I held it to keep it from flapping open. "Call the Palace guardsman on duty, please."

When the guardsman arrived, he saluted and then stared. Ignoring it I said, "The Lady is, I feel, indisposed, and ought not to go out into the cold to see me off. I should tell you that she does not agree with me in this. Therefore, keep her in her rooms until dawn tomorrow, and in the City until I return. Her women may go in and out today and bring her whatever she wishes. Understand?"

"Yes, Majesty."

"Good." The advantages of being an absolute monarch, I decided, were considerable.

In my own chambers the Wardrobe Master and Xalan were waiting for me. Xalan raised his eyebrows at my attire, and remarked, "I hope you had a pleasant night."

"No, I did not," I said. But since I refused to elaborate no further comment could be made.

The Master lifted the borrowed cape off my shoulders, and helped me dress. Then the armor was buckled on. I had ordered a severely practical set, and the design had been approved by both the Master Armorer and Commander Silverhand before I allowed the jewelers near it. The result was both secure and comfortable, but not very grand—a knee-length bronze lamellar coat, fitting loosely and buckled in front, burnished and inlaid smoothly around each finger-sized plate with silver wire. I would wear the Crystal Crown to lead the parade out of the city, so that the people would recognize the Shan King, but the battle helm was similar in design, covering my head and neck and plumed with green and white.

The Master slid the cover from the mirror for me. "Come and give me your opinion," I called to Xalan.

"Businesslike," he judged, "but not very kingly. The thicknesses of metal added to my shoulders and limbs made me a heroic figure beside Xalan in his dark red magic robe. My face, with the fine dark hair hidden under shining metal, looked stern and severe, but his under the peaked cap held only irony. He made a ludicrous face at my reflection, and when I laughed said, "I daresay the artisans would weep at the sight of it, a few weeks into the campaign."

I noticed a fresh bruise darkening my leg just above the

shinpiece, and without thinking said, "I wish Melayne could see it while it's new." Then I regretted the uxorious words and to hide my embarrassment hurried into the main room to say farewell to Sahai. She was hiding in a saddlebag, sulking over all this disturbance, and I turned her out, saying, "You can't come either."

"Everything has been packed, Majesty," the Master of Wardrobe assured me.

"I'm adding a few important items," I said. From a cupboard I took the well-worn scrolls on Caydish. The Tiyal and the Caydish are more or less of the same race, and their languages share many words. Then I brought out the mirror of Xerlanthor, still in its case as I had received it from Warlord Prince Melbras. "What do we hope to get out of this?" I asked Xalan.

"Who knows? But it's sure to be of some help. Magi bind their mirrors to them with many spells."

The main road had been spread from Upper City to the West Gate with green leaves and branches. Spring was in the air, and it was a brisk, windy day, but it was still too early for real leaves. Since they were demanded by custom—they symbolize the power of the Sun our forefather, as seashells stand for the might of Ennelith—leaf-shaped slips of green cloth had been substituted. My warhorse Piril, a gift from my brother, did not like the feel of them under his hooves, and I had to lead him a little way along at first.

My place was almost at the end of the procession. First Commander Silverhand, preceded by the eagle banner of the Sisters, led 300 women warriors who paced behind her proud and sleek as leopardesses. Zofal and the horsemen led the courier mounts, which were draped with cloth leaves for the occasion. General Horfal-yu rode a brown horse before sixteen marching fists of spearmen, an impressive and glittering sight that filled the road like a metallic river, since the Viridese military fist is fifty men armed with heavy spears and shields. I was next, leading the magi, herbals, bonesetters, and so forth who would be in my charge, and with me marched my own guard, a finger of ten picked spearmen.

The Master Armorer himself brought my sword—a new one, the gleaming honed bronze blade wide as my hand. I had allowed the jewelers only to set one stone, a royal emerald, in the pommel. Fisan-shi brought me the Crown, and removing my helm I put it on. In the usual dreamlike calm I was helped onto Piril's back.

With the Crown I skimmed the emotional surface of the hearts around me, starting away from the painful ones that spattered like hot fat. My mother's pride in me, and worry over my fate. The Armorer's complacent anticipation of a profitable summer, arming fists and guardsmen now that we had depleted armories for miles around. My sister's admiration, Rosil-eir's envy. Master Magus Xantallon's lean white face as white as his mustaches, reflecting the labor over magic strategies. The noisy crowd lining the road, quick glimmers of patriotism, excitement, pride, fear.

The flicker and glare of so many vivid fleeting impressions hurt, much as staring at the sunlit harbor would dazzle an eye in summer. The City in its fake greenery seemed cozy and dear, familiar yet brightly tinted, poignant as spring. We hadn't even left, but I was already homesick.

In parade order we passed slowly through the West Gate and the teeming marketplace beyond, and turned onto the road built beside the Mhesan west to Mhee, over the grim mountains to Cayd, and at last to Ieor and Xerlanthor's dam. When we had gone past most of the crowd I reined in my horse and let the endless column march past until I saw Fisan. Signaling to her I took off the Crown and returned it to her casket. My freed perceptions instantly focused, and I turned my horse.

Due east nature's fortification, the rocky scarp of the Upper City, rose high above the puny City walls. On it I could see the white Palace buildings, and the curve of the golden Temple dome beyond. The glory and beauty of it stopped my breath. I could not believe I had once resolved to exile myself from Averidan. Do fish survive out of their native water? I must have been mad.

"Excuse me, Your Majesty."

With a start I looked down to see a panting Palace guardsman at my stirrup. "Did I forget something?" I asked, casting my mind back over my packing.

"No, Majesty, the Lady sent this." He held out a bit of gleaming black and red: a knife, a tiny dagger with a red stone haft and an unusual blade chipped from what looked like obsidian. It was broken, snapped off an inch or so from the hilt.

"How did this happen?" I asked.

"It was like that when the Lady gave it to me," the man said. "There was a message also—to give it to her kin in Lanach."

Puzzled, I took it and turned it over in my hands. "It's really just a toy." Then it came to me. This must have been a memento, a childhood souvenir of her late brother. I didn't know much about Caydish burial rites but it must be a grave-gift, to be sent to the Deadlands with the body. She had wanted to accompany me not only for love but for piety. The realization brought a sentimental lump to my throat. Looking back I could pick out the place in the shadow where the Lady's rooms look out over the cliff, and though I knew even if she watched she could not see, I made Piril back and rear, and waved. The guardsman must have thought me demented.

With a clatter of hooves Zofal cantered back to me. "What have you been doing?" he demanded. "Don't tell me you've changed your mind again."

"No, no," I said, turning westward. "Just waving good-bye."

Chapter 8: The Tambors of Xao-Lan

To Mhee is an easy trip, only a day's march on a wide, well-traveled road paved with the usual oyster-shell and lime. Barges laden with grain or goods floated downstream hung with big copper bells at prow and stern to ward off bad currents, and their steersmen waved at us. Travelers can sail east from Mhee to the City but going west upstream it's less labor to use the road. Booths had been set up at intervals, under convenient groves or where there was a spring, to sell clothing, sandals, food, fuel, drinks, and generally lure the extra coin from the traveler's purse. I had the feeling of riding not with an army but on a holiday excursion with a large and unnaturally ordered family.

Private houses became fewer as we went along. I took note of the house belonging to the Director of City Roadworks—the high wall and geomantically unfortunate house all roofed with red pottery tile. Somewhere on the other side of the river here was my family's estate.

By midday we passed mostly barley fields, spreading flat and brown on each side to the horizon. The seed had been sown, but had not yet sprouted. Whenever the road arched itself to go over an irrigation cut we could see the yoke of plump gray oxen toiling on the treadmills below, raising water from the river to the fields. The mills are usually kept by farm children, who splash in the water, chase frogs, and in their spare time tend the oxen. It seemed a rhythmic, carefree life—the endless fall of water, the regular thud of hooves on the wheel, punctuated, as it was today, by exciting passers-by. Sleek black heads would pop up above the edges of the bridges to look, and then vanish again when I approached.

I didn't want to frighten them, and so dared not simply gallop up and collar a child. At last I hit on the tactic of riding up toward the head of the line, dismounting, and keeping steady watch while the whole line of march passed behind me. They would hide from me at first but the sound of so many feet on the bridge drew them irresistibly to peep over the edge again. As with horses, it did not do to make sudden or threatening gestures, but after a constant yet nonchalant forward progress on my part their shyness would fall away, and I had many odd conversations.

Was I a soldier? Where did my horse come from? What was my armor made of? Was I coming back or going on to Mhee? I told my name and our business, but gave up mentioning my rank since the confession met with disbelief. "Everyone knows our King is tree-tall, and dressed all in gold," one dignified young miss informed me. "You don't even look like him." Told that I planned to go past Mhee, but to come back soon, they would frequently promise to look for my return.

At the confluence of the Mhesan and the Arcet, Mhee is a busy little shipping town, with many bridges linking either bank. Where the grand City and holy Ennelith-Ral are built of stone, Mhee is cozy in wood floated downstream from the north and west. We arrived after sunset and were greeted with torches, flags, speeches, and music.

The next day we left the good road behind. West of Mhee the land begins to rise in earnest, and our way was unpaved and gravelly. The hundreds of marching feet raised thick gritty clouds of dust, but to save the horses' hooves we took them along the grassy verge. It is an unirrigated country where only one barley crop a year is to be had—good farmers can wring two harvests from the richer land downstream. But flax does well here.

Before noon we came to the Felcad where it flows into the Mhesan. Standing on our bank and looking across we could see the power of Xerlanthor. The Felcad's turbulent yellow waters poured over rapids down to the level of the Mhesan and swelled it. But upstream from that point the unaugmented Mhesan was low in its bed. Brown weeds were visible in the channel, waving slowly back and forth as if offended by the stinginess of the icy water. Dry rocks stuck out of the muddy banks. The flow was sullen and quiet, not noisy as it ought to have been this time of year.

We halted while a young hydromant magus girded up his red robe and waded far out into the frigid stream to test the quality of the bottom and measure the depth with a weighted line. Several times he stepped into a pothole and vanished below the surface, but since he had a rope around his waist we could rescue him if necessary. He trod water in the center for a long time, trying the depth here and there, and when he tried to return was too cold to swim properly. So we hauled him in like a runaway dinghy. But he had brought back his measuring line, knotted at the water line.

While the hydromant was dried at a fire and given wine, the Master Magus measured the line. "It's five fathoms at its deepest," he reported. "We know from the boatmen who travel here that about this time of year the channel should be at least five and a half."

"Three feet isn't very much of a drop," I said.

"Multiply that by the length and average width of the Mhesan from here," the Magus said, "and the volume of water will surprise you. What baffles me is what Xerlanthor is doing with the water. He was a geomant in the old days, and we're told he's studying pyrolurgy now. Is he also delving into hydromancy?"

"They do say the rains were light last year," Xalan pointed out. "Perhaps Xerlanthor is watering the sheep of Tiyalor and then selling them all heavier and bloated to Cayd."

"I doubt minor chicanery would be worth his while," I laughed.

When we camped that night at a small town the magi measured the depth again, this time with the assistance of a farmer's rowboat. If I had refused a supper, specially cooked for the Shan King by the town wives, it would have been insulting, but after the meal I insisted on unstrapping the army-issue bedroll from Piril's saddle and sleeping with my ten guards around their campfire, as a rehearsal for harder times to come. It was surprising how hard and lumpy the ground was, and how cold one's feet got. In the morning dawn came far too early, and frost furred our quilts.

What looked like a low bank of gray and white cloud rested on the western horizon, and I pointed it out to the Commander. "Does that mean it will rain today?"

"Look again," she said.

It lay unmoving in a great curve, north to south, and I

exclaimed, "They're mountains, the Lanach range. We're almost there!"

We did not reach them that day, but with buffeting winds and a little sleet they gave us a foretaste of their character. Huddling in my hooded green cloak, I crouched on Piril's back and switched the reins from one hand to the other so that each had a turn under cover. The fists had to hold their shields carefully, else the wind would catch them and wrench them around. Several elbows were sprained before they learned.

We did that day reach the forests of western Averidan. I had never seen so many trees at once. The leaves had not yet come out, and the noise the bare branches made rubbing together in the gusts was a little unnerving, as if they muttered together against us. The woodcutters and charcoal-burners who live there made us welcome with honey and firewood, and built us windbreaks of log sections so that the heat of our campfires was not swept away by the wind. That night I was so tired I never noticed the tree roots beneath me, or the weird forest noises, but slept sound.

"The Sisters say it will be a short journey today," Fisan shi told me in the morning.

"Our last full day in Averidan," I said. "Tomorrow we'll be climbing the pass into Cayd."

Fisan had become very friendly with the warrior Sisters, and while I practiced Caydish with my interpreter spent the days walking with them and listening to their plaivs of war. In the time of the Tsorish invasion they had retreated to these very forests, after Ennclith-Ral and the City fell, and had proved so pugnacious in woodland warfare that to placate them Tsantelekor the Invader, who had named himself King, had married the deposed Shan Queen he had planned to execute. The Sisterhood still had much forest lore, and when the trees came close occasionally Sisters would sometimes walk through the fringe of the forest rather than on the road, to practice silent woodland travel. Although I had seen the women slip into the trees, and knew they were keeping pace with the march, I never could hear them—not a crackle of a dry leaf, or a snap of a twig, or a warning whistle from a startled bird. Fisan said the Commander could slip up to a sleeping squirrel's nest and steal the stored nuts without waking the owner, and I believed it.

Long before we came there we could tell we were nearing the Tambors. Little rafts of foam began to appear on the Mhesan, and a distant dull roar became audible. It grew louder, and when we came to the last big glade before the falls we saw there the

Last Bridge and the garrison lodge beside it. The captain of the garrison came out to meet us. General Horfal-yu and the Commander had been here before, but I had never seen the Tambors, one of the wonders of the world. So leaving them to set up camp I took Zofal and rode over the bridge and past the last bend in the road.

Here at the feet of the mountains even a Shan King was humbled. The peaks rose up, clothed in dark forest on their lower slopes, then snowy trees, and at last snow only, glaring white, where only falcons set foot. The icy wind whistled down off the pass, cutting through our clothes, bringing an odor I recognized but could not place. "What's that, on the wind?" I asked Zofal.

He breathed deeply and said, "Pines, those furry trees you see way up there. Cayd is almost all pines. They never lose their leaves—you should get one for the Palace gardens."

"I wouldn't think one would grow in the City," I said. "The climate is too different." I sniffed again, and it came to me— Melayne had smelled like this on that first day.

"The fall is over there," Zofal pointed, "beside the pass." Picking our way a little north, along a grassy path marked with rocks, we came within sight of the Tambors.

They are named after the first Magus, Shan Xao-Lan, who is said to have built them. This was almost certainly not plaiv, but history, for he had been one of the old sort of magi, excelling in every branch of the magic art. They indeed looked like the work of a deity, not a human—five mighty falls, each as high as the Temple dome, evenly spaced up the pass like steps on a colossal stair. The noise of the water was painful so close, with a high musical note tinkling over the deep roar—the little cymbal-chimes of their tambors. The water curved green over each step and thundered bubbling down to the next, so that at the wide bottom pool the water was beaten to foam like a meringue. The hand of Xerlanthor was even more obvious here. Eroded rocks to either side of the falls bore silent witness to a once much greater flow. The river was less than half as wide as its channel now.

To the left of the fall was a steep narrow path, paved here and there with a log or two, which was the pass to the uplands of Cayd. We would have to go single file. For the first time I realized how difficult it would be to coax Piril up. On our way back I asked Zofal's advice on it.

"If you insist on bringing the poor beast," he said, "you'll have to blinker him. Otherwise he'll get frightened, break away, and fall."

"And I'll stop up his ears," I said, "like I'd do for myself."

"It's not worth your going along anyway," Zofal said. "You're too valuable to risk."

I could not mention the secret battle plans involving the Crystal Crown's powers, so I said, "it's *chun-hei*, Mother says it runs in the family. I'll be safe enough. Not only is there the army and the Sisters, but I have my own guard, and the Crown too."

"I wouldn't rely overly on that thing," Zofal grumbled.

"You may be surprised," I told him, careful not to smile.

That night gathered around Silverhand's campfire we who were in on the secret watched General Horfal-yu lay out battle tactics with little wooden blocks, a store of which he had brought along in a linen bag. "Now, if the earthworks are heavily manned," he said, "then the magi can set the supporting wooden stakes afire with pyrolurgy."

"Not if the earth is packed around them," the Master Magus said. "Besides, pyrolurges are very rare nowadays. I didn't even bring one."

"Why not?" I asked.

"The only true wielder of the wooden wand in Averidan now is in his nineties," the Magus replied. "Too old for war. And his pyrolurgic apprentices are too young."

The General was not deterred in the least. "Or His Majesty's powers could strike at the enemy from the western side, here," he said, stacking blocks on the map, "while the fists swing around this way."

"Have you practiced turning the forces of the Crystal Crown into a weapon?" the Magus asked me.

"Wouldn't the Tiyalor press the attack here?" Silverhand asked, pointing.

"No, because the Caydish archers will be there, to cover the area." The General measured the distance carefully with a notched stick. "Yes, that's well within the range of Caydish bows."

The night before I had accepted a gift of chestnuts from a forester, and was now sprawled on my stomach roasting them in the fire. Waving one back and forth on the tip of my knife to cool it, I answered the Magus, "Of course I haven't. I'd need someone to practice on, and who would be silly enough to volunteer?"

"Use a tree, or an ox," he suggested. "Or someone due for lapidation."

"Never! I like trees, and oxen too. And I haven't lapidated anyone yet." I threw the chestnut peelings one by one into the fire, and popped the sweet nutmeat into my mouth. "Want one? I'll roast it for you . . . besides, I don't expect it will be any more difficult than mending a bone is."

On my other side Silverhand was saying, "I'm sure Caydish archers wouldn't line up like that, all in a row. They would rather run screaming at the foe."

"My dear Silverhand, we can order them to line up," the General said. "Not that their formation will make any difference. Now with spearmen it is important, so that their shields may overlap."

"It won't be as easy," the Magus told me, "simply because you'll be working against the Crown's nature."

"It's always seemed naturally dangerous to me," I said, "but then I had a personal interest."

"There was never any real likelihood of that," the Magus said crossly. "Do you know how geas works?"

I quoted Xalan: "Using pyrolurgy to constrain the soul-fires."

"Yes. Well, it's not quite accurate to say that geas is laid on the Crystal Crown, since it has no soul—did you speak?"

"I beg your pardon," I said. "I didn't let it cool enough." I pushed the chestnut back into the embers with a stick. Of course only I, the wearer, knew of the Crown's beautiful erudite voice. "Go on, Magister."

"The Crystal Crown is a mighty work of pyrolurgy, after all, and its makers knew it was so powerful that limitations would be necessary for the safety of both the Shan King and Averidan. So it is greatly constrained to work for good: to heal and not curse, bless and not damn."

"Then how did my great-grandfather fight with it?" I wanted to know.

"I can't say," the Magus admitted. "But all my magic training tells me it could not have been easy."

On the other side of the fire the General was saying, "If the main goal is to kill Xerlanthor we must get His Majesty close enough to blast him. The assault must be planned with that in mind."

"But he's so cunning," Silverhand reminded us. "Did the Warlord tell you how Xerlanthor escaped when Cayd stormed

Ieor last year? He dressed three Tiyalor in magic red, and himself wore black. So he slipped through their fingers.''

"He can't fool me that way," I boasted. "The Crystal Crown is a touchstone of truth."

The General beamed at me. "We'll show those Caydish how to do it."

The ascent of the pass next day promised to be difficult, and we rose well before first light to prepare for it. All the packs carried by the horses had to be unwrapped and rebalanced for human backs. Only Piril and General Horfal-yu's warhorse were crossing with us, and we could not lade them heavily for fear they would slip under the unaccustomed weight of baggage. Items which had been necessities in Averidan were now, weighed against the steepness of the climb, doomed superfluous, and the garrison captain offered to keep extra luggage here against our return. To my shame I had more baggage than anyone else. I had been wearing a sensible traveling outfit of gray and blue quilted linen, reinforced with soft leather, but the Wardrobe Master had sent along a handsome selection of fancy wear. Xalan pointed out, "In Cayd you'll be expected to put on a fine show. You're the Shan King, ruler of Averidan the wealthy." But overruling him I weeded my packs ruthlessly of almost everything unsuited to a military campaign, and for good measure ordered the captain to send the rejects back home.

Silverhand had hoped the wind would drop, but if anything it was worse, not blowing steadily from one direction but buffeting cruelly from all sides and plucking at our sleeves and coats. The magi could not calm the wind and also travel with us, since it takes time and quiet to work weather magery. As a precaution against being swept off the mountain Silverhand had us link ourselves together in threes with rope. Little rolls of linen or fleece were distributed, so that we could plug our ears against the noise of the waterfalls. Bigger wads were tied around the horses' ears, and they were blinkered. Piril took this very well—a tribute to Zofal's training—but it needed all of Zofal's horsemanship, plus help from me, before the General's brown horse would submit.

The army would need hours to creep single-file up the pass, but I hurried with my packing lest I delay things. Before I plugged my ears I said good-bye to Zofal. "Try not to get into trouble," I told him. "I'll send often."

He embraced me and whacked me on the back, saying, "Don't catch cold, little brother. Don't offend your Caydish in-laws.

Remember it's unlucky to get mixed up in the works of magi. Keep your feet dry and eat regular meals. Don't pick quarrels with bears or wolves.''

"You sound just like Mother," I said.

"Now I'm not there to keep an eye on you, you'll have to take care of yourself," he growled.

In our honor the garrison's ten spearmen had dressed in their best. They stood proudly in a row at the Last Bridge, their shields painted with the same device (five red horizontal bars, symbolizing the Tambors) while we started the climb up. When at last my turn came Zofal handed me Piril's reins and clasped my shoulder once more.

I was the last of my three, to keep the connecting rope clear of Piril's feet. Roped to me ahead was the Master Bonesetter and a Sister named Lioncelle. Ahead of them was General Horfal-yu leading his horse, roped to another Sister and Xalan—the air was too turbulent for the magi to lift, and they had to toil up on foot like the rest of us. Behind me were my guards, their captain Corlis in front. Our progress was very slow. The path was just wide enough for the horses, cut into the rocky side of the falls. While on the left there was a comforting granite wall, to the right the path dropped sheer onto the rocks and foaming water. So we walked on the edge of a precipice, and I almost felt I could do with blinkers myself.

Through the earplugs the thunder and tinkle of the falls was only uncomfortable, and as we climbed higher it was possible to dissociate the roar from the torrent below and blame it completely on the wind. For the wind was a torment—pushing on my brow and body until each upward step was a struggle, and then suddenly whipping around and shoving at my back so that I stumbled forward and grabbed at the stones for fear of rolling off the edge.

We were too far above to be wetted by the river water, which in any case was less of a flow than usual, but the wind whipped the spray up through the air so that our cloaks, clutched tight around us, were soon beaded with moisture. Once wet, the garments seemed to hardly strain the wind, and we became chilled to the bone.

The way was sometimes solid rock, more often a scree of loose pebbles and stones. Wherever footing was too treacherous a few logs would be embedded to hold the stones. They were slippery, and the pebbles hurt my feet through my thin-soled riding boots. I ached for the Master Bonesetter ahead of me, who

was shod in the soft leather shoes most Viridese wear. Behind
me Piril began to favor one leg, and I knew he must have
wedged a stone in his foot. There was nothing to be done but tug
him along. The twisting path was too narrow to allow me to
examine his hooves, and I hoped he would not become lame. I
stroked his black nose and murmured encouraging noises that
could not be heard by either of us through the earplugs. Looking
back, I could see no trace of the garrison or the Last Bridge.
Only the tops of the leafless trees were visible, undulating
brown-grey eastward to the sea.

The Master Bonesetter and I trudged along, hoods up and
heads bowed, too miserable to look up past the next step or two.
The warrior Sister leading us, however, was experienced enough
to watch the progress ahead. When Lioncelle halted the Master
Bonesetter and then I ran into her.

Just ahead General Hortal-yu was in trouble. The brown horse
had apparently decided it had had enough, horses were not meant
to climb mountains, and was backing down the path. We could
not retreat, or not quickly enough to get out of the way, and the
General wrenched at the reins, fighting to lead the rebellious
animal forward.

Lioncelle tugged at my cloak, and then pushed the hood back
from my ear. Plucking out the linen plug she said, "Lie flat and
hug the path, Majesty. Better to be trodden on than knocked over
the edge." I could barely comprehend, over the suddenly loud
roar of the water, but I nodded and plugging my ear again
obeyed. With gestures she commanded the Master Bonesetter to
imitate me, and lay flat herself. I tapped her leg and pointed to
Piril, who certainly could not be stepped over. She shook her
head and drew her dagger, of the bright metal only Sisters use,
from the top of her combat boot.

The brown horse was putting on quite a show, bucking and
kicking out its hind legs. We pulled our helms over our noses
and dug our chins into the gravel. The General seemed to be
cursing it, his face red with fury. He looped the reins around his
wrist before hauling at the plated headstall with both hands,
putting his back into the effort. Released, his green and white
cloak rippled back in the wind, and then was caught by another
gust and twisted forward, snapping like a whip.

Really frightened now, the horse reared. Even through our
plugs we could hear its startled whinny. Not an arm's length
before my face the big hooves trampled and slid, kicking pebbles

down on to us. Shaken off, the General slipped on the gravel and sat down hard, still pulling on the reins.

One hoof descended too close to the edge, and slipped. With a dreadful scream the horse foundered, recovered, and then fell, vanishing over the precipice. The General still had the reins around his wrist, and was dragged violently forward and down. Before he was pulled over, a flash of light caught the corner of my eye. Lioncelle had thrown her dagger, slashing the reins free. Only a Sister's dagger could hold an edge sharp enough to do it at one blow. The General rolled downhill with the force of his fall, but I stopped him before he hit the wall, throwing myself full length on his back.

For a long moment no one could move. Then Xalan and the Sister leading that trio, who would have been dragged to their death with the General, came down. We staggered to our feet, shaking the gravel out of our clothes and armor. The General had bruises, and raw scrapes where he had been rolled over and over on the stones, but no serious injury. The Master Bonesetter took cloths from his pack to bind the bleeding places, and Lioncelle produced a stoneware flask of plum brandy. Fortified by a sip, I knelt carefully at the cliff edge and peered over.

The horse had broken its back, and writhed on the boulders about a spearlength above the foaming water. I could not hear its cries but I saw the bewilderment in the eyes, the wordless pride brought low. Corlis the captain of my guard had crept up beside me, and tugging at his arm I pointed. He seemed to understand. Taking another coil of rope he looped it through his arm, and gave one end to the guard roped next to him. Gesturing for the second man to support him with the connecting rope he lowered his legs over the edge.

Fortunately the cliff was not undercut at that point, and by clinging to the rocks and supporting himself with the rope Corlis was able to clamber down to the fallen horse. Dodging the thrashing hooves he pulled one of the General's spears from the saddle-holders and plunged it into the brown throat. He looked back up at me, and I waved my approval. Somewhat to my surprise he then cut the packs free from the saddle, and took the spears and shield. Thus laden he could not climb, and at last tied the extra line round the baggage. His second hauled it up to the path, and then Corlis worked his way back. With a feeling of disappointment I realized he had made the risky climb not from mercy but to salvage the General's equipment. But there was no time for discussion even if we could have been heard, for everyone had to clear the pass by nightfall. So I clapped him on the shoulder in thanks, and went on.

My legs and feet got heavier as we toiled up. By virtue of my rank I was the only one without a pack, and now was glad I had not insisted The constant buffet of the wind made me dizzy. When I shifted in my cloak it crackled stiffly. The soaked cloth was beginning to freeze. I barely noticed when the path began to level off, and to broaden. The Mhesan roared emerald in its narrow channel far below us, for we had climbed past the five falls and were now in Cayd.

Chapter 9: A Cure for Hiccups

Our path led us around a grassy upland, a strange new sight to eyes used to tamed fertile fields. The ground rose gently to the west in undulations of yellow shrub and yellow grass to the forest fringe. The light of the setting Sun glared in our eyes and tinted the sky yellow too, so that we seemed to have come to the One's own land where light is lord and night has no place.

Between the forest and the field, perched above the cloven river channel, is Lanach capital of Cayd. It is not nearly as big as the City, nor even as Mhee—perhaps eighty wooden buildings of one story with steep-sloped roofs, and another hundred or so humbler dwellings built of sod or cut into convenient hillsides, and roofed with poles and thatch. A runner had been sent to warn of our arrival, and while we waited for his return I was combed and chivvied into the one silken cloak I had brought. It was a rich deep green, embroidered in gold with a peach-blossom design, and in it I must have looked a fool cleaning Piril's hooves. He had picked up three stones, and would need a few days' rest. But first he had to carry me into Lanach.

King Melunael's own herald came to lead us to his palace, which consisted of three large wooden halls surrounding a flagged courtyard where his folk had gathered to greet us. I entered in style, mounted and wearing the Crystal Crown, at the head of the army.

I recognized the King right away from the impression I had garnered from Melbras. Melunael was old as the Master Magus, perhaps, but not hale with his years. His staff shook in his gnarled hands, and the fox color had faded from his sparse hair and beard, leaving them gray as wool. Only his eyebrows, incongruously, were still bushy and red. I dismounted for the presentation, and as was proper greeted my fellow monarch as an equal with an exchange of kisses on the left cheek. The King had once been tall as his brother Melbras, but his back was now bent so that our embrace was face to face. It was peculiar to feel the loose flesh and brittle shoulder bones under my hand and think that from this had sprung Melayne's plump sweetness.

The King's heir, Prince Mor, was next. In Cayd the king chooses his successor from among his sons. The bad feeling engendered by this custom has often led to regicide and civil war, and I was grateful for Averidan's more sensible system—no one dares argue with the Crystal Crown. Prince Mor was a towering fair warrior of the same stamp as his uncle, some years older than myself. He wore the copper necklet that princes bear in Cayd, and his pale restless eyes searched everywhere not only among us but among his kin.

After him there were almost more uncles and younger princes than I could count. Daughters are not introduced to strangers. I had not become fluent enough in Caydish to discuss Melayne's family with her, but it needed no Crown to tell me King Melunael had married a beloved and fruitful wife.

The Army and Sisters were to camp in the meadow, but the magi, the noncombatants, my guard, and I were lodged in one of the three great wooden halls. The low thick walls were padded with dry moss and woolen loomwork to keep drafts out, so that passing through the low door was like entering a cave. The rafters of the peaked roof rising far above our heads were hung with strings of onions, sides of smoked mutton, and skins of ale, very foreign and unlike home.

I took off the Crown and said, "Is the store up there so that they have supplies when they're snowed in, or is it a hospitable provision in case I get hungry at night?"

"You won't get hungry," Xalan predicted. "We're having a royal feast tonight. At least it's warm."

I had never seen such huge stone fireplaces, too wide to span with one's arms and big enough to stand up in. There was one at either end of the long hall, burning what looked to be a tree each, and a long enclosed bed of stones running down the middle of the hall, holding smaller fires for cooking on. The warmth was delicious after a day in such cold, and we gathered as close as we dared to the flames, laughing and comparing tales of our labors.

As my clothes were unpacked and shaken out I asked, "Do I get a bath?"

No one knew, and Melunael's steward at last approached me and said, "Baths are not healthful in winter, O King."

"Nonsense," I said. "I take them all the time."

"But that is in Averidan," the man objected, "land of eternal summer."

Xalan said in my ear, "The truth of the matter is, I think, there's nothing to bathe in except the river, which truly is unhealthful in wintertime."

"What do the Caydish do, then?" I asked.

"They wash in basins, by the fire."

So I did, screened for modesty's sake by a few blankets, but did not feel properly clean at all. I put on my good clothes, a grass green robe sewn with topazes over creamy silk leggings and a matching shirt. The stuff seemed to give no warmth at all, even when the matching embroidered cloak was added, and my thin green shoes let the cold in terribly. I looked with longing at my fur-lined traveling cloak but it was still being dried. When we were conducted across the courtyard to the feast I hid from the wind between Xalan and the General.

The royal hall was built exactly like our own. Long narrow tables had been set out along the sides, and carved wooden chairs faced across the central fire-pits. As guest of honor I was placed where I could be seen, in the middle of one side equidistant between the two great fireplaces—arguably the coldest seat in the hall. In the dim light I hoped no one would notice my shivering.

Ale was poured, and then food was brought. The dark ale was strong, bitter yet warming in carved wooden goblets. The meal was oat cakes and roasted meat, more kinds of meat than appear in our mostly vegetable meals at home—lamb, goat, mutton, each cooked on spits over the central fires. One pointed at the sort of meat wanted, and young boys carved and brought a portion on platters. Not used to such heavy and monotonous fare—herbs or spices seemed to be unknown—I drained my goblet instead of taking another serving of meat. I had never tasted ale before, and did not realize how strong it was.

The king had seated me on his right, and on my other side was Prince Mor. The formal welcome had been managed with the help of the interpreter, but now I delved into my scanty stock of

Caydish and said to the King, "Your daughter Melayne sends her greetings."

"Ah, Melayne." Melunael rubbed his gray beard, making a raspy sound. "The little one."

"Yes," I said. It had not occurred to me before that among this tall nation Melayne would naturally be the "little one." I wondered if the Caydish called us, who were all a head shorter than they, the "little people."

"All my other daughters are so much older than you," the King said. "Melayne is a late child, only seventeen last spring, so we felt she was best. I hope you do not feel she is not well-grown enough?"

I was confused, not sure whether he meant in height or years, and said, "She suits me very well. How many brothers and sisters does she have?"

"Now poor Masgalor is dead, there are fourteen, of which eight are sons." The King nodded as if congratulating himself and then seeing my astonishment added, "But of course I was careful in selecting my three queens."

Appalled, I wondered if they were successive or contemporaneous. But no, I would surely have been told if Caydish custom allowed polygamy. I said, "So your Majesty is twice a widower?"

"Three times," the old King said. "I will not be choosing a fourth queen, however. I have heirs enough."

Looking around the hall I agreed. Almost every other man at table seemed to wear a prince's copper necklet. But of course some of these would be King Melunael's brothers. Turning to Prince Mor I said, "You are a very numerous family."

"The nest is too small for the falcons," the Prince replied. His voice was stiff and shy, as if not often used. Hoping to set him at ease I felt in my sash and took out the little broken knife Melayne had sent.

"I was asked by your sister to bring this," I said, giving it to Mor. "I was sorry to learn of Masgalor's end."

"The fortunes of war," Mor said. His face was more stiff than ever, and snatching the toy he quickly hid it in his tunic. I was charmed to see that even these big warriors were so sentimental. With a noticeable effort Mor continued, "But tell us of the wonders of Averidan. My uncle Melbras was in too great a battle-rage to give an account of your wedding."

The ale had loosened my tongue, and with much help from the interpreter I told of the festivities not from my limited viewpoint but from the perspective of my subjects—the distribution of honey-cakes baked in lucky seashells to children, the new linen robe traditionally presented to every Shan adult so that no one need be underdressed for the occasion, the officially sponsored parties across the country on the day. With some muddled idea of pleasing her kin I also spoke of Melayne's honors—the prenuptial gift of eighty silk outfits so that she would not be outshone by the other ladies, the jewels, the horse.

My words met with a silence that spread slowly up and down the tables until no one else in the hall spoke. Unnerved by this response I also fell silent, fearing disbelief. Seeing that I had finished Prince Mor smiled as he said, "Our word for your city means the Opulent Harbor. We named it well, did we not?"

But I could not escape the feeling that I had been a bit ill-mannered, and I turned the subject, saying, "Where is the Warlord now?"

"Ieor, besieging the Tiyalor. He has received word on the winter activities of the evil magus."

"Indeed?"

"The spies report he is boiling the waters of the Mhesan."

"What?" Sure I had misunderstood, I put down my cup and said, "Say that again."

"Boiling them, in great copper cauldrons." He mimed them, outlining the pots with his hands.

"But what *for*?" I looked down the table to where the Master Magus sat listening. Mor shook his head.

"We hoped you could tell us."

The Magus called to me, "We'll look into it. I had heard Xerlanthor was going into pyrolurgy—such magery is unknown to me."

My hosts had been drinking two cups to my one, and from their example I had underestimated the strength and foaminess of their brew. Now to my horror I hiccuped, a loud, attention-catching hiccup like an unburped baby. I choked down the first one but they did not cease, and in embarrassment I pushed my chair back and hurried out the nearest door.

Instantly I realized my error. I had not stepped into the flagged courtyard between halls, but outside the palace complex altogether. The wind was still blowing hard, and it had begun to snow, great white flakes driven sideways in the gale. Pinpricks of light were vaguely visible from distant windows, but no one was in sight. In my thin clothes I would freeze. But even as I turned back big hard hands grabbed me by the back of my robe, and I was hauled off my feet.

"A light," a deep voice said in Caydish, and a crock of coals was uncovered near my face for a moment. "Who is this?"

"Surely the Shan King," a smoother voice replied in the same tongue. "Look at the clothes. But where's his Crown?"

"He was wearing it before," the first said. The fire-pot had been set at our feet so I could not see the face of the speakers, but I realized they did not know I understood Caydish. "Should we kill him?"

"We need to kill somebody, and he's perfect," the smooth voice replied. "Let's strangle him now, wait for the body to be discovered, and then get what we came for. With any luck the two parties will kill each other, while we get away."

Obediently the first speaker began to shift his grip from my nape to my throat. "It'll only take a moment," he said to the other.

My guards were all within. Summoning all my combat instruction I curled shrimpwise in my captor's grasp and kicked with both feet at where I thought the pit of his stomach should be. One foot missed but the other sunk deep into hard flesh. With a whoop of agony he released me, and I sprawled in the snow. The other speaker cursed in several tongues and drew a dagger—I saw the brief gleam of bronze. My rudimentary training had never progressed as far as fighting an armed opponent, but I knew the principles of turning terrain against my foe. Still kneeling I scooped up the trampled snow and popped a handful into the firepot. The coals died in hisses and steam, and I was cloaked in darkness. "May Ixfel swallow you!" the smooth voice cried in Viridese with hatred. I scrambled to one side as softly as I could, swallowing my hiccups, and groped for more snow.

Before I could gather it the hall door swung open again, throwing an oblong of firelight onto the ground. "Liras? Majesty?" It was Xalan. At his approach my assailants fled into the storm.

"You always turn up at the most opportune times," I said. My relief was so great I hiccuped again.

Xalan grinned and said, "Are you planning to vomit, or have you already?"

"Xalan," I said, as steadily as I could, "I have just been attacked." I looked around, but my foes had even remembered to snatch up their fire-pot. "Look at the snow."

"You've been rolling in it."

"Not all these tracks are mine," I insisted, pointing out the big prints of Caydish boots.

"It's impossible to take you seriously when you're making those comic noises," he said. "And you'll freeze, sitting there."

I tottered to my feet. My robe was torn and snowy. "I can't go through the hall like this. Let's go around to our door. Tell my guards. We can't get lost in the dark as long as we walk near the wall."

Grumbling, Xalan obeyed, following me through the deepening snow. We were chilled through when we came to our hall, and our shoes were soaked. Taking them off, we sat on benches close to the great fire.

"Bring us some heated wine," I ordered the servant.

"Ought you to drink on top of that ale?"

"I'll be fine," I hiccuped. "As soon as I get warm."

"So tell me about your attack." He listened without question or comment until I had recounted my adventure, and then asked, "Were they Viridese or Caydish?"

"They spoke Caydish," I remembered, "but the leader spoke Viridese, too. He consigned me to Ixfel, which is a name the Caydish don't use."

"It couldn't have been a true Cayd national," Xalan said. "Cayd needs you alive, to help against Tiyalor."

"They said they had to kill somebody," I said. "Could it be in the service of some death-demon, Ixfel himself perhaps?"

"No, such cults have no foothold here in the cold west," he said. "I see the hand of Xerlanthor in this. If you were murdered in Cayd, we'd be at war with them, not Tiyalor. His enemies would be divided."

I shuddered, remembering the strength of the hands that had swept me off my feet. "It's the mirror, he's trying to get his mirror back."

"That's part of it too. We'll have to delve into that mirror tomorrow."

The day's physical and mental labor had worn me out, and it was very late. I yawned and hiccuped, saying, "Should we tell our hosts about it?"

"Not, I suppose, until we get to the bottom of it. We can't afford dissension as we go into battle. Unless you'd rather not risk silence."

"The risk doesn't weigh on my mind nearly as much as fearing the Caydish will think I can't hold their ale," I said, but I was really too sleepy to worry about it. "I wish I could shake these hiccups." The snow had melted off my clothes, which were beginning to steam in the warmth of the roaring fire, and at last I was getting warm. The fleece-stuffed pallets the Caydish sleep on in winter were stacked under the benches, and as Xalan brought mine out I waited dozing near the fire.

I had just begun to dream, about climbing an endless waterfall that made the noise of hiccups, when a muffling weight crushed the breath out of me. I started awake, thrashing back and forth to grasp my foe. A woolen pallet was smothering me, and without thinking I hooked a bare foot round the ankle of my oppressor and jerked him off balance. He tumbled backwards over the bench, and throwing off the pallet I leaped to immobilize him.

"Wait! Stop!" Shaking the hair out of my eyes I saw Xalan's startled face beneath me.

"Have you lost your mind?" I snapped. The guards had leaped to their feet, drawing their short swords, and in my confusion I remembered Xerlanthor could lay geas for assassination.

But Xalan impatiently pushed me aside, pulling the right sleeve and hem of my robe out. "Look at this!" The silk was blackened, crumbling away in his hands, and he said, "You set yourself on fire! You've got to be careful with trailing sleeves near these fireplaces!"

"Viris!" I exclaimed. "I fell asleep. I'm sorry I jumped on you, you saved my life!"

"All in a day's work," Xalan growled. He rubbed his bruises. "The Tiyalor have my sympathy. At least I stopped your hiccups."

Chapter 10: The White Queen

When I came next day to look at my robe it was plain the garment would not recover from my treatment of it. Too much cloth had burned away to even be patched. I hoped the Master of Wardrobe would never learn of its fate. One of the herbals offered to pick out the topazes, but I had no other garments. I would either have to wear my still-damp traveling clothes, or armor all the time, or acquire an outfit here in Cayd. I asked Silverhand's advice.

"You'll be considerably more comfortable in the Caydish style," she told me. "Silk and linen are well enough at home, but here thick boots and wool jerkins are not a mode but a necessity.''

"What would the Director of Protocol say?" Xalan teased, but the Commander retorted, "Clothing should serve convenience, not custom," a saying so well suited to my mind that I put it to practice at once. My interpreter, primed with an edited version of the night's events, was sent over to the royal hall to ask our hosts' assistance.

When he returned he brought the complete outfit of a Caydish nobleman: a knee-length coat of thick green-dyed leather, cured with the sheep's wool on to form a lining; a vest to wear over of brown suede thick and supple as velvet; a gold-dipped copper belt to fasten everything with; knee-high boots of smooth brown hide. Two identically irregular pieces of soft calfskin wrapped round my booted legs to become the Caydish snow-leggings that keep one's calves and thighs dry in deep snow. Next to my skin went the woolen jerkin and breeches, cunningly made in a way not known in Averidan. An endless strand of fine yarn was intertwined tightly with itself to form strong stretchy cloth. All these garments are made by Caydish ladies only for their own, and it was an honor for me to be given them even though by Viridese reckoning I had married into the family. In return I wrapped the salvaged topazes in a square of silk cut from the good side of the robe, and sent them to the royal ladies with a message of thanks.

The clothing felt odd and foreign on my body. The wool was ever so slightly oily to the touch, my toes were confined by the stiff boots, and the coat weighted my arms so I had difficulty raising them above my head. But once dressed I was truly warm for the first time since leaving the Tambors. Delighted, I asked Xalan, "How do I look?"

"All you need is a load of flashy jewelry and you'll be a perfect little Caydish gentleman," he said.

A joint meeting was planned for noon, and there I brought Xerlanthor's mirror. By it the magi hoped to descry the enemy's movements and plans. They had spent the morning preparing for the scry, clearing out one of our hall's big fireplaces and screening the chimney opening with cloth. When all was ready Melunael and his counselors assembled with us.

The Master Magus seated everyone at the far end of the hall. "We won't be able to see anything," one of the princes complained, but the Master was firm.

"The energies released may be dangerous," he said. "And

remember Xerlanthor can sense through his mirror, and may notice our scrutiny.''

All magi scry, but the magi's best hydromant was Xorc, who had perfected the art of scrying through another's glass. He was a plump, rosy man, middle-aged, who looked more like an indulgent father than a magic master. With a bow he accepted from me Xerlanthor's mirror, and set it up still covered at the other end of the hall in the cleared fireplace. While he seated himself on the hearth facing it the other magi laid their mirrors a pace apart in a long line behind him. There were almost thirty of them, round and gleaming silver in the dim light. The magi then seated themselves alternately to each side of the mirror line.

There was complete silence as Xorc slid the cover from Xerlanthor's mirror, and a long suspenseful pause while he bent forward over it and peered into the thick glass. At his signal the magi began one by one to open their mirrors also. Xalan, as the most junior magus present, was last in line, and when I saw the Master bent oblivious over his glass at the head of the line I tiptoed from my place to Xalan.

"What's he doing?" I whispered.

"Looking for Xerlanthor," Xalan replied. "That's our first priority."

Without turning Xorc said, "Odd, he doesn't seem to be near Ieor. What do you get, Magister?"

"I feel he's rather nearer to us," the Master replied. "Let us get a few more mirrors into the scry."

The last magi opened their mirrors. Looking into Xalan's I saw neither his reflection nor my own, but rather a moving, shining blur like a reflection in running water.

"Ah, here he is." Xorc spoke with quiet satisfaction. "He's traveling up the river valley with a party of eight Tiyal archers."

"How far away?"

"About a half-day's march, or a little more, from here."

"What was he doing in Cayd?" the King asked, but the magi could give no answer.

The Master commanded, "Xorc, keep a wary scry on him. The rest of you, upriver to the dam. Let us see how the ground is laid."

"Can he see us?" I asked.

"He isn't scrying us," Xalan said. "And he can't block our scrying the dam now. But his own mirror might alert him, even from this distance."

"They are indeed boiling waters," a magus up the row cried. "Hundreds of fires, tended by Tiyal workmen."

"Is there anything being cooked in the pots?" someone asked.

"No, the cauldron I see holds only water, and muddy at that."

"What of the dam and its defenders?" the Commander asked.

"The dam—ah, a mighty sight! The gorge walled across with blocks of stone and the siege tower on either bank guarded with earthworks, three rings of ditches and walls."

Another magus added, "I see the waters of the Mhesan backed up in their gorge behind the dam, to form a rising brown lake."

"Is one bank more heavily defended than the other?" the General asked.

"One is more difficult to approach, up the ravines and rocky cliffs, and so its tower is less heavily manned. The southern bank."

"How many Tiyalor are there?" I asked, but before anyone could reply a wordless cry burst from Xorc.

"Quick!" The Master rose from his place and ran. Even as he reached Xorc a fierce blood-red light thrust from that end of the hall. The source was Xerlanthor's mirror, and it intensified so quickly the power struck on one's brow like a hammer blow. Everyone clapped hands over their eyes and, when that proved insufficient, muffled their heads in cloaks or fell flat on the floor. A ghostly red image of the room burned in a fiery sea behind my clenched eyelids, and tears poured down my face and the back of my nose.

For a dreadful moment it seemed we were all blinded. But after a bit it was plain the scarlet light had waned as quickly as it had waxed. Wiping our streaming eyes we opened them to the comforting dimness of the hall. I blew my nose and hurried to help the magi.

Xorc was either dead or insensible, his eyes burned black by the frightful energies. The Master Magus had dashed to cover the mirror, probably saving us all, but disoriented by the vicious dazzle had then slipped and cracked his head on the hearthstones. The cloth that had blocked the chimney was alight, and sparks and ashy smuts drifted down into the room. I could hardly see for the wraiths swimming black and red between me and everything before me. A nasty smell of scorched wool and smoldering pitch filled the room.

"Was that Xerlanthor?" a Caydish prince whispered.

"He must have sensed poor Xorc," Xalan said. "An old trick to keep people from looking through your mirror, but this time bolstered with pyrolurgy—to kill."

The herbals were called. A poultice of tea leaves was tied over Xorc's eyes, and the Master's head was bound up. "They must stay in bed, in quiet," the Mistress Herbal pronounced, and the meeting was ousted so that the invalids could rest.

We adjourned to the royal hall, and no one refused the ale that King Melunael ordered served. I drank one cupful, in sips. The meeting was greatly subdued, and we determined to join with Warlord Prince Melbras' forces at Ieor and there plan an immediate assault on the foe. After a quiet supper we retired early, to be fresh for our start tomorrow.

After the rigors of our journey west I was not sufficiently tired by a day of talk to sleep well that night. At last I rose and dressed, tiptoeing past the other sleepers to the dim corner beside the big fireplace where the Mistress Herbal watched, nodding, over the two magi in her care. She started awake when I tapped her shoulder.

"To your bed, Mistress," I said softly. "I can't sleep anyway. Let me watch in your place."

"That's not customary, Majesty," the Mistress protested.

"You need your sleep, and I don't," I said, and yawning she could not deny it. "We have a long road tomorrow. What need I to do here?"

"Keep the poultices moist," she said, handing me a bowl of cold tea. "Would Your Majesty like a hot cup for yourself?"

"Surely." She moved the kettle onto the fire and showed me where the tea things were. I took her low seat between the two pallets, and she went to bed. The corner was shielded from direct light by a pile of blankets and luggage, and the fire had burned red and low. The rosy gleam on the pale woolwork hangings made the snaky-human woven figures seem alive, twisting in strange barbaric dances. Somehow the act of getting up and dressing made me sleepy again, so that I nearly let my kettle boil dry. The stimulation of a scalding cup of tea roused me a little, and I looked over my charges.

Xorc's plump face was almost invisible beneath tea leaves rolled in cloths. His breath came and went so shallowly I feared it had ceased, and laid a hand on his chest to be sure he was alive. The Master Magus slept restlessly, his hands twitching outside the quilt. He had given himself a long cut on the side of his head, and the place had swollen under the thick loose bandage so that his head looked misshapen. His long white mustache, braided for convenience, had been stained with the blood. The Mistress Herbal would judge in the morning whether the Master Magus was well enough to go with us. Xorc would stay and be nursed in Cayd.

I turned to set down my cup and when I looked again the Master Magus was awake. Speaking softly so as not to wake the others I said, "How do you feel, Magister? Would you like some water?"

His eyes wandered. "I can't see very clearly," he complained in a faint voice.

"The herbals said you should rest your eyes," I said.

"Is that Shan Liras?"

"Yes. I couldn't sleep." The Master turned on his pillow, straining to focus his vision, and I held a hand over his eyes, saying, "If you overtax them they'll go bad on you. Give them a chance to rest."

"What of Xorc?"

"He's alive," I said.

"Hurt?"

Reluctantly I said, "I think he's blinded."

"Ah," The Master lay quiet for a moment, and I took the opportunity to tuck his quilt in more closely. "Vision is half of life," he told me, "but for Xorc it is far more. A blind scryer has lost everything."

I took my seat between the two pallets and thought about blindness. The darkness of death seemed almost preferable: never to savor the peculiar clear purple of klimflowers, or the rich glory of Melayne's hair. Trapped in the cage of one's skull, surrounded by the void of earth and sky, the world shrunken to the reach of an arm—I felt a momentary impulse to go outside and walk, to escape. But of course I had to stay.

The Magus' hand groped for mine, plucking at the woolen sleeve of my Caydish jerkin. "Do something, you can do something," he said.

"What do you wish, Magister?" I asked.

"The Crown—use the Crystal Crown, to heal him." I felt a fool for not having thought of that before. But the Master continued in a low voice, "Xorc was one of my aptest pupils, long ago before you were born. He is in my charge, and yours too."

The idea was not unfamiliar to me, for I knew that as Shan King my role was to protect and ward my people as a father would his children. But it had never yet come so close to me. An irrational guilt descended on me, as if with proper care I could have saved Xorc today, or negotiated a settlement with Tiyalor, or talked Xerlanthor out of whatever his goal was. The entire burden, the responsibility for the health and happiness of everyone in Averidan, smote me. I could almost feel the weight of the load on my shoulders, squeezing the juice out of my body.

Shaking, I rose and walked softly past my sleeping subjects until I came to Fisan-shi's pallet. The casket of the Crown was at her elbow, and I lifted it gently so that she would not wake. Returning to the magi I sat again and opened the casket.

The Crystal Crown's healing properties are felt by the bonesetters and herbals to be a little suspect. It is true that they are not completely reliable from monarch to monarch, and in any case tend to be more useful for minor wounds than major ailments. Broken bones are easiest, perhaps because the bone itself wants to be one again. I had not previously even seen as serious a wound as Xorc's but I refused to admit doubts as I set the Crown on my head.

I usually wear the Crown in public, and it was a new experience to feel so many sleeping minds around me, in dreams or oblivion too deep for dreams. Only the Magus was partially awake, and I told him, "Go back to sleep, Magister."

With Xorc the difference was palpable. This was not the slumber of health, but coma induced by shock. Bones can be reunited with a touch, but his injury was in the nature of a burn, and I was unsure what to do. Resting my hand on his head I began to delve for his consciousness, but the Crown's voice chimed in my skull, above and behind my nose, saying, "Death is our one bane, until we know it for our one blessing."

"I haven't done anything yet," I protested. "How do you know he's dying? As long as he's not actually dead I have to do something, what would I say to the Master Magus?" The Crown never stooped to argument, whether from pride or, less likely, trust in my judgment. I assumed I had won my point, and turned again to Xorc.

I seemed to travel a long way, in and down, before I found him. He looked in perfect health, and was striding at a good speed up a curving mountain road with the aid of his thick glass wand. His dark red robe flapped behind him with each step.

"Xorc!" I called. "Where are you going?"

"Is that the King? I can't stay, Majesty, I'm late already. The Queen's summons, you know." He waved his wand at me, and grinned happily back before turning uphill again. I had to run to catch up. The path was wide and well-traveled, not as steep as the pass to Cayd, and the air seemed curiously thick and dark, as if it were about to storm behind us. The sky was clear and bright only before, beyond the hills.

I did not for a moment know what he was talking about. The last Shan Queen died eight hundred years ago. Then I remembered, and called, "Xorc, which queen do you speak of? Not—" At the last moment I caught the name on my tongue and shut my teeth on it. It is perilous to name the Queen of the Deadlands at any time, but doubly so to speak it here. For I recognized now from dozens of plaiv the road and the barren mountain we climbed, the close, starless dark. We were walking out of the lands of life, over the hill and down to death's country, where the White Queen sits. With the Crystal Crown I had pierced the division between history and myth at last, and now trod a super-natural road.

"Yes," Xorc was saying. "It was the Queen, I'm sure of it. But there was something, some obstacle or whatnot, so I got a late start."

"You can't die," I said, hurrying to keep up. "There's so much to do, we need you." He bounded uphill without answer, lightly as a goat. As in dreams time seemed to have no meaning. I could not tell how long we had been traveling, but surely the top of the pass was not far ahead. The light seemed quite near now. In desperation I said, "I am Shan Liras King, son of the Sun. The magi are bound to my service. I do not release you, Xorc, you may not leave me."

He heard me, for he walked slower, and then stopped. He turned downhill to face me, but with the light behind him I could not see his face. Then the brightness increased, as if dawn were coming. But there is no dawn, in the Deadlands, and I knew that in naming myself I had made a possibly fatal error. For I had been overheard.

The division between death and life is at the top of the pass. Though the steepness and difficulty of the uphill road is said to vary—for some find it easier to die than others—the peak of the road is marked by a tree, the only tree on the barren side of the mountain, and after this tree the road is always an easy descent, broad and fair through green fields and orchards. In the growing light I now saw that tree ahead of me. While the rest of me panicked, a distant part of my mind functioned calmly, recognizing the tree as not an evergreen but a warm-climate tree of the lemon or orange sort. And under it, on the other side, was a white and shining form from which the light poured.

Xorc turned again uphill, crying, "The White Queen!" I hid my face in my hands, regretting all my folly. But I dared not retreat.

"Welcome, Xorc." The voice was low and cool, sweet as Viridese wine. "And you are the Shan King, young Liras-ven Tsor-melezok, are you not?"

It is well known that to see the Queen is extremely dangerous, but when she spoke my name I had to look up. Her pale face was almost too bright to look at, yet it was not because of the light shining from it. The light was inborn, not borrowed like the light of my Crystal Crown, yet it was only a minor product, the residue of some greater, more awesome quality: divinity. She was beautiful beyond desire, and terrifying as lightning bolts are when they strike at your feet.

When I could not reply she said, "You do not release Xorc from your service? Why is that?"

She spoke without anger or defiance, in a gentle and almost humorous tone, knowing that the fire of her divine life surpassed mine more than the Sun does a candle. Forcing my voice out I said, "Magi are sworn to serve the Shan King, my lady. I still have need of him."

"My claim precedes all others. Your Sun does not shine here, where I am the only light. Will you contend for Xorc with me?"

The ripple of power in her voice was like the undertow off Averidan harbor, that drags ships to their ruin on the rocks. She bore me no malice, but would destroy me nevertheless if I defied her. Yet it was a temptation to fight, and lose as I must. Defeat would be painless and swift, and after she would claim me for hers, if the plaiv were right. She was unbearably beautiful, and her children look always on her face.

I bowed to her, deep and careful as I would to the Altar of the Sun in the Temple, and said, "My lady, I regret any infringement I may have inadvertently made on your claims. Xorc's allegiance passed from me to you long ago, as he assures me, and I was foolish to delay him even for an instant. Let him serve you as well and as faithfully as he did me. Accept him, with my highest commendations."

She did not speak, and I held my breath. Then she laughed, a sound like silver bells or fountains of water, and said, "Courteously ceded, Shan King. When you come again to my realm I look forward to the pleasures of your conversation."

"Thank you, my lady," I said, stuttering with relief.

"Come, Xorc, to me." Xorc skipped up the hill past the tree and fell at her feet. I waved good-bye but he did not look back. She cast a final glance at me, a piercing look from green eyes that held deep light as the shore holds the sea, and said, "Farewell for a time, Shan Liras," before turning away.

"Good-bye," I said. The light faded as she went down toward her country again. I turned back also, toward the land of the living. It came to me then that I did not know the way out and up back to the hall in Cayd. I had followed Xorc here, but he was gone. The mountain was dark and the valley ahead was starless and invisible. On the way up there had certainly been a road, a broad curving one, but now either it had vanished or I had wandered off it into the trackless bare hills. In plaiv the hero is always guided back from the Deadlands by a wise animal, or a clew of thread. But stumbling in the rock-strewn night I could not even be sure of my downhill course. Once you leave the safe, everyday world for the other realm peril is a commonplace.

Then I remembered that so long as I wore the Crystal Crown I had a source of light, and a guide. "How about some illumination?" I asked aloud, but there was no reply from behind and above my nose. Reaching up I felt no Crown on my head. A desolation of loss swept over me, and I began to run— downhill or up, it made no difference. In the dark I missed my footing, and fell head over heels down the mountain, bouncing and sliding on loose rock. I sensed the cliff somehow just before I came to it, but was too late to stop myself from tumbling over into space. This is the end of me, I thought, and shut my eyes. How surprised and cross the White Queen would be to see me again so soon!

I hit something soft, and then something hard that drove the breath from my lungs. A babble of voices rang in my ears, and I opened my eyes. Familiar faces hung above my own, and morning sunlight shone on my face.

"He's awake," General Horfal-yu cried. "He opened his eyes!"

"Oh, thank the One!" Fisan-shi said.

Gasping for breath I sat up. I was on a fleecy woolen pallet in the central courtyard of the King's palace. The Crown was on my head, and although the cold nipped my nose I sweated under blankets and furs piled high over my body.

"What happened to Xorc?" I panted.

"Don't worry about that now," Xalan said, squatting beside me. "Drink this."

"What is it?"

Xalan pressed the cup to my lips, saying, "Milk mixed with wine, the Master Magus ordered it."

It was goats' milk, which is nasty enough, and milk is not a favorite beverage in Averidan anyway. I choked down one sour mouthful and pushed Xalan away, sputtering, "What do you mean, the Magus ordered it?"

"He told us, if you came back you would need to be sealed to life again. So we had this ready, in case."

"I'm too old for it," I growled. Newborn babies are customarily sealed with their mother's milk, of course, with a drop of wine rubbed on the nipple. And heroes in plaiv who journey to Death also need that service. But I did not appreciate the sour chalky taste on my tongue so early in the day. "Let me out, before I bake."

Throwing off the furs I was helped up. My boots had been removed, and the snow was cruelly cold to my bare feet. It was still very early, not much after dawn, and beyond the crowd of my folk our Caydish hosts were gathered to stare. Leaping from bare spot to bare spot to spare my feet, I hurried to our hall.

"Food," I ordered, once inside. "Fisan, take this." I lifted the Crown from my head and gave it to her. I looked over at the corner where the magi had lain, but only the Master Magus was there, sitting up and being fed soup. Going over to him I said, "I'm sorry, Magister, there was nothing I could do."

He said, "I knew you were in trouble. When the Mistress Herbal returned to check on you, Xorc was sinking, and you could not be roused."

"He had gotten too far, and met the White Queen," I said.

Xalan brought me a bowl of oaten porridge, with dried apples mixed in, and tea. "Did you truly see her?" he asked. "What was she like?"

But the memory of her face, which I had never thought to forget, was fading with every word I spoke and every spoonful of porridge I swallowed. Perhaps it is true, about sealing to life. I could only reiterate the usual descriptions, and add, "Xorc wanted to go, I couldn't hold him against her."

"That would have been unwise—and impossible, even with the Crown," the Magus said.

"We wanted to take it off you, but the Magus said it was your only hope," Xalan said. "He made us take you out into the sunshine so that the Crown could help draw you back, and keep you warm so that the blood would rise to your head.''

"You seem to know all about it," I yawned.

"Others have met the Queen and lived to tell the tale," the Magus said. "For a while. But please, don't try to see her again."

"Don't you fear," I said. "I plan to meet her again, but not soon."

Chapter 11: Chasm

My adventure could not interfere with our marching plans, for the Warlord was counting on us. We could not even delay for Xorc's funeral—our first casualty—but had to entrust the rites to King Melunael. After breakfast my gear was packed, and Piril saddled. His feet were better, and I let the Master Magus ride him. The Caydish court regarded me with unease. My two nights in Lanach had not been peaceable and some garbled translation of my journey to the Deadlands had already made the gossip rounds. For many reasons, therefore, they were glad to see us go.

Our way lay through Lanach, now blanketed in snow. The townsfolk had gathered to see us march west, children calling to their mothers, "The foreigners are leaving, hurry and see!" For the sake of warmth I wore my Caydish clothes, and leading the Magus on Piril was taken for a servant. Opinion was divided as to whether General Horfal-yu, splendid in green and white, or the Master Magus on the sole horse, was the Shan King. The anonymity delighted me, and when an old wife in peasant dress called, "Avenge my sons for me, boy, and give this to the Shan King," I accepted the goats-milk cheese in its net from her and promised to deliver it.

But remembering the bright gay crowds in the City I could see why the Caydish called us opulent. The King's household had worn furs, but the poorer folk here were clad in sheepskins or milch-goat hide, woolen leggings or skirts, and wooden clogs. Faces looked hungry and worn, and while we saw dozens of children all were skinny as crows.

"The oat harvest failed here last year," Xalan explained to me. "The rains were light, and there was no river water because of the dam."

Just past Lanach is the only bridge over Mhesan in Cayd. Technically, once over it we would be in Tiyalor, for Cayd has true claim to only the territory south of the river. But this land so close to the capital and river had been annexed by Caydish oat farmers and goatherds, and the main population of Tiyalor lives far away around the lake anyway. The bridge was built in the Caydish style, of pairs of braided hide hawsers supporting rows of planks. I did not like the look of it, especially the way it dipped down in the middle to float on the surface of the rushing green water on logs bolted together. And behind me I could hear my army speculating as to whether earth currents have any effect on braided bridges, or had the thing been constructed without reference to geomancy at all? But with Caydish urchins darting back and forth across it to see us better I could not hang back. There were four plank walks, each wide enough for a horse—two for human traffic back and forth, and two for sheep or goats. About ten feet below the bank the Mhesan flowed low in its rocky bed, and the bridge dipped down to rest on it and then rose again to the far side.

Both animal and human traffic were halted so that the army could use all four walks. I blinkered Piril again, and made the Master Magus dismount so that he could not be thrown. But after all we crossed without incident. The bridge swayed with every step in a very uncanny manner, and although the hawsers were thicker than my arm I could not help inspecting them for frayed or broken places. Piril behaved as if all warhorses of his acquaintance crossed such bridges every day, and when we were safe across I made much of him and fed him a piece of dried apple while we waited for the army to cross.

From there to Ieor the Mhesan bends in a wide curve, but by cutting straight across many hours of travel can be saved. We foreigners would get lost in the hills, but some Caydish were to guide us through the wilds to the camp of the Warlord and his forces. Our guides were led by one of the King's many younger sons, one Prince Musenor. This prince, also, bore little resemblance to Melayne, being so broad in chest and shoulder that in his fur cloak he looked like an insomniac bear. However, in conversation I found he was less close-mouthed than Mor, and because of his relative youth more companionable.

We were marching through snowy pine woods, very different

from the forests of Averidan. At home pines grow only on sea cliffs, where they are wracked by storm and wind and stunted by salt water. These trees, their rich relatives, stood proud and tall under icy coronets, hooded and cloaked in deep green needles, in endless brooding ranks as far as we could see. We passed through in silent awe, like children allowed to attend a sacrifice offered by haughty priestesses.

The cold was shrill in my lungs, frosty on my breath. When I exhaled, the white vapor congealed on the fleecy collar of my jacket, spangling it with white crystals. It was good to be alive, I decided, recalling vaguely the dry barren darkness of my journey last night. I asked Prince Musenor when spring would come in Cayd. He replied, "The weather loremasters, O King, say the Winter Wolf this year had seven moon cubs. It is not quite midway through the fifth now, so there will be more than six more weeks of winter."

"In Averidan," I said, "we call winter a leopardess with a white tail. The animal is big as it approaches, but passes in a flicker of frost, and then it's spring again."

He grunted in his blond beard and said, "Here winter is a wolf, a hungry one. The cold is good only for fur bearers."

In the crunchy snow I could see dozens of cloven hoofprints, and I asked, "Are these the tracks of the goats you keep for fur?"

"No indeed! These are the spoor of food animals, the goats that give milk and meat. The ones you think of are the white ones, the long-haired praswel goats kept in grassy valleys. That is so that nothing tangles or tears their hair."

"They tell me Melayne kept some of those," I remembered.

"She did, O King, in the valley near the pass." His eyes, green as a cat's, glinted at me. "She was a leopardess, if you like. Never was there a more stubborn child, or more fierce and clever."

"She's still stubborn," I assured him.

"She would stick at nothing to win, when we had games or weapons-practice, so we would wash her face in the snow, to teach her honesty."

The picture made me laugh, and I said, "I must think of a substitute in Averidan, we don't have snow often enough there."

The Sisterhood was in its element here, as the warriors slipped through the wood on either side of us, invisible and silent as the frost itself. The army was much less happy, slogging through the snow until the road was trampled to muddy slush. They jostled and slid on patches of ice, complaining to each other in the undertone soldiers use in the hearing of their generals in a long, winding column of discontent behind me. Viridese fists prefer to fight neat battles, of armies lined up on either side of flat, dry battlefields. On those fields they are hard to defeat, when they can overlap their oblong shields and advance steadily bristling with bronze spears. The methods of the Sisterhood, they feel, are suitable only for women—the unarmed acrobatic skill or the strange, unnaturally sharp blades. For the Sisters use weapons nowadays, in battle at least, and their own special weaponry is notorious even in Cayd. Our Caydish guides patronized the spearmen, ogled the herbals, but avoided the Sisters in awe.

The Warlord's force was within a day's march—indeed, Prince Musenor had come from there only a few days before with messages—so we hoped to arrive in the late afternoon. The day had been icy clear and bitter cold, but as the Sun declined leaden clouds gathered and snow began to fall—not a driving gale, but drifting down in a gentle, inexorable progress. It was beautiful, but daunting for travelers in the wild, and without being aware of it everyone picked up their pace a little, pressing onward to shelter.

We heard a warning horn-call when we were, according to the Prince, still more than an hour's march away. We halted, seeing two Caydish axemen waving at us through the trees as they approached.

"Do you know them?" the General asked.

The Prince stared hard and replied, "Yes, they're my uncle's men. Hoy, Gev and Forlim! What news?"

"The Warlord sent us, Highness," one called. "We were to watch for you, to tell you the camp at Ieor has been moved."

"It has, what for?"

"The spring began to fail, Highness, so a better spot was found a little north of here."

"Is it within striking distance?" Musenor demanded.

"Oh, yes," the man said.

The Prince rubbed his yellow beard and shrugged. "Lead us, then, to the new camp."

So we turned a little north, on a narrow valley road that had steep goat pasture on the left, now knee-deep in snow, and a pine wood on the right. But Commander Silverhand was not satisfied. She caught my arm and made me and my guards wait with her until the Caydish had passed. We fell in between two fists, and lowering her voice so that the tramp of feet would hide her words she asked, "Are those two to be trusted?"

"Why not? Prince Musenor recognized them."

"It is exactly how I would direct an enemy into an ambush—were I a magus."

"Ah," I said, understanding her. "You mean they might be under geas?"

"Yes. But how can it be proved? Shall I send my warriors ahead on the trail to search for enemies?"

"That would be as well," I said. "Have them go armed, and silently. And while they do, I have an idea." For the problem seemed ideally suited for the Crystal Crown. With it the sifting of truth from lie is easy; it is by design a touchstone.

The Commander stuck two fingers into her mouth and whistled a shrill, complex signal to the Sisterhood. Those Sisters not already in the woods vanished into the underbrush. Fisan-shi, her face pink with cold, said to me, "I want to learn that. It looks so exciting!"

"You'd have to join the Sisterhood to do it," I said, not really paying attention. "Let me have the Crown."

"Why, what do you need it for here?"

She held out the casket and opening it I lifted the Crown out. "Just an experiment," I told her. "Something I was discussing with Silverhand."

I pushed back my hood and put the Crown on. Because of the cold I sensed a definite period of unreadiness while the Crown took heat from me and awoke. To get the blood moving more hotly in my veins I trotted forward through the deep snow beside the road, passing our fists until I came to the head of the column. My guard followed, swearing in undertones whenever snow got into their boots. When the Caydish saw me wearing the Crown they seemed surprised but not alarmed. All the powers of the Crown are kept close. They might know the saying that it is hard to lie to the Shan King, but that would be all.

As soon as I came near I could sense the difference inside the two axemen. Under a thick concealing layer of normal speech and behavior was rigid fear, choking horror. I pointed at General Horfal-yu and said, "Halt the march, please."

He was puzzled but obeyed me, shouting the army catchwords to bring the column to rest. Prince Musenor frowned and said, "We must hurry, O King, before the snow becomes too deep for travel. Why this delay?"

"I'd like to hear more from your two axemen here," I said in

my stilted Caydish. "How long has Prince Melbras been in this
new camp?"

The two stared at each other, at Musenor, at the whirling
snow, but avoided my eye. The lie was palpable even before one
man voiced it: "O King, a day only."

The Crown's power surged in my limbs until I felt I could
snap my fingers and cast a lightning bolt. Very gently I asked,
"When did you meet Xerlanthor the magus?"

"Never, O King," said one.

The other said, "I've only seen him from a distance, King, in
the battles."

"You are wrong," I said. The feathery snow stuck to my
eyelashes, touched the Crown and instantly melted. "There was
one other occasion, an important one. Was it yesterday, or
perhaps the day before, when the geas was laid on you, to lead
us into ambush?"

Prince Musenor said, "Forlim, is this true?"

For a moment they neither moved nor spoke, and I saw they
could not. Yet Xerlanthor must have made some provision in the
geas in case they were discovered. I said, "They cannot deny
it."

Then the man Forlim exclaimed, "Will you believe this runt
of a foreigner, Highness, before us? My soul to the everlasting
ice if I lie!"

The other added, "They must be in league with the evil magus
themselves! Is he not of their race and nation?"

"You seem to have been well rehearsed," I remarked. The
Caydish had fallen back on either side of us, unhitching bow
cases and fingering axe handles, ready to attack either the two
axemen or myself. My guards fidgeted behind me, but with a
gesture I signaled they should not draw their weapons yet. Prince
Musenor obviously did not know what to think, but as he paused
irresolute another shrill whistle pierced the silent white forest. "I
sent the Sisters for some proof," I said, "and I believe they have
found some."

Down the snowy trail loped two brown-clad Sisters, urging
between them a foreign archer. The man wore black leather
armor and still carried a quiver of black-fletched arrows on his
back. Blood gushed from his shoulder and side, but the Sisters
did not let him stop running until he fell in the snow before us.
"Twenty other Tiyal archers, Majesty, hidden in the rocks," one
woman reported. "We shall kill as many as we can, but the
Commander said to bring you one."

The Prince poked the panting archer with his booted foot and asked, "Who sent you?"

The man said something in Tiyal, of which I recognized only the name: Xerlanthor. The Prince snarled, "May wolves suck his marrow! You were right, O King! Quickly, we must kill them!"

But before he could unhook his battleaxe the geas-ridden two turned and ran, dodging and twisting westward across the snowy pasture like hares. A few Caydish arrows hissed into the snow around them but none found a target. They were swift runners, but the two Sisters gave chase, and were swifter yet, coursing down the tracks fleet as hunting leopards.

As they ran the women each whipped out one of the Sisters' favorite weapons, the bladed rope. A strong silken line several feet long had a many-bladed weight crafted of the Sisterhood's special metal at one end. This was swung around their heads in a deadly blur. Seeing pursuit the axemen split, one running on over the hill while the other doubled back toward us. But the Sisters divided also and inexorably lessened the lead. The circle of death drew closer and closer to the fleeing Cayd's back, and then with a final sprint of speed she caught him. The whirling razor edges cut him in the side, and the snow was suddenly scarlet with arterial blood. The man shrieked and fell, tumbling over to spill out intestine and liver. The Sister's speed was so great she overran him, staining her soft boots to above the ankles. Unconcerned, she wiped them and her blades on a patch of clean snow, like a cat cleaning its claws after the kill.

My own response was unfortunate. I had been too involved in reading the man's heart, and his break for freedom had caught me off guard. Before I could wrench myself free he had been run down and slain. The wash of his death-anguish nearly swept me away also. His agony was my own, it was my guts trampled in the slush, my vision dimming to blackness. It was not like Xorc's end at all, for this man had run from his death, fought against it, feared it. His fear was now mine, twisting in my throat, shrinking in my skin, and the sky spun above me. The blood seemed to drain from my body with his, and I fell to the path insensible.

Later I was told that in the excitement I was nearly trampled as I lay. But my guard stood close around with their shields to keep bystanders off. General Horfal-yu took charge of the army, turning the column to retrace our steps, and the Caydish beheaded the captured Tiyal archer and threw his body into a ravine. Commander Silverhand and her Sisters returned, having slain almost all our ambushers. The Master Magus and the Mistress Herbal examined me, and decided to remove the Crystal Crown. It was returned to Fisan's care, and when I did not revive I was carried on a shield by my guard.

I came to myself with a start. I was alone, on my bedroll in an unfamiliar small tent of stitched goat hide. A copper lamp glowed beside me on the matting. Memory returned in a rush and I sat up and pressed shaking hands over my eyes to shut out the picture of the Caydish axeman dead in the red snow.

Only with my mind had I known wars kill me. Now I knew, in my stomach, in my skin, in my imagination, that I myself might die. All these weeks I had spoken lightly, planning to do this or plant that when I returned to Averidan, promising to watch again for the farm children beside the road to Mhee—but I might never fulfill those plans, or keep those promises. How could I have not seen that my life dangled by the thinnest of silk threads over a chasm of death? A whim of fate—a stray arrow, a sliding pebble underfoot, a touch of fever—and I would fall. When I had followed Xorc the road to death had run gently uphill. But now I knew it fell steeply down before me, so that with one misstep I would slip, as the brown horse had done, to break my bones on the rocks below. The plaiv call my great-grandfather "the Merciful" nowadays, though he had never let the term be used while he was alive. Now I understood. The wearer of the Crystal Crown must feel the pangs of many deaths. His battle prowess must have cost Norlen-yu dear indeed, and the epithet "Merciful" must have seemed cruelly ironic. I had not his courage.

The tent flap stirred and swung back. Xalan came in carrying a covered food platter. "Good, you're awake. Have something to eat while I tell the Magus and the Commander. Everyone is frantic about you!" He set down the tray and vanished. I lifted the cloth, but the sight of the roast mutton revolted me, and I sat shivering until Xalan returned.

"Where are we?"

"Ieor, in the encampment of Warlord Prince Melbras," Xalan replied. "Don't say you're not hungry, everyone else is ravenous."

"I can't eat."

"You have to," he argued. "In this cold you'll make your-self ill if you fast. Look, I'll help—split this with me."

He broke an oatcake in pieces and passed a bowl of spice sauce. Since, as the proverb says, food is fuel to life I took a crust and dipped it. Xalan kept up a cheerful, if one-sided, talk of the afternoon's doings: the blasphemies Musenor had voiced when we found the Caydish camp in its old site; how in Melbras' face rage at the ambush attempt had vied with disgust at my squeamishness so that he had exclaimed, "May he be reduced to congress with his own sheep!" at me before remembering his audience. Alternately coaxing and distracting me, Xalan forced most of the food into me.

However, before I allowed my servants to put me to bed I sent Xalan for Commander Silverhand. When she arrived she looked me over with curiosity, saying, "What happened to you today?"

"It was the Crown," I said in a low voice. "I'm sorry to upset the General's tactics but I can't join the fight. I don't think I can even be near the battlefield."

"Are you certain?" she asked. "Surely you'll feel better after a night's sleep."

"One man's death was bad enough," I said. "Thank the One we never discussed the idea with the Caydish. I'm sorry."

She was silent, searching for some word of comfort, and then she flashed her sweet smile at me. "You oughtn't to have expected that being Shan King would be like being an ordinary spearman. And we ought not to have expected it either."

The next day to an observer I would have looked quite recovered. The snowstorm of the previous day had blown itself out, and the banners flying from the watchtower—the green pennant of the Shan King, the Sisters' silver eagle flag, the Army's green and white, and the Caydish talisman of a ram's skull with gilded horns—were a brave and valiant sight. But I had lost my nerve. The beautiful bronze sword I had to carry weighed on my hip, a weapon borne without right and in deceit. When we gathered around the Warlord's campfire to plan the actual assault my first impulse was to propose that we all turn and go home again. For nothing seemed worth the risk of anyone's death, not vengeance or the dam or Xerlanthor. But of course I did not voice these thoughts.

A detailed map of the dam and its defense was passed around. The Caydish had not had enough troops to block both river banks and thus starve the enemy out, but now, with our help, they proposed to do just that, or more.

Warlord Prince Melbras began. "First we must storm the dam, exterminate the Tiyalor to the last defender."

"My dear Prince!" General Horfal-yu exclaimed when this

had been translated. "The rule of war advises mercy. What if they ask for quarter, or surrender?"

"They won't surrender," Silverhand predicted.

Prince Musenor struck his knees with both hands and shouted, "What quarter have they shown us? We outnumber them heavily now. Let us pluck victory while we have it in our hands, and chase them all the way to Tiyalor."

The Caydish officers and princes applauded this. Another Caydish officer stood up and said, "Let us take the price of the Mhesan river water in blood!" There were cries of approval, and for a moment it seemed that without further ado our allies would simply snatch up their weapons and dash off to fight.

But Prince Melbras swatted at his nephews and brothers, bellowing, "Hold your blood-thirst awhile!" Then he added more quietly to us, "That is an idea I had also. We have many more warriors now than the foe. Once Xerlanthor is slain, Tiyalor is headless." This was almost certainly true, for there were too many rumors afloat of the demise of the last royal Tiyal heir. "All that is left of the army of Tiyalor is here, defending the dam. If we slew them all Tiyalor would be defenseless as well. It would be easy then to conquer and rule them. Your nation and ours could swallow them up."

"Wait a minute," I said. This whole turn of the discussion was unplanned. "The Tiyalor have done nothing to deserve sack and conquest."

"They aid the evil magus," Prince Musenor pointed out.

"I can't believe they meant to," I said. "Our only interest is to remove the source of the trouble: Xerlanthor. After that the Tiyalor may go their own way. Why should we meddle in their lives?"

"They will be weak," Melbras pointed out in cold tones. "Weakness is opportunity for the strong. Does the wolf show mercy to the lamb?"

This whole way of thinking was foreign and horrible to me. The memory of the disemboweled Caydish soldier rattled at the back of my eyeballs, twitched at the ends of my fingers. In this pass I should have consulted Silverhand or the General, should have been tactful and diplomatic. But without thinking I burst out, "Are we wolves or men? We shall not conquer anybody. We shall spare any Tiyal that surrender, except only Xerlanthor. Any other action would be intolerable."

"They tell us your forefathers were mighty warriors once," the Warlord retorted. "One would never know it."

Stung, I said, "If you do not wish to abide by our rule of war, we will have to refuse to participate."

"What!" General Horfal-yu cried, like a disappointed child. "After coming all this way?"

"Certainly," I said. "We can turn around and go home again."

"Insanity!" the General began, but became quiet when I glanced at him.

I turned to Melbras and said, "What is your word, Highness?"

When the head of his nephew was sent to him I had seen Melbras in his hot rage. Now I had waked his cold one. The green eyes flashed icy as the winter river, and the weathered face was set and hard. I remembered the ambition I had seen with the assistance of the Crystal Crown, and feared I had offended it mortally. Through gritted teeth he replied, "It appears we have no choice. Your Majesty owns the sheep, who are we to say how they shall be shorn?"

Silverhand, who is fluent in Caydish, said, "The tactical memoirs of our foundress warn that when you are stronger than your foe you should take care never to drive him to extremity. Always leave an avenue of escape, lest he become desperate." She glanced at me, and I knew she meant this for my instruction as well as the Warlord's. "If we box the Tiyalor too close on both sides there will be a bitter battle. Let us be more subtle."

After a morning's argument it was decided to have the army and the Caydish forces jointly assault the strongly fortified northern side. The three curved earthen walls and their ditches were deadly when manned by determined defenders, especially archers. To even the odds a bit the magi would mount an hierognomical weather attack.

"I can promise you at the least a blinding rain," the Master Magus told us. His thick white eyebrows stuck out incongruously from underneath his bandage, but he seemed otherwise recovered. I was secretly grateful for that, since I dared not don the Crown to heal him. "If the spells work particularly well it may even hail. Not on our forces, of course, only on the enemy. The timing will have to be precise."

"That should spoil their fire completely," the General said with satisfaction. "A wetted bowstring is useless." An organized assault on known fortifications was exactly to the General's taste, and had we not been firm we would have listened to dozens of tactical examples from famous sieges of history.

The Caydish were enchanted with the idea of weather as a

weapon, and Prince Musenor asked, "Will you be brewing the weather yourself?"

When this was translated the Magus smiled. "Not all hydromants are weatherworkers, your Highness. When I was your age my special study was transmogrification." But there is no word for that in Caydish, so the translator was at a loss.

In the relative safety of the rocky southern bank the Tiyalor had based their camps. The Sisterhood would swim the Mhesan in secret and at the proper moment set fire to the tents and stampede the herds. If we prevailed on the northern bank the Sisters would let the enemy pass through, harassing them from the forests in their retreat. They would also kill Xerlanthor, should he escape in the confusion of battle again.

Of course Xerlanthor knew of our coming, and might well have been scrying all this time to learn of our plans. But this had been partially foiled by the loss of his mirror. Since one does not hear through a mirror, as long as we did not write our plans down he could not descry them and would have to rely on spies. Therefore it was important to attack soon, to give him as little time as possible to learn of and counter our tactics. So the main assault was set for next morning.

To my secret shame my role would be to keep the camp. My guard of ten would do all the work, of course. I knew this was makework for a figurehead. Prince Melbras did not contribute much to these plans and after everything had been concluded left his deputies to handle details and vanished sulking into his tent. Silverhand whispered to me, "We've not heard the last of this."

"Zofal was right," I said in misery. "I should never have come."

The magí immediately set about preparing their spells, for weatherworking takes considerable time and skill. The Commander gathered her Sisters and they hurried away to hone their gray blades. They would march upstream to swim the Mhesan, and march back down the other shore to fight in the battle. Such stamina is said in plaiv to be the peculiar gift of Shan Mir-hel to her disciples, but we who had marched with the Sisters knew it was training and hard practice. Our fists lined up to hone their bronze spears at the whizzing grindstone, while the Caydish sharpened their arrowheads with brazen hand files. The bonesetters gathered wood for splints and the herbals prepared drenches and poultices.

Passing all this activity by I eluded my guard and went to hide in the pine wood behind the encampment. In my Caydish clothes

I was warm enough even though the snow was deep. I scuffled through the dry dead ferns where thick-laced boughs had kept the snow off until I came to a fallen tree, and brushing the needles off sat down. As long as I didn't move it was unlikely the watchman in his tower on the small hill in the middle of camp would spot me. I told myself that I had not yet on this journey found leisure to examine a pine tree closely. But this time the old charm failed me.

Counting over the marks of cowardice, it seemed I had them all: fearing death, fearing to kill, refusing to fight. In despair I wondered whether it would not be simplest just to slink farther into the snowy forest and never return. Yet I was afraid to die, too. Alone, without food, money, or destination I would starve or freeze. And a more cynical part of me recalled that the same irrational impulse to flight had seized me when I had been chosen Shan King. "You must have learned something from that," I said aloud, and quoted Sandcomber's words to myself: "Life is perilous." Yet my situation did not seem to be amenable to Sandcomber's methods of solution. I remembered, as from another existence, the Commander telling me that the courageous didn't let fear affect action. Perhaps if it was impossible to help the battle I could somehow be useful tomorrow somewhere. A dogged resolution crystalized in me, to eschew despair.

In this spirit I returned to camp, where I was caught and very politely scolded by Corlis for vanishing into such dangerous surroundings. There seemed to be urgent work for everyone save me. At last I went to feed and groom Piril, the one job I was indisputably better at than anyone else in Cayd, and found that since my illness yesterday Fisan-shi had been giving him the best of care. So I went sulking to bed.

Chapter 12: Storm Over Ieor

Well before first light everyone was up. No fires were lit other than the usual watchfires, to keep the camp as normal-looking as possible. In the unaccustomed darkness the stars seemed to lean down close and bright. The cold was intense but had in it for the first time a hint of mildness to come. Spring was far away, but coming nevertheless.

I envied Warlord Prince Melbras, for he was doing what I had wished to do—striding up and down the lines, inspecting bowstrings and axe handles, exchanging profanities with the sentries, inspiring courage with his strength and confidence. But as with fire, one has to have courage to share it. In any case I had not the face to go and encourage the men to die bravely, when I would not be risking so much as a scratch.

As the fists armed up they formed in their battle column, ready to march. General Horfal-yu had briefed each fistleader on his proper place and the plan of battle. Now in the pre-dawn twilight heavy bronze armor and shields gleamed in rows even as the scales on a snake's back. The column seemed incredibly long, twining around tents and hummocks of rock—a serpent more deadly than any viper. The Caydish archers who would provide covering fire assembled behind and to either side. When everything was ready the Prince leaped to a ledge sticking out of the central hill so that he could be seen. I looked forward to a fiery battle oration, as generals give in plaivs. But in his deep harsh voice he said, loud enough for all to hear, "You all know the terrain and the plans. We can't lose. Let's castrate the mudfoots!" He leaped down again and they were off. The Viridese marched in step, with the stolid and competent air of craftsman at their labor, while the Caydish trotted alongside, joking and bragging of the deaths they would deal today. It took a long time for the combined forces to march past, but I waited to see them all. Then with mingled regret and relief I went around the hill to the magi's pavilion.

The Master Magus had chosen thirty magi to come with us, of which almost half were the geomants who would destroy the dam once we won it. The rest were hydromants and hierognomers, so that three of the four loose magi divisions were represented. The hydromants and hierognomers had been brewing their weatherworks all night, gathered for quiet in a rocky dell nearby. All I could see when I passed was the faint glow of magery from the tips of glass wands and folded fans. The other magi were scrying so that the storm might be broken at the critical moment. When I peeped past the rush mats screening the sides of the pavilion I saw the Master Magus bending over his mirror and tapping his glass wand softly into his palm.

"Do they know we're coming?" I asked.

"You shouldn't be here, Majesty," the Magus said absently.

"We're busy. They must know something's afoot, people are going in and out of Xerlanthor's rooms."

Another scrying magus said, "We're starting through the woods now. Around the last hill and the first men should be in view of the watchmen on Xerlanthor's tower, if they're awake."

"They'll be awake," the Magus prophesied. "Someone get a scry on them, I don't want to lose Xerlanthor. Xalan, run to ask how the storm is. And bring something to eat."

"I can help," I offered.

Xalan said, "If you insist—you'd better get the food, the hierognomers won't want strangers around."

Hurrying to the kitchen tents I gathered skins of ale, oatcakes, and round Caydish cheeses. The one guard deputed to keep an eye on me had to help carry the food back. When we returned the Magus was saying, "There he goes, up the ladder to the battlements. A pity the Caydish bows don't have a longer range. . . . Where are our men?"

"Deploying around the earthworks, Magister," someone replied. "Not ready yet."

Xalan came in and said, "Any time, Magister, just give the word. The Sun's rising, and you can see the clouds hanging over the dam."

"No sign of spreading, is there? We mustn't drench our own men."

"No, the thunder head is stacked almost vertically." Xalan turned to me and added, "It looks like a tidal wave ready to fall."

"Ah . . . the Tlyalor are stringing their bows, nocking arrows . . . what does it look like on the earthworks?"

"The warning has spread, Magister," another magus said. "They're running up to the top of the dike . . . it looks like a kicked anthill."

"Javelin men, too, but mostly archers," another added.

Unable to sit still, I cut into a cheese and poured out ale for the Master Magus. After one sip he set down his cup, and I could see food and drink were forgotten. I could not eat either, and asked, "Have we attacked yet?"

"I have Melbras here," someone reported. "He hasn't given the signal yet, but the horns are ready to sound the assault. . . . He's looking up, at the sky and the clouds."

"He's the one supposed to begin," the Magus grumbled. "I told him to pick his moment and charge, that we'd time the

storm to him. He's not supposed to wait for us. If the rain starts
too soon the Tiyalor won't be sufficiently weakened."

"Why didn't you send a magus with him to advise?" I wanted
to know.

"No point to it, I told him we'd keep a mirror on him," the
Magus said. "We need all magic strength here."

"Wait—he's raising his axe. Yes, there it goes, the horns are
blowing. We're attacking!"

"Quick, Xalan, tell them to loose the storm!"

Xalan dashed out. I followed more slowly, and turned to look
south. The Sun peeped redly through the snow-clad trees. Over
the low pine-covered hill before me was the Mhesan's gorge,
and the dam. But all that could be seen from here was a towering
black cloud, mountain high and threatening as a naked sword. It
was plainly hierognomic, for it rose in a long, narrow cone like
an aerial turnip or carrot, its point poised above the battlefield.

Even as I watched the sullen mass flickered with lightning,
and a whipcrack of thunder made me jump. The clouds began to
writhe and seethe, and I could see the rain cascade down.
Though I could feel nothing here a gale wind was to blow from
our troops to theirs, to drive the rain against enemy faces and
thoroughly soak bowstrings. We have violent brief storms at
home, but I knew this would be like no natural weather. I
imagined the Tiyalor, knee-deep in the red mud that was once
their fortification, squinting into the slashing rain to aim their
arrows, only to have the missiles falter a few paces away because the bowstrings gave no power. Yet if they kept their bows
dry under cover they could not resist our assault. The plaiv tell
of magic storms with hailstones the size of dogs, but I had never
seen one. Nor would I today. In frustration I returned to the
pavilion.

Within, the tension had eased. The battle was now in the
armies' hands. The magi had done their part magnificently. The
Master Magus was looking into his mirror now merely to satisfy
Viridese nosiness. "It's raining hard," he reported. "Xerlanthor
is cursing us, I can tell by his face. He was always immoderate—
brilliant and versatile, but brittle. No self-control. He was never
the same after the Bilcad River disaster. . . . What of the
earthworks?"

"The Tiyalor have lost most of the first redoubt," a magus said.
"They're retreating, slipping in the mud. . . . I can hardly see
through the rain, it must be more like swimming out there. The
ditch in front of the second earthwork is full of red angry water.

There! One archer fell in—oh, I see, he was hit by a hailstone. Holy Viris, they're the size of my head."

"What about our men?" I asked.

"It's muddy going," another magus said after a pause. "But they're only getting a light drizzle. The storm fades to nothing ten yards back. It's a rout, they're getting almost no resistance."

"It's early yet," the Magus warned. "Still, a good beginning. Xalan, run and tell the weatherworkers to pull the storm back and downriver slowly. In a few hours I'll want the whole battlefield sunny and clear."

"Can Xerlanthor do anything to counter us?" I asked.

"He was a geomant, once," the Magus said. "But even if he calls up an earthquake it will be either very weak or very localized. He is only one, and we are many . . . and besides an earthquake would endanger his dam. He's climbing down now, wet as a drowned man washed up on a beach. . . ."

I could not bear my idleness. The battle was going well. Perhaps I could see it from the top of the hill, for the timber watchtower on its crest had been built not only to survey the camp but to look over the treetops. When I got there two of my guard were on duty, watching for sorties or flank attacks on the camp. As I climbed the short ladder I called to them, "How does it go?"

"The storm is passing off, Majesty," Corlis answered.

Leaning over the split-log rail I could see the dense black clouds to the south already calmer and less pregnant with rain. The three lines of dikes curved around the square tower guarding this end of the dam, but the river and the dam itself were not visible from here. Very faintly, when the wind veered toward us, I could smell moisture, and hear a dull noise—the patter of rain, the ring of bronze hewing bronze, the yells of defiance or pain, the grunts of the dying—all melted together by distance into a grinding agony. Straining my eyes I could just see men, bright in metal or dull with mud, struggling on the inmost dike or gathered at the base of the tower. The Caydish had of course assaulted and won the dam once before, and Prince Melbras knew exactly where scaling ladders could be safely set against the tower walls. The earthworks seemed to be won, and here the battle had been scarcely two hours in progress.

A fever of envy seized me, and forgetting my terrors I said, "It's there we should be, with the army, not nursemaiding magi and healers here."

"Don't you believe it, Majesty," Corlis said. He was chewing a piece of dry grass, and rubbing linseed oil into a leather armor strap with a bit of rag. "It's important to guard your rear. Aren't we taking advantage of the Tiyalor's foolishness there? They're relying on the cliffs to keep their bedrolls and tents safe. Won't they be surprised when the Commander fires them!"

I had not thought of it like that, and said, "Then you don't mind staying behind?"

He shrugged. "If it's not my fate to fight today, Majesty, how can I argue? The White Queen knows everyone's end. If she wants me she'll get me somehow."

Faint and hard to grasp as the odor of pressed flowers, the memory of the Queen of the Deadland's face drifted before me, and I remembered Xorc's joy. Perhaps dying was not so painful once it was over. Certainly Corlis did not fear it. I wondered how my two views of the road to death could be reconciled: Is it easy, or hard, to come to the White Queen's realm?

Reflecting, I looked out over the western forest. The outline of the trees against the snow was quite strange, spiky and pointy rather than round and fluffy. How long I stared at a tiny uneven flicker of light among the boughs I could not say, but coming to myself with a start I asked, "Corlis, what is that, over there?"

He stared hard, shading his eyes with one oily hand, and said, "It's men, Majesty, armed men."

"Friends?"

"I can't see their weapons or their armor, but I think those flashes are torches . . . Quick, the horn!" The other guard handed Corlis the horn as I half-climbed, half-fell down the short ladder and slid down the hill. As I raced through the deserted camp the horn blast warned everyone of possible attack. With only my guard of ten and the magi to defend the camp we would need everyone's help to win. In my tent I armed myself in the flexible bronze lamellar coat, and strapped on the shin-pieces. Buckling on the sword I ran to the Sisters' staff tent. Within, Fisan-shi was alone.

"The Crown, quickly," I commanded. "We're under attack."

She dropped the armor she was polishing and said, "Oh, no, Liras-ven! You can't be in the fight!"

"I have to, we're outnumbered," I said. Clumsy in my armor, I knelt beside the casket and opened it. There is always a slight reluctance, a resistance to using the Crown—it is too powerful, too close. But now I could hardly bring myself to touch it. Behind me Fisan said, "You at least shouldn't use the Crown, you had it on the other day when that Caydish fellow died. You nearly died then too."

"I have to," I repeated. "I don't want to, it'll hurt. But we have to win, and with the Crown's power I can win this fight fast." As long as I kept moving, kept acting, I wouldn't have time to get scared—I hoped. Telling myself that if my great-grandfather could do it I could, I put the Crown on.

Perhaps because of my fears there was no effect of distance or remoteness this time. I heard only the thump of blood in my temples and Fisan fidgeting at the front of the big tent. My skin prickled and shrank, as if I were walking nude past a stinging-ant hill.

"You are afraid." The Crown's beautiful voice startled me.

"We mustn't read anyone," I said aloud. I felt my brain curled up tight in the shell of my skull so as not to touch anyone else's pain. "There's a battle going on outside. Don't touch, don't get too close."

Fisan-shi stared at me, but I was too troubled to care what she thought. She peered through the tent door again and cried,

"Liras! They've torched the watchtower!"

Brushing past her I ran out on shaky legs. The Sun was now bright in a cold blue sky. Shouts and yells echoed from my right, beyond the central hill, and orange flames licked at the tower and several tents. As I watched, a tall hairy man in strange leather armor appeared between two tents. He carried a javelin, a torch, and an armload of straw.

I was dizzy and leaned on a tentrope for a moment. This man I would kill. The idea seemed impossible, yet I dared not think it over, for already the Tiyal had laid the straw between two tents across from me and was firing it. A yelling crowd of fighting men was moving closer, and if I did not soon act I would be overrun.

"All right," I said to the Crystal Crown. "Hit him." I pointed at the Tiyal and closed my eyes.

"You are under some misapprehension," the Crown said.

"What?"

"Your destructive capabilities in this mode are subject to conditions."

I felt flattened, as if I had been kicked in the stomach. "Well, hurry, what are they?"

"It's complex," the Crown replied. "Perhaps you have more urgent concerns?"

"Liras, wake up! Are you dreaming?" Fisan shouted in my

ear. I looked for the Tiyal but he was flat on his back, bleeding at the nose. "He was going to spear you," she said, "so I hit him with a rock." Her face was white but she held another big rock, one of those gathered to weight down tent flaps, ready to throw.

"Curse it!" I exclaimed, and dashed back into the tent. Snatching the Crown off my head I shut it into its casket. When I hurried back outside the Tiyal had risen to his knees. His face was masked in blood, and he had taken up his javelin again to menace Fisan, who was spitting out a stream of defiances she could only have learned from the Sisters.

"Just come close enough," she cried, brandishing her rock, "and I'll spread your fat head on this for the rats to chew!"

It was ridiculous as a child defying a sand-leopard—Fisan is slightly built, not coming even up to her foe's chin. "Run, Fisan!" I ordered, and drawing my sword charged the man.

He was not very quick, for as I approached from one side the javelin wavered from Fisan to myself and then back again. Shouting to draw his attention I watched for the throw. The javelin flew at me hard and true but I twisted aside and felt the bronze point scrape past my armored flank. Before he could draw his sword I was on him.

My first blow rebounded from the hard leather shoulder pauldron, and the man punched at my torso. Leather gauntlets protected his hands and I discovered that while lamellar will turn a point it is not proof against a fist in the gut. I gasped and curled around the pain as he drew his blade, but recovered sufficiently to dance away from its blow.

Tiyalor swords are not broad and leaf-shaped like ours, but pointed and slim, more suited to stabbing. With the weight of a big man behind it not even my armor would protect me from one.

Suddenly a big rock sailed past, narrowly missing me and rebounding off the Tiyal's knee. "For Viris' sake, Fisan, run!" I cried, but out of the corner of my eye I could see she had taken charge of the Tiyal's javelin and held another rock ready to throw as well. I turned my head and snapped, "That's an order, cousin, get back into the tent!"

The Tiyal leaped, knocking me to the ground. I writhed away from the deadly sword point bearing down at my throat. More by instinct than sense I wrenched my sword out from between us before it was pinned and hacked hard under the lifted arm where my foe's armor left an unprotected spot. The wide blade bit deep enough to stick in the leather chest-piece. I tugged it free and rolled to my feet.

He was wounded, mortally, but to my horror he was not dead. Blood bubbled out of the wound and he spat and coughed thick crimson spittle, yet he did not die. Sickened, my first thought was to run for the Crystal Crown and heal him again. Then I took a firm grip on myself and raised my sword. It would be cruel to let him choke to death. I owed him a swifter end. He lay face down, trying to support himself on his elbows. Approaching from behind and to the right, I aimed deliberately for the neck bared between pauldron and helm. He must have heard my step on the gritty snow, but did not move. I put my body behind the blow so that it clove through to the spine. The bubbling gasps were stilled. I tugged the blade free. I had to brace my foot on the corpse to do it. The freed sword dripped clotted and sticky, and I felt the same—steeped in slaughter.

Behind me a crowd of yelling Tiyalor burst into the open space between the tents. Drained in body and soul I stood over the corpse and only looked up as they saw me and raced shouting with rage to cut me down. But beyond them a red robe gleamed above their heads, and Piril's battle-scream belled. Xalan thundered up, trampling those who did not leap out of the way, and reined Piril in before me.

"Hurry and take him," he said, sliding off the sleek ebony back. "He's too lively for me. I thought you'd be here. Where's the Crown?"

I took the reins he pushed into my hand. "With cousin Fisan, I hope," I answered. Xalan had not had time to saddle Piril, but with a boost I managed to mount. "What about you?"

"Never worry about magi," he said. "Get that nervous beast out of range and I'll show you." He slapped Piril's rump and the horse leaped away, striking out at the melee with his front feet. The Tiyalor fell away. I hacked indiscriminately at exposed limbs or weapons, for Piril had no armor and might easily be speared. Somehow there was no conflict in me about the relative value of horse and man—Zofal and I had always loved our horses, and now it was easier to defend Piril than myself. As before, I dimly realized that continuous action gives no time to be afraid. I had caught my breath, and was able to close my first kill into a mental room and lock the door.

Several tents down, when we had won clear of the foe a little, I reined up and looked back. More than half of the Tiyalor crowd had run the other way, toward Xalan. The black stone wand in his hand was held with the base a handspan above the frozen ground. The Tiyalor did not know what to make of this very odd defense, and bunched together working up their courage with uncouth battle cries. Xalan waited until they rushed at him before striking the earth before him with the wand.

The frozen ground heaved and split in a long fissure at the blow, gaping right beneath the feet of the charging Tiyalor. Before they could stop themselves perhaps five of them fell or stepped into the crack, which appeared to be only arm deep. With a grinding, dusty noise the crack instantly snapped shut again, pinching the hapless assailants' legs or arms. Rather than helping their fellows the other Tiyalor turned and ran, dodging between the tents back toward the fiery watchtower. Xalan examined his prisoners with cool approval and sauntered over to me. "I think Granduncle will be proud," he said.

"I'm impressed," I said with envy. "Much neater than the way I had to do it."

"They still outnumber us, let's go help."

There were twenty or thirty Tiyalor in all, too few for a sortie. In fact we later learned they were a supply expedition cut off from Xerlanthor by our assault, who had made the best of their situation by attacking us. Although magi have mighty abilities they do not often use them against others, and today the hierognomers and hydromants had already poured out their powers on the main battle. Geomancy was perilous, since earth-tremor might easily shake the flaming timbers of the tower down on us all. So force of arms would decide the issue.

At the foot of the low hill the remnant of my guard had made their stand. Their armor and shields had served against javelins and arrows but in the hand-to-hand fight numbers were telling against them. Taking up a stone, Xalan lifted above the scrimmage, high enough to be out of bowshot, and joined the hovering red-clad flock of magi in the winter sky. Every now and then when a clear target presented itself they would release their stones, which fell on the Tiyalor hard enough to crack bones.

With a scream of defiance Piril reared and charged the enemy. Zofal-ven does the training of war-horses—my role in the business had been gentling riding animals—and I realized he had wasted on me the bravest horse in his stables. Horses do not usually like to step on things that move, but Piril had been taught to trample, and to kick with all four feet, all without unseating his rider. To my surprise we cut a wide swath of devastation through the enemy and right up to my guards' shield-wall. The tired guardsmen cheered, and Corlis shouted, "Come on, let's rush them!"

As the guardsmen pressed forward I reined Piril around to gallop through again. The Tiyal archers had recovered from my first sweep, and black arrows hissed past me on either side. But the pounding hooves, the red blade in my hand, the shouts, intoxicated me. Fear and doubt had been left behind, for now I sat like a god on the moving warm back which allowed me to look over the battle and choose my victim. The added height made my sword stroke invincible. Piril's courage and power lent me heroism too. I saw a big Tiyal aiming a deeply curved horn bow, and spurred Piril toward him.

The black arrow bounced off my chest armor, and I leaned forward over Piril's withers to cut the archer down. He must have been brave, for instead of recoiling he leaped forward under my stroke and stabbed upward with a short Tiyal sword. The point skidded up off the high brazen collar of my lamellar armor and just caught me on the jawline, gouging a long slash up my right cheek. The pain and surprise almost tumbled me off backward to the ground, but my knees instinctively held on while Piril turned and trampled. Then he reared, screaming and lashing at the sky with both front hooves. The archers had learned to aim at the horse instead of the rider. Piril fell with three black-fletched arrows in him, and I was pinned beneath.

PART III: TWO PATHS TO VALOR

Chapter 13: Goats and Death

Only a slight hollow in the frozen ground saved me from a broken hip. But the force of our fall dazed me, and I lay unable to help myself while the fight was won around me.

"All right, together now," the Master Magus said. "Don't let it slip, whatever you do—up!"

The paralyzing weight eased a little, and then went away. Vaguely I realized that the shadow creeping across my face was cast by Piril's carcass, lifted by the combined hierognomy of the magi. Gentle hands turned me over.

"Don't pull him around like that," the Mistress Herbal cried in horror. "Bones might be broken!"

"There's blood all over," Fisan said.

"I'm fine," I said weakly. It was not quite true—I ached all over and sticky blood had run from my cheek into my mouth and eyes. But I was alive. Piril had bled in a wide pool so that I only looked mortally wounded. I sat up, spitting to clear my mouth, and said, "Help me up, will you? I'm all stiff."

I was assisted to my tent, where the Mistress put a stitch in my cheek with silken thread. "Don't shave that side till it's healed," she warned. I felt no inclination to disobey. The place was astonishingly painful, and as it stiffened I could hardly eat or speak.

The dam was still being contested, but the scryers reported that the Tiyal camp was afire, showing that the Sisters were at work. Our little group of assailants had surrendered, and a sheep pen was being converted into a prisoner compound. To my sorrow Corlis had been speared in the final scrimmage. Two other guardsmen had been slain also, and the rest wounded, some badly. The entire little affair had not taken an hour. It seemed to me a lifetime's experience. Worn out, I stripped off my armor and clothes, now stiffening and brown, and slept the afternoon through.

I was wakened at sundown by Xalan, announcing, "We've won! The dam is ours!"

"I feel a hundred years old," I mumbled through my bandages.

141

Every joint and muscle creaked in protest as I pried my head off the pillow. "Did they kill Xerlanthor?"

"Perhaps the Sisters got him," Xalan said. "The Warlord hasn't found his body yet."

I tottered up and collapsed by my brazier while Xalan had food and washing water brought. After a meal and a cat-bath in a basin I felt more myself. "What clothes have I?"

"Everything's over," Xalan said. "Why don't you go back to sleep?"

But I took my Viridese traveling clothes out of my bag, saying, "Were a lot of our men hurt?"

"Now you're not going to try healing them! The casualties weren't unduly heavy, the herbals and bonesetters have everything under control—"

Ignoring his protests I dressed and wrapped myself in my furry cloak. "You want to come or not?" I interrupted. "I have to get the Crystal Crown from Fisan first."

The Sun had set, leaving a saffron haze in the west. It was bitter cold. We had to nerve ourselves to suck the first icy breath into our lungs. Ice crackled and groaned underfoot as we hurried to the Sisters' big staff tent. The camp was busy but very quiet, the quiet that bonesetters impose so that the sick may rest.

Brown-clad Sisters were gathered around a big brazier in their tent, eating their supper. In the darker corners those too exhausted to eat lay under quilts. The Commander rose when I came in, but I waved everyone else to keep their seat.

"My commendations on the victory, Silverhand," I said.

There were smudges of weariness under her eyes, and a dirty bandage was tied round her left hand, but her smile was kind as ever. "I hear Your Majesty did some notable deeds today yourself," she said.

"I did?"

Xalan told me, "The guardsmen would have been overwhelmed and slain had you not charged the foe."

"I told you courage could be learned." The Commander smiled.

"Oh, but that was Piril," I said. "You'd call it bravery, not courage—I did nothing except ride along."

"The effect was good, all the same."

"Originally I had hoped to help another way," I said. "And I might as well begin with the Sisterhood. Has my cousin retired yet? I'd like the Crown."

"No, I'm here, Liras-ven," Fisan called. "Here it is—oh, you've been hurt! Are you going to fix it?"

"It's minor," I said. "But that's an idea, if the Crystal Crown can heal its wearer." I put the Crown on.

No written record is kept by rulers of Averidan of their experiences with the Crown, and plaiv is notoriously unreliable. So I did not know whether my venture was even possible. Healings had never tired me, but I assumed there would be some cumulative toll when I undertook an entire battle's worth of casualties. Aloud I said, "Where are your wounded, Commander?"

"We have several hospital tents," she said. "But you need not worry about the Sisters, Majesty. We are nurtured in endurance."

"Nonsense, you feel pain like anyone. Oh, and while I'm at it—" I took her bandaged hand in mine, reaching in to feel with the Crown's power. "How did you come to break two finger bones?"

"Didn't know the man had a metal collar on, when I broke his neck," she replied. With a slight effort I smoothed the fractures over. Startled, she pulled the hand free and unwound the bandage and splint. Flexing the fingers, she said, "It doesn't even hurt anymore."

"If you insist on doing this," Xalan scolded, "at least save your energies for truly serious hurts. There are almost a hundred of ours wounded, and Viris alone knows how many Caydish."

I didn't reply, for from the center of my skull the Crystal Crown spoke, saying, "There are limitations also on your powers to heal."

"I learned one," I said mentally. "With Xorc—not to try to drag the dying back. What others are there?"

The Crown replied, "Plagues, fevers, and sweats—burns, crushing wounds, and wound rot—brain illnesses, apoplexy, and madness . . . It would be simpler to list what *is* in your power: simple wounds, particularly those suddenly inflicted."

"Well, that sounds exactly what I need now," I said. "I'll worry about burns and brain illnesses some other day." Distantly I was aware of my feet carrying me from pallet to pallet, tent to tent, of my hands touching and healing flowing out. From far away I noticed the truth of what the Crown had said. The spearman under my hand had been scalded through the joints of his armor with boiled bran poured on him as he climbed the siege ladder. He had then fallen off and broken his ankle. The bones joined, but the broad livid blisters were not erased by my touch. But this occupied only a small portion of my consciousness, for the discussion in my head had turned to other subjects.

"How do I do as my great-grandfather? Is the plaiv true, about the white-flaming sword?"

"It is, but the sword is not relevant," the Crown said. "The conditions you must fulfill to achieve destructive power, in whatever form, are three."

"Only three? What a pity you didn't run through them this morning."

The Crown recited from one of the many plaiv in its capacious memory. "In the forges of the First Magus, the words of Shan Vir-yan: 'A riddle: when is it right to kill a man? For I am not minded that any weapon of terror should come into the world by us. Therefore, let the Crystal Crown be so forged that it may of its very nature only be wielded in the cause of justice.' "

"That can't be done," I said. "This morning would it have been just or not to fry that Tiyal? How would I have known, quick enough to avoid being spitted? Do I have to submit every case to judgment, like having a house plan vetted by geomants?"

"The justice of the case may only be determined by yourself," the Crown told me. "You must be satisfied in your own heart."

The question then might be whether the satisfaction stemmed from my own heart or the Crown's subtle influence on my judgment. But since at the moment my head was not my own I shied away from considering the question. "All right," I assented. "Who would be so wicked as to kill someone undeservedly? What are the other conditions?"

". . . His son Shan Xao-lan answered, 'Yet justice alone will not suffice, for if all who were ever unjust were slain Averidan should be unpeopled, and the world also. Let us then forge the Crown so that it may not begin, but only reflect death.' "

I mulled this over. "Does that mean I can only attack someone who is trying to kill me?"

"When your own life is at risk, is the condition."

"That would have been all right this morning," I said. "Even behind lamellar armor, a Tiyal javelin is no joke." Then another thought came to me. "What about lapidation, how does that fit in?"

"It is a different case entirely: society ridding itself of a bad member," the Crown told me. "Did you never hear plaiv about unjust lapidations?"

"You mean the ones where the people refuse to pile the stones up over the victim." I remembered—it is a favorite theme, for a hero to be unjustly condemned and then magnificently vindicated. Feverishly I prayed my reign would never be marred by such a mortification. "Go on, what is next?"

". . . but his grand-daughter Mir-hel, who was Shan Queen after him, said, 'There is death enough in the world, and how shall these questions be judged in time to come? Let us strike to the heart of the matter. Let the ruler of the Shan feel the destruction he calls up, and know the cost of his work in himself, so that the Crystal Crown shall never be wielded lightly.' And so it was agreed."

Appalled, I said, "But then how did my great-grandfather manage at all? Did every person he kill hurt him?" I remembered my vicarious agony when the Caydish axeman died.

"Yes," the Crown said. "For this is the touchstone, the answer to Shan Vir-yan's riddle. When is it right to kill a man? When it is just and necessary and costly." ·

"It's impossible," I protested. "I could never go through something like that again. It hurt too much. No matter how just or necessary it might be!"

"That," the Crown said, "is a matter of your own courage."

That hurt, but I could not deny the truth of it. "I'll never be that brave," I admitted. There is no point in prevaricating to the Crown. It was a concession of defeat—I would never emulate my great-grandfather. But the work under my hand consoled me a bit. "I'll do other things," I promised the Crown and myself. "Healing is much easier for me, and more necessary now too."

From far away I had been aware of some hubbub or commotion, and abruptly the fuss moved closer. Someone was being hit, not viciously but sharp and insistent, around the face and on the hands. They wouldn't let him rest, and I ordered, "Leave the poor fellow alone! What's going on here?"

"Majesty, wake up!" Xalan said.

"I'm sure it's hurting him, what you're doing," I scolded. "After all, he's wounded. Look at that bandage around his face." As I said the words I raised my hand to touch the place and heal. A throb of pain rewarded me, and I realized it was my own face. The two halves of my mind rushed together in a roar of confusion, tumbling over and over like pebbles in the surf. Xalan was bending over me as I half sat, half lay on a snowy heap of rocks which had been gathered to weight tent flaps. Behind him red torchlight shone on the Master Bonesetter and Fisan. Another blow to my left cheek seemed to spin the eyeballs around in my head, and I groped for Xalan's wrist, saying, "Stop that!"

"Welcome back to the real world," Xalan said with a sigh of relief. "You began talking to yourself a little while ago."

"Where are we? What time is it?"

"Your Majesty collapsed while walking from one hospital tent to another," the Master Bonesetter told me. "It is past midnight and Your Majesty has laid hands on almost sixty wounded."

I believed him. I felt sucked dry as a discarded orange skin. When Xalan hauled me to my feet my head swam and firelit fog spun before my eyes. Whatever forces I used in healing I had nearly drained. "Maybe I'll do the rest tomorrow," I mumbled.

"Excellent idea," Xalan approved. "Master, if you'll support his other side—"

The night's cold shook my limbs and the warmth of the two steady bodies on either side of me was good. "Would you like me to take the Crown?" Fisan asked me.

"In a moment," I said, for the Crown was saying, "You cannot heal your own wound."

"Why not?" I asked.

On my right Xalan said, "Curse it, there he goes again."

Fisan said, "I'm sure it will help if he takes the Crown off."

"Your powers over the physical cease with your own body," the Crown told me.

"It's not serious anyway," I said. I could hear my tongue slur the words. "I just won't be able to shave."

"No," Xalan said to Fisan. "Better get him to his tent first."

"It's uncanny," the Master Bonesetter remarked. "As if he's talking to someone invisible."

I am, I wanted to say, but my tongue would no longer obey me. Nor would my feet. Night's darkness overtook me. Faintly I heard Xalan say, "Just a little farther—no? Well! Fisan, can you take his feet?" And I relaxed into oblivion.

Next day we moved camp and took possession of the dam. I slept unstirring until midday, and woke to find my tent the only one still unstruck. My guardsmen kept zealous watch around it, and when I came out I said, "Aren't you all on sick list? Ranoc, how is your leg-wound?"

The man seemed confused, and answered, "But Majesty, you healed it last night. Remember?"

I didn't, but I said, "Oh, yes. . . . Let's go and see the dam, everyone's already there."

It was a gray, windy day but the snow was melting a little so that tufts of tired yellow grass stuck through the ice. When we got closer, the fury of the hierognomic storm yesterday had washed the trampled earth clean. The earthworks were a sticky red expanse of lumpy mud, studded here and there with logs, broken weapons, and discarded Tiyal bucklers. To keep out of the mess, and out of the way of the squad gathering and counting enemy corpses, we circled south to approach the rocky river bank downstream.

The wind was cold but bracing, sweeping away my mental fuzziness of the night before. In my thick Caydish boots I was surefooted on the icy rocks, and strode along feeling enduring and bold. I was Lord of the Shan, and we had won a resounding victory—"What happened to Xerlanthor?"

"No one knows, Majesty," Ranoc said. "He must have got away. The Sisters watched the rout on the other shore, but didn't see him."

"Then the whole battle was for nothing!" I exclaimed. "He could raise another army in Tiyalor and come back tomorrow!"

"That was the problem, Majesty, with the idea of letting the Tiyalor live." Ranoc spoke very meekly and politely. Of course if we had known Xerlanthor would escape, common sense demanded a policy of extermination.

"Did we indeed?" I asked, wondering if on the field Warlord Prince Melbras had not given his own orders.

"The Caydish were sullen about it but on your behalf General Horfal-yu insisted on mercy whenever possible."

"Faithful man!" I had not thought the General had it in him.

"We even took some prisoners, more than a hundred of them," Ranoc continued. "But they're in poor shape."

"I'll see to them later," I said. The guardsmen looked at each other. I could almost hear them thinking that laying healing hands on prisoners of war was too *chun-hei* even for a Shan King. If Viridese love of argument possessed them, though, they hid it well. To turn the subject I asked, "Have the dam's sluice gates been opened yet?"

"Yes, Majesty. Look there."

We had come to the river bank. Far below us the naked bed of the Mhesan was visible—water-worn potholes, dried and frozen water weeds, stones eroded to smoothness, threaded by a line of ice-rimmed silver that was the newly liberated water. All the flow we had seen on our way here was from springs and tributaries.

This, the headwater, was the source, the true river, and now it flowed slow but sure in its old paths.

Passing some boulders and stunted bushes I saw at last, upstream to our right, the dam we had come so far to destroy. It was monumental, so large that àt first my eye saw it as a spur of the southern bank: gray rock cut in rough blocks walled the gorge across, sloping up in a mighty man-made mountain. The top was flat and wide, spanning the gap from bank to bank like a bridge, and had been smoothed for ease in crossing. From the tunnellike sluice gate to the parapet was perhaps twice the height of the Temple Dome in Averidan. I gaped like any yokel, saying, "How did Xerlanthor ever build it? It must have taken tons of stone, years of labor!"

"Magery," My guardsman replied dourly.

Judging from the mighty slope the dam was almost four times thicker at the base than at the top. I wondered no longer that the unsophisticated Caydish had been unable to level it. The low square towers at either end seemed inadequate afterthoughts, mice hoping to defend a great gray leopard. Across the river we could glimpse the other bank, a little lower than ours but full of small cliffs, ravines, and rocky broken ground. Charred ruins here and there marked where huts and store-tents had been burned. No human was visible, but many of the goats and sheep the Sisters stampeded yesterday had returned, foolishly clambering about looking for their masters. We could also see more than a score of great copper cauldrons, each big enough to boil a goat in, tumbled over or leaning drunkenly on their fire-stones.

The little cliff path we climbed ran west, uphill right up to the tower. But every inch was commanded from the tower parapet and the dam's battlement. The spearman on watch above recognized me and waved. We went to the right, around the two-story tower to its double wooden door. Inside, the tiny windowless main floor was crowded with Viridese and Caydish. The Warlord and General Horfal-yu were upstairs.

At my entrance the cheerful buzz of conversation died away. It struck me that I was the only person present who had not fought in the battle yesterday—our skirmish in the camp had slipped my mind for a moment. I had no hood or hat to hide my shyness in, so I ducked my head and walked as quickly as I could through the crowd. The ladder up to the second story was in the far corner. But my way was blocked by a veteran fistleader, a Viridese nearly as old as my mother. Muttering an excuse, I tried to pass by without looking up. But the man said, "Majesty, sir, could I have a word?"

I stopped perforce, and said, "Yes, messir, what is it?"

The man would not look me in the face, and for a moment I feared his contempt. But he said, "Sir, yesterday I had the hamstring cut, here at the back of my leg, and the herbals told me I'd limp the rest of my days. You put hands on it, and it's whole again. So I wanted to thank you, for the use of my leg."

This was almost worse. My aversion to being thanked for the Crystal Crown's work is unreasonable, I know. But such expressions seem imbued with the same unreality of plaiv about myself. Now I felt the commonplace world slip around me, and the blush rise in my face. At court in Averidan, shielded in protocol and custom, it is easy to elude gratitude. To my further embarrassment Viridese within hearing spoke up also, with thanks or pleas for the healing of friends or relatives. The Caydish listeners did not understand us, and thought this some strange lowland custom. But some who spoke a little Viridese began to translate for their countrymen. For fear of a riot, when everyone learned of the healings, I leaped for the wooden ladder that led upstairs.

The foundation and lower walls of the tower were of stone, but the upper floor was made of timber, with slits for arrows and a thick double door leading out onto the dam itself. I panted up the final rungs and swung across the opening to the floor. Yesterday, when the entire defeated Tiyalor army had had to retreat up this ladder and through those doors, the slaughter must have been dreadful. But someone had cleared away the corpses, and only brown splotches on the rough-hewn floorboards told the tale. General Horfal-yu looked up and said, "Ah, Your Majesty. We've been discussing the whereabouts of Xerlanthor."

Warlord Prince Melbras rose from his seat in greeting. His arm was in a sling but one look at the hard brown face suggested to me that I need not offer him a healing touch. Instead I said, "My commendations, your Highness. I hear the battle was managed perfectly."

He was a little mollified, and growled, "That magus escaped us."

"Well, we must all redouble our efforts," the General said when this was translated for him, "and run him to earth."

The Master Magus also rose, looking me over carefully. The wounded side of his head had been cropped to accommodate the dressing, and was now growing out, which gave him a rather untidy appearance. "Our hydromants are scrying intensively," he said. "It will only be a matter of time, unless he's shielding from us." Then he added, "Xalan told me about your work last night, Majesty. Please don't overtax yourself."

"I'm fine," I said. "Are we to wait until Xerlanthor is descried then?"

"We can't afford to wait," Commander Silverhand pointed out. "Every day he's at large he will use to gather another army against us."

"I've thought of something to do about that," I told the Magus.

The Warlord said, "We must leave a force here, strong enough to hold the dam, and search along the roads to Tiyalor. My men have done that once before—the peasants know they cannot hide a fugitive from us."

The Commander said, "He may be wounded, lying up in some forest glade. If so, the Sisterhood will find him."

We thus decided to send the Sisters and a light, mobile force of Caydish archers on the hunt. The Viridese fists, who are no use in forest warfare, would hold the dam until the magi could destroy it. The Prince and Commander Silverhand left to announce the decisions to the troops and ready them for departure, while the General and I prepared to settle in.

"The earthworks must be repaired and re-dug immediately," the General said.

"You must move into this tower then, General," I told him, "to supervise properly. I will take possession of the other." I sent my guard for my things, and taking the Master Magus with me went through the double doors onto the dam itself.

"How will the magi ever level this?" I asked, for as we walked across the dam seemed far too massive for human hands to destroy.

"Geomants will call up an earthquake," the Magus said, "strong enough to shake the dam apart. The force of the pent-up water will sweep the pieces away. It won't be simple—Xerlanthor has learned from his mistakes, and chose the geomantically best site for miles around. The earth currents run close and strong hereabouts, so that the structure is knit into the bones of the earth. But the true problem is undoing the spells that hold the dam together."

The broad top of the dam was laid dry with square blocks of dark stone. It was more like walking along the ridge of a mountain than anything else, for on either side of us rock sloped down and away. I looked over the right-hand parapet to see the pool formed by the dammed waters. Because the silt had not settled out the long, narrow lake was opaque, the reddish-brown of a good redfish soup. The blustering wind that bit at our cheeks did not ruffle the water. The sullen surface was a good way down, for last autumn the Caydish had let much of the accumulated water drain away and the mountain snows had not yet begun to add their melt. We could see successive rings of pale dried mud at the edge, marking old water levels, and trampled paths down to the water level.

"So this was the water he was boiling," I said. "Does that have anything to do with the spell holding the dam together?"

"Your Majesty, I wish I knew." The Magus tapped the stone parapet lightly with his glass wand. "Xerlanthor has explored unheard-of magic areas, fields dealing with life and the use of life. Have you looked at the mortar, here?"

He pointed with the wand at the joint between two of the big parapet blocks. I looked at it closely. The stones were mortared together with a dark brown, almost black stuff. It would have excited no comment whatever in a wall at home, and I said, "What about it?"

The Magus touched the joint, and I did the same. The mortar rubbed off clammy on my fingertips, a damp brownish stain. "The stuff is melting, from the water pressure on the other side," I surmised.

"No," the Magus said. "I can't say for sure, but all my magery tells me it has never dried."

"Then how does it cohere, bond the stones together?"

"You know that light equals life, of course," the Magus said, and I nodded. Everybody knows that. "Blood is also life, at least in men. He's found a way to harness the power of blood in his geomancy. This dam is almost alive."

I snatched my hand away, wiping it on my tunic. "You're joking!" I said, and then seeing his face I asked, "Whose blood is it?"

"I wouldn't care to speculate on that," the Magus said in grim tones. "But he was always too interested in taking things apart to see how they worked. A brilliant man, but grievously flawed. He became cruel."

My pleasure in the morning melted away. Death and the fear of death hung round the dam like a ghastly mist. How many had died in its construction? I looked down at the square stones under our feet and said, "I suppose they're laid dry so that the nerves

of the Tiyalor wouldn't be raveled by bloody footprints whenever they had to cross. Let's go on.''

The dam's top was wider than a city street, and very slightly
curved. At its south end a similar tower's double wooden door
stood ajar. The Caydish archers who had held the tower last
night were now packing up their bedrolls. They did not recognize me, and eyed us with suspicion—someone obviously Viridese
yet dressed as a Cayd and accompanied by a magus. In Caydish I
said, ''Please don't let me interrupt you.'' We passed among
them and climbed down the ladder to the main floor.

The main room of this tower held only more archers and the
smell of sheep and goat. When I stepped outside into the cold a
dozen white and brown goats bleated and leaped for joy, jostling
each other to get close. Their odor was overpowering.

''It must be feeding time,'' I said, pushing downhill through
the flock. ''How tame they are. We'll have to get one of the
Caydish to help take care of them.''

The Magus did not hear me. At the bottom of the rocky slope
he bent to set a copper cauldron onto its three legs, and examined the interior carefully. ''Nothing,'' he reported. ''Bone dry.''

''I have some plans for one of those, if you can spare it.''

The Magus raised one white eyebrow. ''What use did Your
Majesty have in mind? They're too big for cookery.''

''A bathtub,'' I said. ''I haven't had a hot bath since we left
home.'' The goats surged around us both, drowning my words in
their bleats. The Magus was too dignified to quarrel with them,
but I pushed one away with my knee. To my astonishment the
animal whirled on its back legs and butted me hard with its
knobby forehead, tumbling me flat.

The Caydish call our jokes decadent and obscure, but that is
because their own humor is of a rougher and more boisterous
sort. At any rate the tall Caydish archers who watched us from
the tower door howled with laughter at the sight, poking each
other in the ribs and doubling over to slap their knees. In the
cold thin air their noise sounded like baying wolves. The goats
were delighted with the audience's response, and capered merrily
round and round us, while the Magus seemed speechless with
shock. The hilarity of my plight overwhelmed me too, and I
rolled back and forth on the stony grass giggling. Only the
inquisitive nostrils and cool snorty breath of a goat's nose an
inch from mine brought me to my feet. The archers came down
the steep hill and gathered around, laughing and clapping me on

the back. One, a man of middle years, said, "Little man, choose another line of work! You'll never make a goatherd!"

"I will, thank you," I said in Caydish. "But I thought to take charge of these goats to feed the soldiers. What are they calling for, do you know, is it that they're hungry?"

This question drew another round of guffaws. The man answered, "Have you never known goats, that you can't tell these want to be milked? Night and morning, they need it."

"I always imagined that whenever you were thirsty you just went and milked," I admitted. "Like pouring ale from a flask."

"Ho, ho! You have much to learn!" Without more ado the man took off his round hard-leather helm, revealing a shock of straw-colored hair done in a single braid behind. "Here, you hold her head—" Callused hands took my wrists and guided them to a goat's neck. "Hang on, now!" he ordered, and moved around to the animal's flank.

The brown and white pelt was warm under my hands, but not perhaps very clean. The head tried to butt me in the stomach so that I had to kneel beside the beast and put an arm around its throat. Behind me the Magus demanded, "What are you doing?"

"I'm helping milk a goat," I said in Viridesc. The Magus said something about improper protocol but I could not pay attention because the goat's front foot kicked out and nearly caught me in the crotch. When I grabbed the offending hoof the beast squirmed so that the archer said, "For Limaot's sake! Someone give him a hand there!" I was shouldered aside, and at the firm touch of the Caydish helpers the goat instantly became calm, turning to look at me with ironic yellow eyes. "Come here," the milker called. "Maybe you'll be better at milking."

"I very much doubt it," I said, but I squatted beside him to see how it was done. The helm was steadied against a stone by the archer's booted toe, and foamy white milk nearly filled it.

Taking the helm up he brushed the yellow mustache back from either side of his mouth and raised it to his lips. "Very good!" he exclaimed, smacking his lips. "She must have been stolen from a Caydish goat farm. Want some?" He held out the helm.

"No thanks," I said as calmly as I could. "I don't like milk."

He sucked white droplets off his mustache and shook his head. "You would be better grown if you did," he said. "You must be a foreigner, I can tell by your talk. Where are you from?"

"Averidan," I said. "My name is Liras-ven Tsormelezok." The helm was passed around the group and quickly drained. I noticed that questions of fastidiousness seemed to tax no one.

"A mouthful of name! Mine's Gorst, son of Lor. We're farmers, south of here. All right, now it's your turn—" He held out the helm and gestured for me to take his place. The Caydish gathered around to enjoy my attempt, cracking goatherd jokes I couldn't understand and jostling each other. There was no malice in them, but beside them I was short enough to look a weakling. As the Warlord had informed me, weakness is opportunity in Cayd. They had fought a hard battle yesterday, and were now rested and ready for a little amusement—at my expense. Seeing there was nothing for it I took the helm and crouched at the goat's side.

Gorst's instructions were cryptic: "Don't tug, just squeeze gently from top to bottom." He demonstrated, squirting a white stream onto my boot. Setting the helm beneath the udder I grasped the teat and tried to imitate him. It felt warm and smooth and full, like a finger in a fine leather glove, but I got no results. When I squeezed a little harder I did get a dribble of milk, which ran down my wrist to soak my sleeve. The Caydish thought this very funny, and Gorst whipped the helm out to demonstrate it was empty. When he put it back I grimly persisted, and at the cost of sprinkling my clothes and even my face and hair I milked the goat out. Because of my poor aim the helm was not full when I was done, but I stood up, straightening my aching back with an effort, and handed the helm to Gorst.

The Master Magus had wrapped his fur-trimmed red cape around him and withdrawn to sit on a rocky ledge just within earshot. His prim posture, and the long glass wand he tapped on his palm, warned me even before Gorst bellowed, "This isn't milk!"

I rubbed my face clean on my sleeve and peered into the helm. The fluid was no longer chalky white but brown and bubbling with foam.

Another Cayd exclaimed, "It's ale!" The helm was passed from hand to hand in a babble of astonished comment. One man made as if to drink but another warned, "It's witchery, it'll do a mischief to your belly."

"Nonsense," I said, taking the helm. I knew it would taste like goats' milk, since transmogrification alters only appearance. So I took only a small sip, and even so had to concentrate to keep a grimace from my face. I was careful not to smile or glance at the Master Magus, who sat staring nonchalant into the distance.

The Caydish were not soothed at all. "Witchery, he's a witch," they repeated, and would not drink.

It was the first time I had heard the word—I was certain it wasn't in the "Merchant of Quality's" word lists—and I asked, "What does 'witch' mean—not 'magus,' is it?"

They were too busy making overt gestures to answer me, and in my ignorance for a moment I was in real danger, for reputed witches are strangled in Cayd. But before I could grasp the significance of the bowstrings being fingered or unstrung a deep harsh voice shouted in Caydish from the tower. "What are you sheep droppings doing, taking holiday? We're packing to march and here you are not even begun yet!" It was Warlord Prince Melbras himself.

The archers scurried up the stony slope to him, slipping in their anxiety, explaining and contradicting each other in loud agitated tones I took the opportunity to sidle up to the Magus and ask, "What did you do that for?"

"For Your Majesty to fraternize with our people is necessary and right," he said. "But foreigners I think should hold the Shan King at least in respect." He smiled, and smoothed his long white mustaches back. "It's not easy to transmogrify anything into ale. But it was worth it, to see their faces."

"It was very funny," I agreed. "But what will Prince Melbras say?"

"It would be improper to play a joke on the Warlord," the Magus decided. I held out the helm and he passed his wand over it twice to dissolve the illusion. We were just in time, for the Warlord was striding down the slope growling, "Witch, eh? Show me this witch."

I turned, schooling my expression to bland innocence. "Greeting, your Highness. When is your departure scheduled?"

Taken aback he answered, "Tomorrow morning, O King."

Gorst exclaimed, "Warlord, he's a witch! He turned milk into ale!"

In reply I handed Melbras the helm. The Warlord took one look and pushed it under Gorst's nose. "Turd-brain, does this look like ale? You must have taken a blow to the head yesterday!"

The other archers murmured in confusion and once more passed the helm around. "He must have witched it back." "It was ale, wasn't it?" "You saw it plain as I did." "But we didn't *taste* it."

Finding his voice Gorst said, "Sure as my mother bore me, Warlord, it was ale!"

"You milk-mouthed yokels," the Warlord snapped. "Don't you recognize this 'witch'? This is the Shan King, and his Magus; they're all wonder-workers."

The archers fell suddenly silent. Gorst's eyes bulged, as if he had bitten a chunk of ginger by accident. So that they would not be punished for impudence I said, "Your men were just teaching me how to milk a goat. I thought we might do something with these animals, since the Tiyalor won't want them anymore."

"That's not a bad idea," the Prince admitted. "But your people don't know anything about goat-keeping."

"No," I said. "I hoped your Highness would loan me a Caydish goatherd."

"Of course, O King." He poked a big finger into Gorst's belly. "You, you mutton-skull—and you can learn to be a little less gullible about foreigners and their powers, while you're at it."

"But Warlord," Gorst pleaded. "I wanted to go with you and fight the Tiyalor."

Ignoring this the Warlord continued, "And this is yours too." He took the helm and righted it onto Gorst's head. The goat milk splashed over his hair and down his face, dripping off his beard and into the back of his woolen jerkin. The others bellowed with laughter at the sight, and to my surprise the Warlord and even Gorst himself also laughed heartily. The archers shoved and whacked each other to emphasize their delight, and Gorst shook milk out of his hair and shouted, "Then let me give you the embrace of farewell, Prince!" Like a herd of playful colts they all thundered up the hill, chasing each other around boulders and calling names.

The Magus and I looked at each other. "Cayds are odd people," he said at last.

I agreed. "If I did that to a Viridese soldier he'd commit suicide."

Chapter 14: The Work of the Magus

So I settled into the south tower and took Gorst into my service. My guard and staff had the ground floor, and I slept above. After the arrow slits were chinked the thick timber walls were cozier than a tent, and despite the grisly structure outside the door we soon made ourselves at home. In part my content may have been founded on the reinstatement of my daily hot bath. With the help of the guard and lengths of rope, a salvaged copper cauldron was hoisted up the narrow ladder. Hot bathwater was carried up in jugs. That first evening the pleasure, after these many days of cold washcloths, was so great I steeped in the tub until my skin became wrinkly and heat-reddened. At the sight of my head lolling on the cauldron brim Xalan told me I resembled a stewed chicken, and offered to fetch herbs and wild onions to improve the flavor of the broth.

Overriding Xalan's arguments and Prince Melbras' suspicions I laid hands on some of the Caydish wounded that evening, so that they could strengthen the Caydish search expedition. I was careful to pace myself, and not waste energies on wounds I knew were beyond me. The Caydish were both reluctant and eager, and I heard muttered again the epithet "witch." Most, however, were willing to drop their mysterious scruples to gain in exchange the use of legs or arms again, so I decided it was a minor kink of the Caydish mind and gave it no more thought.

The following day the Tiyalor prisoners were released. The morning was bright but windy and cold. Lean gray clouds scudded across a cold blue sky so that the Sun flashed like a guttering lamp. In my plain clothes and the bandage half-hiding a two-day scrub of beard I did not look like a king but I reckoned the Crystal Crown would lend royalty enough. Tiyalor surrender only after being cornered, and many of our prisoners had severe wounds. They were brought or carried out to the open muddy area between the north tower and the remnants of the inmost redoubt while I waited with my gong-bearers just out of view inside the tower door. Outside, my official interpreter stood on a section of log and made the prepared speech in Tiyalene:

"Hear, oh you warriors of Tiyalor, the word of the Shan King of Averidan, Son of the Sun, Child of Fire, Lord of Light.

"Grievously has the evil magus Xerlanthor misled your nation with fables of dominion and temptations of wealth, for he has now brought destruction upon your heads. You had neither the right nor the need to hoard up the river waters. By the laws of both civility and war you have won only a hard death."

When I peeped out of the arrow slit I could see the bearded, carefully impassive faces of our prisoners. But the Crystal Crown on my brow showed me their true hearts. They expected death by torture, which indeed some Tiyalor had received when captured by Cayd in the past, and were sullenly resolved to deny us the pleasure of their agony by dying with fortitude. The interpreter's words had little impact, since they did not admit the justice of our cause. Like the Caydish they believed what could be done was equivalent to what should be done.

"However, because like children you have been led astray by one greater than yourselves, the Shan King is disposed to mercy. You shall return to your homes and never bear arms against Averidan or Cayd again."

At this announcement the Tiyalor shifted and whispered among themselves. Such things are never done in Tiyalor, or Cayd either. From my listening post I felt their bewilderment congeal into suspicion. Either the offer was an opening ploy to tortures more unnaturally subtle than ever heard of, in which case the proper response should be fortitude, or Averidan was a nation of fools, in which case they should swear whatever oaths demanded and then hurry home to join the new assault on us. They would wait and see.

"And in token of this a sign shall be set on you, so that you may know the power of the Shan."

To my disgust and irritation the image of red-hot bronze immediately leaped into many minds. "I think it's going far enough," I told the gong-bearers. "Let's make our entrance."

The gong was not the man-high instrument that usually precedes the Shan King, for it would have been too much labor to drag one up the Tambors. This one was three buckler-sized bronze discs suspended from a pole borne by two men. Smaller chimes hung below and to either side. The whole thing could be dismantled for transport. Now the beater raised his sticks and struck an intricate brazen melody. Xalan came forward with the long green banner of the Shan King, and at my silent command the Crystal Crown flowered into cool white light on my head.

Blue-black shadows instantly flowed out behind everyone's heels, and the gong-beater was so startled he struck several wrong notes. Every joint in the rough stone walls was harshly revealed, and the soldiers and magi shaded their eyes and squinted against the light.

My impressive entrance inspired as much awe as I could wish. Even the Viridese soldiers in charge of the prisoners gaped, and Gorst and some of the other Caydish—these were men the Warlord had deemed not wood-wise enough for a forest hunt—actually fell to their knees. I could sense the Tiyalor were overwhelmed, some in confusion associating my corona with the red-hot bronze they expected, and some exclaiming "Ornast!" which is their name for the Morning Star. Those who were able knelt, and the rest groveled flat on their faces. I picked my way in until I stood among them like the sole survivor of a sudden plague, and said, with due pauses for translation, "The penalty for opposing me has been death, from time out of mind. But because I have had slaughter enough I will remit your blood. And in token of this—"

At my signal my guard came forward. I pointed to a likely-looking Tiyal whose leg was broken in two places, probably in the retreat off the earthworks. Two guardsmen took him under the arms and hauled him up from his prone position. The man was the youngest present, little more than a lad. At the sudden grasp he squealed thin and shrill, involuntarily, like a trapped piglet. In the Crown's perceptive power his fear seemed rank in my nostrils and his humiliating despair wiped the rest of the pompous speech from my mind. My own leg throbbed at ankle and thigh in sympathy, and quickly I bent to put a hand on the fellow's limb. The bones knit at the touch and my guards set him on his feet. The stunned bewilderment on the pink face nearly made me laugh aloud, but I kept him fixed with a solemn stare as he staggered about and tested the leg. I could tell the Tiyalor around us did not understand what had happened. Slowly and loudly I said, "In token of my mercy I have healed your leg. By that limb I now adjure you, go home and tell truly of what befell you when you bore arms against the Shan."

The man was near fainting from terror and awe, I sensed. Also he had stood up too quickly. So leaving him to recover I turned to the others. Around me an unseen sea of emotion roiled and foamed: mostly a teeth-chattering fear of the supernatural, under-shot with suspicion and hatred not only of us but Xerlanthor. They thought me an offended demi-god, and were angry that

Xerlanthor had not thought to warn them of my power. In many minds I sensed a determination forming that next time Xerlanthor wanted to pick quarrels with a divinity he could do so alone.

It took all morning and part of the afternoon to lay hands on everyone, for I did not want to overtax myself. As I progressed the Tiyalor no longer had to be forcibly brought up by my guard but crept forward humbly to be noticed. Those already healed huddled back near the watching soldiers. As I have mentioned, Caydish and Tiyalene are similar, and although I could not understand the whispered Tiyalor questions I did catch some of Gorst's lurid replies. He assured the unfortunate prisoners that I was a witch of the most appalling power, who could pluck out and eat a man's soul easy as licking milk custard from a cup. From my distant mental vantage I heard the fables embroidered and elaborated with unwilling admiration. The fellow was utterly free of any petty convention of truth-telling. He should have been a rhetor. Furthermore I could see the Tiyalor believed every word. Of course Viridese also lie, but at leasst we have institutionalized the vice—in plaiv.

When I was done I signaled to the interpreter, who shouted, "Take warning! Today the Shan King blesses. If he finds you against him ever again, that blessing will become a curse!" The deliberately vague threat—after all I had no intention to seek out and punish the disobedient—was followed by another series of gong strokes. The Viridese and Caydish soldiers reluctantly reformed to allow the prisoners passage. The Tiyalor were at first disposed to suspicion, and in my exhaustion the emotions pricked and fluttered, disjoint, at the edge of my mind: arrows in the back, home! the pleasure of painlessly flexing fingers. I coaxed the Crown to a final intolerable flash of light, and pointed the way. They did not dare turn their backs, but edged shyly down the aisle until they felt clear of my scrutiny. Then they ran. When the last were gone I took off the Crown, returning it to Fisan, and wearily climbed the two ladders to the tower battlement. By the time I got there the Tiyalor had run quite a long way, and in the thin chilly afternoon sunlight the dark-clad figures were barely visible against the pines north and west.

"Lovely bit of work," Xalan congratulated. "By the time they get home you'll be nine feet tall with fangs and claws. Rumor is the best yeast in the world."

"They'll be clemmed," I said, being hungry and cold myself. "We should have given them some food."

"What? Waste good food on a Tiyal?" General Horfal-yu

exclaimed. "Hunger will merely spur them on their journey. We should have lapidated them all."

"Think of the bloodshed and trouble I've saved everyone," I said. I was a little smug, for I had done not only a cunning deed, but a kindly one, entirely consonant with the intentions of the Crown's makers. "I wish I could be there when Xerlanthor tries to recruit a new Tiyal army."

For the next month the magi scried daily, searching systematically through the forests for Xerlanthor. Xalan complained that the images of pine trees had been permanently engraved on the back of his glass. Of course no one now dared use Xerlanthor's own mirror to track him. Only Xorc had really had that skill anyway. The Caydish had no better luck scouring villages and roads, but a small scroll, cut from pliable tree bark and sealed with a dab of pine-pitch, was delivered to us by one of the Sisters. It was from Silverhand, who said they had been questioning stragglers on their way back to Tiyalor. Xerlanthor had certainly survived the fight and was said to be lying low in disguise. So we should beware of strangers, and watch for the geas-laden. At the bottom, writ small, the Commander had added, "Some of the Tiyalor say they are prisoners released by the Shan King. They have many unusual tales."

One notable occurrence about this time was the arrival of a messenger, not one of the military couriers from Zofal at the Tambors but a rhetor all the way from the City. He was a bold, bony fellow, small even for a Viridese, and hid his astonishment at the Shan King's odd appearance under a facade of politesse. In my tower room I had ale served for this rhetor Bochas-hel, and when everyone of importance in camp had assembled I asked, "What news of Averidan?"

In answer he took from his pack a bundle of scrolls wrapped in oiled silk against the wet. I undid the bundle, turning the cylinders to read the red labels on each case and passing them to the appropriate person. As I had expected, there was nothing from Melayne, who could neither read nor write. Yet I was disappointed, and could not help asking, "Is there any token from the Lady of Averidan?"

Though Bochas was on bent knee before me he contrived to bow gracefully, and said, "I suppose, Majesty, I'm the token. The Lady selected me as the messenger because of my newest work, a plaiv on Your Majesty's marriage and war in Cayd."

I sighed and hoped someone had enlightened Melayne about

rhetor narrative conventions. Rhetors are a peculiarly Shan institution—without help she would be lost. While official chronicles embody Viridese history, rhetors dispense plaiv, the vehicles of myth, easily rearranging past and present events to suit their fancy. The constant inflow of fiction has a curious effect even on the chronicles themselves, and indeed the very oldest chronicles all have a sound of plaiv. We all half-know the cold history and half-love the bright myth in plaiv, and sometimes we cannot say which is which. This process was now come to me, as I knew it would someday, and I resigned myself to hear Bochas' plaiv.

"Wouldn't Your Majesty prefer to have your Caydish hosts hear it as well?" he suggested. "Perhaps at dinner."

His opportunism irritated me, and I let him see it. "Everyone Caydish of note has accompanied the Warlord. Furthermore, a tale about me would spoil my appetite."

Chastened, Bochas rose to his feet and began his recital. It was an entirely typical work, grandiose in conception, long on action, short on depth, but I heard the first lines with dismay. The events of my scant year's reign had been recast beyond recognition: the Shan King, to rescue fair Melayne of Cayd, battled an evil magus. Naturally he won. When the nonsense had reeled to a hackneyed happy ending—the King married the Princess, as I recall, and had three sons and a daughter—I exclaimed, "But it wasn't like that at all!"

But my objections went unheard in the general applause. The guards called, "Pung!" which is the proper acclamation to offer rhetors when you don't have money, and General Horfal-yu gave the man the gold-plated brassard off his own arm. Xalan later informed me this was not as extravagant as it looked, since the General had lost its mate in battle. Rhetor Bochas bowed to either side and grinned boldly at me. Smothering my negative reaction I said, "And what did the Lady say to it?"

"The Lady's Viridese was not yet fluent enough for her to grasp all the finer points," Bochas said, "but she enjoys heroic accounts of any sort, we hear."

"Who hears?" I said jealously.

"The rhetors' Guild, Majesty. We perforce keep in touch with the tastes of possible patrons."

He smiled again but I refused to take notice of the hint. "See to it that your plaiv in Ieor are of older vintage," I commanded.

Later Xalan asked, "You don't like plaiv?"

"I enjoy them tremendously," I said. "But when they're

about me it makes me worry my memory is unreliable. Doesn't it confuse you?''

"Not at all," he said. "You're over-sensitive."

The herbals worried over my face-cut and insisted on anointing and rebandaging twice a day. "Even so," the Mistress Herbal said, "there'll be a scar." What I thought was a very fair crop of dark beard had developed and stuck unevenly out from under the bandage that encircled my head and chin. It was a shock one day to glance into Xalan's mirror as he was closing it up and see that I resembled an alley cat with a bad case of mange. Every day I saw so many magnificent beards among the Caydish that I had forgot most Viridese are not gifted with abundant body hair.

"How does everyone keep from laughing aloud at the sight of me?" I asked Xalan. "No wonder the rhetor stared."

Xalan took the glass I returned to him and said, "Well, we've had a chance to get used to the sight of you. And it would be impolite to guffaw."

"Alas, the Mistress won't let me shave yet." I fingered the thin, ragged black fringe on my chin and began to laugh " 'This goat is insufficiently hairy.' "

The geomants selected a clear day following a week of snow and rain for their attempt at shaking the dam apart. "That is so that the planes of earth will be well moistened," I was informed.

"I would have thought rain would make them heavy enough to stick together," I suggested.

Only Xalan was bold enough to hoot at this idea. The other geomants gathered on the dam kept serious faces, and one politely said, "Such matters must be studied for many years, Majesty. It is our honor to apply our learning in your service."

For safety's sake the General and I had moved out of our respective towers. Working up such a major quake would take all day, and they say it is unlucky to get in the way of magic works. So to pass the time usefully I inspected the redug inner earthwork. The General had incorporated all the latest tactical improvements, and I walked on neat timber trestles covering clay drainage ditches. Each man stood on or near his own handiwork, and I wished I had Sandcomber with me to invent endless flowery compliments for log supports and earthen walls.

When I returned to the river bank there was an indefinable change in the air. Some of the magi had moved off onto either bank, and some stood spaced irregularly on the dam itself. I knew each geomant stood above an unseen current of force deep in the earth, ready to twist them in the hard, sudden wrench that would drag the dam's foundations out. From where I stood upstream on the lake shore, only their red robes proclaimed their Order. I could not see the black stone wands I knew were clenched in their right hands, ready to strike the earth.

Behind me Fisan-shi asked, "When will it be, Liras?"

"I don't know," I said. "But surely not until the rest of the magi move off the dam." We settled down to wait. The lake shore was muddy, and we perched on logs and camp chairs near a pine wood on a hill above the gorge, well upstream. Dreary leaden skies glowered over us, and the wind mourned in the pines. It seemed that winter is eternal in Cayd. No fire or brazier could be lit, for heat might affect the course of the geomancy. So blankets and furs had been brought, and also food and skins of ale so that we should not be dry or hungry.

Gorst's flocks had been penned safely out of range, and he sat with us, smelling a little goaty. "I don't know where you find these people, Liras," Fisan said to me in Viridese. "Are you going to bring him back home too?"

"There's an idea," I grinned, picturing Yibor-soo's expression. "You remind me, I ought to write home." Couriers had been going back and forth, and one was to leave for Averidan tonight bearing news of the geomancy. If I wrote a letter today it could reach Zofal-ven in two days, Mother and Siril-ven in four. Calling for my scrivener I borrowed from him writing tools. I had filled two panels before Gorst asked me, "What spell do you work?"

I spent a long while explaining the idea of writing to him but in the end I think he grasped only the idea that I was conversing with those far away. It did not take much effort to maintain my reputation for witchery in Cayd.

I had directed that Melayne should be taught to read but even she would hardly have made much progress yet. So I could not write her, and cast about for a gift to send instead. Then a thought came to me, and turning to Gorst I asked, "How long do those cheese keep, the round goats-milk cheese they carry in string nets?"

"You should ask a farmwife that, O King," Gorst complained. "I don't know. But they're smoked in the fall to keep them sweet and we eat them all winter long."

"Then they would keep a week. Find me three or four of them today."

"You won't be able to eat more than one," he warned me, but I didn't want to explain and sent him off with a note to the cooks.

The magi had all left the dam now. Here and there on the downstream banks to either side we could see the red robes bright against rock or earth or yellow grass. Very slowly, feeling for the currents, they paced away from what would be the heart of the quake. When they stopped I knew the moment was at hand. "Everyone sit down," I commanded "The quake is coming. General, you'll want to set that aleskin down."

"Shall we feel it here?" Fisan asked.

"Probably not, but you never know."

There was a long suspenseful interval. We watched intently, straining our eyes to catch the descent of the stone wands. No one spoke, so that the birds in the grove behind us took courage in the silence and began their small conversations again. Then I saw an almost imperceptible movement of the red figures. The response was out of all proportion with that tiny gesture: the earth on both banks heaved and twitched, like the hide of a gigantic horse plagued by flies. Trees waved their tops but did not fall, and a cloud of birds rose up from either side, their complaints shrill and faint in the distance. Yet the earthquake was so perfectly focused that upstream we felt nothing.

But although the banks and the bed of the river itself writhed in torment, and red-ocher ripples chased themselves round and round the narrow lake, and stones fell into the gorge, the dam did not break. The rough-hewn gray stones shifted and moved in their places, balancing themselves against the surge. The structure as a whole seemed bound together by its mortar, as teeth are by their gums. Twisting and bucking, riding the shock, the dam was whole as ever.

"I don't believe it," the General declared.

"It's Xerlanthor's magery," Fisan said. "Not even all our own magi can best him."

"Please don't say that to the Master Magus," I said. I stood up. The earth-tremors had died away, and the tiny red-clad figures were clustering together to discuss the problem. "That's all for today," I announced. "Let's go back."

"But what will happen, what shall we do?" the General sputtered.

"There's only one solution now," I said. "To track Xerlanthor down, and twist the secret of the dam out of him."

Chapter 15: Fire and Water

After the stray livestock had been rounded up and penned by Gorst I suggested that since Viridese don't drink milk the sheep and goats be slaughtered one by one and roasted.

"That's madness, O King," Gorst said, scorn and respect in his tone. "The ewes are almost ready to drop their lambs! It would be a wicked waste. And most of these goats are too old to be toothsome, even if you stew them a week. I'll cull out the youngest for you, but that's all."

Like most Caydish farmers he was a good herdsman, grumbling over the little flocks like an enormous yellow cat with kittens. So I gave way, and in the weeks that followed learned a great deal about livestock. Gorst had whittled himself a tall shepherd's staff, deeply hooked at the top, and with it he snared and held sheep by one leg so I could learn to evaluate the thickness of the fleece. I knew nothing about it, but tried to ask intelligent questions.

That day I asked, "Does it hurt the sheep to lose its wool?

"Only when the shears nick them," Gorst assured me. "A low-lander would ask such a question! They leap for joy to be free of the weight, in the summer heats."

It was a cold, foggy day, and we had to stand behind boulders to hide from the wind. A fine misty rain, not quite snow, fell invisibly to spangle the sheep and the grass and our cloaks with cold droplets. Summer heat seemed distant as a dream upon waking. I said, "When will the lambs be born?"

"Any day now. Look at this one, you can tell by her flanks she's almost ready. Either twins or a very big single lamb." The yellow brows knotted together and I saw a glint of blue as he glanced sideways at me. "I don't suppose the witchery could tell you which it will be?"

"Of course not."

"But you're the Witch-King," he said, a little disappointed. "Haven't you been learning Caydish spells? What did you want the cheeses for, otherwise?"

I had not heard my new title before, but I wasn't really

interested in gloomy Caydish superstition. The edges of my wool jerkin were soaking up so much damp that the sleeves flapped clammy against my wrists. I suggested, "Let's go in, it must be lunch time."

"For such little people, you eat very often," Gorst said, but without malice.

"You enjoy it as much as we," I said, and indeed meals are far more regular with the Shan than with Melbras' expedition.

The pines to the south were fleecy in curds of thick white mist. No sound carried through the cloak of moisture. Among the wind-raveled streamers of fog we and the sheep seemed to be the only living creatures in Ieor. As we clambered up the stony hill ice gleamed between the yellow grass tufts, so that we had to choose our footing carefully. The sheep would not follow us, but huddled together in the shelter of the valley. So we were startled when a shrill, cracked voice spoke to us suddenly out of the fog. "Shepherds, what place is this?" it asked in Caydish.

I jumped, and Gorst brought his crook to bear, stepping between me and the speaker. "Who are you," he demanded, "a rock troll?"

"No, no!" The speaker moved closer, and I saw that what we had taken in the mist for another boulder was a hooded and cloaked old man, bent nearly double with years and toil. He was dressed much as we were, in dark Caydish style, and leaned on a wooden cane carved with twining vines. "An old man only, no danger to hearty fellows such as yourselves."

I did not care for his slyly humble manner, but there was certainly no harm in him. He looked at least eighty years old, frail and brittle as last year's leaves. I said, "You are in Ieor, not far from the dam across Mhesan built by the mage Xerlanthor. It is now held by the forces of Averidan and Cayd. What business do you have in these parts? It is no season to be traveling for pleasure."

The oldster cackled at this. "Nor would I, whatever the season! Old bones are meant to rest, not labor up hills and through forests with messages for the Shan King!"

I became acutely conscious of our solitude, here at the north end of the farthest sheep pen. If this were a geas-ridden assassin no help was even within shout. The fog would hide everything. But on the other hand Gorst towered head and shoulder over the old man, and could no doubt crush him in a moment. "You have a message?" I asked. "Deliver it."

"No, no." The old man shook his head slowly, a cunning

gleam in his watery blue eye. He patted the enormous greasy leather bag slung over his shoulder. "What would they say of me, if I gave a king's message to a shepherd lad?"

His smug assumption was a relief. Obviously I was not to be waylaid and murdered today, since he did not recognize me. Back in camp if he had geas he could be dealt with. I elbowed Gorst in the ribs to keep him quiet, and said, "Then let us lead you to the King, old father."

We set off up the hill. Through clearings in the wooly fog a bright red-orange gleam flickered above and to our right—the brazier of the watchman at the top of the south tower. The old man made quite a business of the climb, grumbling about the trampled slippery snow and leaning heavily on his cane. When I made to take his arm to help him over a ravine he started and hit out feebly at me with the cane. So I let him be. I remembered the Caydish woman who had sent the Shan King a cheese, and resolved not to tell him my rank but to let someone of sufficient authority, General Horfal-yu perhaps, take the messages. Otherwise the surprise revelation might startle such an elderly man to his death.

The narrow pasture rose ever steeper until it ended in a low stony cliff. At the top Gorst had built a rough wall of loose-piled stone to keep the sheep in. After that the slope was gentler and less rocky. The pasture was a little upstream of the dam on the southern bank, and when we came to the top of the ridge the sullen red lake was visible beyond the mists. Out of the hill's shelter the wind drove fine rain deep into the weave of our clothes. At the sight of the lake the old man mumbled, "No, Ieor wasn't like this in my day! A lake! Sheep pasture only, it was in my youth!"

"It will be again," I promised, but he mumbled the words over and over into his straggling gray beard. "How far have you come?" I asked. "Who sent you?" But the old man seemed genuinely in fear, and would say only, "It wasn't like this in my day."

"I recollect last year, when the Warlord won his first victory," Gorst reflected. "I'd never even seen the King's house in Lanach. I joined the army on its way here. The sight of this thing—" He nodded toward the dam. "We were knocked all of a heap. It was so big—we didn't know people could *build* that big. All of us thought this Xerlanthor must be big as a pine tree, lackeyed by ghosts, and powerful as a lightning bolt. That was how he got away, that first time we beat him—we were all looking for a demon. When we actually had him in hand no one believed it.''

"Too bad," I said. There had been no word of Xerlanthor in all this time, and we feared he might be dead, of fever in some woodland hole, or eaten by wolves.

When we came to the tower I had Gorst keep the old man in the lower room while I climbed up the ladder, ostensibly to fetch the Shan King. The wooden floor above creaked and moaned under my weight. Neither tower had been shaken down by the geomants' quake, but every joint and peg had been loosened so that on a windy day the upper floors swayed and complained like a drunk man. At the sound of my step Xalan looked up from the scroll in his lap.

"Here he is, ask the linguist," he said to Fisan-shi.

"Oh, Liras-ven," she cried. "What is the Caydish for 'left side'?''

I told her the phrase, adding, "What do you need to know for?''

"The Commander told me to check over the Sisters' climbing gear," she said. "So I told the servant to oil all the boots, but when I looked in on him all the left boots were gone!''

The image of an army's worth of right boots was comic, but seeing her genuine distress I did not laugh. I said, "You'd better let me ask the man, I'm sure there's a reasonable explanation.''

Xalan spun the scroll tight between his palms and slid it into its red case. "These things aren't very helpful," he complained, and then began to laugh "What did the Lady say of them?''

"Thank the One, she couldn't read them," I said. "Did you bring the Crown, Fisan? There's a messenger here I want to read for geas.''

"Right there," she said, pointing to the casket in the corner. "Who is the message from?''

The creaking of ladder and floor ought to have warned of anyone's approach. But without any noise at all a blast of scarlet light fountained from the ladder's corner, blinding all three of us. We fell back dazzled as a smooth voice answered Fisan: "From the Magus Xerlanthor, little maiden, to the Shan King!''

The ferocious red glare faded quickly but our vision was slower to recover. Through burning watering eyes I dimly saw our assailant float up off the ladder to alight in the middle of the room. I could hear him stride across the creaking floor, unerringly to my pack, and the clink of the buckles. "How kind of his Shan Majesty to bring my much-traveled mirror back to me!

These are his rooms, of course?'' No one spoke, and he commanded, ''Answer me!''

As my eyes cleared I made out a small, lean man of Viridese race. Although his sardonic face was smooth and proud, his hair dark under the hat, I recognized the Caydish clothes, the staff carved with twining vines in his right hand—a pirolurge's staff. ''You're the old man, the messenger!'' I exclaimed.

''Very perceptive, shepherd.'' With his free hand he grasped my hair at the crown and waggled my head around to face him. ''Now, I asked, these are the Shan King's rooms, yes?''

I called to mind the Sisterhood's combat precepts and prepared to kick the staff out of his hand. But Xerlanthor had some magery I had never seen. A white jewel set in the head of his wand glowed white, and I could move neither hand nor foot. It was as if I had been wrapped and baked in clay, and a sweat of supernatural terror chilled my forehead. Only my facial muscles obeyed me, I suppose so that I could speak. I rolled my eyes to glimpse Fisan and Xalan. Fisan was frozen with shock, but Xalan grasped the situation immediately and said, in exactly the right lordly tone, ''The only topic that one knows is his sheep. These are the Shan King's rooms, but you must be mad to come here! Guards!''

But even as he shouted Xerlanthor released both his hold and his magery on me, and turned to take Xalan by the throat. ''None of that now,'' he said. ''I'm particularly anxious to meet His Shan Majesty. One gets so tired of hobnobbing with minor Caydish princelets. We have many subjects of mutual interest to discuss. Don't think I haven't appreciated his malign influence on my Tiyalor friends. We're almost destined to meet, wouldn't you say?'' His courtesy was a horrible contrast to his actions. The jewel in his wand shone like a tiny star as he waved it before Xalan's purpling face. There was something familiar about that glow, and also about Xerlanthor's voice, but I had no time to cudgel my memory. For Xerlanthor was saying, ''You are new since my time, young Magus, but you must be one of the King's friends since you have the run of his chambers. So tell me, where is he? When will he be back?''

''Renegade,'' Xalan choked, and then was silent again as Xerlanthor squeezed his windpipe.

''I supposed for efficiency's sake I ought to lay geas on you to go and lure him to me,'' Xerlanthor mused. ''But I've perfected a few impressive tricks with my toy, here.'' He waved the wand in a circular gesture. ''I haven't had a chance to show anybody.

You'd be a perfect subject—knowledgeable, able to appreciate the finer points. And you'll find me very persuasive. Just nod when you're ready to be informative, will you? I need both hands for this stunt, so you'll pardon me if for now I paralyze your tongue as well as your legs." He released Xalan's throat and stepped back. Xalan slumped in the camp chair like a dead thing. Only his eyes were alive, gleaming at me and then to the double door opening onto the dam.

The white gem flickered as Xerlanthor swung the wand back and then forward again. No blow was struck, but Xalan's arm jerked and sagged. The magery would not let him speak but he gasped with the shock. I saw that there was a new bend between elbow and shoulder—the bone had been snapped.

"The Order taught me, as I'm sure they taught you, that there are 365 bones in the human frame—one for each day of the year," Xerlanthor said. "As in so many other areas, they were wrong. I only counted 206 myself, in the skeleton of a Caydish archer last winter. I'm sure you won't force me to work through all 206 of yours. So, tell me—where may I find the Shan King?"

The Sisterhood of Mir-hel trains its novices to practice total awareness. A Sister never overlooks a foe in the most confusing battle, or gets taken by surprise. Xerlanthor had obviously never learned this art. As he focused his magery to break another bone he seemed to forget Fisan and me. I leaned near her ear and whispered, "Only the Master Magus can defeat him. Do you know where he is?"

She nodded. Gently I edged to the double doors, and lifted the latch. But she held my arm for a moment and bent softly to pick up the casket of the Crown. I tucked it under my arm and breathed, "Ready?"

Even as I whipped the door open she was running. We dodged across the causeway as fast as we could, and the misty rain hid us. But in the empty north tower chamber I stopped.

"Oh, hurry, Liras!" Already she was lowering herself down the ladder.

"He knows we recognize him," I said. "He'll escape. He'll kill Xalan."

"That's why we have to hurry," she said impatiently. Only her head stuck above the floorboards now. "Come on!"

"I have to go back," I said.

"What!"

"It's safe enough," I told her, setting down the casket. "I

have the most powerful weapon in the world here. Now I've learned the trick of it I can beat Xerlanthor.''

"You're crazy," she said.

"Hurry and fetch the Magus," I commanded, and to forestall further argument put the Crown on and turned back.

My only fear at this point was that Xerlanthor would see or hear me return. I watched for him to appear at the south tower's door, which still swung ajar, and ran. To my surprise when I dodged to crouch behind the closed half of the double doors I could hear him, smooth and polite as ever, saying, "Now this bone is a rather important one. Your pelvis, you know, holds your legs to the rest of you. In my experience a broken pelvis never mends. One simply gives up walking, copulating, and so forth.''

Sickened, I called silently on the Crown. "Quickly! he deserves it, and I accept the pain of his death. Quick, before he kills Xalan!''

"But remember, there is a third condition," the Crown's beautiful voice said. "Your own life is not at stake.''

"Don't be silly, of course it is!" I exclaimed. "Can't you hear him trying to find out where I am? What do you think he wants me for, a dinner party?''

The Crown did not reply. Inside I could hear Xerlanthor lost in a digression: "But, you may ask, is there not more to life than locomotion and sex? At least eating should be included. And drink, no Shan would exclude that. You've no idea how I've missed the good wines of Averidan. All this ale, thin as urine— give me red wine, the blood of Viridese grapes. Yes, drink, definitely. . . .''

In my fury of frustration I could have pounded the Crown into powder. Xalan was the first friend I had made as Shan King, and the most faithful. He supported me even in my follies. If I let him die now, not ten feet away, I would never forgive the Crown or myself. Keeping my head low I peered into the room, but could see only my armor, wrapped in oiled silk against the damp, and leaning on the wall behind the javelin of the Tiyal I had killed the day of the battle. At the sight of it a new and horrid idea took shape in my mind. If I grabbed that spear and threw it at Xerlanthor I might kill him. Or I might not, and he would turn to kill me. But then the Crystal Crown would save me in a flash of fire. It would be easy, and safe . . . almost. I knew now the truth of what Silverhand had said, in my garden so long ago: Xerlanthor was no common foe. His magery was of a power unheard of in the magic circles of Averidan. He might well be able to best even the Crystal Crown.

I set my teeth. It was a gamble. But now I called on the betting streak all Viridese possess. To wager my life was only increasing the stake. From within I heard Xerlanthor working up his final oration. "But if you persist in intransigence you won't be able to enjoy any of these good things, will you? Keep in mind that the Shan King will sooner or later return . . ."

Making a flat dive through the open door I rolled over the bundle of armor with one shoulder, snatched up the javelin, and threw in one movement. At this range even I could hardly miss. The bronze point took Xerlanthor full in the chest as he whirled to face me. To my dismay the javelin rebounded harmlessly—he wore armor beneath his tunic. I shouted, "You seek the Shan King, Xerlanthor? Know me, then!"

Xerlanthor's face was suffused with astonishment, but he made as if to raise the wand. Behind him Xalan had slid off his chair and lay crumpled on the floor. I pointed at him and felt the power of the Crystal Crown surge up with the fury in me, inexorable as the incoming tide.

But even as I was about to stab my power into him Xerlanthor dropped his wand and snatched at his big leather shoulder satchel. "Haven't you heard," he exclaimed, "that it's unlucky to meddle in the works of magi?" Before I could dodge he threw the satchel's flap back and flung the contents at me. Soft slushy snow hit me full in the face. I gasped and staggered back with more than surprise. The sudden cold struck at the union between the Crown and my mind. The hot, righteous power melted away faster than grease in a hot skillet, and icicles of pain drove like spikes into my temples. I reeled back against the wall, fire swimming in my eyes. Even as I stumbled the wand was in Xerlanthor's hand again, glowing with the magery to keep me pinned. Dimly through the roaring haze I recognized at last the white gem at the tip. It was the same color and light as the Crystal Crown itself.

"Well, well! How very unobservant of me!" The voice above me was now genially triumphant. "Even now I wouldn't have believed the Shan King could present such a scruffy appearance. But the Crystal Crown can only be worn by one, and after all my call took you unprepared."

A tremendous yet invisible weight sat on my chest, crushing me to the floor. The tendons and cartilage of my limbs screamed in anguish. Every breath was a rib-creaking effort, and I found I

could get enough air only by panting in short gasps. When
Xerlanthor took me under the arms and hauled me up to sit
propped against the wall the shift nearly cracked my heart. Cold
sweat ran down my face to soak the high neck of my jerkin. The
Crown was deathly silent on my brow, and Xerlanthor ensured
its continued emptiness by balancing his satchel with its remain-
ing slush on my head and shoulders.

"Lovely, perfect! Now we can talk in peace. I hope that
posture isn't as uncomfortable as it looks, but there are some
advantages in it for me. You recognize this, of course?"

The cruel dark eyes smiled not a foot from my own, while the
jewel tip of his wand shifted and shone between us. With an
effort I kept my eyes focused on his face rather than the wand,
so that he should not have the petty satisfaction of seeing my
eyes cross. I had gambled and lost. It was no longer a question
of knowing the worst—the worst held a crushing hold on my
ribs, bent laughing over my pain. Now the same dour defiance I
had read in the Tiyalor prisoners smoldered in me. He had won,
but would get as little out of the victory as I could contrive, if I
died for it.

"The very same material as your own Crystal Crown, you
want to say? Pardon me for conducting both sides of our
conversation, but I never underestimate an enemy but once." He
stood, pushing Xalan to one side with his foot so that he had
room to pace back and forth. "My story begins—oh, don't fear,
I'm not going to say, 'when I was born'! It begins when I left
Averidan to journey up the Mhesan to the Tiyalene Sea. A vile
trek, you say, why did I undertake such an arduous expedition?
Well, you should know that I have had an abiding fascination
with your Crystal Crown. In fact, my tragedy may be rooted in
the fact that the Collegium of the King's Counselors selected
your predecessor, Shan Eisen, instead of me, when they chose
the Shan King."

I wished they had, so that the Crown could have assayed him,
found him wanting, and fried his brains. But he continued, "As
you no doubt have experienced, the Shan King keeps his Crown
very close. I could not come at it, either through the King or
through the Order of Magi. So I turned to research delving into
the archives to learn how the Crystal Crown had been made."

Out of the corner of my eye I saw a movement. Someone was
coming up the ladder. Xerlanthor saw him also and waved the
wand in a casual gesture, stepping forward. It was Ranoc, my
guardsman. I could neither speak nor move to warn him, but to

my surprise Xerlanthor spoke first, in a cracked voice: "I've been waiting for the Shan King this long time now. If he isn't here I'll go find him."

Ranoc said, "He was right here. Gorst said so. Rest yourself, old man, he'll be back soon. If we see him on the north side I'll tell him you wait." He looked around the room but his eye passed right over Xalan and me. He went out the double door and was gone. Xerlanthor had moved to keep between him and us, and now tidily shut the door after him.

I suppose despair showed in my face, for he chuckled and said, "Really, the Crown is wasted on you. Look at how much I've done with my speck, in such a short time. You didn't know about how to deceive the eye of a watcher? No? Much easier to handle than a wig, or some such disguise . . . where was I? Ah, yes, how Shan Xao-lan made the Crystal Crown. The source of this stuff—" He tapped the Crown on my head with his wand. "—is not recorded, in chronicle or plaiv. Wherever Shan Xao-lan got it, I would suspect there is no more in existence today. But as its latter-day discoverer I have provisionally named the substance 'phlogiston.' Most of the phlogiston in the world, I postulate, was made into the Crown. But a piece was left over."

He almost skipped with delight at his own words. I wondered if he had confided this to anyone else under the Sun. It did not seem likely I would enjoy my exclusive knowledge long. "Now, where was this leftover phlogiston? Shan Xao-lan had disposed of it in the safest, most remote spot he knew—the Tiyalene Sea. So there I journeyed with nought but my wand and my mirror." He had set the round covered mirror on the table, and now patted it fondly. "I spent a year scrying the sea bottom, searching for any trace of the phlogiston. For I knew such a deeply magic substance could not be forever lost. But I found nothing, and nearly despaired. At last it came to me as in a dream what had happened. The phlogiston, immersed for more than ten thousand years, had dissolved."

He pointed at me. "Did I surrender? I did not! I realized that what is dissolved may be distilled back again, as salt is evaporated back out of sea water. It was then that I conceived the idea of boiling, to gather together the tiny atomies of phlogiston. Why the dam then, you say? Why not just dip the lake or river water out and boil it down? Do you know how long it would take to get anywhere, kettleful by kettleful? No, I see you don't. I did the calculation. Suffice it to say that no one lives so long! I needed help. So I contracted with the King of Tiyalor, to trade

him the labor of his people for conquest of Cayd. All this—"
He waved the wand toward the dam. "All this is incidental to
my real work. Almost two years' worth of boiling by nearly the
entire population of Tiyalor got me this little flyspeck of phlogiston.
I immediately began experiments. And I learned many things
which you, young king, never dreamed of."

The speck of phlogiston twinkled merrily at the end of his
wand. "For instance, do you know we've met before? No? Cast
your recollection back, Shan King, to your first night in Cayd.
What an opportunity I missed then! I should have had your neck
broken right away."

For a moment he seemed quite cross. In despair I recognized
now the smooth voice I had battled in the snow outside the
King's hall in Lanach. "Of course I had to try and get my mirror
back. But when I saw you and your Crown I realized my
incredible good fortune. Instead of dealing in specks of phlogiston I would simply steal the largest specimen in existence from
you."

Now indeed if I could have spared the breath I would have
wept. With great labor and care I had brought the greatest and
oldest treasure of Averidan, the heart of the realm, right into the
hand of the foe. But Xerlanthor continued, "The core of my
discoveries is the power phlogiston has on living matter—one
can fool the eye, break or mend a bone, and so on. To cause a
hiccup in you that night was a little delicate, but quite feasible.
Because my bit of phlogiston was so small—I've added to it a
little since then—I had to heat it quite hot to realize its full
power. Foolishly, I thought a compartment under a crock of
coals would be safe and warm enough. You have no idea the
pleasure it gives me, to turn your snowball trick back on you!"

The hatred, so long veiled by sardonic courtesy, was naked
now in his voice. I thought he would strike me, but thinking
better of his dignity he said, "You'll be a perfect pass to safety
for me, under the proper geas. I've never laid geas on a king
before, it will be fun to be served by royalty. I don't really want
to deal with the spirit Shan Xao-lan built into the Crown, so after
we get home I'll take the Crown apart. . . ." And I knew he
would have no reason to keep me alive after that.

Suddenly he was all business. He had gloated enough. "Close
your eyes," he said. "The geas will sit easier on you that way."
I was certain my comfort was not foremost in his thought, and
stubbornly kept my eyes wide open. I had nothing to lose
anymore. Seeing this he said, "Have it your own way, then. It's

the last time you will." He took a handful of powder from his belt-pouch and threw it into the coals of the brazier beside me. A stupefying cloud of bluish smoke rose up. Raising his wand he began to mutter the formula. The cloying drugged smoke made my eyes water. I held my breath as long as I could. I knew I was lost, but doggedly refused to give in.

But my head was bursting, and my lungs ached for air. With a sobbing gasp I exhaled, and drew in the blue vapor Xerlanthor fanned into my face. Instantly haloes of strange color glimmered around the arrowslits and braziers. My head seemed to float on Xerlanthor's chanted spell. The sparkling jewel on his wand, surrounded by ghastly rainbows, hovered over my head, preparing to descend and seal the geas.

I saw but could no longer grasp the appearance of a new light and halo around the door. Only when the Master Magus entered and kicked the brazier over to scatter the coals did I understand.

"Now, renegade," the Magus thundered. "Yield yourself up."

"Xantallon, how nice to see you again," Xerlanthor exclaimed, his voice suave but wary. "You may have heard I've been exploring the further ranges of pyrolurgy." Again the red light flamed, from his wand to the palm of his left hand and then straight at the Magus.

The Magus dodged the bolt and pointed his own glass wand not at Xerlanthor but at the door. It was ajar but swung wide open as three tall forms shouldered in. Their heads and bodies were globular, red-brown and quivery like meat jelly, and their stubby arms had round elbows and round hands. The Magus had animated the lake water to do battle for him. Xerlanthor shot another handful of light at the first globular warrior. It hit in what would have been the abdomen of a human, and for a moment there were two globes of murky water one above the other. Then the globes ran together again, as droplets of mercury do. Xerlanthor cursed and took up a chair. The bigger missile broke the water-warrior into lumps of ruddy water that rolled themselves together again more slowly. The other two rolled closer on their round feet, trying to embrace Xerlanthor between them. If they could envelop him he would drown in their conjoined bodies. I saw the fight would be a near thing.

All Xerlanthor's energies were now turned against the Master Magus. The terrible weight on my chest was lifted, and I found I could move again. The satchel of snow water fell from my head with a splash as I rolled to my hands and knees and crawled to the door. Cold clean air whistled outside, and I collapsed onto the dry-stone pavement, breathing slow and deep to rinse the drugging smoke from my lungs. My sodden woolen jerkin flopped icy against my chest at every gasp.

Fog hid the northern shore so that only the top of the north tower showed. Low clouds veiled the Mhesan to east and west. I could not have been more alone on a solitary mountain peak. The Crystal Crown was cold and silent on my brow, and I feared the spirit of knowledge imbuing it had been destroyed or driven off. The emptiness where there had been life was peculiarly devastating, as if a large and gracious mansion had been sacked and put to the torch. Not until I had lost its shield did I realize how deeply my mettle had been rooted in a confidence that the Crystal Crown was mine. I had been borne on its power as I had been on Piril's back, or on the battle skill of the soldiers and Sisters. But the masque was over, and bereft of my borrowed finery I had to face an enemy in nakedness. Now I had to go back inside, help the Master Magus defeat Xerlanthor, with nothing but what was in me.

Silverhand's words came again to me, that courage could be learned. Shivering, I defied my own fear, repeating the resolution aloud: "I am going to be brave." But it was hard, the hardest thing I had ever done, to turn again to the door.

The room was hot as an oven. The spilled coals, and Xerlanthor's fire-bolts, had ignited the straw stuffed into the arrow slits, and flame had spread to the timber framing. Reeking black smoke obscured everything. If Xerlanthor could heat the air sufficiently the water-warriors would evaporate, pass out of the Magus' hydromantic control. From above I could hear the man on watch yell, "Fire! Fire! Help!" But to forestall interruption Xerlanthor had seared away both ladders. The man was trapped. The Master Magus was trying to draw more water up from the lake but that and the management of the water-warriors was straining his power. I crept behind the overturned table and took up the leather satchel to smother out the nearest flame.

Xerlanthor had to win quickly and escape before the guards below found a way up. Changing tactics, he raised his wand to cast not fire but deception, and stepped softly past the water-warriors who now battled an illusory foe. As soon as he was clear Xerlanthor raised the wooden wand to blast the Master Magus from the flank.

Peering past the table I saw his intention, and groped for a weapon. The table itself was too heavy for me to hurl, and the wreckage of the chairs was beyond reach. But fallen from the table was Xerlanthor's mirror, still in its case. I snatched it up.

It was hot to the touch, and on impulse I slid the bronze cover off, still careful not to glance into the thick glass. I had meant to throw the mirror between the magi and reflect Xerlanthor's bolt back at him—just the sort of thing a hero in plaiv would do. But as I threw my free hand came to rest on a bit of burning wood. With a yelp of pain I jerked off balance. The mirror flew high into the smoky air just as Xerlanthor poured bloody light from his wand into his other hand. With a sound of log striking log the mirror fell solidly onto Xerlanthor's head.

The peak of a magus cap would have turned the blow. But the thick felted hats of the Caydish were no protection. Xerlanthor staggered and stared around. The mirror bounced to the floor and broke. Seeing this he screamed, "May Ixfel eat you!" and leaped at me. Too late he brought his wand to bear, for the water-warriors had gathered around him. They seemed to join hands, circling Xerlanthor like children at play. Then they flowed into each other, and Xerlanthor was engulfed in an enormous bubble of ruddy lake water.

It took him a long time to drown, bobbing there in the middle of the burning room, but the Master Magus strengthened the skin of the bubble so that Xerlanthor could not break through it to get air. His fists hammered at the rubbery skin, weaker and weaker, and his face showed bluish where he pressed it close to mouth curses or pleas. At last he was still, twisting over slowly only with the forces that suspended the water-globe in mid-air. The crackle of hungry flame was the only sound, for neither the Magus nor I could speak. I wondered after if Xerlanthor had heard it, the last sound of his life, through the water.

The Magus was the first to recover. He went to the roof-hole and shouted, "Watchman! You, up there!" The man called something in answer, and the Magus replied, "The ladder is gone, can you jump? I can catch you." At his glass wand's gesture the great globe of lake water divided again, the greater portion bearing Xerlanthor's corpse out the door while the other bobbed over to the roof-hole. When the man at the Magus' urging leaped the globe moved to break his fall. "I am too weary to quench the fire," the Magus coughed. "Let us take what we can of Your Majesty's gear, and go."

I had already wrapped Xalan in a fur cloak. While the dripping watchman carried him out onto the dam I took up my sword and armor, and some bedding, the Magus called to those below to flee. We left just as the floorboards caught.

The bobbling globe collapsed when we got out onto the dam, the water leaking away to leave Xerlanthor's sodden corpse on the pavement. Those on the north bank had noticed the smoke and flame and now approached. The Magus sat panting on the parapet and wiped smoky grit from his face. General Horfal-yu turned the body over. "My dear Magus, what a tremendous feat! You've quite wiped the Army's eye, and the Sisterhood's too!"

The Magus replied, "Without the assistance of His Majesty we should have been lost. A brilliant magus, but immoderate."

We sat exhausted in the drizzle and watched the fire burn itself out. On the south bank we could see my guardsmen and Gorst's taller form. As I sat in the sweet cool rain and sucked the burnt spot on my palm a feeling of detachment came over me, as if this violent fulfillment of our long journey had happened generations ago, to a quaint and foreign people, preserved now only in the stilted illustrations to a folk tale. The dust of crumbling parchment was sour in my nose, and the stained yellow scrolls with their faded tints and spidery characters were brittle and dry in my hands. Closing my eyes I said, "Welcome back."

The voice behind and above my nose was shyly apologetic, as if it were not used to being caught off guard. "Cold is the only weakness," it said. "That is why the Navel Room was built, as a collector of the Sun's warmth."

"We'll avoid these chilly western climes in the future if we can," I promised. "But now we have work."

Xalan had been carried to the north tower. When I entered the Master Bonesetter was examining him and the herbals were brewing a pain-draught. "How is he?" I asked them.

"The young magus will mend," the Master told me. "His back isn't broken. But if magic fractures are like others he'll be bedridden for many months."

"We can't have that," I said.

They had straightened and set each limb so that Xalan no longer resembled a smashed toy. Although his skin was unbroken each place where a bone had been snapped was livid with a swollen bruise. Even after my touch smoothed and joined the fracture beneath, the purple-black mark remained, and when Xalan came to his senses midway through he criticized this failure.

"And it still hurts, too, the bruises I mean," he panted.

"What does it feel like when I mend the bone?" I asked. I had always wanted to know but had been too shy to ask.

"Unpleasant," Xalan said. "A shivery feeling, like the air just before a thunderstorm."

"Stop a moment, Majesty," the herbal commanded, "while he drinks this."

Xalan blew on the hot herbal brew and made a fantastic face at the smell, but the herbal held the wooden cup close to his mouth and forced it down. As the draught took hold he relaxed. "Kindliness isn't really supposed to be a kingly trait," he whispered when I bent over him. "Lucky for me . . . Never knew a magus could be so nasty. What happened to his wand?"

"Burned, I would think," I said absently.

"If it is, and Xerlanthor is dead, the dam's spells should be gone."

"I'll mention it to the Magus," I promised, but he had dozed off and did not hear me.

Chapter 16: The Moonkeel's Voyage

In the end the rafters fell before the fire died away. The weather-workers assisted by calling up a very localized downpour and by evening a steep sooty path could be laid over the blackened timbers and stones to the south shore. The afternoon's events were announced to the camp, and messengers dispatched to Warlord Prince Melbras and Commander Silverhand with the news. At the General's insistence the body of Xerlanthor was hung by the arms and shoulders from the dam he had built. "It's the proper thing to do, Your Majesty," he told me. "Especially for a dastardly foe." But I was revolted and yielded only to the Master Magus' argument that the body's presence would some-how aid a geomantic earthquake attempt.

To my surprise Fisan supported the General completely, declaring, "Let the Tiyalor, if there are any spies about, see what opposing us means." And she added, "At least the weather's cool enough so he won't go bad on you right off." This calm comment appalled me and I went to append a line to the Commander's scroll urging her to hurry back.

The second earthquake attempt was delayed a few days until the Warlord returned. I thought that after all his labor he should be present at the dam's final destruction. The geomants were optimistic and gave explanations of earth currents and Xerlanthor's life-blood forces that I did not understand.

On their return the Caydish nobility found the tale of Xerlanthor's end hard to swallow. With many protestations of trust and reminiscences of the dead magus' cunning Melbras and his staff even insisted on pulling the body up to identify it. The Master Magus gave me what I felt was an undue share of the credit, and I needed no help from the Crown to sense the Warlord's incredulity. But lately I had learned to know and value what I truly was, rather than what opinion and protocol demanded I should appear to be. So I offered neither false modesty nor the boasts and strutting the Caydish expect from a surprise victor.

The next day it was certain spring was on its way. It no longer froze hard every night, and that day the thin crust of old snow was pierced from below by the short stalks of vivid yellow-orange snowflowers. The pastures were scattered thick with plump thumb-high candle flames that scorched no sheep and melted no ice. I was fascinated, and on this day scheduled for the earthquake, when we again retreated upriver, I whittled a stick to a point and dug one up to see whether it might survive transplanting to Averidan. The Caydish did not know what to make of this, and at last Prince Musenor approached to ask me, "What do you hope to discover, O King?"

I had dug down several handspans, and since the soil was hard with ice until melting into sticky mud, I had dirtied myself all over. "Do you never see a beautiful thing and long to make it your own?" I asked.

Confused, the Prince answered, "Not I, no, but one hears of others who suffer the torments of lust."

"They should get married," I advised. "There, I knew there must be a bulb or tuber, you see?"

The Prince squatted politely to inspect the bulgy brown root embeded in frozen soil. "How does this further your possessing?" he asked.

"Oh, to do it right someone would have to dig them up after the flowers go by, whenever that is," I said, eyeing the Prince hopefully. But the hulking blond warrior did not look the sort of person amenable to such commissions, and I decided to entrust the task to Gorst. Levering my prize out of the hole I wrapped the bulb in a cloth, remarking, "It's just possible, though, that this one will survive being dug up out of season and carried home."

"But why should you want such things in Averidan?"

For a moment I feared Musenor was hinting the bulbs were virulent weeds that would crowd out all my other plantings. Then I saw he had no such knowledge of horticulture. "They're beautiful," I tried to explain. "I want something from Cayd."

"You should have saved the skull of Xerlanthor," the Prince said.

I gave it up. "What are the magi doing?" I asked.

The Prince relaxed a tiny bit and said, "Your subjects say the quake will be soon."

I joined the spectators at the top of the hill. The Master Magus had judged Xalan not recovered enough to participate in the geomancy, so he now sat on a fur rug regaling the Commander and Bochas the rhetor with an account of my introduction to goats. The rhetor was both shocked and amused at the tale, but Silverhand was disturbed. When I sat down beside her she turned to me and asked, "Do you know what it means, Majesty, when they name you 'witch'?"

"No," I said. "There's no Viridese word for it, it's some Caydish term."

"You might translate it as 'necromant,'" she told me. "They're calling you a wielder of the spirits of the dead."

This seemed so preposterous I could scarcely credit it even as superstition. "That isn't even possible," I said. "Why should the White Queen allow any such thing?"

"The Caydish think of death as a malignant spirit, a hungry wolf seeking life to devour," she said. "Their Death will lend power to evil men."

I dismissed her worry. "They compare everything to wolves."

"It must come of holding all their wealth in sheep," Xalan laughed.

"Furthermore, I've been there," I said. "I know the Caydish are incorrect. I met the White Queen myself."

Xalan's ready wit supplied endless disputations. "Why would being dead render you more able to work wonders? Do witches use only magian ghosts? Why would anyone, once dead, want to come back? Especially to cooperate with a witch? How do ghosts work their magery? Does one learn the art after death, and if so from whom?"

Silverhand interrupted to ask me, "Do you know the fate of witches in Cayd?"

I was uncertain. "Do they join a sodality or fellowship?"

"They're strangled on sight," she said.

I could not help loosening the high collarband of my jacket. "Gorst didn't say anything about that," I said.

"A reputed witch was executed in Lanach only a few weeks before we came," she said.

"I'm sure they wouldn't hurt you," Xalan argued. "You healed so many Craydish wounded, they must be aware of your good will."

The Commander sighed. "Perhaps it won't matter. We'll be leaving Cayd shortly anyway, if all goes well."

"Thank Viris," Xalan said. "I'm sick of snow. And mountains. And pallets. I want to sleep in a proper bed again, on a platform up off the floor, with quilts."

"I miss a bathtub big enough to lie in properly," I said. "And seafood. A baked redfish, or tunny in sour sauce."

"Oh, don't let's talk about it," Xalan moaned.

The lake had been growing in the past weeks as snow melted and ran into the Mhesan. We sat this day on a different, farther hill, too far to really see what the geomants were doing. So it was when we had all become tired of watching and no longer attended that the quake struck. Again it was the birds that warned us. They rose up from their trees with shrieks of alarm and dismay, an almost musical clamor at this remove. Again the river banks writhed and heaved as we watched breathlessly. But this time the dam did not ride the shock. It seemed to quiver, rigid, and then a chunk of stone fell out of the top to splash into the lake. Another followed, and a crack widened where the dam and the south bank joined. The pressure of the pent-up water did the rest, pressing through every leak. With a slow, inexorable roar of fury the liberated waters swallowed up Xerlanthor and his work. The mighty structure sagged to one side so that we could see the river channel beyond, a chaos of foaming brown water and tumbling blocks of stone.

Stupefied, we sat or stood motionless. One never sees geomantic destruction of this magnitude in Averidan anymore, for each house or building there is old. Every foundation was aligned for luck with earth currents by magi long dead. Most unlucky structures were rebuilt so long ago the City is more set in its ways than an old man's bedtime habits. The Caydish were also awed by this display of power, but recovered quickly. It was entirely characteristic when Melbras exclaimed, "And the magi *do* nothing with their might!"

When I translated this to Xalan he said, "Of course we do things, but we don't need to. It's enough to *be*, we don't have to *do*." But the nuances of this were beyond my feeble mastery of tongues, so the Warlord never heard it.

Cautiously we began to walk downstream. Closer the change was frightful. We had come to think of the dam as a work of nature, not man. Its overthrow seemed like a convulsion of nature, a tidal wave or devastating fire. On this the north side the entire cliff had crumbled into the water, taking its tower with it. Nothing was left but elaborate earthworks guarding emptiness. No one dared approach the unstable edge, but we could just see the raging brown torrent worry at the ruins of the dam, loosening a boulder here or a stone there.

The magi met us near the earthworks. It was queer to watch them push their peaked red caps back and congratulate each other with slaps on the back—to see them as only men. We recognized individuals as our friends or relatives or companions, but magi in the mass were awe-full. And it was wierder yet to recall that the Order of Magi is bound to the Shan King's service. Such power was too heavy for me, and I shied away from the thought.

"Beautifully done, Magister," I congratulated the Magus.

"The spells were bound up in Xerlanthor's own life," he said modestly. "Most geomantic spells are. Once he died, it was simple enough."

"Now we can go home!" Xalan rejoiced.

"Home." I rolled the word on my tongue, and suddenly the homesickness hit me. Like the Mhesan I ached fiercely to hurry to the sea by the shortest path, to sweep away obstacles in the path downcountry. Winter lingered endlessly here, but in Averidan it must be spring, the most boisterous and extravagant season of the year—a busy time for gardeners. My garden ought to be in first bloom, the new beds I had laid out and planted around the Palace, and soon it would be time to prune klimflowers again. I rubbed my hands, in anticipation and also to get the dried mud off. There was what looked like a scar on one finger, but the mark rubbed off on my woolen breeches. Then it came to me, why I had expected a scar. Melayne had bitten this finger, hard enough to draw blood. I hadn't seen Melayne in weeks, hadn't even thought of her in days, but the memory of her now was so vivid, so tactile, that I felt blood mount in my face. My cozy Caydish outfit seemed choking hot, and my skin remembered the sensuous feel of loose robes, cool and flowing, clothes meant only for sitting in beside a beautiful and beloved woman.

General Horfal-yu was saying something to the Master Magus about the ceremonies planned in Lanach. I interrupted to say, "We must hurry home as fast as we can."

"Why ever for?" the General asked. "There's no urgent business in Averidan, is there? And I understand King Melunael is planning a tremendous celebration."

I wanted to exclaim that Ixfel could have the celebration, that I had been wed scarcely a season. But of couse I couldn't say all this to a good and faithful subject, especially one so much older than myself. Shyness, impatience, and the battle between what I wished to say and what I ought not made me blush hot, but Xalan as usual put in the saving word. "You forget," he said, "the Shan King has many of the kingdom's cares in his charge. Royal business can't wait forever."

"Of course, of course!" the General agreed. "We must simply explain the urgency to the King."

"I'm sure he'll understand," Xalan said, with such a milky, serious face that I knew he had read my trouble.

We had packed up everything to move clear of the dam, and now I proposed it would be simplest to march to Lanach today. I was overruled by Prince Melbras and Silverhand, who pointed out that their troops had been working hard the last month and deserved at least a night's sleep. So we unpacked and pitched camp again.

Spring is a bad time for travel in unpaved Cayd. Silverhand reported that the roads were nearly impassable with thick red mud that came up to one's knees. The Sisters had tied flat pieces of wood to their feet and glided over the ooze, but such skills were beyond the untrained Caydish warriors and they had worn themselves out ploughing through. The Master Magus noted this at the festive dinner that evening, and said, "What would Your Majesty say to the magi's staying in Ieor a week or two, until the roads dry out? The geomants would like to map out the earth currents in detail for the Order's records. And the hydromants are interested in how quickly the Mhesan will recover its full flow."

"If it's agreeable to his Highness I have no objection," I said. I signaled to the interpreter to pass the Magus' request to the Warlord, and added, "In fact I have a commission to execute here in Cayd, and there is no one I have more confidence in than Xalan.''

"What is it?" Xalan asked from his seat across the table.

"You remember the bulb I dug up this morning? Well, just before you leave Ieor, I want about a bushel basketful dug. . . .''

Across the trestle table Prince Melbras boomed at me, "O King! Is it true, what this one says, that your magi wish to stay awhile in Cayd?''

"Unless it is inconvenient,'' I said in Caydish, surprised at his vehemen e.

"Of co se not!'' A good deal of ale had flowed to that side of the table, and the Warlord's red beard bristled with emotional excitement. He leaned over and hugged Xalan, who was the nearest magus, to his huge armored chest, shouting, ''Visit with us as long as you wish!''

Xalan pleaded faintly in Viridese, "Liras, somebody, get him to let me go!'' But I was laughing too hard at the sight of Xalan dandled in the big arms like a toy, his red cap askew and his robe rumpled up to show cross-gartered leggings. The Warlord laughed too, which set the whole company off, and the smoky tent rang with merriment.

So it was agreed. Only Silverhand thought to ask me, "Why is the Warlord so pleased?''

"What difference does it make?'' I asked. "The Caydish have a great respect for power. Maybe he likes magi.''

The next day dawned fair and mild. As a farewell present I gave Xalan a list of detailed instructions on how to pack and transport bulbs. He was not pleased, and complained, "I'm an invalid, I'm no good at digging.''

"Get the Caydish to help you," I said. "And get as many as you can, we have to allow for some to die. Have a pleasant stay—I'll see you in the City, in a few weeks.''

"Oh, good-bye, go,'' he said. "Before you think of any more plant life to be imported.''

The road was every bit as bad as the Commander had reported. My Caydish boots were knee-high, and were further covered by the leather leggings. But, neither liquid nor solid, the mud came higher yet, and crept coldly in so that my feet were wet and heavy. Worse yet, unless I walked at the head of the column and so on fresh mud the stuff was so sticky from the passage of many men that my feet nearly parted company from their boots. The first time this actually happened, to a Caydish axeman, it was funny. The man hopped one-footed on a drier spot, cursing the mudhole to complete destruction, while his hooting companions explored the mire with their own feet to find the lost boot. It was recovered only when Ranoc lent them his javelin to probe the utmost depths. But the second and third time it was not so humorous. The delay was maddening. The sky was blue and fleecy, the west wind no longer cut at us but brushed sweet and gentle through our hair. I wanted to be with Melayne, and the week's journey stretched before me like a sandy desert. The green country was behind view, and I pressed passionately toward every hilltop, around every turn of the road, to come closer to home.

Warlord Prince Melbras had sent a messenger last night to his kin, so at sunset when we arrived at the four-fold bridge most of the population of Lanach turned out to greet us. The men, farmers and herders in the dun-colored work clothes, cheered Prince Melbras their Warlord, but I walked beside him and accepted from wives and mothers yellow-orange blossoms, a little limp from having been plucked so long. Only by my position next to the Warlord was I known, for I was muddy to the eyes, plainly dressed, and in any case not tall enough to be marked as royal in Cayd. But this no longer weighed on my mind. We had done what the tall Caydish could not, and when the menfolk chattered to the Prince of plunder and adventure their women gave me silent gratitude for water, crops, the safety of their sons.

At the Palace our old quarters were ready for us. The low walls and woolwork hangings seemed quite homelike now. Our arrival had been late, so the king's celebration did not commence until full dark. Tables had been set up in the courtyard, which had been entirely tented over with untanned goathide. A bonfire was lit outside, and further cookfires were set up beyond that, for King Melunael had invited the entire joint armies to the party. Well-born menfolk crowded the tables and sat cross-legged on the flagstones, since their women had banished them from the halls so they could cook without interruption. The many bodies, the steam from the cookery, and the reflected heat from bonfire and torches, warmed the courtyard almost unbearably. One would hardly know it was early spring.

I had doubted Xerlanthor's boasts about his wand's power, and therefore was still cautious with Caydish ale. But I never again got hiccups from it. It was one of those long-winded parties, that wind up and go on forever. By the time we had eaten our fill and worked through the pledges of eternal friendship and battle-brotherhood it was well past midnight. Our hosts showed no signs of fatigue, whooping across the courtyard and calling for yet more food or drink, but as the night showed signs of wearing through to morning I cast about for some respite. At last Bochas-hel's polite hanging-about bore fruit, for catching his eye I rose and offered King Melunael some genuine Viridese entertainment.

The Caydish were now in a mood to enjoy anything, and roared with delight at the suggestion, beating on tables with belt-knives and axe handles. Sweat gleamed on Bochas' face but his manner was composed. Stepping into the central space between the tables he announced, "This is a traditional plaiv, the story of Tsantelekor the Sea-Reaver who sailed from his homeland to win a kingdom and a fair Queen."

When the translator rendered this his audience applauded heartily, and I joined in. The Tsorish invasion was 800 years ago; there could hardly be anything controversial to say about it at this late date. And Bochas had gauged the sophistication of his audience to a nicety. I recognized from the opening that it was a version now recited for youngsters:

"Tsantelekor's ship was named Moonkeel, after the crescent Moon, and had a prow carved in the shape of a griffin's head. On a day he and his twenty spearmen were asea, and the Moonkeel's head spoke, saying from its carven beak, 'I know a far land, green and rich, ruled by the fairest Queen the Moon ever shone on.' And Tsatelekor said, 'Let us see this land and this Queen.' So the Moonkeel steered itself toward Averidan, and after many days bore Tsantelekor through the straits and into the harbor. Now on the day of their arrival. . . ."

It is a simple and romantic version in which Tsantelekor is lover and savior of the Shan Queen—the Sisterhood of Mir-hel has another tale entirely, and so does the Army. When I was a child I relished this plaiv because the ship Moonkeel manages the Queen's rescue (from a plague of rats) so cleverly, but Bochas had calculated the Caydish would enjoy the battles, a shipload of stalwarts conquering a far nation.

The truth of the matter, as I understand it, is less savory than any of the plaiv, involving the sack and conquest of the Shan by shiploads of sea pirates. But since the Caydish plainly knew nothing of our history they were enchanted. At the conclusion, when Tsantelekor and the Moonkeel's brave crew are asked by grateful Viridese to stay and marry the comeliest ladies of Averidan, most of the audience leaped from their seats to embrace Bochas, and first among them was Prince Melbras himself. My folk clapped and shouted, "Pung!" Prince Mor sent a pageboy for gold, asking me, "Is money appropriate for such performers?"

"Money is always appropriate for rhetors," I replied with the old proverb. Bochas had indeed been excellent. I also would have to gift him. But first I had to rescue him from Caydish enthusiasm. Leaving my place I wormed through the press of big Caydish bodies until I was able to pluck Bochas' sleeve. The rest of him was invisible in Melbras' boisterous bear hug, and I said in Caydish, "Don't squeeze the life out of him, your Highness, he may still have plaiv in him!" In Viridese I added, "You're a hit, rhetor, perhaps your guild should schedule tours in Cayd more often."

The noisy mill of fur and leather-clad bodies seemed to raise the temperature to roasting pitch, and when Bochas was released, damp and crumpled, he staggered and almost fell. "I'm going to have to learn Caydish," he panted. "I can tell they like it but that's all I understand."

"If that is truly your wish I have just the gift for you," I said.

We retired soon after this, knowing we would have to travel next day, but the party lasted till dawn. The din was only slightly muffled by the thick timber walls of our hall, and we slept by wrapping our heads in our cloaks.

Though we did not make an early start the next day, only King Melunael was awake when we left. He had also left the celebration early, and now embraced me in kingly farewell. "You have saved Cayd, as neatly as the sea-reaver in the tale last night saved your folk," he said.

"That was just plaiv," I said, embarrassed yet proud. "And recall, you have given me a great gift in exchange." He blinked at me in confusion, as old men do, and I reminded him, "I greatly value Melayne, your daughter."

"Ah, Melayne. The little one." He seemed a little embarrassed also. "For my part, Cayd shall always be Averidan's ally. But I would not have you leave us without a word of warning." He glanced around the courtyard, strewn with last night's wreckage—upturned benches, mutton bones, flattened aleskins, crusts of oat bread—but no one Caydish was awake yet. "Royal policy changes with a new monarch," he said.

This did not strike me as very important, and I said, "So it is in Averidan also." Although that was not quite true, since for the Shan the Crystal Crown lends continuity. But I could not explain all this now to Melunael.

He laid a thin speckled hand on my arm. "The next is too small for the falcons," he said. "You know our race came to Cayd from the western wilds?"

"No, I didn't," I said patiently.

"You must ask Melayne," he said, "since you have won her love. Now remember to do that."

I promised I would. General Horfal-yu and the fists were already marching eastward out of sight, but the Sisters waited for me, and I had to hurry. I looked back once, for my last glimpse of Cayd. The morning was clear and cold, and the Sun behind me brought out the first faint wash of new green on the distant hills. For a moment I was almost sorry I would not be here to see a Caydish spring.

The descent of the narrow pass was tedious but not nearly as uncomfortable as it had been earlier in the season. Perhaps we had been hardened by the tail end of the Caydish winter. The ferocious wind had tempered to occasional playful gusts, and of course it is always easier to go downhill than up. Through our ear plugs the Mhesan falls rejoiced more thunderous than before. The water was rising; spring was here. I looked for the place where General Horfal-yu's brown horse had lain but the spot was hidden in foaming yellow-green water.

When we reached the head of the fifth fall we could at last see Averidan. The distant trees were in full leaf, so that the vista was startlingly green. It was as if we had stepped through some mystic portal from winter into summer. A lush, fruity breeze blew gently in our faces, so that my mouth watered at the memory of peaches and sun-ripened apricots.

If I had a little more patience a messenger could have gone over before us, to announce our return to Zofal-ven and the garrison. As it was our arrival took everyone by surprise. The watchman at the Last Bridge was asleep on duty and was roundly berated by the General. The Sisters took swift possession of their old camp-site and with easy competence began to unpack. I recognized the bay riding mare hitched in front of a new timber addition to the garrison lodge, and hammered on the door before throwing it open. "Zofal!" I shouted. "We're back!"

From a handsome wooden bathtub flanked by copper braziers Zofal-ven gaped at me. I had caught him at the evening bath. He lunged for the sword propped on his clothes stand, and nearly upset himself. With a splash he sat back down in the steaming water and whipped the broad blade out of its scabbard. The firelight gleamed yellow on the honed bronze edge as he pointed it at me and snapped, "This is a Viridese military garrison. Have you legitimate business here?"

"Zofal, put that thing down and get out of the tub," I said. "It's me, Liras-ven, and I haven't had a bath like that since I left." The sight of his hard wary face shook me, as if some plaiv had come true while I was away and wiped me from existence here. For a moment the real world seemed to waver and thin, showing the myth underneath. Then I recalled my clothes and beard, and pushing the furred hood back from my head exclaimed, "Don't look at this face hair, I can't shave until the scab comes off. And I borrowed these clothes from my in-laws, I lost all my Viridese stuff when the tower caught fire."

I suppose more than anything my disjointed explanation convinced him. Zofal stared hard and exclaimed, "Viris above us all, it is you!"

"Of course it's me, who else?" I bent laughing over the tub to embrace him, wet as he was.

"Did you just arrive? Why didn't you send word? We would have gotten up a little ceremony. What happened to you? You look dreadful!"

I said, "These are the honorable wounds of war, believe it or not. I should have Xalan here to give you the story of the fight—or no, you can ask cousin Fisan."

We both talked at once, I a jumbled account of all my adventures and he the story of his doings here. He dried himself and dressed, and the captain of the garrison came by, flustered and apologetic, to invite us to a late meal. My bath, with proper herbs in Zofal's big tub, was delightful, and Zofal lent me an outfit so I even had clean clothes after, only a little too short and tight.

Our meal that night felt more truly a victory celebration than the Caydish party, for we were able to relax, to speak our own tongue, and discuss the campaign freely. It was too early in the season for fruit but we had fish in greenspice sauce, barley groats, and spring vegetables cooked in every possible mode. As on my return from the Deadlands, every bite seemed to seal me to Averidan. Cayd's snowy pine forests and steep hills faded with each sip of sweet purple wine. I mentioned this to Silverhand, saying, "I don't remember things very deeply. Is that bad?"

We were by this time all a little drunk, with homecoming as well as wine, and she answered, "Well, you're alive and not dead, Shan, and not Caydish. Naturally you're happier here—Averidan is in your blood and bones, as with all of us." She refilled my porcelain cup and her own. "And when you're actually in a place or situation you feel it close to the heart, don't you?"

"Oh, yes," I said. "Dreadfully."

"Then if anything it's an advantage," she said. "If you remembered everything with its original intensity you would go mad. Don't worry about it."

"Enjoy it," Zofal-ven put in. "The headlessness of youth passes too soon." He reached over to rumple my hair, now badly in need of barbering. "Don't grow up too fast, little brother."

"Can it only be a year ago that everyone was urging me to grow up fast?" I asked. Right now I did not feel old at all. The joy of life, of victory, of success, hummed in my veins, and I said, "How many horses do you have here, Zofal?"

He was instantly suspicious. "Why do you want to know?"

"I'm not going to walk four days home," I announced. "Lend me a few mounts and I can ride to the City in a day or so."

"What! You have to lead a triumphal entry into the City," General Horfal-yu objected.

"I can't put on a very royal show like this," I said, and certainly any Shan seeing me now would be disappointed. "I'll go home quietly, and ride back up the road to join you again when you arrive, all dressed up."

Many objections were advanced—that it wasn't protocol, that I might be waylaid, that the gate-keepers wouldn't let an oddly dressed foreigner into the Upper City—but I was entranced by my inspiration and insisted on my own way. In the end Zofal reluctantly consented to lend me the necessary horses. "But someone must go with you, Majesty," Silverhand declared.

"There aren't remounts enough for your guard," Zofal said. "And I suppose I'm the only other competent rider present anyway."

The General made a few throat-clearing noises but I said, "I'd be glad of your company, Zofal."

So the next morning very early I rolled Zofal off his pallet and sent him out to saddle horses. My guard also rose to see me off, and I said to Ranoc, "You may tell the men my plans, since they'll know anyway. But have them keep it to themselves. I don't want it commonly known up and down the Mhesan that I rode ahead."

The dawn was rosy and cool. The little glade was dim with

long blue shadows cast by the forests, but above us the mountain peaks were pink and gold in the Sun. When I went out to help Zofal tie our scanty luggage onto the horses the smell of leaf and water was good enough to eat, refreshing as rain after drought. To my surprise Silverhand and Fisan-shi were waiting for me outside.

"You can't go away without the Crystal Crown," Fisan said.

I had almost forgotten it, something that would have been impossible once. "I'm sure I won't need it the next few days," I said.

"That's not the custom, Majesty," Silverhand said. "The Crystal Crown never leaves the Shan King."

"We haven't horses enough for you to come, Fisan," I said. "It's impossible."

Remembering the last time I had meant to leave Fisan behind I dreaded another scene, but she said, "No, Liras-ven, I don't want to come. Here, take the Crown with you. I resign as your Bearer."

I took the casket she handed me, so surprised it nearly slipped from my fingers. Zofal said, "If my wayward little brother has offended you somehow, cousin, Shan King or no I'll throw him in the river."

"Oh, no, Zofal," she laughed in protest. "Liras has been so kind, helped me find my true home."

An awful idea occurred to me. "You haven't fallen in love with a Caydish axeman, have you?"

Even the Commander laughed at that, and Fisan said, "No, if anything the opposite. I'm entering the novitiate of the Sister-hood of Mir-hel."

No one in the family has done that for years. Zofal said, "What will your father say? And what will Mother say to *us*? We were supposed to be taking care of you!"

The Commander smiled, very sweetly. "We can deal with them." She stood poised and serene in confidence, and I noticed that Fisan had the same air about her.

"I don't doubt it," I said. "I'm delighted for you, cousin, you'll make a wonderful Sister, I'm sure."

The Crown's casket was tied behind my saddle. We had two horses each, and would exchange them for fresh ones at Mhee. To smooth our way I wrote chits authorizing us to pass guards and gates on royal business. "I knew someday it would be useful for you to be Shan King," Zofal said. We waved to Silverhand and Fisan, and spurred our horses toward the homeward road.

Our mounts were bred for speed, not war—slim swift horses, born to run. It was a relief not to have to walk anymore, and our speed was exhilirating after so many days at a foot's pace. The road was wide enough for us to ride abreast, and neither muddy nor dry to dustiness: a perfect day for travel.

Couriers take three horses, and ride at a steady canter to get to the City in a day, switching mounts often. Zofal and I would go more slowly and spend the night in Mhee. After we came to the river road we let the horses run, and whooped and shouted so that the squirrels and birds in the surrounding forests scolded us. The Mhesan chuckled and rejoiced to our right, green and cold as the heart of a yellow melon, and on the farther shore more trees clustered near the water to see us pass. "I'm glad you didn't get yourself killed, Liras," Zofal shouted at me. "Mother would have been so cross."

"Me too," I replied. "Although I came close once or twice. Did you keep up with the dispatches?"

"Of course." Zofal's incredulity showed plain on his face. "Are you sure that rhetor Bochas-hel didn't help you with some of them?"

"I'll admit portions of the campaign sound like plaiv," I said, "but it was all sober fact."

We were trotting past woods, in full leaf and rustling with small busy life. The Sun's light made the forest glow jewel-green, and somewhere in the distance rang the faint sound of a woodcutter's axe. Zofal shook his head. "The family still hasn't recovered from your being Lord of the Shan. Now you're a hero, and what shall we do?"

I laughed at the idea. At the moment I was safe in my own country, in reality. The occasions I had slipped over the edge seemed past. "I'm no hero. Come on, let's gallop again."

As we moved east the forests gave way to undulating fields sown with flax. The plants were well up, and to north and south generous Averidan smiled in tender pale green. I rubbed the long narrow scab on my face, and knew that the campaign had been worth all our pains. An emotion that Caydish shepherds must feel rose in me at the sight of the increase, the fertility of what we had fought for. We had sown death but through some grace abundant life was our harvest.

Chapter 17: Homeward

In spite of frequent changes of horse we grew sore and tired as the day wore away. "How was I ever cajoled into this," Zofal grumbled.

"Keep in mind I have a new wife at home," I said. "I'm anxious to get back to her."

"At the rate we're going you'll be too tired to do her any good," Zofal predicted.

We passed the confluence of the Felcad and Mhesan before sundown, and came to Mhee in time for a late fish supper at an inn that catered to river men and merchants. I discovered to my embarrassment that I had brought no money—someone else always deals with the Shan King's expenses—so Zofal had to search pouches and pockets for the coin to pay our way. To preserve the incognito we hired a room there, and Zofal exchanged our horses at the garrison next morning. The garrison captain recognized Zofal and looked over the chits, while I sat humbly watching our baggage by the horse trough and waited for the fresh mounts to be brought.

Because yesterday had been my first on horseback since Piril's death, every muscle in my body groaned as I climbed into the saddle of a thin sorrel mare. Observing this Zofal mocked, "Your sojourn in sheep country enfeebled your horsemanship!"

For answer I dug the thick heels of my boots into the sorrel's ribs and yelled in Caydish one of Prince Melbras' favorite vilifications, "May you be reduced to congress with your own sheep!"

My mount started violently forward at this sudden noise in her ear, and the stableman in his surprise let the reins of Zofal's horse slip from his grasp. The animal caught my own horse's skittishness and shied away from Zofal's attempts to grab the bridle. Only when I shouldered the sorrel alongside to crowd the runaway into a corner did the stableman recapture him. When Zofal threatened to walop me for fraternal irreverence I made the sorrel wheel and dance around him in a tight circle, and laughed at him until he had to join in.

To an aide the garrison captain remarked, "For a Cayd he rides very well." So we made our departure quickly, before he could deduce more.

The barley fields downriver were clothed now in sunlit silvery green. As far as we could see on either side they spread, like shimmering silk, shot through with gleaming threads of canals flowing with the life-giving water. Although we had risen early the farmers were earlier yet. All the water wheels were already aspin when we trotted over the irrigation cuts. The farm children mostly did not recognize me and only peeped over the edge of the bridges at our approach. But one discerning lad remembered, and called to us, "How many Tiyalor did you kill, messirs?"

I pulled the sorrel over and dismounted. Zofal sighed but said, "I suppose we should breathe the horses anyway."

"At least two," I told the lad. "And maybe more."

"Two isn't very many." Early though it was, he had already been swimming, and dark hair stuck out in wet points over his black eyes. "Did you do it with this sword?"

"I did indeed." It occurred to me that a lad with so sharp an eye might be useful, but he was too young to take into my service. I drew the blade and let the boy hold it—it was almost as tall as he, and he could just keep it off the ground. "Be careful, it's very sharp." When he returned it to me I sheathed the blade and climbed again into the saddle. The lad waved, and I called, "Good-bye!" as we cantered away.

The Sun rose higher and hotter in the azure sky with the first taste of summer heat to come. In my thick wool and leather clothes I sweated like a horse. To no avail I opened the lined leather coat and pushed up my woolen sleeves. At last I had to rein the sorrel over again and dismount.

Zofal said, "I thought you were in a hurry."

"If I don't shed some of this stuff I'll faint," I said, wiping my wet face on my sleeve.

"It's a lovely day, I don't know what you're talking about." Of course Zofal was wearing a light linen robe, Viridese in cut, dark green with black sleeve linings and embroidery. I took off my vest and coat, and the woolen jerkin clung so oppressively I stripped it off too. "I hope you don't intend to peel right down," Zofal said, avoiding his eyes politely. "As I recall Warlord Prince Melbras was dressed just like that, at your betrothal."

"So he was," I said, startled. Casting my mind back I recalled the Warlord had worn only the leather vest over his bare chest. I would certainly be cooler that way, but not properly modest at all. For a moment an echo of Yibor-soo's possible remarks floated acidly to my ear. Then I remembered that no one would recognize me in any case, so what I looked like made no difference. Rolling the coat and jerkin together I tucked them under the straps of my saddlebag.

Zofal exclaimed, "You're not riding into the City dressed like that! Or at least not with me—I don't want it known I'm related to you!"

I knotted the laces of the brown leather vest around my bare waste and said, "No true Cayd would be deceived, I don't have a hairy chest. But to a Viridese I look completely foreign. Just be grateful I'm keeping the breeches and leggings."

We made good time after this, now passing occasional parties of other travelers to the City. I strained my eyes east and south for the first glimpse of home. A bright flash of gold on the very horizon— "There! It must be the Temple Dome!" I cried, and set spurs to my horse.

We tore down the road at a gallop, kicking up bits of oyster shell and raising powdery white clouds of lime. Vendors and others beside the road swore at us, and shook their hems and sleeves to get the dust out. Slowly the Upper City bulged above the horizon, crowned with white and gold. But well before we came to the marketplace outside the West Gate the crowds became too great and we had to rein in to a walk.

"It isn't a big market day, is it?" Zofal asked me.

I leaned forward over the shoulder of my horse and repeated the question to an oil seller, trudging Citywards leading a low dog-cart stacked high with stoppered flasks of linseed oil. Two tired brown canines tugged the cart along at an easy walking pace. The driver glanced up at me in surprise! "You've learned our tongue well, stranger! The nibblers are running, and we're all going to town to eat their spawn while it's in season."

"Nibblers!" Zofal exclaimed. "How fortunate we came back early!"

Nibblers are a pest—snappy, inedible fish with spiny fins and strong wide jaws. In the spring they awaken from their river-bottom sleep so hungry they will pry barnacles off docks and ship keels. Barnacles are pests too, but when the nibblers wrench them off ships they remove and eat the caulking also, so that barges and fishing boats spring sudden fatal leaks. The plaiv say that Ennelith became sorry for all the drowned sailors the nibblers brought her, and so gave the seamen a gift—a song that would charm the fish to the surface so that they could be speared. It may only be used once a year, and the fishermen of those days sensibly elected to use the gift at spawning time, so that the only edible parts of the nibbler—the eggs or roe—should be at their prime.

Impatiently I stood in the stirrups to see how far the crowd extended. The warehouses and slips for river barges were to my left, and from there rose the sound of the nibbler song. Brass gongs were struck to mark the end of each verse, and at the end of each rendition there were shouts of excitement and praise as the fish spears were flung into the water. To my right were the walls and gates of private homes. I looked again, at a town house with a red-tile roof peeping over a red-tile wall. "Zofal, is that a new addition going up on that house?"

"Seems so," he said. "About time too. You didn't have to be a geomant to see the house needed something. The arrangement of the windows and doors is so obviously unpropitious."

Very slowly we were borne in the press to the market square. The booths had been moved to one side and the central area was almost completely blocked by an enormous heap of dead spiny fish, nibblers stripped of their spawn and ready to be hauled away. A delicious smell of nibbler roe steamed with garlic filled the air. Laughing noisy people crowded to the booths holding flapping fish on light tridents high above their heads. The fish merchants with one deft slice would cut the fish open at the proper spot so that the eggs or roe poured into the clam shell the customer held out. Then with an expert flick the fish was flung off the trident over the heads of the crowd to join its fellows on the discard heap. The trident was returned to the customer who either ate his prize raw on the spot or took his clam shell to one of the cookery booths. Every now and then proceedings would be enlivened by a misdirected fish which would hit someone in the face, and the quarrels engendered by these mishaps kept the marketplace abuzz. Neither eggs nor roe keep at all, so for the day or two of the nibbler run every Viridese within walking distance of water eats as much of the delicacy as he can hold.

My mouth filled with water, and a sudden hollow place in my stomach clamored for attention. Zofal leaned close and shouted in my ear to be heard over the crowd, "Everyone's down by the river anyway, why don't we stop awhile too?"

"No," I shouted back. "I want to see Melayne."

"You refer to the Lady of Averidan, stranger?" The oil seller had followed us close because his oil flasks were in less danger of accidental breakage when preceded by two horses.

I said, "Yes, the Shan King's Caydish bride."

"This is my second trip today," the man said. "Earlier this morning I saw her down by the river gate, helping with the hunt in the fashion of her people. The strangest thing you'll ever see—she uses a bow and barbed arrows, with a fishline attached. . . ."

"Thank you!" I told him, and wrenched my horse's head around. "Here, Zofal, take my horse. I'll go faster in this crowd on foot."

"You shouldn't be doing this," Zofal said as he took the reins. "I'll meet you by the cookery booths."

A jostling crowd streamed out of the marketplace onto the path that runs at the foot of the City walls back to the river bank, and I turned to my right and joined them. Everyone was wet and happy, having a good time—City business would grind to a halt in the next few days. But my hunger to see Melayne outweighed even my fondness for nibblers. I jostled forward as quickly as I could. The river gate is rarely closed these days, and tolls are collected from a toll-barge tied up at the foot of the great square fort where City wall meets the river.

I could not see the river-gate on my left until I actually came to the water's edge. Dozens of barges and boats had been moored there. They rocked and thumped hollowly against each other as eager fishers leaped along them and crowded close to the water, tridents in hand. A small barge anchored in mid-stream held the singers and gong-men. They kept up their music in shifts, so that the nibblers were continuously charmed to the surface. The goddess-given song is wierdly sweet, with both a sea-wave rhythm and the droning, buzzy quality of very old prayers.

And there, on the boathouse of the toll barge, was Melayne. Clad in pale green she had knotted up the wide trailing sleeves and bound back her dark red hair so that she could wield a deeply curved Caydish bow. As I watched she nocked and aimed a triple-barbed arrow into the murky water, and loosed. The arrow vanished with a tiny splash of foam, and then a deeper watery commotion marked the death throe of a nibbler. She hauled in the attached line, and allowed her attendants to admire the fish before handing it to the fish cleaners. Most well-to-do Viridese at this season will hire cleaners and cooks, and have nibbler parties on river banks or beaches, but only the Lady of Averidan could command the roof of the toll-barge boathouse as a picnic ground.

At the sight of her a sort of madness possessed me, so that later, although I could remember perfectly well what I did, I could supply no sensible reason for my actions. The boats and barges were tied or chained in many rows to rings set into the walls of the fort or to each other. I leaped from one to another as fast as I could until I was leaning over the gunwale of the very farthest vessel, a small pearling dinghy. If I had had a trident or gaff I could now catch nibblers, and indeed to either side of me professional fishermen speared nibblers with easy economy of motion and shook them off into wide shallow baskets for sale later.

I stared downstream over the glimmering green water to the merry party on the toll barge. I was still not close enough. Over the gongs and splashes and laughter and music Melayne would not hear my shout. No thought was necessary— I did the obvious and necessary thing. I drew my dagger and chopped through the ropes that tied the dinghy to its fellows.

The fishermen did not notice at first what I had done. The Mhesan runs strong and deep hereabouts, and the current plucked at the boat until it drifted out into the center of the channel. With yelps of dismay the fishermen lunged to hook the anchor lines of the last moored boat as we drifted past. But I struck down their boat hooks and said, "We're going down past the toll barge. You may fish if you want but don't stop or turn this boat."

"You are overheated in the head!" one declared, but not very loudly. For a Shan I am both tall and strong. Furthermore I stood with a wide sword on my belt, and my determination was so plain that they acquiesced. Unguided, the dinghy spun slowly in midstream. We were carried down right to the toll barge, and as we drifted closer Melayne's attendants pointed and waved.

"Melayne!" I called. She leaned forward to see better. Somehow through beard and scar she recognized me, but I was not at all surprised.

Her eyes were wide with astonishment, and a little uncertainly she said, "Husband?"

For me that word was sufficient. The dinghy would soon drift past. I stepped onto the gunwale, causing the little boat to dip alarmingly. The fishermen shouted, "Wait, you can't do that!" but were forced to throw their weight to the far side to counterbalance the boat. In a straight leap up I jumped for the rail of the toll barge above me.

Several months later when I returned to the river-gate I noticed the distance the toll-barge sets above the water. It astonished me, for it is considerably above man-height. Yet that day I leaped up and caught it, and then drew myself aboard. Below, the dinghy nearly capsized and shipped a lot of green water, but did not quite founder. The fishermen cursed me heartily before bailing out and rowing back upstream to their mooring place again. I looked wildly around for a ladder or stair leading up to the roof, but even as I turned Melayne flew into my arms. "It *is* you! How did you come here?" she cried, in clearest Viridese, but I could not answer. Caydish and Viridese bubbled together in my head but refused to run down onto my tongue. Wordlessly I folded her in my arms and tucked her head under my chin, muffling her questions on my chest. I had not known until this moment I had been so long away.

That was my true homecoming. The rest of the day—being whisked to the Palace in the middle of a group of Melayne's women; the stupefaction of the Director of Protocol; Sahai's suspicious sniff at my horsey, fishy boots; the unseemly shriek of dismay that escaped the Wardrobe Master when he saw me—all these passed too quickly to be noted or answered. Unresisting I let the flow of homely incident sweep me along, and was not roused from my joyous daze until after the bath, when the Chamberlain showed my barber in.

"The Mistress Herbal said I wasn't to shave," I protested.

The barber set his jaw so stubbornly that his lower lip stuck out. "It would be my reputation's worth, Your Majesty, to let you be seen like that," he declared, so after extracting a promise of gentle treatment I gave way. Sahai purred on my lap under the clipping sheet, and it was as if I had never left.

But when the mirror was uncovered for me after, I did not see my old face again. The damp dark hair was short and neat as before, and a heavy silk bathrobe gleamed dark purple at my throat. But wintry winds had burnished my pallor, and new wary lines deepened my eyes. The dry brown scab ran up the side of my jaw to my cheekbone and pulled at the corner of my mouth so that the smile was a little lopsided. A year ago I had seemed young for my twenty years—now I looked older.

"Lords of the Shan don't live many years," I said. "They just pack more into the time they have."

"Your Majesty is in the flower of youth," the barber assured me. "The scar merely adds romance, distinction."

The Master of Wardrobe had assuaged his horror by selecting supremely elegant attire for me. His assistants bowed and held out for my approval a long robe of deep orange satin embroidered with gold thread and little, clicking amber teardrops, and a loose blouse and trousers of pale yellow silk to wear under. The sensuous satisfaction of once again slipping long, wide sleeves up off my hands, of instinctively cocking my shoulders against the drag of heavy hems, was increased by the sight of my Caydish outfit in the arms of the lowest-ranking wardrober.

"Have those cleaned and laid away," I ordered.

"Why ever for, Majesty?" the Master asked. "Viris forfend that you should ever need them again!"

"They are a memento," I said. "Furthermore they are a gift, from my royal sisters-in-law."

Melayne had ordered supper to be served in her wing. Sahai refused to be parted from me, so I carried her on my satin shoulder. I was shown into a cozy little chamber plastered in velvety peach tones, and Melayne rose to greet me from her seat near the tall triple-arched window. I set Sahai down.

Once I would have waited for the attendants to withdraw before taking her into my embrace. But somewhere on the journey to Ieor and back I had lost my shyness. Now I took my time, breathing in the distinctive aroma deep in her hair and savoring the warm goodness of her mouth. The glow of her seemed to pulse through the layers of rosy silk under my hands, and when I pressed her to me an almost pyrolurgic shock ran between us.

For my part I would have quite forgotten supper. But she turned her lips from mine too soon and said, "Let us dine, we're having roe-cooked-in-eight-spices, from the nibblers I caught today."

"You're getting quite Viridese," I said, taking my seat. "We're all passionate about food too. And you speak the language better now than I do Caydish."

She smiled, tipping her head a little so that candlelight ran along the silver rods in her hair. "I had real incentive to learn," she said. "But say something for me in Caydish."

"How beautiful you are," I said in Caydish. "You are perfect, in every aspect."

She laughed aloud, but not unkindly. "You must have been talking to the farmers!" she said in the same tongue. "The term 'perfect in every aspect' is used in sheep breeding, to describe purebreds!"

It was odd, and a little disturbing, to hear her converse and fluently order the servants about. "I'm not sure I didn't like you better silent," I teased.

She scowled, hearing words and not tone. "If you want a pet you have Sahai," she declared. "I have a great deal to say. You wouldn't listen before."

"You can't still be vexed at me," I said. The servers were bringing in the meal, and its fragrance made my stomach grumble for its first taste of nibbler. "Viridese never discuss things of substance at table, it spoils digestion. Can it wait?"

"The Caydish do," she said in that tongue. "And we also remember grievances. Speak Caydish, and tell me why you came back before your army."

"To see you, of course," I said, smiling.

She thought this over, with a wary expression that reminded me of Sahai cautiously examining a new toy. The servers uncovered the deep porcelain dish between us, releasing a puff of fragrant steam. "I didn't expect to see you," she said at last. "I expected rather to be slain before your return." When I gaped at this she went on with annoyance, "You are too stupid or too kind to see that anyone plotting for your throne would kill me and seize power while you were away."

Astonished, I forgot to fill my plate, and after a polite pause the servers helped me to red nibbler roe and clear pink sauce freckled with spices. "Why would anyone do that?" I demanded.

Now she seemed astonished in her turn, staring at me with wide gray-green eyes. "Are there not many aspirants to be Shan King?"

"Certainly," I said, remembering Xerlanthor. "But no one could achieve the office by hurting you, or me either."

"What of your half-nephew's attempt on your life?"

Of course that whole episode of my attempted escape had been glossed over, and appeared in no official chronicle. But I should have known that lack of an authorized version had simply encouraged the growth of fantastic rumors. "I assure you," I said with a smile, "poor old Rosil had no part in anything of the sort. Despite our quarrels, the Shan have a good deal of family feeling. Mother only hints at Rosil's complicity to annoy Yiborsoo." Melayne frowned at me, not believing a word, and in my most reassuring tone I said, "I know that's how royal succession works in Cayd, but we don't need regicide in Averidan, so long as we have the Crystal Crown."

The pathos of her supposed predicament touched me. She was so young, so helpless, and when I, her only protector, had proposed vanishing on a hazardous enterprise for an indeterminate time she must have been terrified—unable to speak the language, not knowing whom to trust. "I'm sorry you had such a scare," I said. "How dear of you, to worry so about my safety! But you see after all nothing happened, and here I am safe with you. Why didn't your brothers speak to me of this? Ought they have let you wed a ruler thought to be in danger of revolution?"

She met my eye with a cool, considering gaze. "No one in Cayd would have said anything to you," she said. "They're quite proud of their clever deal with Averidan. I'm not considered a matrimonial bargain, you know."

"Well, they did call you the little one," I said. "But you are the right size for me."

She smiled at that, but the gray-green eyes were still cool as jade. "I am also thought disobedient, dangerous."

King Melunael had been mildly surprised, I remembered, when I had told him of my satisfactory marriage. But like a fool I protested gallantly, "Nonsense, you are the sweetest, most delicious little morsel—"

She wiped her fingertips on the napkin the server held out and twisted one of her slim silver hair ornaments free. In a bewildering blur she flicked it from one hand to the other and tossed it at me. In a circle of shining metal it struck the carven arm of my chair and stuck fast. I snatched my hand away and then tugged at the missile and nearly cut myself. It was a dagger, the blade finger-sized but honed like a razor. Melayne tossed me the other half of the hair-rod, which twisted into its fellow with a cunning click to hide the little blade. Stunned, I slid the little knife in and out of its sheath until Melayne remarked, "You should eat, this is too good to let spoil with standing . . . Has the question never occurred to you, whether I wished to wed?"

"No," I had to admit. A wife had been one of the amenities of kingship, like my good cooks. I had expected Melayne, like the cooks, to wish to be so employed. My appetite for dinner had quite gone but it came to me I might be wise to comply. So I took up some barley bread, and asked, "Did you?"

"Of course not," she said. "All they wanted was a Caydish influence in Averidan. And they liked the idea of foisting off a recalcitrant on a foreigner. If you had been cruel or depraved," she reflected, "I would have killed you immediately. Or unfaithful, like my uncle Melbras." She glanced at me severely, as if still uncertain on this point. "And of course I was not going to sit quietly to be murdered, either."

An intense feeling of unreality possessed me, as if I were

stuck in someone else's plaiv. No doubt Xerlanthor's dam had felt the same when its foundations were wrenched out. Apparently all this time I had been intimately amusing myself with a potential assassin. The misestimation, from a monarch whose main function is to evaluate and assess people, was appalling. An error of that proportion in my official work would lead to injustice or, worse yet, the disgrace of a failed lapidation.

How had I blundered so badly? The question, once articulated, was easy to answer. I had slipped into using Melayne as a sort of living plaything, a more exciting pet than Sahai, to be sure, but not really human, not a being with thoughts and fears and desires. Now I remembered her brother Musenor's description: stubborn and fierce, sticking at nothing to win.

The servers brought me back to myself with a start, by asking if I was finished with the course. At my nod they removed my scarcely touched plate and ladled out green abalone soup flavored with seaweed. Finding my voice I said, "I'm glad you didn't find me unpleasant enough to kill. And do you know, I was afraid you would resemble your uncle too."

That made her smile for a moment, but she met my eyes with wounded yet unwavering pride. "I tell you all this because as my spouse you ought to know," she said. "If you are displeased you must take it up with my kin, for I will not change myself."

Her courage took my breath away. Last year when I had been forced to alter my life I had rebelled for a week or so but then surrendered. And on the whole that had been worthwhile. But Melayne, all alone, handed over to foreigners as bad merchandise by kin who would water their sheep before sale, refused to alter. To see such a proud and dignified little person held so light was like watching a cat forced to draw a cart, and I hastened to soothe the hurt.

The meal was not nearly over but I rose from my place and went around the table to her chair. "I'm sorry I didn't learn Caydish more quickly," I said. "Or you Viridese, for if I had been able I would have told you this before. You are the most wonderful person I have ever known—competent and brave and clever. No one except Shan Vir-yan himself is worthy of you, and of all the women in the world I would have chosen you." I laid the little rod-knife on her silken lap and brushed the loosened red-brown hair back to see her face. "If you'll teach me knife throwing I'll show you how to ride," I offered gently.

Her wary expression melted, and her eyes were soft with sudden tears. "Your Caydish accent is dreadful!" she said, and hugged my head to her breast. My arms slipped around her silky waist, and her fingers softly traced the scab on my cheek. "Does it still hurt?" she whispered.

"No." The warmth and nearness of her, the rise and fall of soft flesh under my cheek, was distracting. I rose and drew her up with me, out of her chair and toward the bedchamber door.

The silver rod fell clattering to the marble floor. The Chamberlain picked it up, exclaiming, "But Your Majesty, the next course is fish baked in grape leaves!"

"No more need be served," I commanded over my shoulder in Viridese. "The Lady and I have finished supper."

Chapter 18: A Wish and Its Granting

For once Xalan had been wrong and I right—words are necessary for real love. That night was entirely different from others I had spent with Melayne, for as she had told me there was a great deal to say. My Caydish vocabulary increased tremendously, and when I exclaimed, "Where do you learn these things?" she laughed and said, "I have eight older brothers, all lusty and boastful men."

The next morning I awoke before her and watched her open her eyes, blinking at me with sleepy contentment like a cat. She nestled herself smiling against me and fell back into slumber while I examined the delicate pink curve of her ear and brushed the glorious hair away to see the fuzz at the nape of her neck. All this busy, secret life, an entire and wholly other personality rested beside me under the light quilt. She turned and murmured something I could not catch, and I wondered what she was dreaming. In spite of their fears I had never used the Crystal Crown to read the hearts of any of my family, for I had known them all since childhood. Nor did I need to read Melayne now, her clever female thought and fiery stubborn heart. I possessed all of her already, sleeping and waking, body and soul.

The thought of possession reawakened desire, and I stroked the tender underside of one upflung arm. Without even a twitch of surprise she said, "What hour is it?"

"Early enough," I said. "Since I'm not officially here I have no schedule." So she bit me in return, rather hard on the side of the neck.

Much later I had bathed and lay on a couch drowsily enjoying the coolness of bath-moisture evaporating from my skin. When there came a discreet tap on the door Melayne slipped on an embroidered robe, but I did not move and, laughing, she threw a quilt over my nakedness.

"His Majesty's brother is here," the Chamberlain said to Melayne, "inquiring after his health. Is the King officially at home to him?"

"Of course I am," I called, sticking my head out from under the quilt. "Send him in—no, send someone for some clothes first. He can come to breakfast."

The Chamberlain blushed. "It is nearly noon, Majesty. Would not a midday meal be more appropriate?"

"All right, whatever you say."

So when Zofal-ven was shown out to the terrace we were quite seemly, I in a loose morning outfit of pale blue and Melayne in thin white linen. Zofal set the casket of the Crown on the table and announced, "The way you abandon this thing, on the back of a tired horse down by the docks, one would never know it's a national treasure."

"I knew it was safe with you," I said.

Curiously Melayne lifted the lid. She had never seen the Crystal Crown before, except from a very great distance the day we had marched for Ieor. "So this is the symbol of royalty for your folk?" she asked.

"Yes, and much more," I replied. I would have to tell Melayne a little more about the Crown and its role in Viridese life. But there was not time now, for the first course—sectioned fruit—was brought in, and nothing of importance is discussed during meals.

Zofal seated himself at the round table and looked me over. I hoped the red mark of Melayne's teeth was not too obvious on my skin, but he said only, "What a transformation! Yesterday, a dirty, rather undersized Cayd, today an overgrown Viridese nobleman."

"Yes," Melayne put in. "When did you change your dress? The dispatches said nothing of it."

"Well, it was because of your father's dinner party," I began.

The tale made her laugh, and Zofal said, "That sounds much more like you. Setting yourself afire is all of a piece. Even as a child you were clumsy."

"Was he really?" Melayne asked. "And what happened to you then?" So I recounted everything in order: my visit to the Deadlands, the ambush, the battle, the first-hand account before, and from the corner of my eye I saw servers and Chamberlains stretching their ears at windows and behind shrubbery. But I spoke mostly for Melayne, for the wonder in her bright eyes and her exclamations of sympathy and acclaim.

The meal was long over when I concluded, saying, "So tomorrow when the army marches in I have to meet them outside the City, suitably dressed."

"I'm so glad you brought him back early," Melayne said to Zofal. She smiled at me so mischievously that I blushed. Zofal set down his teacup and pushed his chair back.

"I'll remind the keepers of the West Gate," he said, "so that when the message comes from the General we'll have warning to dress and set out. Brother, Lady." He bowed to Melayne.

"Sometime tomorrow afternoon," I promised, and punched him in the shoulder in farewell.

The attendants were putting Melayne's suite in order, so we walked arm in arm along the terrace to my rooms. Sahai twisted in and out between my ankles until I handed the casket of the Crown to Melayne and took the cat up in my free arm. The gardens were glorious in full flower and leaf. Fruit blossom and early lilies scented the air, and the many shades of purple klimflowers shone from wall and trellis like living amethysts. Beyond the verdant lawn the flower beds I had planned with such care were more perfect than I could have imagined. As when we had come to Lanach after long toil I seemed to walk now in the estate of some deity, one who cherished life and beauty. The lush exuberance around me was not of my doing. Some other, greater gardener had mended my work.

The leisured in Averidan traditionally eat four or five small meals a day. So when we came to my wing the smell of nibbler eggs sauteed in sweet oil wafted out to greet us. The Lord Chamberlain ushered us into the white-and-green Tsorish salon, saying, "Your Majesty must eat well now you are returned home."

Melayne sighed at the gleaming porcelain tableware laid out for us. "How is it you all eat so much?"

"Not much, often," I corrected. "We say it's bad to let the belly empty, that food is the fuel of life. And of course the nibbler season will soon pass." I slid my hand from around her waist up to the tender breast and armpit. ''They're supposed to promote vigor.''

We had finished the nibbler and come to the barley groats when the Lord Chamberlain bent deferentially at my elbow. ''The Warlord of Cayd is here, Your Majesty. Do you wish to be officially at home to him?''

''You mean Prince Melbras? What is he doing here?'' I set down my bowl and rose, but even as the Lord Chamberlain turned, Prince Melbras bulked like a thundercloud in the doorway. The Lord Chamberlain squeaked in astonishment—protocol demands that callers wait to be shown in—but I said, ''Your Highness, what a pleasant surprise! We thought you would be resting from the campaign in Lanach. Join us, have you eaten?''

Melayne had also risen, but her face was milk-white. In Caydish Melbras said, ''I bring urgent secrets, O King. Let us be alone.''

But Melayne exclaimed in Viridese, ''No, Liras, let me stay!''

''I've traveled a hard journey to be with my wife,'' I said indulgently, waving the Lord Chamberlain away. ''So you must excuse me if I won't be parted from her just yet. How did you come to the City so quickly?''

The Prince wore not the usual leather and wool but his bronze battle armor, still dented and dirtied from the Ieor campaign. He shut the green-and-white paneled door and leaned against it. ''I and my men caught up with your army last night in Mhee. We came here overnight by barge.''

The odd tone of the deep voice should have warned me, but my mind was running on Xerlanthor. Surely he could not have been revived, his corpse had hung three days on the dam. Or— ''Has someone found that bit of phlogiston?'' I exclaimed. ''I should have had the ashes sifted.''

''What are you raving about?'' Melbras growled. An enormous hand grasped my shoulder in a dreadful grip, so mighty the bones creaked in protest. I must have gaped like a speared fish into the bearded face above my own, for he bared white teeth in a grin and said, ''Limaot is surely on our side! For plainly you did not know, little Witch-King, that we in Cayd have long lusted for your rich Averidan.''

The exaltation in his voice appalled me. ''But we are allies!'' I protested.

''You are weak and wealthy, and we are strong,'' he corrected. ''And such strength that you have, you left behind you—your magi in Cayd, your army at Mhee. When they return they shall find a new Shan King—myself!''

The other hand caught my embroidered waist-sash and twisted it so that I was almost cut in half. With unbelievable ease he raised me by my arm and waist like a toy above his head and hurled me across the room. I hit the green-figured wall and fell helpless to the floor, bringing the glass table over in a resounding crash with me. My left shoulder had taken the impact and was now stabbed with an agony that made me faint and sick. Through pain-blurred eyes I saw Melbras approach me not with his battle-axe but with a sheep-gut bowstring in his hand. Strangulation is the fate of witches in Cayd.

A white linen sleeve whisked between us, and Melayne said in Caydish, "No, uncle, he loves me, I won't have him killed."

"You won't!'' Melbras' voice was exasperated but patient. "Love has nothing to do with it, leave this to your menfolk.''

"I don't care what your plans are, he's mine!''

"Did you know he's a witch? By his power he defeated that Xerlanthor, where we could not ''

"I don't believe it,'' she said. "He is sweet and good. And how should so powerful a witch come to be surprised in his own home?''

"It is fated, he has to die,'' Melbras argued. "Consider the history of our race. And of his own will the Witch-King came home without his magi and army. How can we pass up this opportunity? We shall be like the reavers in their past, a few that invaded a great realm.'' Melbras' uncharacteristic patience vaguely surprised me, but I supposed even he would consider the wishes of his blood kin. But then he continued, "And you even sent the broken dagger to Mor, the signal for invasion, by his own hand. How would he do that, except by the will of the gods?''

"I sent it because I feared assassination!'' Melayne exclaimed hotly. "Why didn't you declare war quickly and save me?''

"We had our own war to manage!'' Melbras shouted. "Were we supposed to let the evil magus off just to rescue an undergrown female? Now be sensible, he shall die and you shall be queen—the bridge between the old rule and the new.''

But I hardly took in Melayne's response. For the entire plot was plain to me now. The perfidious Caydish had planned to take Averidan from the very first, had sent me a bride known to be willful and violent to either kill me or head a puppet government after conquest. When I had arrived in Cayd after a fortnight of marriage in good health they had set invasion plans in motion.

And in everything, from Bochas-hel's plaiv to carrying the deadly token to my speedy return, I had assisted them.

Suspicion and rage flooded into me. I wouldn't give them the satisfaction of dying. The broken bits of my shoulder-bones grated horribly together as I pried myself free of the glass table fragments. Uncle and niece were calling imprecations down on each other, but among the spilled barley groats I caught sight of a wooden casket adorned with chased-gold plaques—the casket of the Crown.

"The runt should have whipped some obedience into you," Melbras shouted. "If you won't be a biddable queen you may die by his side."

"You try it," Melayne hissed. The hair-rod was in her hand, and before Melbras could dodge the little blade had sunk deep into the bend of his right elbow. With a bellow of rage and pain Melbras swung his unhurt arm at Melayne's head, knocking her to the floor.

At the sight of her blood on his fist an icy anger consumed me, freezing my heart but leaving my head clear. Awkwardly with one hand I scrabbled the Crown out and put it on. Outside the door the Lord Chamberlain called, "Your Majesty, is everything all right?" Melbras shoved a chair against the door and bent to recover the bowstring he had let fall. When he turned again to me I was ready.

The Crown's power ran cool right down to my fingertips, and white light cloaked me as I reached into Melbras' skull to stop him in mid-stride. Red-hot pincers dug into my left shoulder, and dozens of little pains from bruises and glass cuts shrilled at me, but only from far away, for I was Melbras now and he me.

Coldly I sorted over emotions and impressions: Ambition fueled by the exaltation of the god-chosen, of one riding with destiny. The force of Caydish history, the dimly remembered ages of journeying by all the race—Cayd, Tiyalor, and countless unnamed others—from the bleak heart of the continent to rich and fertile shore country.

And once again I saw myself and my people through his eyes. I saw our arrival in Cayd, wealth and ease touring a crowded hungry land, with no pity but only mild curiosity and amusement. Our easy, almost careless defeat of a foe that had cost Cayd dear in both labor and lives. When balanced against our slight build, the queer dark eyes and hair, the weird customs of magi and Sisters, the fragility of so many of us—here there was a confused mix of memories, the Shan King lying senseless on a shield borne into camp by his guard, the weaponless magi, the way Commander Silverhand came just up to Melbras' copper necklet— all this added up to witchery, supernatural help. It was good and right to kill witches, to take their wealth, their women, their land. A hot lust plucked at me, a desire to kill, to take, to rape, to possess all I could understand and destroy all I could not.

But this hot flood of emotion did not thaw the ice that ran in my veins. He had to die, if for no other reason than to deter other ambitious Caydish princes. The safety of Averidan and all her people rested with me. Coldly I reached, as Xerlanthor must also have done in his kills, into the big hairy body past armor and skin and lungs to the heart. A squeeze, a command to stillness, and instinctively I knew it should be done. He would die without a mark on him, and vaguely from the other half of my consciousness I was aware that witches did indeed slay without external sign.

I listened, but the Crown spoke no word. Only my external ear heard the sound of Melayne's sobs. At least Melbras had not slain her. The throb of his heart was in my chest, the heat of his desire in my blood, but deliberately and coolly I closed my power on him.

Melbras convulsed, as if to wrench himself free, but it was already too late. A quick pain in his chest, and the pulse of life faltered and was still. Consciousness ebbed into blackness—the blackness of the road to the Deadlands—not with fear or hatred, for I had hold of his perception, but with that same envy and lust I had frozen him in. The strain on me was almost unbearable, but I persevered, hanging grimly on to my own battered body while I watched Melbras' soul slip away from me into the starless dark, the close mountain valley and the uphill road to the tree.

When he was gone I blinked, and noticed that the big red-bearded form had fallen to the mosaic floor. Every step jarred my shoulder to anguish but I tottered to the body and turned it over. The green-yellow eyes glared up at the ceiling, and I shut them. He was quite dead. Yet the frost still trammeled me, and for a moment I could not think why. Then I heard behind me a sniff, and turned.

Melbras' blow had cut Melayne's delicate eyebrow, and the eye beneath it was swelling. Her loosened hair tumbled over her white robe to the floor, and her shadow streamed out black behind her in the light of the Crown on my head. When I stepped toward her she fell to her knees, whispering in Caydish, "Great lord, have mercy."

"The Crystal Crown is not necessary for you," I said in Viridese. "Know that in Averidan the fate of a traitorous wife is lapidation."

From a very great distance I saw her set her jaw and glare mulishly one-eyed at me, and the courage I had won with such labor loved her for it. But I had to know her part in all this, for the safety of the realm, and without considering the consequences to myself I reached out in the Crown's power to read her heart.

Fear, fear of witchcraft, fear of my anger, fear of dying by the Crystal Crown filled her, yet only defiance showed on her face. She had learned in childhood to fight against long odds, she, the smallest of a numerous and violent family. Because she had seen none of the reputed signs in me she had not believed the accusation of witchery. But when the white unearthly light had surrounded me, when Melbras had fallen dead without touch of weapon, she had believed perforce, and feared.

I brushed past all this surface turmoil and peered deeper. She had said she married me unwilling, and it hurt now to see how true it was. Commander Silverhand had been right, Melayne would have made an excellent Sister, vowed to virginity and war. She had felt sorry for my denseness, confidence that she could manage me, affection even, but not love. Only where she respected could she love. Even last night, my gentle words had been a mild exasperation. A proper husband would not have been so soft.

Caydish women join their husbands' clan at marriage. But when I had left Melayne in (as she supposed) mortal danger she had shifted her loyalties swiftly, sending the token to her kin hoping to prompt an invasion in time to save her life. When neither conquest nor murder attempt appeared she had set herself to learn Viridese well enough to evaluate my political importance, fearing I was a mere figurehead.

The revelation of my own ignorance and foolish trust scalded like knives of ice. But the realization that I had loved her more than she did me hurt worst of all, far worse than my shoulder. Only the three constraints of the Crown held me from sending her to the Deadlands after her uncle, and for a moment I gave serious thought to ordering her lapidation on the charge of treason, for my heart was frozen in fury and pain. But with astounding bravery she had risen, and now approached me.

"You're hurt," she said gently in Viridese. "Shall I fix it? I've set dislocated shoulders before."

Her hands reached for me but I flinched away as if she and not I were the witch. "No! The bonesetters will see to it!" And I pushed past her and thrusting the chair aside stumbled out of the room.

The Lord Chamberlain gaped at me but I gave him no time for questions. "There is a group of Caydish in the Palace, those who accompanied his Highness here," I said. "Send a guardsman for them instantly, in the Prince's name." He hurried to obey, and while he was gone I tore with my teeth and one hand the hem of my long trailing left sleeve, and knotted the ends around my neck to form a rough sling. When the Lord Chamberlain returned I ordered, "Have all the available guardsmen come here. And have the Lady's people come and escort her back to her rooms. Quickly!"

One glance at my face and the Lord Chamberlain hurried away again. Behind me I heard Melayne crying softly, for me or for her uncle, but from the distant vantage of the Crown it seemed to have nothing to do with me. The guardsmen came almost immediately, and at my gesture stood around the green-hung walls of the anteroom. Melayne's escort appeared, and when she would not come out of the salon I had her forcibly extracted and led sobbing away. Perhaps she feared she was being taken to execution, but I would not look at her and so did not know. I had Melbras' body brought out and laid on the anteroom's mosaic floor, and covered with a cloth.

As the Caydish were brought in I read their hearts. They were all men who had heard the plaiv of Tsormelezok's conquest, and were hot to do the same. Melbras had promised them estates and loot, for they were to be the core of the new Caydish realm. One even carried their emblem, the ram's skull with gilded horns, all ready to be displayed above the new monarch.

When they saw me, shining in white glory like the Sun himself, they feared the worst, and when I nodded to the Lord Chamberlain to uncover the corpse they fell on the body with cries of grief.

"Let it be known in Cayd," I said coldly in Caydish, "that all who oppose the Shan King must die. Take your fallen back to the land of his fathers, for I will not have him or any of his in Averidan."

Perhaps when I took off the Crystal Crown I might feel sorrow for friendship that could not ever be, but I was now unmoved when the man who bent over Melbras raised his blond head. It was Prince Musenor. "And what of my sister, you witch?" he cried, dashing the tears from his cheeks.

"You gave her to me," I replied. "To seal a bad bargain that you did not mean to keep. I have not yet decided her fate, but she is mine, to lapidate if I wish. As for you, you will lay down your arms. You will go home. And you will never return."

Musenor snatched at his battleaxe, shouting some battle cry, but at my signal the guardsmen leveled their spears, some at Musenor and some at the twenty other Caydish. With the Crown's power I forced Musenor's fingers apart, so that the axe fell clanging to the tile floor. The guardsmen easily disarmed the rest, right down to their belt knives. "Send to the Army barracks," I commanded, "and let a fist of men escort these prisoners west. They shall be driven right up over the Tambors, and this body with them."

The guardsmen saluted me and led the Caydish away. Bonesetters and herbals attended me in my chambers. "Before I begin treatment, Your Majesty," the bonesetter said, "would you remove the Crystal Crown?"

I was in such a state that I almost struck out at her. But some lingering sanity held me back, and when I looked down at my hands, glowing like molten silver, I knew she was right. As soon as the Crown left my head I expected the chill to leave me, but it did not. I was ice not in my body, nor even in my mind, but in my heart. The bonesetter chattered cheerfully at me, and I did not realize what she was about until she took my left arm and wrenched it sharply round. I shouted with the agony and almost fell off my chair, crying, "What are you doing?"

"It was only dislocated," she soothed. "It will be fine now, just sore for a week or so."

"So Melayne was right." I wanted to weep with desolation and pain, but could not. The herbals were there with a quieting draught, hot and bitter. But it could not warm me. Unresisting I let them take my torn robe and salve my cuts and bruises.

"Sleep, Your Majesty," the herbal urged me, and I needed no more encouragement to collapse into bed.

Before dawn the next day I awoke. My shoulder had been tightly bound with strips of linen and the arm set in a sling. A painted porcelain nightlamp glowed beside my bed but the darkness pressed close all around its yellow light. And with it icy wanhope hemmed me round so that my hands shook with cold. In vain I struggled against the frost in my heart. Each beat seemed to pump thick cold blood slowly through my body. I caught up the lamp in trembling hands and padded barefoot to my wardrobe. With my own free arm I struggled into my old gardening clothes. The night guardsmen saluted sleepily as I went into the bright-lit hall and down the wide marble stairs to the terrace, and so out to the garden.

A gibbous moon shone low in the west, and klimflowers were closed in sleep. By tradition every portion of the Palace is lit with candle and lamp at night, but when I caught myself looking back toward the Lady's wing to see if there was a light in Melayne's room I turned away coldly furious at myself. I had given her my trust and love and she had not returned them. It was ridiculous. A year ago I had not known she even existed. How could her perfidy affect me so?

I wondered whether it was not my duty to order her lapidation for treason. But it was plain to me that even if I did so the sentence might never be carried out. If she had endangered Averidan so had I. Not only had I left my army, carried the treacherous token, missed dozens of hints and warnings—I had deliberately never enlightened Melayne about our customs, most especially about the Crystal Crown, underestimating her intelligence and will, keeping her in my power. For a moment a crazy vision of my own lapidation for treason danced before me: the rocky bed, the hot insupportable weight grinding my bones down. But a year's practice gave me strength to parry the old fantasies of inadequacies. I was what I was, and Averidan would have to make the best of it. But there was no solution for us. I had slain Melayne's uncle, by "witchcraft," and defeated her kin. Yet we had been indissolubly wed. How should we ever recover our happiness?

In the darkness of cold despair there is only one help for a Viridese. Higher even than the white Palace the golden dome of the Sun Temple gleamed softly at me in the moonlight. I plucked a branch of blossoming peach and threaded my way through the dozing garden to the little entrance from Palace to Temple. The quiet bustle of preparation for the dawn sacrifice was in progress in the courtyard, and I slipped into the main sanctuary and sat on one of the benches around the walls until one of the Sun Priestesses could see me after the rite.

It is a touchingly naive belief in Averidan that the Sun our forefather shines with particular favor on women ever since his epiphany to Viris our foremother. The dawn gong tolled its deep brazen note in the courtyard outside, announcing the arrival of a new day, and the sound flowed in past the golden columns until the great circular room was filled from mosaic floor to plated dome with one rich golden voice. The priestesses, women chosen for comeliness and wisdom, entered in twos singing the morning hymn in high clear tones. A sparse congregation trooped after them, mostly humble people who had to work all day and could not therefore attend a later rite.

The sacrifice today was spring flowers and, in honor of the nibbler running, a live nibbler in a big pottery bowl of water. As the ultimate source of life the Sun cannot be offered death, so no blood is ever drawn in his Temple and only flowers which can be plucked without destroying the parent plant may be brought. Only a scale of the nibbler would be burnt; the spiny fish itself would be returned to the harbor. Even confined in its bowl the nibbler was not about to give up a scale, and the ceremony was held up for a bit while three priestesses in heavy gauntlets wrestled with the splashing, flopping fish. At last flowers and scale were cast into the flames, and the prayers said. The little crowd drifted away or accosted priestesses for advice or personal offerings. One priestess approached me, saying, "Do you need counsel, young man, or a wish?"

"Both," I said. "I have devoted this past year to my country's service, and find that the work has estranged me from my wife. Is the marriage ended? Would she be happier without me?"

The priestess smiled. She was a hearty woman of perhaps forty years, with the strong beautiful bones and deep wise gaze of such holy women. "From your viewpoint, at least, your second question answers your first," she said. "You would not consider your wife's happiness, did you not love her still."

"No, that is not true," I said. "She has hurt me mortally."

"In your love, or in your pride?" She watched my face and when I could not reply she took the flowering branch from my hand. "Come," she said. "Let us ask the god whether he will grant your wish. What shall it be?"

You will find fools in every nation who will consult before blowing their noses, or petition before crossing the street. But the more sensible and reverent reserve the attention of the deity for major requests. So I had to wish for the true desire of my heart, if I could discover it. The priestess waited patiently while I leaned my forehead on my one good hand and searched my soul. At last I muttered, "For my wife's love."

The priestess smiled again, very kindly, and led me to the central altar. On a chest-high roundel of polished granite the holy fire has burned since the founding of Averidan. We stood close while the priestess invoked the Sun and tossed in the blossoming branch. In her wide rapt eyes the dancing flames were reflected, little and bright, as she watched the offering turn to ash and crumble away. At last she turned to me and said, "If you are patient you will have your heart's wish."

I could not believe it. "Are you sure?"

"Quite." Confidence was plain in her voice, and also a touch of annoyance. There is no point to receiving a wish and then not believing it. When I apologized for my incredulity she said, "Let me know what happens."

"If all goes well I shall bring her here, to make a thank offering," I promised, and took my leave. I was still unhappy, but the hard icy lump had gone from my chest and I was at peace with myself. After all I had, all by myself, saved the country from sack and invasion. Any personal unhappiness was worth that. The feat would have satisfied my hunger for glory completely, a season ago. So wishes do come true.

The day promised to be clear and warm, the new-risen Sun beckoning merrily to the east and sending clear yellow spears down through the ornamental trees. Since it was still quite early and I was wearing my work clothes I went into the Palace gardens. Near the wall I found a tray of seedling onions ready to be set out in their bed, and applied myself to the work, dibbling rows of holes in the cool earth and setting each plant in, not too deep. The labor was not impossible for a one-handed worker, and when I was done I stacked the tray and tools neatly beside the walk. I was just in time, for Zofal-ven came down from the main building calling my name.

"Here I am," I replied.

He hurried up, waving a scroll. "They'll be here before sundown. If the gardeners hadn't seen you I'd be looking for you yet!" Then, catching sight of my sling, he said, "What happened to you?"

As soon as the army came back I should have to tell the tale to the Sardonyx Council, for the invasion attempt would affect our foreign policy for years. But until then I didn't want to discuss it, and said so. Zofal urged me back to my rooms, complaining, "You're getting so secretive, I remember as a child you were transparent as water."

I was bathed, combed, and put into my battle armor, which had been shined and cleaned to look like new. The bonesetters rebound my shoulder and substituted a festive green silk sling for the linen one. Before I was helped onto my horse—a fine gray battle stallion, again from Zofal's stables—I gave Zofal the casket of the Crown, saying, "Carry this for me. I need my one hand for the reins."

"You had better appoint a new Bearer," Zofal said. "This thing makes me nervous."

With plain linen cloaks belted over our finery we looked ordinary enough, and we rode out the West Gate without incident. We met the army well up the road, where they had paused to unfurl banners and get into parade order.

"Well met, Your Majesty," Commander Silverhand hailed us. She came close to my stirrup before saying quietly, "We met twenty Caydish prisoners and their escort on their way to Mhee today."

"You told me this before," I said, "and it bears repetiton—we're not done with them yet."

"When necessary we'll deal with it," Silverhand replied.

Word of the returning army had been announced as soon as Zofal and I had left the City, and as we marched down the oyster-shell road people were gathered to cheer. I had put on the Crystal Crown, and felt for the first time the difference between my folk and the Caydish, or even the Tiyalor. We were used to holding two opposite truths at once, where the westerners were single in mind. The Viridese seemed soft and gentle, a pampered race for whom life was slow and rich, to be savored and enjoyed rather than bent to one's will. All of a sudden I was afraid for us all, our follies and petty squabbles. We had lived so long the same. How could I safeguard my people, ensure our continuity?

Very softly the Crystal Crown's beautiful voice answered me. "I am that continuity, down through the ages," it said. "So long as you act in me, Averidan has the same ruler."

It was a werid thought, that I had not only succeeded, but indeed was Shan Vir-yan, yet not utterly strange. Perhaps some-one had told it me when I wasn't listening, or perhaps I had always known it. "Search your memory," I asked the Crown. "Are we become decadent?"

"The Shan have been more so, and also less."

"How shall I foster our vitality?"

"You are the Son of the Sun," the Crown chided gently, "not the deity himself. Leave that to the god. Your own duty is plain."

"Ah, and I see a neglected one," I exclaimed, I reined in the gray horse and waved the parade on down the road, for I recognized the red-tiled home of the Director of Roadworks. With unbelievable folly he was perched with his family at an upper window, waving and enjoying the show. With spur and rein I guided my mount right under the window. The children were ecstatic at my notice, tossing flowers and leaves, but the Director himself let his hand fall and turned to flee.

"Hold!" I commanded, and reluctantly the man returned to the window. "Tell me, Director of Roadworks, of the new addition to your house."

He began some incoherent tale of a geomantic imperative to alter his home and thus his fortune, but in the Crystal Crown's power I saw the truth of it. He had not learned a lesson at all, had not immediately but bit by bit edged over into dishonest accounting again. The usual Viridese two-mindedness had allowed him, once the money was in hand, to spend it as if it were honestly come by, on publicly visible extravagance.

The Sisterhood had gone by, and the fists of spearmen filled the road behind me with their even-measured parade step. To my left and right the noise of the joyous crowd rose up, but the spectators close enough to see what I was about were silent so as not to miss a word. The day a Shan minds his own business is the day he's dead.

There were plenty of guardsmen in the crowd, on watch for cutpurses or handkerchief snatchers, and at my gesture several came forward. I pointed up at the Director of Roadworks. "Lapidation," I ordered. The guardsmen bowed and departed to carry out my command. Spurring the gray horse to a trot I caught up with my place again at the head of the parade. The whole business had not taken three minutes.

Against our victorious return sachets of mint and other fortunate spices had been prepared, and our every step now stirred up sensuous, nose-tickling scents. The marketplace, hastily cleaned and adorned, was redolent with spicy odors which did not quite mask the smell of fish. A fine linen canopy had been set up just outside the West Gate for our official welcomers: my family, government dignitaries, priestesses, among them the Sun priestess who had counseled me this morning.

With a lamentable lack of self-control my relatives broke ranks as I approached, surging round until I feared my horse would tread on Mother's very toes. "Oh, Liras-ven, you've been wounded," my sister Siril cried. "Are you going to lose the use of your arm?"

Rosil-eir laughed at her. "What a tactless question! And

hadn't you heard he was back early?'' He punched me in the thigh and added, ''I told you she'd be able to fold you in half with one hand!''

But I no longer needed the awe that the Crystal Crown could lend me, and fixing Rosil with my eye I replied, ''On the contrary, this is an honorable wound of war received in defense of the realm.'' I did not need to add, And where is yours? for he immediately retreated.

In the press beyond my chattering family was one incongruous red-brown head. It was Melayne, and the same force that draws waves up onto the beach drew me to her.

She wore a robe as vividly yellow as Caydish snowflowers, encrusted with silver embroidery at hem, sleeve and sash. Cosmetics hid the discoloration of her eye but not the swelling, which gave her a false air of jocularity. She came forward into the sunshine glowing like a living flame, and I recognized the pearls in her hair as my gift to her. She rested one hand on my booted foot in its stirrup and looked up at me.

Through boot leather and hose I felt her touch, and blushed like a fool. I reached down to her not with my hand but with the power of the Crystal Crown, and felt, sweet and firm as a ripe peach, her fundamental good will. The shift of female loyalty in Cayd from blood-clan to marriage-clan is so often sealed with violence that blood is instinctively reckoned into the marriage-price. I had killed Melbras to win her, and thus permanently earned her allegiance. And she was far too sensible to transfer loyalty without love. Furthermore, she had been able to come to terms yesterday with the power of the Crystal Crown far more quickly than I had last year, for strength to the Caydish is always admirable.

Now she said to me in a low voice, ''It doesn't matter if you're a witch.'' The lopsided green-gray gaze searched my face timidly to see if I was offended. All in a rush, so softly that with all the crowd noise I could understand her only by listening with the Crown as well as my ears, she said, ''I love you anyway.''

As with the Sun priestess I almost didn't believe it. But no one can lie to the Shan King. A wild, impetuous happiness leaped in my chest, and as I reached down for her hand I saw my limbs shining not only with bronze lamellar but with the exultant white fire of my joy. Melayne hesitated at the eerie sight, but then set her chin and held up her arms. I caught the wrists and gently hoisted her up before me on the saddle. At the extra burden, the gray horse backed and shook his head with a jingle of bits, and I spurred him on toward the West Gate.

"Wait, Your Majesty!" the Director of Protocol called. "There's an official speech of welcome yet!"

"For me there's a more important rite," I said. "I owe the Sun a thank offering." And I smiled at the Sun priestess' surprised face.

Do you long for the great novels of high adventure such as Edgar Rice Burroughs and Otis Adelbert Kline used to write? You will find them again in these DAW novels, filled with wonder stories of strange worlds and perilous heroics in the grand old-fashioned way: